Nicholas Griffin is twenty-nine. He was brought up in England and currently lives in New York. His first book, *The Requiem Shark*, was published by Little, Brown to much acclaim and won a Betty Trask Award.

'A confident and beautifully plotted excursion into eighteenth-century London and love . . . Griffin has done his research and thoroughly understands the literary culture of the period' *Independent on Sunday*

'Griffin's novel is a clever exercise in historical re-creation and, implicitly, a disturbing fable about scientific arrogance' *Sunday Times*

'Thieves and cut-throats, whores and mountebanks abound in what is a completely absorbing tale of the dankest, darkest underbelly of eighteenth-century London . . . Griffin's explorations of good people forced to do bad things through the pursuit of love, fame and money are both compelling and emotive. Wonderful' *Manchester Metro*

'A fascinating novel, which combines history, science, myth and fiction in a tale of ambition and deception' *Bookseller*

'Full of atmosphere, mystery, medicine and intrigue: a truly gripping tale' *Publishing News*

'An unputdownable evocation of London life and medical practice in the early eighteenth century . . . wonderful' *Ms London*

THE
HOUSE OF SIGHT
AND SHADOW

NICHOLAS GRIFFIN

ABACUS

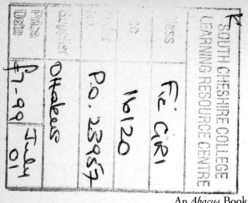

An *Abacus* Book

First published in Great Britain by Little, Brown and Company 2000
This edition published by Abacus in 2001

A CIP catalogue record for this book is available from the British Library.

ISBN 0 349 11318 1

Typeset in Cochin by M Rules
Printed and bound in Great Britain by Clays Ltd, St Ives plc

Abacus
A division of
Little, Brown and Company (UK)
Brettenham House
Lancaster Place
London WC2E 7EN

www.littlebrown.co.uk

For O.B.

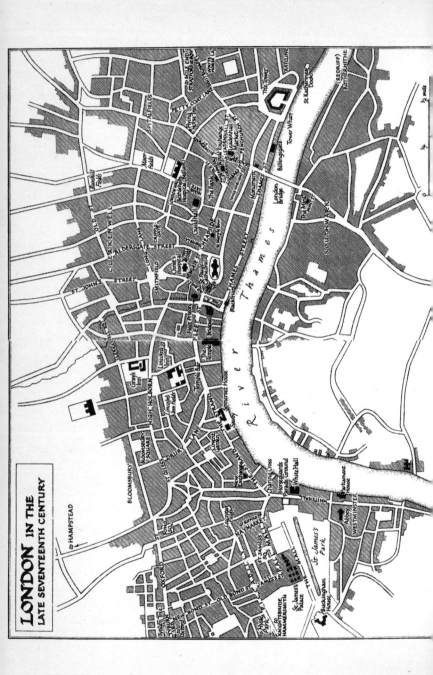

LONDON IN THE
LATE SEVENTEENTH CENTURY

Question your desires,
Know of your youth, examine well your blood.

William Shakespeare
A Midsummer Night's Dream, Ii, 67

'Tis Money guides the World and Fate,
Makes Virtue Vice, makes Crooked Straight.

Daniel Defoe
The Commentator, 1 August 1720

Nobody – All the people in Great Britain, except
about 1200.
Worth – Power. Rank. Wealth.
Wisdom – The Art of acquiring all three.
World – Your acquaintance.

Henry Fielding
A Modern Glossary, 1752

CHAPTER ONE

Joseph Bendix looked down upon London from the heights of Blackheath. A musty warmth had parted the skirts of smoke above the city, illuminating her fresh brick, her tight alleys. The sun had baked the surface of the mud, creating a thick crust for their carriage. At noon there were no shadows. Reluctantly, Bendix climbed back into the coach, taking the same position between the two elderly ladies that he had held all the way from Dover. Sharp spokes of light lanced the perforations of tin-sheeted windows, so that all could see the choking dust they breathed.

Their descent into London was accompanied by the eruption of conversation that Bendix had so carefully quelled through the miles.

'They say,' said Mrs Sexton, 'that there are leopards in the Tower . . .'

'Perhaps,' continued the flat-nosed Mr Harper, 'they still show the two-legged dog that was so prominent during my last visitation.'

'My sister writes,' continued Mrs Sexton, 'that they now display the entire skin of a Moor. Tanned. With the hair on it. Shall you be seeing it, Mr Bendix?'

'No, madam, I shall not,' said Bendix, and stared straight ahead.

'Was there much entertainment in Paris?' inquired Mrs Sexton.

Bendix held his silence and cursed the lack of funds that condemned him to travel in so ungentlemanly a manner. They bumped and walloped and knocked against one another as the horses strained down the hill. They picked up two more ladies at an inn in Deptford, put one down by the horse ferry at Southwark, and at the death of the day finally entered the gates of London.

An old Englishman in Paris had told him of London. How she had been racked by plague, freshened by fire, rebuilt. Up went a thousand houses, narrow passages returning where men had dreamt of the wide boulevards of Paris and the majesty of St Petersburg. There were parts erected that held splendour: the embankment of the Thames, the precise angles of Soho Square and St James. St Paul's shone above the city, but even her beauty was not so far from Pudding Lane, from the warped rooftops of Blowbladder Street. But Bendix saw none of this, gazing only on Mrs Sexton's yellowed fingernails and the tempered rind of her cuticles. Had the coach not carried all his belongings in the world, he would have leaped out and walked alone.

He could hear carriages travelling both in front and behind him. The air was thick, dirtier than Paris, thought Bendix, weighed with the heavy smell of horse dung and the laboured breath of driven cattle. Mrs Sexton held a handkerchief to her nose. The remaining lady from Deptford laughed at their affronted sensibilities.

Mr Harper leaned forward and tapped Bendix upon the knee with his cane.

'You visit family?' he inquired.

Bendix shook his head in reply. 'My father is long departed.'

'Dead?'

'Merely Northumberland,' replied Bendix with the start of a smile.

'And you shall practise here. Good, good, sir.'

By the time they pulled up at the Black Horse, a portion of Bendix's good humour had returned to him. He helped all of the women down from the coach and hired a broad-backed porter to sweat his belongings up to the room. Opening his chest, he removed his writing case and immediately scratched a brief note to the doctor, letting him know of his intention to call the following day. He strapped his hangar to his side and descended with his missive. The landlord advised him not to trust the evening post and proposed two link boys, sitting by the empty grate. Bendix gave one a pair of pennies to deliver his note and letter of recommendation and hired the second for a stroll up Drury Lane.

He walked for a mixture of edification and amusement – to take a turn about the city in which his parents had been raised. It took him no more than one stretch upon Drury Lane to deduce why his father had abandoned London in favour of the North. The street was abustle with a confused mingling of peoples. The silks of gentlemen, the sight of beggars, children cursed with misshapen limbs. More frightening was the concentration of the unplaceable. Persons he suspected might be actors, ladies he presumed to be whores, noblemen he supposed as penniless as himself. London, he decided, was a fallen honeycomb, the bees long ago ceding their territory to flightless grubs.

He returned to the Black Horse, paid his link boy as he extinguished his torch in a bucket of water, and vigorously patted the dust from his breeches. In his room Bendix undressed quickly, sipped at the wine his landlord had left, and finally removed his peruke. The hair beneath was closely shaved, a sphere of stubble flecked with grey. He blew out the candle and walked naked to the window with his glass. Beneath him, in the dim light granted by the tavern, ran a thoroughfare of shadows. He watched the affectionate touch of hand on hand and felt the sharp pang of the lonely. Bendix knew not a soul in the city. Having lost his father's letters of recommendation many moons ago, he now relied upon a single connection. Awaiting his meeting with the doctor, he slept fitfully throughout a hot and anxious night.

The morning found Bendix ensconced at a table in Tom's Coffee House, a short walk from the Black Horse. He read the *Daily Courant*, noted the upcoming trials and politicking, and held the news-sheet high to disguise his loneliness. In Paris he had had a small circle of friends, fellow students of medicine. They had drifted from Bendix during his rise, then stood back and crossed their arms to watch him fall.

Mocking Parisians had laughed that London now thought itself the centre of civilisation. All agreed that Hanover was now established and, as the monarchy began to flourish, Bendix believed King George would encourage his nation with money. Where there was money, there was advancement, opportunity. Great men were only found in great nations. In truth, Bendix's return was not simply a matter of coin, though he would have insisted on the lie had anyone asked. In the circles in which he had moved, money was a more understandable excuse than love.

He had heard of the doctor, Sir Edmund Calcraft, from his own tutor, Bertrand LeMaître, who had attended the doctor's lectures on lithotomy at the turn of the century. There was, LeMaître insisted, no man like him. None with the disrespect necessary for the advancement of knowledge since the days of Boyle and Hooke. But Calcraft had not taken a student in twenty years, had not operated in twenty years. Rumour, said LeMaître, declared that Calcraft had not left his house in a decade.

'Why,' Bendix had asked, 'would he even consider me?'

'Why does a man marry if he has no need of children or money?' answered his tutor.

'For love,' replied Bendix immediately.

'Or,' said LeMaître, 'for companionship. I shall write you a letter.'

'What does he work on?' asked Bendix.

LeMaître shook his head. It didn't matter what Calcraft was studying. Bendix had to leave. 'You shall find his observations most interesting.'

By four the next afternoon Bendix had received no answer to his solicitation. With the sun still bright above, he hired a hackney and directed it to Lincoln's Inn Fields. He had rustled enough gold up from the patient LeMaître in Paris to ensure a worthy appearance. Indeed, all his money was invested in appearance. A dozen fine suits, each a silken key that might open the doors where the shabby were restrained by servants. They passed down Great Queen's Street, Bendix admiring the regularity of the facades of fine red brick and heavy wooden eaves. Lincoln's Inn Fields was an extension of this perfection, broken by the odd arabesque fancy.

The door to Dr Calcraft's house was black and freshly painted. Bendix rapped upon it with his knuckles, then quickly examined his sober dress of dark silks. His frock coat remained clean, despite the dirt of the hackney. The silver buckles of his shoes gleamed. There was no answer at the door. He rapped again, then attempted to peer into the windows. They were drawn and curtained. Scratching at the skin beneath his peruke, Bendix walked along until he found the mews, then doubled to the back of the house. It seemed dark. Once more he returned to the front, and knocked for a third time.

The door was opened, guarded by a short man who bowed briefly before Bendix. He was at least as wide about the waist as he was tall, with round, ruddy cheeks that cloaked his eyes. Bendix feared he might pop.

'If you would tell Dr Calcraft that Joseph Bendix calls upon him.'

The spherical servant raised a hand to his face and masked a smile. Bendix noted his extraordinary fingers, fine and tapered like a starfish, and realised at once his mistake.

'Dr Calcraft?'

'Or else, a very presumptuous footman,' said the doctor and offered Williams one of his starred hands.

'I apologise for my . . .'

'Understandable, quite understandable.' Finally he released Bendix's hand. 'Come in, sir. 'Tis uncommon warm today, and there are fevers about. If you should catch one, I would charge you for your visit.'

Calcraft let Bendix pass before him, studying his face. The false curls of the French wig, his angled nose, dark eyes – brown or grey, but very alive. Almost Greek, thought the doctor. Deportment: brimming with confidence, a necessary trace of arrogance on an otherwise kind face.

Bendix entered a long hallway of burnished oak and followed his host deep into the house. Though the solemn grandeur of his surroundings was not lost on Bendix, it was muddied by the pervasive odour of wet clothes left to dry in a damp room. No movement of air. Bendix overcame his desire to search out a window.

'You know LeMaître well?' asked Calcraft, following him down the hallway.

'Three years,' said Bendix. 'I considered him one of my closest friends in Paris, though he was, of course, my superior in learning.'

'Poor child,' said Calcraft, 'I trust you have more ambition than he. Delightful man, delightful, but an ordinary mind. Has he told you much about me?'

'He said that you would grant me an audience. I doubted it myself.'

'To your left, sir,' said Calcraft and they passed up a flight of stairs that led directly to a study. To Bendix's relief, the curtains were parted. A faint breeze accompanied the last of the sun. There was only one chair in the room. Bendix stared at it. 'A drink?' asked the doctor.

Bendix nodded, and the doctor poured him a large glass of brandy and tempered it with water. The setting sun lent the woods an orange hue. The red leather chair on which Bendix was asked to sit seemed black.

Calcraft paced back and forth before his guest, as if it were the most natural manner in which to conduct the interview. He dressed plainly, thought Bendix, lacking all pretensions of the day, bowing neither to French powders nor English perukes. Bendix realised how wrong he had been to judge him a footman. No house-proud man would have let such a sight represent his kingdom. Simple breeches, maroon and silk, a chemise of light cream, a pair of tarnished buckles upon his shoes.

'You did well to doubt your admittance, but while LeMaître shall always teach and never practise, he is a master in the art of flattery. He will force a memory upon you. A warm one, uncommonly warm, and while you bask in its light, will ask a favour that seems trivial in comparison. Thus, you sit before me.'

'Might I ask upon the memory?'

'No,' said Calcraft, and then conceded. 'He accompanied me, as my assistant to Oxford, a long time ago. We spent the summer chasing up villagers for sixpence. Each of us met ladies. His was temporary, mine divine.'

'I . . .'

'No more, sir. We must speak about you. You are a curious specimen.' Calcraft wagged a finger at him.

'Says LeMaître?'

'Naturally, sir. He knows something of the changes I have undergone since last we met. This information, I presume, he has passed to you.'

Bendix nodded slowly. 'It seems, though, as if all that I hear is rumour and gossip. The only certainties, and therefore the only evidence that can be considered in judgement, is of your life before your retirement.'

'Judgement,' chuckled Calcraft, 'this is most excellent. Yes, why not? You should judge me, and I, you. What do they say of me?'

'You are considered a worthy anatomist.'

The doctor peered up at Bendix. 'Come now, man, if you wish to last one minute more in this house you shall have to forget your Continental manners. Politeness, sir, is insincerity. What do they say?'

Bendix took a breath. 'They say that your house is built upon bones, curtains stitched of women's hair, and pillows sewn of eyelids. You are a monster.'

Calcraft paused in his wanderings and sat upon the edge of his own desk. 'The common folk, Mr Bendix, are much afeard of anatomy. More so than of Tyburn rope. To be dispatched by justice is a crime indeed, but to be studied for knowledge is barbarity.'

'It is also against the law.'

'Of course,' said the doctor, 'the law grants that six bodies a year belong to the college for dissection. One for every other month. Would be difficult in the coldest months, but imagine the putrification this July. And the crowd, man, imagine the crowd. Two thousand doctors and surgeons crushed about the body, tearing at it like dogs. Arrangements are made. It is necessary.' Calcraft walked over to the decanter, and returned to fill both their glasses. In the uncomfortable silence, Bendix itched at his head through his thick peruke. 'Remove it, sir,' instructed Calcraft as he sat. With some relief, Bendix unpinned his wig and placed it on the desk. Calcraft looked down upon his grizzled, close-shorn hair.

'Some more, sir. Tell me more of yourself. I know why LeMaître says you come before me. Tell me in your words. Truth, sir. Trust in it for now.'

'You know where I am from, Doctor. I have attended the most reputable courses of anatomy in Europe. I have learned much with my ears and almost nothing with my eyes. Mostly, we studied from the carcasses of dogs.'

'Dogs,' interrupted Calcraft. 'A dog is no good, no good at all.'

'What I wish from you, Doctor, is an apprenticeship of the most visceral kind. As Dr LeMaître points out, though I have much to learn from you, perhaps I also have knowledge that you would find desirable.'

'He wrote of your theory,' began Calcraft. 'The body's subservience to the mind. A bold treatise, I will grant you. And, more impressively, offensive to our Greek ancestors.'

'Indeed,' smiled Bendix.

'Tell me,' asked Calcraft, 'what do you believe to be the purpose of the brain? Is it filled with vapours, as Galen says? Does it leak, as Aristotle claims?'

'I do not know.'

'Do you agree with Stahl as to the existence of the anima?'
Bendix shrugged.

'You do not have opinions?' asked Calcraft sharply.

'My opinion is that I do not know enough to propose a theory on the substance of the brain that you could not, at once, smite down. If it is thought that fills the brain,' continued Bendix, 'I am here because mine needs fattening.'

'And yet you proposed your theory to LeMaître on which he granted you your licence. "The body is subservient to the mind." How did you conclude such a thing without opinions?'

'If I take anything from any man,' said Bendix, 'it is from Descartes's reliance on what we can be sure of and from Boerhaave's willingness to cut into a dead patient. My own theory is born of my own eyes. I may discuss . . .'

'And if, sir,' interrupted Calcraft, 'I were to let you absorb my learnings, what will you pay?'

Bendix shifted in his seat. 'I have little in the way of income . . . there was an annuity from my father. It has been withdrawn.'

'Gambling?' asked Calcraft.

'Of a kind,' said Bendix, summoning a brief helpless shrug that was designed to show past weaknesses were no longer present.

Calcraft managed to mask his sympathy with a stern facade. At Bendix's age he had fallen into debt. He couldn't help but see his guest as a young and impecunious reflection of himself. 'Stand, sir, stand and leave,' said the doctor. 'Be back tomorrow, in the light. You shall keep your money. And I shall keep my time. Not all of it, of course, but I shall continue about my business. And where I decide it is allowable, you may attend with me.'

Bendix rose from his seat and could not suppress a smile of elation.

'You have a fine temperament,' said Calcraft and shook Bendix by the hand, 'but this is a quiet house, Joseph. I shall be a poor introduction to London. You are young, sir, and I suspect shall find your own way. You may begin by accompanying yourself to the door.'

Bendix wandered in a happy stupor back towards the Black Horse, dismissive of the doctor's concerns of London society. As for 'youth', he now despised the word. According to his father, youth had connotations of ignorance, neglect and insensitivity. Bendix knew what he really meant. Ignorance of money, neglect of its management, insensitivity to the patron. It was not until his thirtieth birthday that it occurred to the son that he had not only ignored and neglected his family, but also his own career. Suddenly he sympathised with his father's concerns, several years too late for his father's understanding.

In France, money had become a most peculiar thing for Bendix because it was tied, in a tight silken knot, to love. Money had brought him to the attention of his first love and his lack of gold had cast him from her realm. The Comtesse had been, in many ways, the perfect first love: older, more patient, kind in doses, most deliberate. Perhaps Bendix was a little too old for first love. Fine-skinned, bright-eyed, an odd mixture of easiness and intensity, he had been used to receiving attention, but never reciprocating it.

The woman he saw as an equal viewed him as a foreign diversion. He was a worthy affair, at twenty-seven, ten years her junior. Apparently moneyed, he was also handsome enough to cause ripples of jealousy in her circle. The ladies teased Bendix for his accented French, inquired of his medical knowledge, of his acquaintances in England and then, behind the Comtesse's back, trilled his unworthiness and placed small wagers on how long he would last. That the

Comtesse kept him for two years spoke much for both his conversation and his earnest tenderness in love-making, something that even the garrulous Comtesse could not adequately describe to her friends.

However appearances required a heavier purse than Bendix's. Gold given by his father was only a brief respite. Tailors in various corners of Paris unwittingly combined to support Bendix, until eighteen months later his credit was stopped. So sure was he in the mutual bond of intimate love that he waited only a day to ask the Comtesse for a loan. It was, of all things, what the Comtesse feared the most. In her eyes it immediately reduced Bendix from a lover to a whore. The years swept across her face and Bendix saw something frightening and motherly in her eyes.

'Money?' she repeated, plucking the single word from his soliloquy of love and translating it from its smooth French to give it a rapacious English bite.

Bendix nodded and understood his mistake, but the word hung over them. When Bendix left her that evening, his approaches resisted, he knew that he would not be allowed back in her presence again.

So involved had he become in her life that he had few friends to turn to. Only LeMaître stood by, advising that the surest way to stitch a broken heart was to put water between oneself and one's desired. At first, Bendix had not listened to his professor. Instead he had put pity on his back and bent beneath it. For a full year, his clothes had grown dirtier, his creditors more aggressive. It was LeMaître who had forced a loan upon him.

Finally, Bendix's self-disgust had exceeded his love. He remembered how, before the Comtesse had interrupted his life, the world of medicine had been his sole obsession. Having once more convinced himself that the real truth of life lay not in love, but in work and progress, he had consented to leave Paris behind him. Women were to be ignored. His final days were spent in deep conversation with LeMaître. Theories that had been forced by love to the peripheries of his brain were now harnessed and dragged forward. By the time that his coach had reached London, his only remaining regret was for the two lost years he had suffered through the Comtesse's manipulations. Bendix could not afford to thank LeMaître in anything but words.

CHAPTER TWO

On his first day in Lincoln's Inn, Bendix was introduced to the three members of staff who formed the household. The upper butler, Mr Lemon, showed him to his room, a breathless chamber, a level below the street, with a fine view of buckles and ankles and the tips of canes. His living arrangements were apart from both the doctor and his servants.

Bendix was not the sole person who felt himself stifled by the heat. The cook, Mrs Hemmings, viewed her fire and pans with the horror of betrayal. Her young cousin, the housemaid Julia, moved with an unearthly sluggishness. When she was introduced to Bendix, her curtsey was so slow that he feared she might never rise. Though Calcraft possessed an energy that could not be tethered by the weather, his cheeks became a little brighter, his breath quicker, his body a touch bloated. Still, he retained the whiteness of a newborn throughout the burning July, and found no reason to move beyond his walls.

It was Julia who first informed Bendix that he was living in not one house but three. Calcraft had purchased the three buildings over the span of five years. The centre house, split by a large atrium, held the drawing room, the breakfast parlour, the library and a pretty spiral staircase made of rosewood, inlaid with intricate pearl. The staircase did not lead to Bendix's bedroom, but to the central basement area, sealed from his quarters by a thick layer of brick.

The eastern wing, built over the kitchen, belonged almost exclusively to the servants, save for the large, narrow dining room that sat beneath their eaved quarters. Calcraft kindly granted Bendix a private study on the second floor where, said the doctor, the young man might continue to exercise his theories. It was a room in which Bendix intended to spend much time. He had a broad view of the Fields. Above his head, on the flat roof of the building, lay a spice garden. Bendix had direct access through a simple trapdoor that opened to the rooftop. The doctor took great pride in directing his apprentice through the sere garden, yellowing under the relentless sun.

'You are so close to the Physic Gardens,' said Bendix, after murmurs of false admiration.

Calcraft looked confused.

'Why do you not use their land?' insisted Bendix.

'It is better to be contained,' replied Calcraft strongly, as if he thought his apprentice very deaf and perhaps a little stupid.

Bendix marvelled at the size of the house, its weave of rooms and passages. Drums and masquerades in Paris had let him poke his nose about the residences of counts and princes that far exceeded Calcraft's, and yet Sir Edmund was but a doctor and they had all been born to their wealth. Visiting the western wing was prohibited, save for Julia's presence on attending her master's levee. It was Calcraft's domain, and one that he insisted on keeping to himself.

Bendix had long been warned of the intensity of the doctor's private nature. He considered himself of the highest fortune to have access to the doctor and was willing to accept the conditions of restriction without question. In truth, he was not interested in the idiosyncrasies of Calcraft's private life. It was the chamber in which the doctor conducted his work that intrigued the apprentice.

The household servants were a silent group, who communicated in nods and gestures of familiarity without tenderness. As a man who had studied and intended to practise medicine, Bendix had little regard to the barriers of society. Where illness travelled, he planned to follow. And though he was willing to make his first London friendship with Lemon, and brought a cheerful countenance to the kitchen on all of his early visits, he found himself tolerated but not embraced. Mrs Hemmings, he discovered, was a cook fond of keeping spirits near her dishes. They were not ingredients, but stimulants taken to relieve her varying ailments. Her gin breath, noxious to Bendix, was ignored by Calcraft, who gave little concern to his household. Indeed, it seemed as if he encouraged a sullen lethargy and thrived in the resulting listlessness.

On first descending to the central cellar, Bendix's worries that LeMaître's recommendation was misguided were immediately dismissed. It was, to Bendix's surprise, the brightest room in the house. All about the room were lamps, shielded by canopies of clear glass. An inch of sawdust lined the floors, marked by the imprints of Calcraft's ceaseless pacings. The walls, painted in a handsome scarlet, were lined with shelves, save for the large fireplace and mantelpiece against the northern wall. To the west lay books of medicine, as impressive a private library as Bendix had ever seen. On the eastern shelves lay a series of bones, stretched out in quiet disorder, as

if a paupers' grave had been robbed and ridiculed by dis-
memberment. Beneath the bones sat a line of buckets and
vessels, some closed, others spilling sawdust, spices or herbs.

The shelves were no more than an audience to the large
oval table that rose from the centre of the boards, old and
stained and marked with cuts. At the head of the table was a
pulley, lowered from the ceiling, a design borrowed from
the Royal College to enable the surgeon to hold the head of
the body taut while cutting the eyes and back of the skull. It
gave Bendix a strange exhilaration to find himself standing
in such a room, with the doctor talking freely of his work. It
was a space large enough to teach twenty men. An extraordinary venue, thought Bendix, for one man's education.

'Joseph,' said Calcraft, calling his attention away from
the oval table to a stout desk to the right of the fireplace.
Sitting atop the desk was a lamp, a microscope and its
accompanying stotoscope, a brine-filled globe.

'Look,' ordered Calcraft as he lit the lamp. The salty orb
focused its light on a thin glass plate.

'At what?' asked Bendix.

'Hooke's animacules,' said Calcraft. 'Could be any form of
living matter, even a being within a being. In this case,
simply a water gnat.'

Bendix peered into the eye-piece. There, in seeming con-
tentment, sat the smallest being that Bendix had ever seen.
Minute and perfect, Bendix could see through the gnat's
transparent shell, observing the pulsing motion of its head,
thorax and belly. It was an intricate black bead, the simplest example of life the apprentice could imagine.

'Beautiful,' murmured Bendix.

'Notice the internal organs,' said Calcraft, 'such clarity.'

'No need to even cut.'

'Exactly,' answered Calcraft. 'The first thing that your

institutes should learn. There is much to gain from observing even the lowest insect. The perfect beat of the heart. After this, you can cut into your dogs.'

'You avoid vivisection?' asked Bendix.

'No, no,' said Calcraft. 'All men with microscopes progress to dissection of one sort or another. An inevitability. It is tempting though to see the intricacy of nature, to attempt to unravel it. Take the finest works of man, look at them through this lens and they shall seem clumsy. But creatures, down to this scrap, are wondrous.'

'And the dead?' asked Bendix, pointing to the oval table.

'Still beautiful,' replied the doctor, 'but no longer perfect.' He signalled Bendix to follow him up the stairs.

The presentation of the microscope puzzled Bendix. It was too simple a thing for Calcraft to concern himself with, unless for a purpose other than amusement. Any man who had shunned society for so long must have a focus, thought Bendix. Everything he had seen in the basement he knew to be connected, but the lines remained invisible to him. At the very least, it forced the Comtesse further from his mind. This was the laboratory of a self-made man. For a moment, Bendix was as excited as if he had just been passed the ancient secret of alchemy.

CHAPTER THREE

He saw little of Calcraft the first week, except at meals, where the doctor picked at food, plying himself with drops of laudanum and complaining of his vexation with various calculations and texts he worked on. He recommended many of his books to Bendix, examining his pupil on Heister or Vesalius at breakfast time with a series of questions that astounded Bendix with their consummate mastering of the text. He had yet to talk openly of his discoveries and only once during the week did the doctor express any interest in Bendix's own theories.

'Can you,' asked Calcraft, 'reduce your ideas to lines so simple the king and his limited English might understand them?'

'I . . .'

'No matter how complex the theory, no matter the weaving of complications, you must present with simplicity. They have pockets filled with gold. You, merely a dedication in your opus to grant them. So let us pretend me the Duke of High Nose, and you a consummate quack.'

'Well . . .'

'Quick, quick.'

'I propose . . . your Lordship, I propose a method of understanding the relationship between the working of the mind and the mechanics of the body.'

'Go on.'

'The mind, your Lordship, is divided into many parts. Our senses are regulated by many governments. You will grant me, sire, that sometimes you find a man who cannot see, but he talks sweetly. Or you may find a fine painter who sings no better than a crow. I propose that the mind might be mapped. Divided into properties and estates, such as your own, your Lordship.'

'Good, good,' said Calcraft and clapped his hands. 'Fine indeed.'

'Moreover, sire,' continued Bendix and Calcraft's enjoyment evaporated at the prospect of this uncalled for elaboration, 'you will admit that hypochondria is a disease afflicting many of our men. I shall prove that if the portion of the mind we term imagination can cause sickness, then a doctor might also use the imagination to cure sickness.'

'Does it not feel fine,' asked Calcraft, 'to talk of one's own beliefs?' There was a trace of sarcasm in the doctor's words that made Bendix hold his tongue. 'You speak well,' continued the doctor, 'but shall find that is the last to be said of your own theory. It is yours and has my respect but, as Harvey proved, vessels through which blood flow move only in one direction. The same must be observed in learning. You are here to learn *from* me. When the knowledge is imparted, you may do with it what you will. Only then may you return to your own theories. Do we have understanding?'

'I wish only to learn,' submitted Bendix.

'You're a good man, Joseph,' said Calcraft standing and regaining his smile. 'Like the dawn, the light of our work shall rise slowly. You will understand it all, but it shall require all of you. When I am gone, there shall be time for your own work.'

Bendix's sole consolation was a hearty pat on the back that Calcraft delivered before retiring early for the evening.

Bendix spent the better part of the day pondering the doctor's words, concluding that it would be churlish to take offence. Though he was student to the doctor, apprentice if he so wished, it was hard for Bendix to forget that at thirty he had already obtained his doctorate. This, however, was merely an undercurrent of pride and Bendix recognised it. Such was Calcraft's reputation and wealth that he would have endured a set of fetters for the opportunity to stand by his side. Compared to the last two years, where his mind had conceded his body entirely to the demands of his heart, the past week had proved engrossing. His brain was ticking once more.

There was no doubt in the difference of their theories. To Bendix everything began and ended inside the mind. To Calcraft the mind was vital, but only in so far as it aided the search and understanding of disease and cure. Calcraft believed in instruments, in symptoms, in diagnoses and cures. He believed in trepanning and lancing, in sawing and cutting, bleeding and blistering. Bendix was the more open-minded, educated in all the dread cures that universities dared pass on, and yet doubtful. Or rather hopeful that there were better cures buried within one's own mind.

How many kings and queens had cured scrofula, pondered Bendix, merely by touching the anguished? Had not the greatest royal cynic, Charles II, borne witness to his own cures? His surgeon published sixty accounts of proof and more. What could explain this, thought Bendix, but the burning belief of the sufferer? God, concluded Bendix, was asleep within each mind. If Calcraft could have read his apprentice's thoughts, he would simply have replied that surgeons lied to flatter kings, curing the afflicted to keep their positions.

During his first week in Lincoln's Inn, Bendix kept his opinions to himself. A surgeon who practised only with his mind would not be paid in coin and it was Bendix's intention to secure his own path of gold. If he might learn the secrets of the doctor's physicking, then he might return to his accustomed life of comfort and to the possibilities of love. Until then he was an apprentice, open to all knowledge that might lead to patients, gratitude and gold.

He would admit to have taken true delight in peeling back the pages of the *Platonis Opera*, printed on spotless vellum.

Or sipping at beer while purveying Boccacio's *La Teseide*, a unique print of 1475, in Calcraft's library. However, books were not friends but tutors, and the relentless onslaught of teaching dried him out. He had hoped to practise, to use his hands, and as faded print and candlelight conspired to weaken his eyes, so his spirits dipped. It almost seemed as if the richest life he had encountered during his time in London had been the pulsing water gnat under Calcraft's microscope. So, it was with great pleasure that he accepted an errand for the doctor to visit Mr Streatham, an apothecary on Lewkenoor's Lane, where Bendix was to purchase those herbs and spices that the sun had reduced to ashes upon their roof.

Dressed in his finest silks, bewigged and lightly powdered, Bendix marched along the darkened hallway towards the front door. It was only when he opened it, and the summer light spilled through, that he noticed that he had walked right past a gentleman in the corridor. Recovering from surprise, Bendix bowed low.

'My apologies,' intoned the apprentice.

'No, no,' said the man and stepped forward to shake Bendix by the hand. 'Was quite lost in thought . . . awaiting the doctor you see. Quite used to the waiting. Pleased to be making your acquaintance, Mr Bendix.'

Bendix stared at the tanned hand he shook, fingers tapered, nails manicured yet long. The voice was foreign, but the accent long obscured by London twangs.

'You have my advantage,' said Bendix and offered another small bow.

'Abram Mendes, Mr Bendix. They that know call me by Sixes.' Bendix considered himself a tall man but Sixes was half a head higher, even with sloped shoulders that bled into arms. Though wrapped in a blue cloak, far too heavy for such a suffocating day, the man's leanness was apparent. As Sixes emerged from the shadows, Bendix fancied him a long-legged spider.

'And you have business with the doctor?' he asked.

'Between him and me, sir.'

'Of course.' Bendix bowed for the last time and offered his hand once more.

'I fancy we shall see each other,' said Sixes.

'Let us hope.'

'Associates and all,' smiled Sixes. 'Now off for your spices.'

The door shut behind Bendix and he stood upon the steps for a moment in amazement. Without a constant footman and in such a peculiar household it was hard to determine the etiquette. Most families of consequence would have abandoned London for Richmond a month ago. Yet, he could not prevent himself from hatching the suspicion that he had just been mocked.

Turning, Bendix presented his face to the sun and strolled idly along the edge of the Fields, heading towards Covent Garden. The piazza was, he thought, as splendid as any of Paris's offerings, though it was simplicity that brought it to life; the order of the arcades, the handsome and noble facade of St Paul's Church. For eighteen months he had appreciated nothing. He had presumed every head empty, every colour bland and that beauty and kindness were a pair of mocking illusions. Now, walking behind driven Smithfield swine, he found himself amused by their twitching tails and began to revel in the day. His week within Lincoln's Inn had been a muted affair, and while his mind may well have been stirred by the contents of Calcraft's library, he missed simple everyday gossip. By the time he turned along the Strand, he had already transformed his dark memory of Sixes into a portrait of novel acquaintance.

The apothecary, Streatham, asked kindly after the doctor when Bendix presented him with his bill of fare. He complimented Bendix on his suit of beige silks and his fine French cuffs. Asked him where he had found such a stylish peruke, then expressed many favourable opinions over the abilities of French tailors as compared to their English counterparts. Bendix received the compliments with the smoothest good humour, paid for and received the small parcel of spices and secured directions to the nearest barber. He had met the apothecary as a lonely apprentice and closed the shop door in the full knowledge that he remained a worthy gentleman.

The barber recommended by Streatham was a small, busy shop, directly behind the church. Bendix relaxed in the chair, and with closed eyes luxuriated in the application of lather to his head, the gentle massage of hands. It was an inexpensive form of human contact, though the mere shake of a hand would have been enough – shared complaints over coffee, meandering conversation, memories recalled and examined. He had never thought of the minutiae of friendship before; in their absence they were made obvious.

After his head was swept of stubble and the barber had bled him of four ounces, Bendix paid his shilling, disguised the pain of its departure, and returned to the street. He did not rush home, but snaked his way along unfamiliar streets, absorbing the commotion, constantly surprised by the busyness of the masses. The only people who stood still were those engaged in selling wares; news-sheets, oysters, nostrums. Bendix hid from the sun under the shade of a large sign and stared at a pair of women approaching a sedan chair. Such gentle steps, such affectations. Three years ago he might have presented himself. Now he pressed

homewards, hands in empty pockets. Had anyone observed
the apprentice, they would have thought there was something a touch pitiful about his downcast look. Yet there was
a visible confidence in him that suggested the only pity he
could abide was his own. He shook his head gently, as if he
had survived the brief but tempting call of sirens.

He was still scrubbing a cold cloth against his brow,
scouring his red scalp with water, when a knock fell upon his
bedroom door. It was the first such knock in his tenure at
Lincoln's Inn and, despite his relative state of undress, he did
not hesitate to open the door. Calcraft stood before him.

'Good evening, sir. I thank you for Streatham's wares.'
With one hand the agitated Calcraft gestured him forward,
while with the other he forbade movement. 'You must meet
an acquaintance. Come with me. No, no, stay.'

Bendix stood rooted among the contradictory orders.

'First, alter your equipage. You shall be stepping out
within the hour. Work to be done. Simplest clothes might
prove the best.'

'Simple?' inquired Bendix.

'Simple,' repeated Calcraft, 'as those of a porter.'

A look of confusion must have passed over Bendix's face,
for Calcraft smiled widely, 'Do not find it so disturbing, Mr
Bendix. Do you not possess such dress?'

'I do not.'

'I shall have it sent up. Quite necessary, I assure you.'
And then, when Bendix stood speechless before him,
Calcraft added, 'It is what you desired. What you are to do
is what you desired.' The doctor bowed, then retreated.

Lemon arrived within minutes of Calcraft's departure,
depositing a small parcel of clothes and then leaving Bendix
to change. The breeches were tainted with mud and a layer
of mill dust, the coarse shirt reeked of stale sweat and the

stockings and shoes were potent enough to make Bendix's nose twitch as he stepped into them. The tricorn hat that had crowned Lemon's parcel was far too large and fell about his eyes. He managed to angle it behind his ears and, refusing to pause long enough to consider how he might look, he walked up the servants' stairs in search of Calcraft.

The doctor was sitting in the breakfast parlour by the empty fire grate talking to himself. It was not until Bendix came through the door and the doctor paused in conversation that Sixes rose from a large armchair to acknowledge the entrance of the apprentice. He was dressed no differently, except for the absence of his great coat, which reduced him to the angles and planks of a marionette. There was, however, something graceful in his movement, even in his bow, as if he knew men well enough to adjust his behaviour in any company. Bendix noted the dark, loose skin beneath the eyes, clouded shadows of exhaustion.

'Mr Bendix,' intoned Sixes and made a slight bow in the apprentice's direction.

'Sixes,' said Bendix, and returned the bow, less a few degrees.

'Quite the dandy,' said Sixes and Calcraft allowed himself a brief, enjoyable snort.

'You look the part, Joseph. High as a dead horse. Where do you find these clothes, Mr Sixes?'

'We must be going,' replied Sixes.

'Where?' asked Bendix.

'To work, sir. Is it not what you wished?' The doctor stepped towards him and would have given him a comforting pat on the back had it not been for his costume. Instead he waved at him and pointed the strange couple to the door, then settled into his seat before the fire.

In the mews behind Lincoln's Inn Fields lay a pair of bony

horses and a beaten cart. Without a word, Sixes mounted it and signalled for Bendix to walk beside. Bendix looked about him. The streets were beginning to empty at the first sign of darkness. Those who remained did not look as their sober parade wound east to Moorfields. The cart creaked through unmarked lanes, past the trees that sheltered the booksellers who had disappeared with the sun. Sixes paused to wrap the horses' hooves in sackcloth to silence their tread. Then along the edge of Sodomite's Walk and to the ditches that held suicides six inches under dirt. Bendix let his hand rest on the flank of one of the horses, drawing comfort from the snorting beast. Heavy-bellied clouds were gathering. They grew thicker and thicker until the moon was replaced by the mute promise of rain. Bendix could barely see the figure of Sixes above him. Now he kept his hand upon the horse for guidance.

When, finally, the horses slowed and stopped, Bendix stepped back towards Sixes as he descended from his seat. They walked to the rear of the cart, where Sixes raised a cloth and handed Bendix two wooden shovels, more laborious than metal but much quieter. Draping the cloth over his shoulder, Sixes turned and walked into blackness. Bendix followed so close as to clip his heels. Sixes paused and handed him one end of a short rope.

'Will the horses be stolen?' whispered Bendix to break the darkness.

'Can you see them?' asked Sixes and tugged him forwards without waiting for an answer.

While Sixes adjusted his pace to large flat steps, Bendix could not prevent himself from a constant stumbling, accompanied by the steady beat of oaths. He did not know how long they walked, perhaps ten minutes, perhaps half an hour. He believed that they had passed through two gates, crossed one slatted bridge, inhaled a powerful fetor of decomposing flesh, then briefly risen on a slight slope.

Bendix was stopped by Sixes's flattened palm against his chest. A second hand touched him lightly on the mouth, indicating silence. Ahead was the faint sound of voices. Bendix tried to hush his breathing, but it seemed so loud to him that he could not determine a single word that came from ahead. He felt the touch of Sixes's lips against his ear.

'We wait.'

Bendix nodded. He was in another man's country and could do little but acquiesce. They held their vigil for an hour of blackness, Sixes so still and quiet that twice Bendix had to reach out to confirm his presence. Finally the faint voices dissipated. There seemed to be nothing about them.

'Do we move?' whispered Bendix.

'We wait on the moon.'

'And should it not come?'

But it did, and to their eyes, so accustomed to darkness, the weak light was enough to illuminate their immediate environs. Bendix could see the different line of night that was Sixes's shadow. He followed it until he heard the soft sound of the spade cut the earth, then joined Sixes in their endeavour.

The body was not buried deep, but the night was so warm that their efforts forced a heavy sweat on Bendix that revived the odours of his clothes. He could also smell wet soil, perhaps a trace of urine about the coffin. It was a roughly constructed box, a gesture of the poor. Sixes stood atop it and prized the board from its head with his crowbar.

'Come now,' he said. Bendix followed him down and together they tore the lid away.

Even in the dark Bendix could see the marks that burned the dead man's unbroken neck. A slim strip of dressing had been wrapped around his eyes to hide their blood from mourners. Still his face was swollen from his slow death, cheeks bloated as if filled with air, mouth open in contradiction. He wore the fine clothes he had been hanged in, dark silks that mocked his lowly demise.

The dead did not bother Bendix when their eyes were covered. He gripped the flesh, surprisingly warm – temperature of the night rather than of the deeper soil – and slipped a rope under the arms of the body. Together the two men heaved the corpse over the lip of the grave. Once more, thought Bendix, he has entered the world head first, but this time in silence. Sixes came about and grasped the feet and led them towards the cart.

The horses pulled them from Moorfields, and, unfamiliar as Bendix was with London, it was obvious to him that their journey would be more peripatetic than before. It was so easy, mused Bendix, to be fond of past happiness and forget that it had rejected you entirely. He looked down at his hands. Though he could not see the dirt, it was there in the crease of his knuckles, under his fingernails. Again, he remembered his exile from the moneyed classes and thought them vein and shallow. To be rich through birth was an easy, lifeless gift. There was no talent in spending, no skill to whoring. It was animalistic. Magpies scavenged, deer rutted. How much more rewarding to stain one's hands, to pull one's own subject from the soil rather than await delivery in the school courtyard for the bodies of dead dogs. He was earning his keep through mud and sweat. Bendix wiped his dirty hands against his coat.

The further they were from Moorfields, the warmer Sixes became, even hailing Bendix to join him atop the cart as they passed a large, darkened inn. The mask of order and silence that had controlled his movements throughout the

night now fell, and it seemed to Bendix that Sixes had quite
forgotten the illicit nature of their cargo. Sixes inquired after
the fashions of Paris and, while Bendix half suspected he
was being antagonised, there was much relief for him in conversation, yet he grew impatient with the frivolity of Sixes's
questions.

'. . . and yet Indian lace is never so fine as Spitalfield.'

'What do we possess?' interrupted Bendix, motioning
over his shoulder to the cart.

'Well done,' said Sixes. 'Well done.'

'Tyburn?' insisted the apprentice.

'James Pink of the Waltham Blacks,' whispered Sixes,
'the man the doctor wished for.'

'It was a particular request?'

'It is what comes from such devotion to a single pursuit.'

'Anatomy?' asked Bendix and had to wait for his answer
as they rolled past a pair of horsemen moving at pace from
the city. The apprentice would have confessed to the holding
of his breath.

''Tis hard,' breathed Sixes quietly, 'is it not, that honest
men such as ourselves must scurry in the night for the sake
of knowledge? You can ask a man, shall your soul stay
within your body when you depart, and he shall say, no sir,
it shall rise and join the Lord, and yet there is much concern
with the flesh. I think it almost unrighteous to stop such
men as you and me. We are those that enable the expansion
of the mind. Why put us down?'

Bendix nodded in agreement. 'These are the doctor's sentiments?'

'I wouldn't know, sir. Our discussions are simple and do
not elevate themselves on to such high plains. He saves such
words for his weekly dinner.'

Bendix turned towards Sixes in the darkness. 'You must

be mistaken, he cannot have a weekly dinner. Ten days since I arrived and not one dinner has been presented.' His tone was a touch aggrieved.

'That would be on account of Mr Defoe's stones. They were uncommon bad last week. He shall return.'

Bendix nodded with interest. 'Defoe and Calcraft are familiar?'

'Uncommon close. I cannot speak on behalf of Defoe, yet I swear he is the doctor's sole confederate.'

Bendix translated his surprise into silence to ease the digestion. That he should have a single friend should not seem incredulous. That he should be a man of some reputation and knowledge, even less so. It was only Bendix's vision that had been altered. Or rather, the dream that LaMaître had originally suggested to him: the doctor, helpless with loneliness, draining his mind for the benefit of his apprentice. Finally, Bendix said, 'I have read Defoe's *True-Born Englishman*. A wily cull, at the least. Shall he be in attendance this week?'

'I would not presume the information,' smiled Sixes, 'but would venture it depends on the acuteness of his stones.'

'Does he not beg the doctor to cut for them?'

'I believe he has.'

'And still he will not?'

'He shall have to soon enough if he wishes to keep Defoe from the state of our Mr Pink,' said Sixes glancing over his shoulder. 'I beg your silence for a moment.'

They approached the gates of London and were challenged by an elderly member of the watch. Broken with colic and propped against a staff, he could only manage a dying, 'State thy name.'

'Wild's man,' said Sixes and it provoked a low bow from the watch as they passed. Bendix was seized by a boyish appreciation of wrongdoing, a strange mixture of titillation coupled with the certainty that they would not be stopped.

'And who would Wild be?' inquired Bendix.

'I am made of particular knowledge,' said Sixes. 'That is a question you may ask of any.'

'Then why are you his man and not the doctor's?'

'When a man has but one master, he is bound to their desire. Choose many masters, Mr Bendix, and you shall have none.'

'There are words for such men,' said Bendix. 'None of them complimentary.'

Sixes made to reply, but chose silence. Bendix, confirmed in his righteous interpretation, abided the quiet all the way to the mews behind the doctor's house in Lincoln's Inn Fields.

CHAPTER FOUR

Sixes placed a wooden block the size of a church kneeler on the long table, then, with Bendix's aid, heaved the body atop so that it rested face upwards, chest protruding as if Mr Pink was caught in the arc of a spasm. Taking a small drill, Calcraft bored an inch-wide hole through a large wrinkle above Pink's eyes and pushed a sharp hook inside his skull. The doctor grasped the rope above him and, reeling the pulleys downwards, brought the head up to attention. The angle seemed merciless to Bendix and he was thankful that Pink's eyes remained covered. Still, he felt a curious pride. He had cut bodies before, felt no disgust dealing with the dead. He knew that bodies were obtained illegally, but never known how. It was not a talent he had ever expected to acquire.

'As a student of the body,' said Calcraft, clearing sawdust from the table, 'you have possibly observed that the diameter of the pupil of the eye is the only aspect of man's anatomy that does not alter in size from the moment of birth to old age. You see, Mr Bendix, this ties closely to your theory of imagination. The way we observe does not change a penny for all our years. It is the interpretation of what we see that is in flux. The mind is still the greatest lens.'

Bendix bobbed his head in constant nodding.

'The eye,' continued Calcraft, 'is of great consequence through the lore of myth and history. Most prized.' He peeled off the strip of bandage that had hid the eyes of James Pink. Blood vessels had burst, leaving hundreds of scarlet spots that lent him a desperate sadness. The strain for survival had been frozen, a despairing imprint of the desire for life.

'It always seems strange to me that it should be the eye that is destroyed by the Tyburn Tree, as if the condemned could not stand to see his fate.'

'Or did not deserve to,' added Bendix.

'Fortunately for us,' answered Calcraft, without looking up, 'the eyes are of no concern.' He dragged his knife across the flesh, cutting from both shoulders to the breastbone then down to the pubis. It was a long, delicate blade, almost a foot in length, that Calcraft wielded as if it were no more than a sixth finger.

While the doctor backed from the body to grasp his saw, Bendix stepped forward and began to remove the muscle and soft tissues from the chest wall. The apprentice dragged the man's skin upwards and shrouded his face. Calcraft opened the ribcage, cutting furiously with a handsaw, sur-

prising Bendix with his vigour. Finally the doctor removed
the chest plate, leaving the organs exposed to their view. It
was only when Bendix looked up to examine the boulevard
of ribs that he noticed Sixes had departed. Within the
moment, Bendix refocused his attention on the fascinating
movements of the doctor as he cut lower, exposing the
abdominal organs in their teary sheen.

'Do you wish me to remove the brain?' asked Bendix.

'Of no interest,' replied the doctor.

'Always, or merely in the case of Mr Pink?'

Calcraft ignored him and continued severing pelvic liga-
ments. Bendix was astounded with the speed at which he
worked, certain that his movements were memorised from
many dissections.

Taking a pair of silver-handled scissors, Calcraft began
by snipping the lungs from the heart and trachea, handing
them to Bendix to weigh on the hanging scales. The doctor
remained undisturbed by the slip and scratch of chalk and
blood as Bendix noted the weights upon a small blackboard.

'Take care,' said Calcraft from the table, ''tis of greatest
importance.'

The liver, the spleen, the intestines soon followed, each
snipped or sliced with considered delicacy by Calcraft, then
raised like offerings from the cavity and presented to his
apprentice. Bendix stood by a bucket of water, squeezing the
intestines of faeces and vomitus. The smell shook Bendix,
rising far above his own potent clothes. He had cut his way
about a body, but never been present at the initial moment of
dissection, never smelled such freshness.

Concentrating on his duty and not his disgust, he soon
emptied the intestine and returned to the doctor to relieve
him of the stomach, pancreas and kidneys.

The body lay empty. Mr Pink stared down at his plundered

flesh but Bendix would not meet his eyes. Calcraft had washed his hands and was scrawling notes in a hurried hand. The journal that the doctor wrote in, observed Bendix, had been drawn from a stack of brethren. How like LeMaître, thought the apprentice, to take note at every turn and trace the patterns of progress on paper.

'Do we incinerate the organs?' asked Bendix, looking away from Pink towards the fleshy piles that lined the long table.

'We are not anatomists,' said a horrified Calcraft, wagging a bony finger at his apprentice, 'we are natural philosophers. We keep the organs, but dispose of the body.'

'How?'

'We may call for Sixes again if you do not think yourself up to the task.' Bendix did not answer. 'I believe they end in the Fleet Ditch.'

'I will ready it for him,' compromised Bendix.

'Leaves of Hyoscamus,' said the doctor and smiled at his apprentice.

Bendix cocked his head.

'From the roof,' said Calcraft pointing upwards. 'Hyoscamus. As much as you can find. Now.'

Bowing in obeisance, Bendix rinsed his hands in the tub of pink warm water, and headed up the stairs. Despite the lateness, he felt refreshed by his minor mission. Already a sense of accomplishment had blanketed him in comfort and he was heady from sharing in the dissection with the doctor. And yet, as he walked up the stairs, through the breakfast parlour and then up towards his study, he knew that the true excitement of the night had not yet begun. The dissection had been a selective process. He had presumed, perhaps because of his own theories of imagination, that special importance would be paid to the felon's brain, and yet it had been ignored. The question remained as to why they had cut so particularly. The need to know propelled him upwards through the trapdoor, on to the roof.

The weed, Hyoscamus, was not so easy to find in the dark. He had left his lantern on the steps to the trapdoor, and in the chromed moonlight the varied greens of vegetation were indecipherable. He paused a moment and looked down upon the fields, the law courts to the west, small glimpses of the river, miles ahead. Turning, he could see back across the house, across the atrium to the doctor's wing. Against the window a pale hand, a gentle wave that was not a wave at all. A distant female face veiled by the sweep of a curtain. Then stillness. Bendix remained transfixed for a full minute. It was most certainly a woman.

The hand *belonged*, he was sure of it. Its quiet grace was unworried, a mere withdrawal from what he was not supposed to see. From what she was not supposed to see. He felt eyes upon him still and did not retreat but stood openly, welcoming the intrusion, unwilling to hide. A minute and it was gone. A sudden embarrassment stirred him. He blushed to be an open statue upon the roof, the Hyoscamus leaves in one hand, staring at an empty window. Turning, he traced the weak light of the lantern to the trapdoor and pulled himself under.

As Bendix moved through his study he caught sight of his watch sitting upon his desk, and was staggered to find that only an hour and a half had passed since they had begun to empty the corpse. It was, considered Bendix, the most vital ninety minutes of his life. He could remember every second, every smell, every suspicion. Indeed, he could not tell what caused more excitement, the sight of the lady's hand or the division of Mr Pink.

Calcraft had placed the various organs into jars, leaving

only the lungs, blackened and shrivelled, upon the table. For the first time, Bendix noticed the burning coals of the fire, the small kettle that sat above them. Calcraft followed his apprentice's stare.

'Decoction, Mr Bendix,' he said, 'the reduction of what is, to its essence.' He scooped the lungs into his hands and walked half the length of the room to the fire and placed them in the kettle.

'You wish to obtain an extraction of the constituents?' inquired his apprentice.

'The essence,' repeated Calcraft, and continued his peregrinations to the water barrel where he enthusiastically scrubbed his hands.

'What else to do?' asked Bendix.

'For me?' asked Calcraft. 'Sleep. For you, sir, a pair of restless days ahead. But first you must see to the disposal of Mr Pink.' He closed his journal, placed the collection of calf-skin books under his arm and turned for the stairs.

'Shall I send for Sixes?'

'He will be in the kitchen,' said Calcraft. 'I shall alert him to your discomfort on my way north.'

As Sixes descended some five minutes later, Bendix put aside the thought that had been obsessing him. He had no right, no business to ponder who might have held their hand to the window. Yet, it made Bendix think of his Comtesse for a long moment, and he was warmed by the foolish thought that she had followed him to London, all the way to Lincoln's Inn. You child, said Bendix to himself, and was plunged into a pool of disappointment that the Comtesse might still force her way into his mind so easily. Whoever the figure was, it was the third time in ten days that Calcraft had surprised his apprentice with the extent of his circle.

The garrulous Sixes who had ridden besides Bendix on the cart only two hours ago was long gone. Bendix was faced by a methodical man, who detached the corpse from the pulley, folded it so that the knees pushed into the vacant abdomen, then threw the graveyard cloth about it. He accepted Bendix's help to carry the remains of Pink as far as the mews and tipped his hat most graciously.

'Tell me,' said Sixes, 'you apprentice to a doctor who does not practise his living. Apprentices I know find scraps of favour from master's employers, so how do you survive? Your father is a landed man?'

'Landed but undistinguished,' admitted Bendix.

'Many brothers?' sympathised Sixes.

'A warren,' smiled Bendix.

'Means you should be fond of money.'

'I worship from afar.'

'Come Joseph,' said Sixes, 'Doctor was well rewarded in his day. Does not matter what he says or thinks now, but at your age he was thick with coin.'

Bendix shrugged. 'The apprentice is not bound to imitate the master.'

'But it is a trait that would be most wholesome to share.'

'What is it you wish?' said Bendix finally.

'Merely in the position of doing yourself a favour. Didn't want to press my advantage.'

'Most kind.'

'If I told you where for little work there was much reward,' said Sixes leaning forward, 'would you take an interest?'

'If it did not temper my studies, and if Sir Edmund were to give his consent.' Bendix's voice swelled with eagerness.

'No need to ask, he don't expect you to rub your nose against pages night and day. Best part of labour is it happens at your command. Your services are wanted, an able physician such as yourself.'

'I am hardly practised,' confessed Bendix.

'But you are ready. These are men who are in need of health and your discretion. If you were to find yourself a lady, and you are not exactly the youngest of students, work might provide a foundation for your independence.'

'You are an able vendor. We shall do this once and proceed from there. Commission, of course.'

Sixes geed the horses forward. 'From you, sir,' he called, 'I expect nothing, nothing at all.'

CHAPTER FIVE

There followed two long days of decoction, every organ taken from its jar and boiled to a potent extraction. They were mostly viscous, dark substances that Bendix was forced to scrape from the kettles then spoon into small pots until Mr Pink began to resemble a miniature ceramic city. Twice more, Bendix had returned to the roof for spices, only once upon the doctor's orders. On both occasions he had seen nothing, neither had he sensed eyes upon him.

He entertained himself with his memories of Paris before the Comtesse, of students and marked cards, of wine swallowed and vomited. His past deeds amused him, but only as tales told of another man's life. His determination to commit himself to the doctor was complete. He harboured no doubts and held his own theories so thoroughly in check that he often wondered if they would evaporate under the weight of new knowledge. The flames burned through the day, Bendix's mundane responsibilities of wood-toting and fire-tending slowly beginning to chafe his pride. Had he known the reasons for his actions, he might have felt compensated for his time. Instead he was only grateful for the brief glimpses of sleep he snatched between the decoctions. During the morning he bothered Mrs Hemmings for bites of brick-heavy pies, always returning to the underground fires before the doctor's frequent visits.

'You are tired, Joseph?' asked Calcraft.

Bendix nodded. 'Perhaps it is the lack of air.'

'Stop, then,' said Calcraft. 'A few hours' rest and you may return. Perhaps we should eat. Or else you must take a turn towards the river.'

'We might combine the two,' suggested Bendix, 'and dine together at the Pineapple in New Street.'

Calcraft opened his mouth, trapped between resistance and discourtesy.

'It is,' said Bendix, wishing a chance to inquire of the exact nature of their business, 'a cook shop where the Prince of Wales is said to have sat beside a cooper, the Master of the Guild beside a ferryman. It is the beef that brings them together.'

Though Bendix's words were designed to appeal to Calcraft's sense of social detachment, the doctor's expression did not change. If he rarely ventured from the house, Bendix would have to make the offer more appealing.

'It would be my honour if you would consider yourself my guest,' attempted the apprentice. Bendix had indeed been told of the Pineapple in Paris. It was, he had been informed, a clean cook shop where a man might eat for a shilling if he held back from his drink. It was information aimed at pockets as shallow as Bendix's.

'I should be delighted,' said Calcraft, overcome by a forgotten sense of propriety. What gentleman would humiliate another over a cut of beef?

The Pineapple was a dim room of hunched shoulders and teeth and gums shredding flesh. Waiters wound their way from the four great spits above the fire, delivering beef, veal, pork and lamb, cups of broth and breaks of bread. As Bendix had been told, the divisions of class were abandoned at the door, an idea the French would never have brokered. Men in the finest silks sat at the same tables as journeymen and labourers. They waited a moment for a pair of chairs to become available at the long central table that cut the room. Bendix watched the men of London eat. They simply consumed more than the French, digesting beasts and leaving bottles of varied spirits rolling beneath their chairs.

Calcraft sank his teeth into a fatty piece of beef and nodded at Bendix in satisfaction.

'As good as home,' he said, then kindly added, 'perhaps better.'

'It is a sea change,' said Bendix, 'a quickening of the gait.'

'You are already weary of Lincoln's Inn?' smiled the doctor.

'No,' protested Bendix, 'merely weary. The air, at least, was invigorating.' He did not add that he also found the meat reminiscent of their day's work and was not finding it easy to divorce from the memory of Mr Pink. He chased his lamb around the plate with a spoon, then grabbed the coat tails of the waiter and ordered two more bottles of beer.

'Do you never eat in cook shops?'

'Never dine abroad,' said Calcraft, 'not with Mrs Hemmings so constant.'

'And has she always been with you?' pried Bendix.

Calcraft laughed. 'No, sir. I was not so different from

yourself a hundred years ago, all bread and begged oysters.
The days of debt, long past.'

'You were in debt?' asked Bendix, amazed.

'Worth less than a button on your coat,' smiled Calcraft.

'So how the rise?'

'Through reputation, innovation and the sense to hold my
tongue.'

'We talk of physicking?'

'Of course,' said Calcraft. He chewed a portion of gristle
then removed it with tapered fingers from his mouth. 'There
are the ways the Ancients tell us to cut a man and there is
mine own manner. It was favoured enough to carry me
across Europe. I was wise enough not to share my aptitude.
The cost remained high.'

'What is your manner?'

'Perhaps you shall see it, Joseph. Patience, please. Above
all, it is precision and speed that have rewarded me. The
sufferers know they must submit to pain for their cure, but
they do not wish it to last. Any man will part with gold to
avoid anguish.'

'You were esteemed?'

'In Liepzig,' said Calcraft, 'I was once given a thousand
pounds for removing the stones of a certain baron. His gen-
erosity set a standard that many attempted to equal.'

'Yet you have not cut in twenty years.'

'Money,' said Calcraft, 'is an odd girl. You must work to
your bones for a family of gold, yet once there it spawns on
your behalf. Doubled my gold in the South Sea. And what
was that? Speculation. Having gold enough to risk and luck
enough to retreat.'

Calcraft took a small glass bottle from his coat pocket and
uncorked it. He introduced a slim river of the liquid into his
beer. When he looked up, he saw Bendix's questioning eyes.

'Laudanum,' said the doctor. 'I am unused to being about. Calms me.'

'You shall fall asleep in your dinner,' chided Bendix with a smile.

'No, no,' said Calcraft, 'I have always found that a little tends to sharpen the mind.'

'And a decent dose brings rest?'

The doctor nodded. 'Often fitful, only a heavy dose guarantees sleep.'

Bendix raised his glass. 'How did you come across your method of cutting?'

'Experiment and practice. Theory and determination,' shrugged Calcraft, sipping on his beer, unwound through the chatter of the room and the prospect of his opiate.

'Yet we do not cut?' said Bendix. 'Mr Pink is intended for elsewhere?'

'Cutting was not vital to me. I am adept at it and it rewarded me, but just because a man enters one door, may he not knock at another?'

'Your theory for Mr Pink is not connected to cutting?'

'You are familiar with the work of Jean Baptiste Denis?'

'Acquainted,' said Bendix unconvincingly.

'Physick to Louis the Fourteenth, a man of some vision. He opened a vein in a madman's arm, ran a silver tube from the lunatic to the leg of a calf and let a cupful of blood flow. The mildness of the calf, he thought, would calm the heated blood of the madman. Twice Denis repeated the process. There were complications, vomiting, but the following day the lunatic displayed great presence of mind and a surprising calmness.'

'You seek a cure for madness?'

Calcraft laughed and patted Bendix on the knee. 'Nothing so dramatic, sir. No, no, not madness at all. What I am suggesting, what Denis discovered, was that blood carries character. This is only half of the solution to the problem I have set myself.'

'The rest?'

Calcraft wiped his hands against his breeches. 'LeMaître said you were the most searching of his students, but knowledge is earned. Unlike blood, it cannot be passed from one being to another.' Calcraft had had enough of his interrogation. It had amused him to share his thoughts, fragments of his past, but Bendix was too new to him, too unproved for a clear sight of his intentions.

Conversation remained dense with words of medicine and anecdotes older than Bendix himself. The remainder of the meal passed in pleasant banter, the opiate slowly reining in Calcraft's tongue. The quieter the doctor appeared, the more benevolent his smile grew until it seemed that the Pineapple revolved around his bright and blissful face. The apprentice was satisfied with the scraps gathered from the doctor and happily withdrew a pair of shillings for their meal and two pennies for their waiter. When Calcraft rose in his haze, Bendix signalled the waiter that his money lay upon the table. Both the doctor and the waiter turned away. Bendix looked longingly at the pennies, but he could not allow himself to retrieve them.

On returning to Lincoln's Inn, Calcraft ushered Bendix down the stairs to the basement. Just before the entrance to the central space of the oval table was a door that Bendix had presumed was used for storage.

'An experiment I wish to share,' said the intoxicated Calcraft, making two attempts to turn the handle of the door. He paused half in and half out of the room, then rummaged in his long pocket and pulled a pair of pipes from within, offering one to Bendix.

'I smoke rarely.'

'For me.'

The room was little bigger than a country larder, and Calcraft crossed it in four modest paces. On either side of the room was a shelf jutting from the brick walls. On either shelf sat three lamps covered by glass cases, one transparent, the other stained a deep red. Calcraft lifted the cases and lit the lamps, suffusing the room in surprising brightness. The unsteady doctor, pipe gripped between his teeth, bent over to raise a pair of light tin contraptions that had been hidden by the open door. Each fitted exactly over the glass cases. Calcraft shut the door and plunged the room into utter darkness. It took a moment for Bendix's eyes to adjust, but he soon saw that each tin sheet was perforated by tiny holes that aimed their beads of light at the ceiling. A match flared in front of the apprentice's face. He dipped his head forward to light his pipe, then watched Calcraft repeat the procedure and wave the flame out.

The doctor stared down into the orange bowl of his pipe, sucked in a mouthful of smoke and blew it upwards to the ceiling. Bendix followed suit. Thin pillars of light, invisible in the darkness, waxed and waned according to the density of the smoke. Within a few minutes the pair were rewarded with a series of interconnected beams, the plain light sharper and crueller, severing the shafts emitted by the red-stained glass.

'What is it,' asked a bemused Bendix, 'that I am supposed to observe?'

Calcraft continued to puff.

'The beauty?' questioned the apprentice.

'Light,' said Calcraft, 'and its behaviour. We are looking for a combination of weaknesses and strengths. The depth of staining. It is an alternative to our studies.'

Had Bendix known what their true studies were, he might have found the occasion more illuminating instead of just artificially beautiful. He had seen the transparent shell of a water gnat, the carcass of a thief and a room full of smoke and light. It was as if the doctor was daring him to connect the theories. Perhaps he was wrong. After all, thought Bendix, there was no connection between Newton's pursuit of cartography and his interest in alchemy other than the basic root of human curiosity. They stood together for a dozen minutes, each fascinated by the play of the intersecting shafts, structures resurrected and silenced by the play of pipe smoke and coloured light. At the end of the bowl of tobacco, Calcraft opened the door to the room and, with a suitably large cough, waved a goodnight to Bendix and headed towards the west wing.

Bendix blinked the smoke from his eyes and set about completing his tasks of decoction. His tobacco-clogged mind turned to their dinner talk of Denis and the transfusion of blood. The doctor's conversation had hardly enlightened the apprentice, for decoction and transfusion were alien to one another. However it had been enough to excite him to the potential of Calcraft's brilliance and remind him of the doctor's wealth. His memory bore only the vaguest smudge of the doctor's constant sipping of laudanum.

At the end of the night, when the reduction of the spleen was all that kept Bendix from his bed, Calcraft descended, the aroma of Virginia tobacco still heavy in the basement. The warmth of the fire had stoked the temperature of the room and the ceramic pot balanced on the grid trembled from the heat. Before Calcraft lay his apprentice, coat folded across his lap, head cocked back, Adam's apple bobbing in the lazy rhythms of peaceful sleep and malted beer breath.

Had Bendix been awake he would have seen disgust

spread across the doctor's face. He looked as if he might spit fire, should he open his mouth. Taking a thick linen cloth, he removed the pot from the fire and peered inside to find the remains of the spleen, charred and brittle. Calcraft placed the pot on the floor beside Bendix and walked back up the stairs, in search of laudanum to calm him from assaults of anxiety and anger.

It took another hour for the apprentice to wake, but only seconds for him to understand the scene before him. He had not been racked by such guilt or worry since he had broken his father's favoured glass, twenty years before. The man had turned red with scarcely suppressed fury. Bendix had not been able to suppress a terrible burst of laughter that erupted from nerves. A beating had been delivered with a leather strap that had drawn blood from the backs of his legs and his stream of tears had taken a night to dry.

Bendix reasoned that there should be no such fear in the mind of a grown man. He climbed the stairs to the library, where the doctor sat before an open window.

'Do you know what you have done?' asked the doctor calmly, without so much as looking up.

'I must apologise,' said Bendix softly.

'You do not understand,' murmured Calcraft, 'the extent of your error. It might take another month, a six-month until the process may be repeated.'

'The next sessions?' asked Bendix.

'We do not seek merely a hanged man,' said Calcraft. 'Were it that simple we could hang a dozen error-strewn apprentices. It is a question of merit. What crime it is that hangs the man and not the man himself.'

Bendix nodded and then offered, 'The sound of the fire, sir. I believe it sang me to sleep.'

'Go,' said Calcraft. 'Clear this house of Mr Pink. We shall see each other with company at dinner.'

'A lady, sir?' asked Bendix and regretted the question immediately.

Calcraft turned to deliver a look of mild disdain. He took a long breath, knowing it would speed the coursing of the laudanum through his body, 'No ladies, Mr Bendix. Merely an acquaintance whom it might amuse you to meet.'

Bendix managed the correct variation of smile, expressing humility, gratitude and a measured degree of subservience. He bowed deeply and retreated.

Defoe was ushered in by Lemon, but instead of being led to the door of the library from where Bendix spied his progress in sartorial elegance, Defoe was shown to the right. He was the first person, other than Julia, whom Bendix had ever seen enter Calcraft's private side of the house. There was an unaccountable stirring of jealousy that Bendix could not comprehend. He watched as Lemon returned alone, before retreating to his port and fidgeting among books.

His spirits were revived somewhat when, as the pair finally entered the library, he was introduced to Defoe by the doctor as 'my young man'. A weight fell from Bendix's shoulders. Their guest was between master and apprentice in height, perhaps sixty or so in age, or at least well lined and well lived. His eyes blinked seldom and slowly, his vast, shaggy peruke almost a decade and a half behind fashion, as if the wealth and position that he once possessed, had never been improved upon and never been forgotten. Large about the waist, fat ankles overflowing shoes, he was an unfit man in obvious pain. LeMaître had always told Bendix that a fellow with stones might be spotted at a hundred paces. Defoe was given to the occasional, excruciating wince that

made him draw his breath sharply then bow to the pain
before he might resume his sentence.

The manner between Defoe and Calcraft was entirely
familiar, two brothers who tolerated Bendix as a distant
cousin. Only when Lemon entered quietly to announce
dinner did Bendix understand their small company were the
full extent of Mrs Hemmings's culinary worries and that no
one else would be joining them for dinner.

The long wake table was headed by the doctor with
Bendix and Defoe opposite one another on either side. The
deep red of the walls seemed pink where touched by candles,
the table top a parade of silver: candlesticks, an array of
serving spoons, trencher salts and a delicate bowl, shaped as
clover, that sat between the doctor and Defoe. It was not
until Defoe plucked the dropper from the table and
squeezed five drops on to his tongue that Bendix was sure
that the liquid condiment was laudanum. Defoe actually
sighed with anticipated relief, closed one eye against a flicker
of pain and complimented Bendix on his fine lawn shirt.
Lemon entered, a thin belt of sweat illuminating his bald
head, and placed a cairn of oysters before them.

'What news of Applebee?' asked Calcraft, then turning to
Bendix, added for his information, 'Mr Defoe is my only
source for the world of London. Excepting yourself, of
course, but Defoe is everywhere.'

Bendix marvelled at the doctor's prompt acceptance of
his terrible error in ruining their experiment and nodded
appropriately.

'*Was* everywhere,' corrected Defoe.

'Hindered by the stones of course,' Calcraft's hand span
the small pot of laudanum again and again. 'Yet, he has
known and survived the affairs of state for thirty years, Mr
Bendix, as long as you have lived and breathed.'

'I have read your work, sir,' began the apprentice. Defoe allowed himself an expectant smile and Bendix understood that he was not immune to flattery. 'Own a print of *The True-Born Englishman*, was most entertaining and illuminating, especially to one in French exile.'

'And did you consider it comment or satire?' asked the writer.

'Both, sir,' said Bendix cautiously, 'weighing towards satire.'

Defoe nodded.

'There is nothing in London, in . . . Europe that our friend has not expressed a written opinion about,' continued Calcraft, scooping a dozen oysters upon his plate.

'The doctor is too kind, or perhaps teases. To express an opinion is often no better than passing wind – a brief trumpet of attention. So much is written without understanding. I confess many interests,' said Defoe nodding, 'yet, of your world of natural philosophy, I remain ignorant.'

'We both stand in the doctor's shadow,' said Bendix inclining his head towards his master.

'Let us raise a quick glass to the end of flattery. Enough, enough.' While Defoe and Bendix hoisted their glasses, they exchanged grins and recognised something familiar in each other's sincerity. Calcraft swallowed twelve quick drips of laudanum.

'What do you write of now?' Bendix asked Defoe.

'I have discovered that there is much money to be made where there is none to be found. I talk of our prisons – Newgate, Bridewell, the Fleet. The tales told before Tyburn.'

'Do they sell well?'

'At the hanging of the Waltham Blacks,' said Defoe, 'my publisher, Applebee, ran four separate prints of a thousand copies.'

'At what price?'

'A shilling.'

'From flattery to economics, it is all quite indigestible,' protested Calcraft.

'Forgive us, Edmund,' said Defoe, reaching out for the oysters while considering how far to swing the conversation. 'You have heard of Sheppard, I presume?' he asked. 'Of course, you do, for the deaf know his name, sir,' continued Defoe. 'It is sung from every corner. I have seen four columns in the *Courant* within the week.'

'The deaf may know the name,' said Calcraft, 'but alas, not the blind. Some detail if you please.'

'Merely a housebreaker,' said Defoe, 'and not a bold one. Caught twice by Mr Wild, and twice escaped. Ergo, the fame.'

'The *Courant* called him a fermenter of revolution,' chimed Bendix, catching sight of an immediate redemption.

Defoe laughed. 'If you could but see the man. We sat together in Newgate only a week ago. He is no taller than my boot. Nimble, of course. Very nimble, amusing even, but no leader of men.'

'One does not have to lead men to be chosen as a symbol,' said Bendix. 'If I were a porter, or cooper, or some poor Newgate soul, I would take great relish in the tale of a man who could not be held by prison walls. He is the very essence of freedom.'

The doctor looked up at Bendix in the most suspicious manner. 'What is it you say?'

Bendix saw the challenge of the doctor's eyes, but could not think of any remark that might have given offence. 'Freedom, sir. The people, they see him as an embodiment of freedom. Though is it not true, Mr Defoe, that he is also suspected of practising the black arts?'

Defoe pinched the squirming flesh of an oyster between his fingers and paused. 'Aided by the Devil, perhaps.'

Calcraft stirred. A trifle more encouragement, thought Bendix, and we might have an understudy for Mr Pink or at least an antidote for the temporary affliction of guilt.

'Is there truth in this?' asked Calcraft.

'It depends on your own beliefs, does it not?' answered Defoe and swallowed the oyster. 'If you believe in the Devil then there may be some substance in the matter. An extraordinary cull, to be sure, is our Mr Sheppard. To elude Jonathan Wild, you might well think a man needed divine or infernal assistance.'

'You mentioned Wild,' said Bendix, turning to Defoe, 'a name I have heard without understanding where it derives its power.'

'Indeed,' said Defoe, 'you are fresh in London.'

'Indulge me, sir,' urged the apprentice.

'Once,' said Defoe, ' a debtor, bailiff, an assistant to the watch, now the General of all Thief Takers. According to his own exhalations, he is the scourge of every thief in the city. I would wager that there are few either end of London town that Jonathan Wild does not know of. I myself lost a silver cane on a Thursday. I applied to Mr Wild upon the Friday morning. The next Monday, he sent me word that my cane had been recovered.'

'Were the thieves hanged?'

Defoe shook his head. 'They were paid, sir. Mr Wild arranged a meeting. I passed a man a guinea, he returned my cane, worth four times such.'

'No talk of money,' said Calcraft lifting an oyster to the ceiling and draining the shell.

'Does this make him thief, or Thief Taker?' asked Bendix.

'It is a hard answer, but it *does* make him damnably useful.'

Defoe winced from pain again, and clenched his eyes tight in agony while the spasm racked him. Calcraft stood and reached for his arm.

'It has passed,' said Defoe, and his features unwound. Still, he poured ten drops of laudanum onto his tongue.

'Mr Sheppard and Mr Wild are not among each other's favourites?' asked Bendix.

'No,' said Defoe, 'there are those who say that Wild simply postures as this instrument of law. Perhaps he runs his thieves as a guild. Sends them on their business, pays them in silver. When the victim applies to the Thief Taker, they must pay him in gold. Wild reunites us with our canes, we are all content. Mr Sheppard does not conduct his business with the Thief Taker. Works at his own pace, and it is a profitable one. Not the sort to attract Wild. Yet Mr Sheppard's escapes mock him. He wishes him hanged.'

'I should like to meet Mr Sheppard,' said Bendix.

Defoe was in the middle of a shrug when Calcraft slapped an oyster shell upon the table and cried, 'A capital idea.'

Defoe sought his friend's eyes with his own to establish his gravity. 'It can be done,' said the writer.

'I look forward to it,' smiled Bendix with ultimate relief.

Defoe resumed his feast, and in the absence of a new topic added, 'Both Mr Sheppard and Mr Wild are the sons of carpenters, like our own Jesus Christ. It is, however, all they share in common, Mr Wild believing that greatness is defined by the number of men who work for him, Mr Sheppard considering his greatness on the number who work against him.'

'Mr Sheppard fascinates,' encouraged Bendix.

'He remains a thief,' intoned Defoe.

'And sooner or later,' added Calcraft, 'thieves shall be hanged.' The doctor called loudly for Lemon. The slap of

footsteps approached slowly, Lemon dipped from shadows
to candlelight, removing the shucked shells. Within minutes
they were replaced by a tower of jugged pigeons, a lamb's leg
and a lobster the size of a lap dog, framed in quivering jelly.
There were many protestations from Defoe as to how
spoiled he had become, how he was not used to such riches,
how he would have to be bled to even his humours.

They talked and sipped and poured, a languid Bendix
taking a considerable liking to Defoe but mostly relieved to
be in eloquent and garrulous company and not sentenced to
books. Defoe encouraged him in his descriptions of the
boulevards of Paris, of the latest styles of court, the play-
wrights and penmen. It was an evening of great success
until Lemon sneezed while his hands were full of empty
plates. They teetered for a second, and Calcraft and Bendix
watched him closely to see if he might control his balance
through the second sneeze, and when he did they gave him
small applause. Yet, turning back to Defoe to praise Lemon,
they found the writer doubled in pain. It was neither wince
nor spasm but a full contortion, where Defoe's head,
already bright with wine, was now afire. He did not
respond to any of their urges, but kept his head low upon
the table, until the doctor stood and walked to the back of
his friend's chair.

'Bendix, Lemon.'

Bendix held the front legs, Lemon the back and, like over-
worked chairmen, they hoisted the heavy writer into the air
and struggled back towards the hallway. The doctor preceded their progress, opening the door to the private side of
the house. Bendix, overcome by his sudden entrance to the
forbidden, banged the chair against the hinges of the door,
eliciting a low accusatory grunt from the writer.

They entered a second hallway, which led to a narrow set

of stairs, lit by a long window, already shuttered for the evening. The teetering sedan followed the doctor down the only turn from the corridor. Bendix and Lemon backed into a skinny room and set the writer down in the middle of stacks of books and papers that sprang from the wooden floor like termite hills. Calcraft's own journals, in their familiar calf-skin bindings, lay over in the corner. Obeying the doctor's instructions, they lowered Defoe on to the only other piece of furniture in the room, a low sofa of crushed blue velvet that held the deep imprint of a reclining body.

'Breathe, Daniel,' chanted Calcraft. 'Concentrate on air.'

'Bleed me,' whispered Defoe.

'May I fetch my instruments?' asked Bendix. The doctor nodded, then calmly took a seat by the wretched Defoe and laid a hand upon his shoulder.

After collecting his silver bowl and lancet, Bendix returned up the stairs and boldly strode into the private side. It caught him before turning into the study, a sweet spiral of gossamer perfume that brought him to a stop. An unfamiliar feminine scent. From within the study. Perhaps one of the doctor's potions, uncorked to revive Defoe. With a blush of expectation, the apprentice entered the room.

Bendix stood above Defoe in a disappointed stupor, barely noticing as Calcraft removed the lancet and bowl from his hands. Not a soul. Indeed, Lemon had retreated. The perfume dissipated, was never in the room to begin with. He had been close in the corridor, believed the wake had even washed down the stairs over him. Been wished in his direction.

'There,' said Calcraft. Bendix looked down to see Defoe's blood brimming the bright silver. The writer had opened his eyes for the first time in minutes, looking composed, a touch embarrassed over the disruption. When he closed them again, it was in peace. Calcraft motioned for Bendix to follow him, then walked him out into the corridor.

'I think Mr Defoe shall rest the night in my study.' He handed Bendix his instruments, the bowl still bright with blood.

'Soon he shall need his stones cut,' said Bendix.

'Of course,' returned Calcraft and then to his apprentice's tacit question. 'Naturally, I will. Goodnight to you.'

CHAPTER SIX

Bendix rose early and found Mrs Hemmings preparing chocolate in the kitchen. Her eyes were rimmed with redness, her waddle distinctly drunken but her demeanour altogether improved by alcohol. Julia entered, in her unhurried gate, picked up the silver tankard of chocolate and turned to go up the stairs.

'Is Mr Defoe too frail for breakfast?' inquired Bendix.

'He's had it,' said the glowing Mrs Hemmings, sweating freely from heat and drink.

'In his delicate condition?'

'He was well enough to call for me two hours ago, well enough for breakfast and a chair home.' The speech was conducted by a pudgy, wagging finger that drove Bendix from the kitchen.

Despite his momentary passage into his master's side the night before, Bendix found that when confronted by the closed door he lacked the audacity to open it. Instead of confirming Defoe's departure, he retired to his study with a copy of Geoffroy's *Table of Relationships* and spent the morning having the weight of the text dissolved by his distracted mind. Geoffroy contended that objects have sympathies with one another and therefore a desire to unite. Bendix considered the theory fair enough when turned to matters of the heart, or even of the purse, but he could not grasp this alchemical suggestion. How could an object desire unity with another object? Perhaps it was the mind that unlocked the keys to the world and not inanimate metals and powders.

No matter how hard he concentrated upon the pages, his eyes flicked to follow flies about the ceiling, then drifted towards sleep. London was overcast. Pear-shaped clouds seemed to force the taller buildings to the ground. Bendix ran a sweat without movement. He dozed, awoke and dozed again, walked about the roof garden seeking the motion of the wind, then returned below to rest.

Little time had passed when Calcraft knocked and entered to find Bendix leaning over the book in apparent concentration. Sensing the doctor, Bendix sat upright and stared first at his stockinged and shoeless feet, embarrassed by the state of undress, before matching eyes with the doctor. Calcraft waved a piece of paper in front of him.

'I have had a letter from our guest, Defoe, thanking us for his evening and for our extended kindness. He repeats his offer to take you to Newgate, but allows that his health forestalls his intentions.'

Bendix was buttoning his shirt, while his toes sought out his shoes.

'We must, then, cut for his stones.'

The apprentice paused in his dress.

'You have cut before?' asked Calcraft.

'No, sir. I have attended many operations of course, but LeMaître thought it wise . . .'

'And is proved wrong. We shall learn much.'

Bendix bobbed his head twice in an eagerness that Calcraft immediately mistook for doubt.

'You are sure you wish a life as a surgeon?'

Bendix nodded.

'You must be positive,' said Calcraft, 'for when a nation abounds in physicians, it grows thin in people.'

The apprentice smiled broadly, 'It is also said that, "God heals and doctors collect their fees." But you and I, sir, we know there is more to physick than constant bleeding and pithy nostrums.'

'*We* do,' smiled Calcraft. 'I suppose that you have also heard the difference between consulting an old physician and a younger one?'

'Tell me, sir,' said Bendix.

'The younger will kill you,' intoned Calcraft, 'and the older will let you die.'

Bendix ground his right foot into the remaining shoe to complete his costume.

'We are to cut Defoe tomorrow,' continued Calcraft. 'It shall be a bloody business and it shall be brief. Where most fumble in the guts for minutes, I shall open and close him in such time. There shall be much pain. But most shall be experienced in anticipation.'

After hearing the word 'tomorrow', Bendix's mind effectively closed for the day. Calcraft observed the sea change sweep his apprentice and left with few more words, advising his charge to spend the remainder of the day walking in the town. Bendix's departure was preceded by a crackling thunderstorm, sheets of rain that ran up and down Lincoln's Inn Fields in visible cavalry charges and swirling formations. The rains stopped suddenly, the threat of the clouds remained, but the humidity had abated to the point where

Bendix readied himself without perspiring. He did not smother his face in the customary powders for fear that they would melt and stain his dress, but picked up his physician's cane and left the house.

Though eager for the morrow to arrive, he suffered no fear or anxiety. His role would be little different to the operations he had attended in France. Calcraft would be the man who cut, Bendix remaining a mere observer. The only change that he could surmise would be the proximity. Before he had sat among his fellow students and members of the public in the operating theatre. Tomorrow they would operate on Defoe in his own house, and there would be nothing to separate him from the experience. If anything, it was an occasion for potential atonement, where Bendix might make amends for his previous error and regain the doctor's trust.

He wandered not far from the Fleet, then turned and moved in the direction of Newgate Prison. It was so busy a corner of the city that at first Bendix believed that he had been misdirected and found himself at Smithfield. A steady flow of people passed beneath the blackened stones of the Gateway, many heading down the Newgate Road to the Old Bailey. Bendix paused, head cocked upwards to observe the five storeys. Crowning the Gateway was a small windmill, ventilation for the prisoners, supposed Bendix, and yet a contraption incongruous with the sombre building. Despite the absence of sun, the crushed glass that lined the edge of the crenellation winked at him. As he cast his eyes from the roof to the arch of the gateway, he saw something that far exceeded the windmill in absurdity. Adorning the arch were the mocking statues of Liberty, Peace, Plenty, Concord, Mercy and Truth.

He wound his way along a narrow, filthy street behind the prison, untouched by the afternoon sun. The morning rains had raised a black, gelatinous mud in the centre of the street. Heads bobbed by, few sedans, no horses. It was altogether a blackened flue of a passage, connecting the chimney stack of the prison to the comparative freedom of the Fleet. Thirty yards ahead, he believed he saw the sharp angles of Sixes walking next to a squat, bewigged gentleman. He was about to call his name when Sixes turned off the street and entered a tavern. Bendix passed the Baptist's Head and followed Sixes through the door of the Blue Boar, following the scent of lonely curiosity.

Bendix was surprised to find himself in a room of some respectability. Dark curtains draped the windows and a single bench traced the walls of the room. There was fresh sawdust about the floor, a mixed clientele of porters, lawyers and clerks. However, Sixes was not in sight. Bendix turned to a pair of porters sitting by the door.

'I am searching for a cull named Sixes.'

'Who are you?' asked the man.

An affronted Bendix declined to answer the question and merely repeated his own inquiry.

'Nonesuch,' said the man at once.

Bendix considered this for a moment before insisting, 'You are saying the man does not exist?'

The man nodded slowly and broke into a wide smile.

'If you asked me who Obadiah Crest was,' began Bendix, 'I would say, "I do not know. I have not heard the name before." I would not say, "Nonesuch." Because, by denying the man's existence, all you are doing is confirming that he not only exists, but is at hand. Kindly point me in his direction.'

The man nodded in appreciation of the argument but did not answer, demonstrating to Bendix that even the most nimble of inquiries faltered against silence. Bendix stared at the man's partner, then about the tavern, but he could only see a dozen smiles and not an eye cast in sympathy. Discomforted, he retreated and avoiding the thick mud of the middle of the street managed to find his way home while keeping his breeches spotless.

Lemon disappeared to clean Bendix's still warm shoes while the apprentice set about examining his creased print of Geoffroy. Once more he became lost between the tables of quicksilver and aqua fortis, the notions of affinity and attraction. He preferred experiment, enjoyed debate, cherished questions above answers. No man could argue with a staid text, nor could he fight it, nor even cut it. It sat there and expected to be ingested whole. Learning through texts was irrelevant when compared to learning through practice. The best he could do was to ignore Mr Geoffroy. Instead he suffused his head with a pleasant delirium of premonitions of tomorrow. Bendix put down his book and, noticing his slight tremors, picked up his pipe, packed it and headed for the roof.

The sun never emerged from behind the clouds to set. Instead the sky dimmed slowly, promising that tomorrow would be nothing but an echo of today. Bendix sat beside the herbs, feet in thyme and tangled weeds. He faced the west wing of the building, thinking of Defoe, of the feminine scent of the previous night, of pain, of Calcraft, of success. There was no wind to remove the smoke of his tobacco and it hung over him like a private rain cloud. He sang, quietly at first. It was a release to him, had always been, but once he had started he presumed he should stop lest he disturbed someone. Instantly it occurred to him that this might be the very reason to continue.

He sang in French, a mournful tune for a lost child. And yet he smiled as he sang, to present his fairest face. He repeated the tune, improvised a verse, then repeated again, shuttered by darkness and amplified by the lack of competing sounds from the ebbing city below. When he saw a figure at the window, his song was trapped in a moment's hesitation before being released fainter, more emotive than before. Finishing the song for the fourth time, he ceased his singing and sat, staring at the silhouette. It occurred to him that perhaps, after all, he could not be seen. He was looked through, dissembled by the gaze. Bendix raised a hand towards the face, but there was no reaction. The figure remained frozen. Only when darkness fell between them did Joseph Bendix descend to his study.

He struggled with the letter, knowing only that he was alone and that the figure at the window had also appeared to be alone. No matter how tenuous the link, Bendix viewed the writing of the letter simply as an effort to communicate. He understood there was something evasive about the enterprise, a frisson of illicitness that made Bendix scold himself. After all, he could approach Calcraft and ask who the figure was. However, he presumed that if the doctor had wanted to grant him an introduction, it would have happened weeks ago. In a manner, Bendix had communicated with the figure before. If he was to be betrayed, it could be only her doing.

Madam,

It is indeed an odd letter to write, having no introduction nor knowledge of you. I do, however, make the presumption that we live under the same roof, having observed you on three occasions. If this inquiry seems bold, know that it is written only in curiosity. If you might grant me the vaguest notion of your circumstance to allay my senses, I would forever, be Your faithful servant,

Joseph Bendix

The most difficult part of the enterprise was how to get the letter safely into her hands. He could not guarantee delivery, no matter how he approached the problem, and resolved to place the letter in the only place he knew her to frequent: the window sill that faced the spice garden. Despite knowing that he would have to be well rested, Bendix decided to deliver the letter at once. Folding it and sealing it with wax, Bendix waited some hours, his mind pushing constantly between Defoe and the lady in the western wing. Finally, when he deemed it so late that all were asleep, he ascended the stairs and opened the door to Calcraft's domain.

With his eyes of little use in the darkness, his other senses soon sharpened and he believed that he could still smell the traces of perfume from the previous evening. Barefoot, Bendix walked upon the sides of his feet, so that his soles were twisted to face one another. It lessened his weight on the floorboards and with blessed few creaks he groped his way to the banisters of the stairs he had noted yesterday and, step by step, scaled the stairs.

At the top of the stairs, he could turn only left or right. Imagining himself a blackbird circling above the house, Bendix concentrated on his whereabouts, turning left to keep to the inside of the house from where a view of the roof garden might be gained. He hoped that the sweat of his hands would not blur the word '*Madam*' scratched across the letter. He could hear a mouse in the boards beneath his feet and wished he might grow as small and silent. In comparison, his own breath sounded like gusts of winter wind. He kept to the corridor, and turning once again was relieved to find a pair of windows that oozed a grey light to the passage. The second window looked across to the spice garden. Bendix put the letter between the curtain and sill and, consigning its delivery to fate, turned and stole away back to his room.

CHAPTER SEVEN

Bendix and Calcraft had travelled separately, the doctor leaving some hours earlier. His departure, so rare, had disturbed the household, bringing the sleepy tongues of Julia and Mrs Hemmings to life. Why had the doctor not simply cut for the stones in his own house while Defoe was present? The inconvenience was terrible, they insisted, and Defoe's household was not one half as well run as their own. Bendix felt a touch of importance when he mounted one of the doctor's horses and threw a small wave goodbye, but it was mostly a relief to be away from the anxieties of the house that caused his smile. The letter remained a warm memory. With Calcraft abroad, fate had provided an open moment for its accidental discovery and Bendix's smile broadened as he turned north.

Daniel Defoe lived in a large, thick-walled house of red bricks in Stoke Newington, an hour's carriage ride from Lincoln's Inn Fields. It stood amid four acres of lime trees and orchards, with a kitchen garden extending from the rear walls of the house. All of this was visible from the deep window seat that Bendix sat upon that Wednesday morning while the doctor gave a final consultation to his friend.

It surprised Bendix that a writer might live in such a comfortable house. It was hardly grand, no more than a dozen modest rooms. He thought for a moment and decided that the most striking thing about the house, and it applied to Lincoln's Inn as well, was that they had been earned. His father's wealth had been handed down with dull regularity through the generations. Wealth had been stripped of importance because to Bendix it had seemed hereditary.

However, diseased branches of the family tree, economic dangers such as himself, were lopped off. He could not blame the family. Oldest sons were suppose to thrive, youngest sons span dizzy circles until they were either broken or disowned. A writer could earn a modest pot of gold. A doctor could own three houses in Lincoln's Inn Fields. Finally a smile cracked over the apprentice's face. He was among men who knew about money. If he were to walk beside them, would he not face the same sun?

Bendix was not alone in the room. Defoe's wife, who had begun the morning by hurrying about the house chasing their maid, had settled into a low yellow chair in deepest contemplation. Three daughters, all prim and pretty with their father's sharp eyes, hustled about the house, sometime stealing glances at the well-dressed apprentice. Bendix would not allow himself to return their appreciative looks, chastising himself with thoughts of the Comtesse. The remainder of the window seats were occupied by two attendants (selected by Calcraft and the elderly Mrs Defoe) chosen for their strength. One seemed awkward in his grand surroundings, the second merely stared out the window embarrassed by the flurry of women.

Calcraft had had a bench constructed for lithotomies sent a day ahead, borrowed for several pounds from an old acquaintance at the Royal College. It had stood at the foot of Defoe's bed, terrifying him throughout the night. When, finally, the three men were called up to the bedroom by Calcraft, they found Defoe absurdly dressed in a fine lawn shirt and a frock coat. And yet his head was bare of his habitual full-bottomed wig and he was nude beneath the waist. Somehow he had contrived to keep hold of a touch of pretension despite his predicament. The wrinkles of his sixty-five years were kept at bay by a general distention brought on by daily drinking. Only a wave of dark flesh beneath the eyes and two heavy lines that dropped from either side of his nose betrayed his age. Calcraft took his arm and led him gently to the board that lay at the foot of his bed. He lay back and let his eyes move from doctor to apprentice. Never had Bendix seen eyes so wide, so inflated with sober fear. Bendix did not know how to react. He nodded what he hoped was a comforting sincerity.

'Come, Daniel,' said Calcraft, and encouraged his friend to lie back against the board. At a signal from the doctor, the two men stepped forward. The heavier set of the two took a thin rope and ran it in a figure of eight over Defoe's wrists. The second attendant pushed the patient's legs up and apart, so that his knees were splayed, then took the rope from his colleague and lashed wrists to ankles. The effect was almost comical, the exposed writer's sagging testicles contracted in fear, his pale thighs gripped tightly by the attendants. Their biting fingers began to redden his flesh. Bendix heard a small moan come from Defoe and looked away to see Calcraft opening his case. Bendix brought the lanterns closer, positioning them on a table so that the shadows of the attendants would not obscure the doctor's view. The silver-handled instruments reflected the warm lights on to the oaken ceiling. The apprentice hoped they proved some distraction to the now sobbing writer.

Bendix took hold of Defoe's penis and forced himself to concentrate as Calcraft inserted a long silver catheter through the opening. Though Bendix had read of this before, knew it to be the surest way to locate the urethra and the bladder, he could not help but wince at Defoe's helpless spasms. Calcraft felt no such empathy, but took his knife and, lifting the scrotum with his left hand, made a small incision close to the anus. Bendix almost jerked the catheter. He could see that the doctor had cut with a lateral incision, not the vertical cut that was taught to every student in Europe. He watched as Calcraft immediately pushed a second catheter into the cut. Defoe shook mightily, and the doctor paused until the attendants had resumed a sure grip. Placing two fingers in Defoe's rectum, Calcraft manipulated the offending stone forward. He paused, removed his fingers, inserted a pair of small forceps and, with a happy click of the tongue, pulled the pebble forth. Within moments, he cleared the catheters and forceps. Bendix knelt to sew the cut, while Calcraft wiped his hands in the waters of the adjacent tub.

Though the entire procedure had taken less than four minutes, Defoe lay twisted against the backboard as if he had endured an eternity of damnation.

Calcraft leaned over him. ''Tis done, Daniel.'

Too exhausted to reply, Defoe was wrapped in blankets and carried by the attendants to his bed, where he lay speechless but breathing. Bendix and the attendants carefully closed the windows, banishing all light and air from the room, lining the sills with damp blankets to absorb any drafts that might creep through. On retiring, Bendix completed the clotting by laying a cloth at the bottom of the bedroom door and pushing a punch of wax into the keyhole.

Calcraft and Bendix returned to Lincoln's Inn Fields together, the apprentice's horse tethered to the rear of the carriage. The case of freshly wiped instruments bounced between them as the coachman led them home at a fast trot.

'If I may ask you, sir,' said Bendix, 'the lateral incision is your own invention?'

'It is not an invention, Joseph, merely a practice of mine.

It eases the manipulation of the forceps. If the stone is of good size, but not great, the procedure is quick.'

'Why do you not publish a paper on this matter?'

'What brings a doctor to the apex of his profession is not skill, but celebrity,' said Calcraft. 'I have had celebrity. Celebrity contradicts the privacy required for progress. It is the applause of one's own generation and means nothing, Joseph. Take what you have learned today, twist it, seize a thought and impregnate it with another. Mix substances and ideas that make no sense to mix.'

'Would the publishing of your method not benefit ten thousand men a year?'

'And bring fame, Joseph. You are not listening. Defoe yes, the rest no. They shall be saved their minutes of agony when I am gone. Posthumous publication is entirely preferable in this case. I would be heralded, Joseph. I would sit upon velvet cushions and be demanded, once again, in the courts of Europe. It is a low goal for a man to set himself.' Although Bendix listened, listened carefully, he could not help but observe that this lecture was delivered from a carriage with six horses and a velvet seat.

'And what is a high goal for a man?' he asked.

'The lateral incision,' concluded Calcraft, 'is a matter of little importance.'

When recalling their conversation that evening, Bendix could not understand how a man of such obvious intelligence might contradict himself so freely. How could he spurn celebrity and its trappings, yet admit he had taken advantage of them in his past and still lived in a world where he was denied nothing? How could he evoke a world of progress and keep such an important discovery as the lateral incision to himself? His own defence, that it was a trifle to him, seemed both weak and callous. Bendix wished to

excuse the doctor and berated himself for his lack of understanding. After all, for a man to consider the lateral incision
of no consequence meant that he must be standing on the
edge of a far greater discovery.

It was an operation that he could learn to emulate, that he
too might build a fortune about, and yet it remained unap-
pealing to him. Not only was it another man's idea, but he
found the prospect of enriching himself through fumbling in
a patient's guts quite repellent. Fascinating to witness, perhaps challenging to perform, but dabbling day in and day
out in blood and faeces was not Bendix's ideal path. When it
came to manual labour, he retained the attitude of a gentleman. Despite his recent application to work, practice and
experience, he remained devoted to thought, only driven to
action by necessity.

The final act of Bendix's evening was to smoke his pipe
upon the roof. He could not bring himself to sing that night,
so ingrained were Defoe's cries and contortions in his mind
that his attempts to play siren seemed trite in comparison.
Still, a part of him wished for the presence of the now familiar silhouette and when, after an hour had passed it did not
come, he retired, disappointed.

The days of the following three weeks passed with pleasant echoes of one another. On the first two mornings after
the operation, the doctor and Bendix rode to Stoke
Newington together to check upon the health of their
patient. Thereafter the job fell to Bendix alone. Finding
Defoe the most interesting of company, Bendix attended to
his business with great care, changing the dressings twice
during his daily visit and supervising the writer's diet.
Bendix's only disappointment during these dying summer
weeks was that he had received no answer from the western
wing. On the tenth night after the operation, he had crept

once more along the passage to find that his letter no longer rested against the window pane. How long it had been gone he could not be sure, as he had had no view of it from the garden. If he had been discovered by Calcraft, he was positive that the doctor would have mentioned it by now. The only alternatives were that it had fallen into the hands of a member of their limited household, or that it had reached its intended destination. If it had then he could only presume that she had deemed it inappropriate and, in her kindness, destroyed it.

On their two mornings together at Stoke Newington, Calcraft had advised Bendix to take note of his bedside manners. The apprentice was instructed never to stand at the foot of a patient's bed, for even if the patient was not superstitious, some sharp-eyed servant might accuse you of trying to block his master's soul should it wish to depart during your visit. On the whole the instruction was simple common sense and yet it comforted Bendix to receive an immediate chance to prove his ability and redress his earlier error.

From the third morning through to the end of the fourth week, Bendix spent five hours of the day alone with Defoe. He rode back and forth between Lincoln's Inn, always travelling in light, though the days were showing signs of shortening. The summer had already dispensed of the worst of her heat and relented with a clarity and breeziness that Bendix could not recall of England in his childhood days. He would trot happily at his horse's chosen pace until he was within two miles of Stoke Newington and then would drive the beast into a furious gallop so that the orange and yellow hue of the country bled together in a blushing streak.

The patient's consumption of two eggs and oxtail broth marked the meals of the day. In between, Bendix followed the doctor's orders, dosing Defoe with antimony to prevent the return of fevers and the syrup of oranges, because the patient was unusually fond of them. In addition, Bendix provided Defoe with a plenitude of senna to combat the constipation from his self-prescribed doses of laudanum.

The patient was sitting up in bed within five days, able to stand within ten, and wrapped in a fur coat tottering about his orchard by the beginning of the third week. He confessed to Bendix that he was most eager for his recovery so that he could leave his own house. His wife and children were well loved, even doted upon, but he avowed that his mind span so fast that he found the constancy of home life constricting. Bendix could see relief spread across Defoe's face every day as he entered. It bothered Bendix. How could a man admit to being content and yet deny his own happiness?

Defoe was a garrulous man and finding that Bendix had read little of his work, save his major poems and the *Life of Robinson Crusoe*, was able to quote himself endlessly. Every time that Bendix's face betrayed some astonishment at his wit or depth of knowledge, Defoe brimmed with a healthy warmth and could feel the surge of recovery.

The closer the two became, the more often Bendix would try to steer the subject of Calcraft and their friendship to the fore, but Defoe would resort to pithy superlatives and the apprentice knew that no new information would be gained so easily. If the writer would not even discuss Calcraft, it was useless to pry into the mysteries of the western wing.

Defoe was fond of talking, but he was no less intrigued by learning. During the fourth week of his convalescence, when their stays in the orchard were no longer confined by Defoe's exhaustion, their talk gradually centred on Bendix and his desires.

'In England science is a service to society,' said the writer, speaking from under his full-bottomed wig, 'while in France – during your studies I am sure you observed this – it is service to the truth, or, if you like, pure knowledge. The result is that France shall be ruled by philosophers and England by pragmatists. As a man who enjoys the pleasures of this life, I feel we should be glad to be English.'

'In *The Tale of the Tub* . . .' began Bendix, shifting uncomfortably with the thought that, in concerns of science, he was more French than English.

'Tub?' asked Defoe.

'Swift,' replied Bendix, 'Jonathan Swift. Do you not keep an eye upon your rivals?'

'I do,' answered Defoe, 'and therefore, read little.' He delivered this with a large wink and Bendix laughed graciously at his comic arrogance.

'Do you consider yourself a rival to your Sir Edmund?' asked Defoe. Bendix stared at him, insulted by such directness. 'Between ourselves, Joseph, I would only think it healthy.'

'I ask you,' said Bendix slowly, 'how an apprentice is supposed to compete when he is not even aware of the focus of his master's work? In the future I shall pursue my own conceits. I am developing a treatise on hypochondria. How if the imagination can cause disease, it may also cure it.'

'So disease,' inquired Defoe, 'is imagined?'

'Just so.'

'And therefore,' said Defoe, 'are we to presume that pain is also imagined? For I would have to testify against you upon that point.'

'No, sir,' answered Bendix, 'but what if your stone was created by the suggestion of your mind? What if your mind brought that stone into being, conjured it from your body?'

'Explain,' said Defoe and reversed his course along the

aisle of the orchard as if to tell the apprentice that there was a limit on time for his description.

'We are told that heavy drinking and eating might cause such a condition. So the man who eats and drinks well, who hears these reports every week of his life, slowly comes to believe that he is the very man who should have such a stone. Within months, perhaps years, it comes to pass.'

'Unlike the stone,' added Defoe. 'My mind is a little broader than most, Joseph, so I listen. I have learned my philosophy in the school of affliction.'

Bendix suspected that his charge had spoken these words before.

'I have seen the rough side of the world as well as the smooth,' continued Defoe, 'and have in less than half a year tasted the difference between the closet of a king and the dungeon of Newgate. On the same day I have written either side of an argument for opposing publishers, so while I will not dismiss an assertion outright, I should like to be convinced by something as solid as evidence.'

'It would take years to prove that a stone might be conjured. And even then it would be impossible to prove it had arrived by suggestion,' confessed Bendix.

'So your theory cannot be proved,' smiled Defoe.

'Nor disproved,' said Bendix.

'Then you must imagine yourself a surer experiment,' concluded Defoe. 'Perhaps your mind shall be fired by the sight of Newgate.'

'I have already visited.'

'Did you pay your two pennies to visit your most dangerous Mr Sheppard?' smiled Defoe.

'I did not enter the gates.'

'There is much to look forward to.'

'When do we go?'

'Within days, my friend.'

'And do we meet Mr Wild?'

'You sound like a child, Joseph. I think you shall be in agreement with me when we depart that, of all the criminals within Newgate, it is the Thief Taker General and not the thieves who cause a man to fear.'

Bendix nodded with excitement.

'Do not mock him,' said Defoe. 'A General only becomes a General by causing the deaths of many men. He runs a corporation, he runs an army. With not even the official power of a magistrate, he has appointed a Clerk of the Northern Roads, a bruising giant named Quilt, and a skinny Jew called Sixes who controls the south of the city.'

Bendix's eyes were wide enough with excitement not to betray his surprise.

'He has devised a system. There is a minimum permitted interval for thieves appearing in the same tavern twice, routes to be followed when returning from robberies, buttons to be left undone to signify failure or success, strawbooters for hire, books of account, warehouses of storage. Altogether a system that's complexity is only equal to its corruption.' Defoe had now worked himself up into a similar state to Bendix, so that they had generated a curiously sexual pitch between them that could only be allayed by a visit to Newgate.

'All this,' said Defoe, 'while posturing as an efficient arm of the law. Perhaps we shall attend next week.'

CHAPTER EIGHT

Bendix had not been home long from attending Defoe at
Stoke Newington when Lemon interrupted dinner to inform
Calcraft that Mr Sixes was calling for his apprentice. The
doctor looked only mildly surprised and asked Lemon to
bring their guest in. Sixes held his hat before him, but
despite his look of subservience he wasted no time dabbling
in politeness.

'I have come for Mr Bendix,' said Sixes. 'I have a friend in
Edgeworth in need of physick. Was hoping for his assistance.'

Calcraft turned to his apprentice. 'Go, Joseph, go. Is this
not what you wish for?'

Bendix did not even need to answer to show his eagerness, but put down his fork, rose from the table and
descended to his room to gather his instruments. His tongue
felt thick, his mouth dry. An apprentice did not have a reputation to lose, but a man who practised alone was to be
judged and leveraged on his good name.

Sixes relieved Bendix of his instruments and led him
through the kitchen to the door to the mews. There was no
carriage, but a pair of saddled horses tethered to a porter's
rest. Bendix paused in confusion.

'We're not bound for Edgeworth,' said Sixes. 'Up now.'

Bendix climbed on immediately, indeed he would have
followed Sixes to Land's End if he might secure a patient of
means.

They galloped east for the better part of an hour, crossing

over the Bow Bridge, through the thickening villages of Stratford and Wansted. Bendix leaned over his horse to stretch his aching back. He had ridden little since his return from France, had done little exercise apart from his London diversions. Sixes seemed to melt into the saddle ahead of him, so that it seemed as if the apprentice followed a centaur and not the thin and raw-boned man who had led him from Lincoln's Inn.

They paused once in the darkness, by the inn on the Great Road, where Sixes threw silver at a stable hand to water the horses. The two men waited by a trough of black water while their mounts were attended. There was the faint smell of the damp soil and dead vegetation of marshland.

'Where are we?' asked Bendix.

'By the Whalebone,' said Sixes. When Bendix showed no sign of understanding, 'By the river,' he began. 'The year Cromwell died, they pulled the rib bone of a whale from the Thames. Seen it myself when I was 'tween knee and ankle. Five times the size of man.'

Bendix did not comment.

'The country is different to the east, not like your northern parts. You go down to Dengy or Cricksea and you'll find those that have married a dozen wives. Women in those parts, they tend towards rotting. Not fond of the wet lands.'

The apprentice allowed himself a smile to acknowledge that perhaps he was teased.

'You know your physicking?' asked Sixes.

'Am I able?' said Bendix as much to himself as to Sixes. 'I believe so.'

'Our names stand together. Remember.' He patted Bendix upon the back. 'You keep the same theories as Sir Edmund?'

'We both are fond of digressing from the accepted. I have yet to prove my own theories, but shall practise.'

'What do you believe?'

'That the imagination is often the cause of sickness.' Bendix scooped a handful of water up into his own mouth. 'I wish to prove that it can also cure.'

'Hold your words tonight, Joseph. A stable manager was thrown from his ride.' Sixes dipped his own head under water and resurfaced with a smile. 'Lest, of course, it were the horse that he imagined.'

The estate manager, Sexton, greeted them at the gate-house. He mounted one of the largest mares Bendix had ever seen and set a canter northwards. Two miles of drive separated the gatehouse from the mountainous shadow of the hall, yet it was another long mile to the stables.

The familiar London smells of manure and wet straw seemed lightened by the country air. There were two stable hands awaiting their arrival, one carrying a bull's-eye lantern that he focused upon their horses as they pulled up. Passing the lantern to Sexton, the hands held the bits of the horses, and the estate manager led Sixes and Bendix inside. They were met by a chorus of mares' coughing, which to Bendix, sensitive in his position of practising apprentice, sounded much like the scoffing of the board of surgeons.

On his first attempt to obtain his licence Bendix had gone before the examination board without sleep or any hint of sobriety, having spent the previous night in Boulogne with the Comtesse and her golden throng. To have passed his exam and left the academy in his third year would have brought pride to his family and left him with the immediate prospect of being expected to return to England to earn a living. At the time the thought of abandoning his love had horrified him. He had refused to speak French throughout the brief interview, except for one question that he had found himself answering correctly by habit. Fortunately, he had saved himself with a well-timed bout of spontaneous giggling. The board had pushed their spectacles up the bridges of their noses and signalled for his removal. As long as his father continued to pay his fees, they would not expel Bendix from his studies. He remembered his sole friend upon the board, LeMaître, looking at him with a sad-eyed loathing.

Ahead, one of the stalls lay empty, save for a table where a body lay at rest.

'His name is Blair,' said Sexton.

The prone subject was a young man, a crop of blond hair matched with an uncommon musculature that even in unconsciousness had a natural pride like the thrusting chest of a sleeping rooster.

'When did the accident occur?' Bendix asked Sexton.

'Three hours ago,' said the estate manager.

'Were you present?'

'He was thrown then kicked. I must report to his Lordship,' said Sexton. 'I shall return within an hour. You shall be well paid. Save him and your fortunes increase.' Sexton bowed, turned and left.

'To ask for fresh news in the dead of night?' said Bendix from standing over the young man. 'He is a good lord to care so for his servants.'

'For his son,' smiled Sixes.

'A bastard?' guessed Bendix.

'One of four, if rumour is to be halved,' said Sixes. 'Every family has its secrets, Joseph. Wealthier the family, dirtier the secret.'

'I suppose, then,' said Bendix, dabbling in his instrument case, 'that if you do not know your family's secret, the chances are it is you.' He brought out his lancet.

'What are you to do?'

'I think,' said Bendix, 'that he must be bled from the temple at once. The pressure is quite extraordinary. Note the shape of the back of the head. 'Tis like a wen. I should perform a trepan but I regret that I have not the instruments.'

'Shall he live without it?'

Bendix cut at the temples and bled the man of twenty ounces. A bruise crept about the perfect face of the lord's son during the course of the night. Another welled about his breast, the vague outlines of a hoof print confirming Sexton's tale. There was little for Bendix to do, save sit beside his patient and pray to God. Despite his years in Paris attempting to do nothing but drink, gamble and whore, he had absorbed a vast amount of knowledge, though only LeMaître had been acquainted with the fineness of his mind. There was no cure for Blair's condition.

Sixes was not as concerned, poking his way about the stables, commenting on the size of the mares, filling the low roof with the sweet smell of his Virginian tobacco. Blair died with the rise of the sun. Sexton was present when Bendix confirmed his passing. A servant was dispatched to the main house, returning within the half hour with words of thanks and a small purse of gold that Sixes insisted Bendix keep for himself.

'We must share it,' insisted Bendix without conviction.

'No, sir,' said Sixes, 'M'Lord will repay silence in the currency of favours. 'Tis my favoured specie.'

'I suppose,' mused Bendix, 'that you receive your gold directly from Mr Wild.'

'Merely one of my masters.'

'I have heard you are of much importance to him.'

'Look at me, Joseph,' said Sixes and spread his palms in supplication, 'and have the sense to judge me for yourself.'

Bendix rode home just before the height of noon,

exhausted, rumpled and defeated. Sixes had treated him to
a breakfast of Colchester oysters, but their richness had
done little to revive him. To lose a patient was not unusual
for any doctor yet, though he knew he had been called in
desperation and for appearance, it disappointed him that he
could do nothing to prevent or even delay the end of life. He
drew some comfort from the burden of gold and understood
that earning it had given his guineas a most marvellous
weight.

Calcraft regarded his apprentice with black humour, presuming that Defoe would be awaiting his arrival. Blessed by
the return of his memory, Bendix broke the news of his
imminent visit to Newgate Prison to the doctor, propelling
him into a realm of high excitement. He reached for the laudanum and gave himself a small dose to calm his agitation. It
occurred to Bendix in his stupor that institutions as
voyeuristic as Bethlem or Newgate incited a feral appetite
for affliction.

Never had Bendix seen such cold professionalism as when
Calcraft had cut into his friend and yet the prospect of his
apprentice's visit to Newgate had stirred the doctor. Bendix
felt a twinge of guilt for his deliberate goading of Calcraft
with tales of the black arts of the escapee Sheppard. He had
spoken at dinner to relieve himself of the guilt of his sins and
now wondered at the appropriateness of his deception. Or
perhaps not his deception but, moreover, Calcraft's enthusiasm.

'I shall not go before tomorrow,' said Bendix, seeking to
dampen the doctor's excitement. 'Perhaps the day after.
Whenever Mr Defoe chooses.'

'You must,' intoned Calcraft holding his apprentice's two
hands in his own, 'observe Mr Sheppard most closely.'

'What is it that I search for?' asked Bendix.

The doctor squeezed their hands together. 'Everything. Give me a sense of the man. How dark a soul is he? They sing about him do they not?'

'In every tavern in London, according to Defoe.'

Calcraft nodded and, tearing his hands away, patted him on the back. 'Sleep now and you shall take my coach tomorrow, Joseph. You must take my coach and hurry back when you have had your first taste.'

Bendix did sleep and slept throughout the day, untouched by dreams. It was an afternoon of heavy greys so that the small intervals of alertness that Bendix suffered were soon absorbed once again by the weight of his exhaustion. He did rise, once, to bother Mrs Hemmings for a slab of cold lamb pie, but it sat like a stone in his stomach and forced him to lie down again. He woke at dawn the next morning and was not altogether surprised to hear from Mrs Hemmings that the doctor had spent the previous afternoon sending a messenger to Stoke Newington, urging Defoe to take the apprentice to Newgate the following morning.

CHAPTER NINE

It was the darkness that affected a man. During the carriage ride, Bendix could not have been in a more buoyant mood, pocket weighed with gold, inflated with trust and the idea of joining Defoe, who knew that gaol as well as any living. Yet within a pace of the gate his gallantry was forgotten, replaced by a hollow turbulence centred in his stomach. The noise in the taproom outside the condemned hold was excruciating. It was where every man or woman who passed into the gaol had their irons removed, if they could afford the garnish to bribe the turnkeys. In Bendix's life, when metal scraped against metal, it had usually been gold or silver, but never before had he heard the sounds of iron ringing off iron so close. Beneath it sang the cries of outraged men and the familiar, boisterous laughter of drink. Focusing on Defoe's voluminous wig, Bendix paid his eighteen pence for admission and followed the writer through a hatch and down the steps of the condemned hold. With the cacophony above and the crushing darkness about, Bendix imagined that he had entered an underworld.

It was not a large room, fifteen by twenty feet, and had a single wooden barrack bed and cold stone floors slippery with the damp. To the right of the hatch through which they had descended was an aperture, protected by spikes, where prisoners could converse with their visitors. It allowed a grey light to spread among the stone. Aside from the visitors, there were four figures present, all condemned at the last sessions and attached by irons to ring bolts fastened waist high to the walls. Defoe pointed to the barrack bed and, whispering instructions to the apprentice, had him drag the bed towards where the smallest of the prisoners was leaning against the wall. The figure had a child's face and a child's build with thin brown hair swept over his head. His eyes were large, white hands prominent against his chains. Defoe had referred to Sheppard as a fox, but to Bendix he looked much more like a dirty squirrel.

'Mr Defoe,' said Sheppard, adjusting his filthy neck tie, 'welcome. You are my most frequent visitor.'

'Good day, Jack,' returned Defoe.

'I'm seeing you've brought your footman,' continued Sheppard, motioning with his bound hands towards Bendix.

Then ignoring the apprentice, 'Defoe, I congratulate you, your friendship far exceeds the fashion of the times, yet no manners, an introduction if you please.'

'This,' said Defoe, turning, 'is Mr Joseph Bendix, a friend.'

'Friend with physician's cane. Always hiding, never sharp, Defoe. As long as you've not brought one up from Surgeon's Hall.'

It had not taken Sheppard a half-minute to determine the true cause for the stranger's visit. Bendix lost his ability to speak for a moment, while he considered his mission: to examine the future prospect of decoction.

'A dumb physician,' continued Sheppard, 'where'd you find these men, Defoe? A dumb physician is the man who can charge no fees.'

'I am,' spat Bendix at last, 'merely an apprentice.'

'As was I,' said Sheppard, and bowed his head in apparent sincerity, as if to let his visitor know that he would relent.

'Mr Defoe,' said Bendix, 'sings greatly of your abilities.'

'And is kind of him,' answered Sheppard, 'but nature does-n't give a man an appetite without the means to feed him.'

'They tell me you are to be hanged in five days,' said Bendix, 'so whatever it is that nature did grant you, she is about to take away.'

Sheppard nodded. 'You don't hear me clearly, but soon we shall fix that, shan't we Daniel?'

Defoe, who had been sitting with his chin in his hands, smiling all the while, nodded. 'Mr Bendix is correct in one respect, Jack.'

Sheppard cocked his head at the writer.

'God may have granted you much, but he has also bur-dened you with the terrible weight of the absence of friends.'

'We've talked of this before, Defoe.'

'Every man should find another in which to place his trust,' said Defoe slowly. 'Some will seek a wife and share child and bed and secrets from the outside world. You have Bess, Jack Sheppard, and twice she's turned you over. Others won't step outside their family, but you have had your own brother turn evidence on you. Others will form a family without a family, a gang determined against the world. You Jack, have been betrayed by that too. Poor choices, for you are alone.'

Bendix noted the absence of interruption, the silence of respect and knew all that Defoe said to be true.

'I am the only person you may trust,' continued Defoe, 'and it is a guaranteed trust, Mr Sheppard, for we are in the fortunate position where we may do one another a favour. Remember this, for it is an even trade.'

Sheppard nodded and pulled at his nose with a chained hand, while Bendix turned to face Defoe to see if he would elaborate on his suggestions.

'Bendix,' said Sheppard. 'They keep an Ordinary here, he has an apprentice too, helps him pass the message of the Lord. More aged than us, because God takes his tolls. He comes about like spectres to press confessions from all caged birds. Now he does not speak as well as this one here.' He jabbed a finger in Defoe's direction. 'The Ordinary has concern for your soul, while Defoe appeals to a man's life and pocket. 'Tis an easy choice, is it not?'

'Depending on a man's priority,' said Bendix.

Sheppard directed his laugh to the stone floor as if it were a joke that no one else in the hold might share.

'The fright,' said Sheppard, continuing to address Bendix, 'is that Defoe always *seems* right. Must be age. Whether or not events proceed as we expect, I'll grant you as smooth a tongue as the slyest of court talkers.'

Defoe bowed his head in acceptance. 'We shall see each other again,' said Defoe and pushed himself upright.

As Bendix stood, Sheppard tipped his head politely. 'Delighted to have the pleasure of your company. By the time we meet again, Mr Bendix, I hope to deserve grander surroundings in which to entertain you.'

Emerging through the hatch, back into the high sun that sat over the tower, both Defoe and Bendix held their hands up to shield their faces. When his eyes adjusted, Bendix was shocked to find Sixes not ten yards ahead of him, in conference with a stout, broad-jawed man dressed in the finest of black silks. His broken nose and scarred cheek seemed to belie the neatness of his dress. A mild look of confusion came across Sixes's face but he did not turn away from Bendix's stare. With the smallest nod of his head, imperceptible to all but Bendix, he moved his thumb against his forefinger in rapid succession, before dismissing the apprentice with a nod. Bendix interpreted this as a sign that he was not to be approached now but that they would talk later, at Sixes's pleasure.

Defoe took Bendix by the arm and marched him past the two figures. When they were some yards away, he leaned close to the apprentice and whispered, 'Jonathan Wild and his Jew.'

'You will not make an introduction?' asked Bendix, only half seriously, should Defoe wish to take his request in jest.

'They are not strong men of Bartholomew's Fair, to stare at for a penny,' said Defoe. 'I would sooner have you shake hands with snakes than hazard an introduction. You do not listen to me well enough, Joseph.'

When they were safely ensconced in the doctor's carriage, Bendix propped both their canes on the cushions between them and asked, 'Do you visit Sheppard often?'

'On five, maybe six occasions. I have recorded his entire confession.'

'Does London really sing of that child?' asked Bendix.

''Tis a duet,' said Defoe, 'but soon a raging chorus.'

Bendix shifted in his seat while Defoe shouted orders to the coachman to take him to his home in Rope Maker's Alley before continuing to Lincoln's Inn Fields.

'Within the day,' continued Defoe, 'Sheppard shall be gone. I did not lie when I told you he has escaped before. From the New Prison, by Bridewell and at the Round House. When he flees from Newgate, the city shall know his name.'

'And how does a man escape from the condemned hold?'

'That I cannot tell you,' said Defoe. 'He asked only for a file. That much I granted.'

Bendix stared at the writer.

'A small one,' smiled Defoe, 'happened to let slip from my sleeve.'

'And that is the limits of his black arts?' asked an astounded Bendix.

'I would wager neither you nor I would escape with a saw, hammer and seven days,' answered Defoe. 'This Thursday, the morning after his escape, he shall send a letter to the *Courant* that will be published upon the front page, addressed to Mr Wild, inciting the rogue to capture him.'

'And you shall write this letter on his behalf, I suppose?'

'Indeed,' said Defoe, 'you begin to understand the creation of sensation.'

Bendix had barely ordered his thoughts by the time he returned to the doctor's house. He believed that he would practically be assaulted by the doctor in his excitement to learn of Sheppard, but instead he was greeted in the kitchen by Mrs Hemmings, who informed him that the doctor had retired for sleep and looked forward to his company at dinner.

They sat together for over an hour, during which time the doctor pushed his quails around his plate in a slow dance and cracked his oyster shells together merely for the sake of hearing them crack. Bendix suspected correctly that Calcraft had indulged too much in the numbing effects of laudanum and had not fully emerged from his stupor. He was wan, floating in an indiscernible aura of jigsaw thoughts, hands trembling if they lay idle. When conversation began, it was not until Lemon arrived with the third course of jugged pigeon that Calcraft mentioned the word Newgate.

'What manner of rogue is he?' inquired the doctor.

It was the question Bendix half dreaded. Sheppard, thought Bendix, was certainly a thief, a sly chit of some charm and winning manner, but at no stretch could he be considered the dark soul who deserved the hanging that Calcraft sought. Bendix had met many in Paris with blacker souls. He even believed his own soul blacker than Sheppard's, at least until he had been delivered by his epiphany of responsibility and had cast off friends, women and idleness. However, to inflate the doctor's opinion of Sheppard and then disappoint him might bring their relationship to an inescapable nadir. Besides, it was not the man's life that they weighed, but merely the breathless body of a criminal.

'A peculiar rogue,' said Bendix. 'Shrewder than a fox.'

'What does he resemble?'

'A child,' continued Bendix, 'with eyes quick and lacking in all innocence.'

'Daniel called him a fermenter of revolution,' questioned Calcraft. He raised a shaking hand to his face and ran a finger under his nose. '"Tis fair?'

'Men might rise up about him, perhaps,' muttered Bendix. 'They say he fired a pistol at Jonathan Wild that flashed in its pan. Would be murder, were it not for Lord's luck.'

Calcraft considered the words and nodded. 'I thank you,' he said, 'Daniel often succumbs to the charms of the needy. You, despite country birth, have smarts about you. 'Tis not want of sense, but want of suspicion, by which innocence is often betrayed. You are different, Joseph, and have seen the truth well enough. Your days in Paris, I presume, have sharpened you.'

'Thank you, sir,' bowed Bendix. If his fall from grace had been accidental, this new ascension was most deliberate. He knew it was simply the telling to a man of what he wished to hear. If it brought peace to the house and the opening of the doctor's mind to his apprentice then it was worth the feathered weight of guilt that settled on Bendix's shoulders.

Rising from dinner, the doctor's shakes commanded his movement and he accepted Bendix's offer of a steady arm. The apprentice had not considered the doctor vulnerable until this moment, but as they entered the western wing the concept of Calcraft's susceptibility seemed to grow upon Bendix until he was quite pregnant with maternal affection. He lay the doctor back upon his sofa of crushed velvet, and stood over him as the laudanum dragged him back into sleep.

Bendix cleared an area within the stacks of towering books in which he might lie. He moved aside the bound collection of Calcraft's journals then, taking a heavy volume of Galen, pushed it under his head as a pillow and relaxed in thought. Dinner had left the apprentice less shaken than his master, but now he was perturbed by a new question. He had heard how much all the hanged feared anatomy and had thought it mere superstition, but never had he known a condemned felon. Since he had already completed his return to the doctor's trust, was it necessary for Sheppard to be reduced and decocted? Perhaps, perhaps not. It was now, he decided, the doctor's quest, and if he might maintain a neutrality then his conscience would be assuaged.

Falling into a brief, uncomfortable sleep, Bendix convulsed and contorted his body according to the darkness of his dreams. He woke, less than an hour later, among the ruins of a fallen city of books. He had contrived to upset three towers, scattering the debris in every direction and yet the doctor continued to sleep soundly above. Bendix rubbed the back of his stiff neck with both sets of his fingers, massaging it to looseness.

He had been woken by the whirring of his mind. Why a body? Why the body of a criminal, of a particular criminal? Between the human carcass and the decoction Calcraft sought was a line of logic that eluded the apprentice. He knew the subjects of the experiments, but could not guess the purpose that would unify such divergent activities. Rising, he reorganised the books according to the best of his memory and, desiring his bed, relieved the doctor of the room's only candle and hastened along the corridor.

At the foot of the door to the western wing lay a small white shape. As Bendix stooped to pluck it from the floor he blocked the candlelight, casting a vast parodic shadow on the ceiling above him. Standing, he held what appeared to be a letter to the light.

He hurried to his bedroom, almost extinguishing the candle in his haste. He read the letter. In fact, it is fair to say that he reread it, again and again, trying to decipher an undercurrent of intention, delaying the probable answer that there was none at all. In truth, it was not a letter at all – not in so far as it resembled anything else that Bendix had ever read. Folded within the page was a collection of words or phrases cut from a book. They had not been pasted in any order, but lay loose. He arranged the seven clippings in what he presumed to be an appropriate order.

'Neighbour'
'My patron entertained me like a prince, he made my safety his peculiar care'
'no longer'
'needful'
'just reflections of a kind I have not yet made'
'hand influenced from above, governs all our actions of every kind, limits our designs, orders the events'
'I am very much obliged'

Before unfolding the paper Bendix had presumed that it would answer every inquiry that had spun through his brain in the preceding weeks, and yet, though it allayed several suspicions, it simultaneously created a new host of questions. Why not write the words, rather than cut them from a book? Still, the tone was one of kindness and formality and though the words were borrowed, the effort of communication was her own.

Despite the clipped word *'prince'* Bendix did not doubt that he was addressed by a woman. Yet there was little suggestion as to whether it might be the doctor's mother, wife, daughter or mistress. If he could not rely on his eyes, then perhaps he might trust his sense of smell, for was there not the gentlest plume of perfume escaping from the paper? It was the same smell that had captivated him in the western wing. And yet it was an old trick of aging coquettes, to shroud their demise in heavy scents as if they might cause a squint that would prevent a gentleman from seeing the spreading wrinkles. How often in Paris had he danced with a lady and sniffed her skin, marinated by day for the night's sweet deceits.

No matter what interpretation Bendix gave to the paper, the scent or the very words, one thing was certain: she had voluntarily established a covert correspondence with him. They were already, in some way, linked. It was an innocent communication but intrigue, combined with his own lonely position as London apprentice, magnified his curiosity and when he slept that night, he closed his eyes and dreamed of an unknown face.

CHAPTER TEN

If Bendix's heart had beat hard the night before, there was a significant increase in palpitations when the doctor greeted him at breakfast with the news that a letter had arrived for him. Bendix stammered his acknowledgement of the information, believing that his correspondence had been discovered, and brushed the cuff of his frock coat across his brow, yet the letter that lay to the left of his fork had been delivered by a footman who awaited his answer in the kitchen. Bendix opened the letter and read what was not a request but a demand for his presence. The letter was signed, in a sweeping signature of black ink, by the Thief Taker General, Jonathan Wild.

For the third time in the week, Bendix headed to Newgate, this time on foot. The first day of September greeted him with an ebb of summer heat and breath of winter wind. It would have been a comfortable, even pretty walk, had the destination not been the Blue Boar Inn, within an echo of Newgate. He did not notice an elderly gentleman in a great coat, who might ordinarily have tickled his notions of fashions and seasons, but proceeded along the Fleet and over the bridge to Newgate Street. Bendix was nervous to the point of upset, his stomach queasy and unsettled. His greatest fear was that Sheppard had escaped and the file had been found. He had been recognised by Sixes and blame was easily attached. The apprentice passed behind the prison, along the same tight street cluttered with signs that had been so muddy only days before. Now it seemed altogether fresher. It was as if autumn had arrived in a single day, bringing a freshness and clarity that swept everywhere except through the chaos of Bendix's mind.

Bendix was aware of every strand of his being and struggled to control them. Even a simple matter, such as walking across the threshold of the Blue Boar, was achieved with awkward dislocation. It was a particular kind of anxiety that consumed him, as if he were an actor caught before an expectant audience without the slightest memory of his speech. Concentrating on simulating a fluidity of movement, Bendix was shown through a door at the rear of the half full tavern, led along a candlelit corridor and into the office of Jonathan Wild.

The Thief Taker sat beside a gate-legged table, slumping forward in thought, while Sixes perched on a walnut stool beside the hearth, tending to the birth of the first fire of the season. Bendix, who knew something of furniture from his stay in Paris, could not help but notice the finer pieces in the room: the beech chair that held Wild's stout figure, the mirror inlaid with boxwood, ebony and ivory. The panelling of the room was of fine Baltic oak. A framed picture of

Laroon's *Mountebank* hung to the right of the fireplace. Within a shout of Newgate, but a room equal to any in Lincoln's Inn. The elegance acted as a balm to the apprentice, lowering his anxiety to a more manageable level. He now believed he might, if challenged, be able to conceive an appropriate lie. At any rate his uncertainty, the terrifying thought that he might prove coward enough to betray Defoe before the inquisition, was now quelled and he stood in silence as the door closed behind him and the three were alone. The heavy smell of chocolate clouded the room.

'And you are?' said Wild looking up. The Thief Taker's peruke sat on the table beside him and Bendix could not help but stare at the uneven dome of his shaved head. It was clearly cracked in at least three places. A surgeon had soldered a silver plate to the deepest of the fissures so that a child might suspect that Wild was made of precious metals. There were other scars about his face, none hidden by powders, and though Defoe had painted him as a man of deceit and manipulation, Bendix knew he was staring at the visage of a veteran.

'You are?' repeated Wild.

'I was sent for,' mumbled the apprentice.

'Mr Bendix? I thank you for attending my levee.'

Bendix could not calculate how such finery and taste might end up in the room of a man whose accent was unrefined. In fact, it seemed obvious from Wild's tone that he delighted in the contradiction between his birth and his position, his scars and his presumption. Had he been a coachman along the Dover Road, Bendix might have expected better elocution.

'Your letter led me to believe that it is a matter of urgency.'

'Indeed,' said Wild. 'Urgency indeed.' He paused, dropping the room into silence. Bendix looked around nervously for some support from Sixes, but he tended his fire as if he were the only man in the room. He wondered if this was the moment they were expecting him to confess before announcing the escape of Sheppard.

'I have a problem of a delicate nature,' smiled Wild.

'And you associate it with me?' said Bendix, the first half of the question begun in a whisper, the latter galloping towards loudness.

'I do,' said Wild.

'Why ever?'

'Because I have heard from Sixes that you are a fine young thing, a man of learning.'

'I must thank Mr Sixes deeply for the recommendation,' said Bendix with not the least trace of sincerity.

'Come now, Mr Bendix,' said Wild with the greatest of warmth, 'we are all gentlemen here. I seek to engage you professionally. I am attacked relentlessly by a disease of Venus. Sixes says you may be relied upon, if not for experience, then discretion. I wish to dose myself, but not without consultation and not without oversight. While this might offend a more established physician, I presume that you have no such qualms as a student.

'In the last year,' continued Wild, 'I have been bled, fed with emetics, swallowed unholy amounts of guaiac and suffered from quartern fevers. I have been prescribed a daily bolus, filled with calomel, and have coughed three pints of spit a day. My teeth, sir, loosened so that I could not take a bite of beef. I am told by Mr Sixes that you have recently returned from France, and have been thinking that since they say the disease is French perhaps these people have discovered the cure?'

'You have suffered,' murmured Bendix with a drop of sympathy.

Wild shrugged, but managed a regretful nod. 'I fear, Doctor,' said Wild and Bendix did swell with pride to hear the moniker so applied, 'that soon it shall eat my nose.'

His first instinct after being called 'Doctor' was to comfort his patient, regardless of his true thoughts, and yet he contained his sympathies and instead resorted to the sensible remedy of considering Wild's individual case.

'How long have you suffered from the burning?' he asked.

'Two years,' said Wild.

'Unfortunately, sir, in France the fashion is similar to the methods you have pursued. Aside from a prescription of salutiferous herbs, I can only recommend the mercury ointment.'

'And how is it applied?' asked Wild, with a modest smile of supplication.

'To the body.'

'Where?'

'To . . .'

'Show me how it is done,' said Wild with a sudden gruffness, 'as if you were applying the ointment in the here and now.'

And so Bendix found himself in the odd position of removing Wild's boots, helping him out of his stockings, then demonstrating how flannel might be wrapped about first his feet, then his calves, thighs and arms. Wild's toenails were thick and yellow – pedlar's feet.

'The breast, belly and back are best omitted,' said Bendix, 'for fear of paralysis.'

'Tell me,' said Wild, as Bendix sat on the floor at his feet, 'of your interest in Jack Sheppard.'

'I have none,' muttered Bendix, his gaze riveted to the cloth that he was wrapping in imitation of flannel about Wild's right foot.

'Come now, Joseph,' smiled Wild cheerfully, 'we are too close, patient and physician, for lies. Tell me.'

'For the last weeks,' said Bendix, meeting his gaze and refusing to blink, 'I have been attending the writer Daniel Defoe, since my master cut for his stones. During this time, he has told me of his work for *The Newgate Calendar* and his intention to write of Sheppard. As you know, Mr Wild, I am a recent arrival from France, and having few friends or interests in this city, I accepted Mr Defoe's offer gladly.'

'And so you did,' said Wild chewing over the information. 'We are sad that you have found few friends and are pleased to have made your acquaintance. We shall stay friends, I believe?'

'Our introduction is professional,' said Bendix coldly.

'You are right, you are right,' replied Wild, 'I forget myself. I am a Staffordshire man and forget my place.' He reached within his pocket and withdrew three gold moidores. 'We must keep ourselves professional and, being a man adverse to debts, let me settle our account.'

He pressed the gold into Bendix's palm, then shook him by the same hand so that the gold cut uncomfortably against their flesh.

'Good day, Mr Bendix,' said Wild. 'I look forward to renewing our professional acquaintance.'

Bendix bowed low and hurried from the room.

Very calmly Bendix traversed the floor of the tavern and walked up to Newgate Street, where the comparative width and scarcity of signs enabled the full force of the weather to alleviate his angst. He filled and emptied his lungs with protracted breaths, encouraging the purity of the air to refresh his harried mind. Letting his hands rest against the top of his cane, he leaned forwards, allowing it to absorb his weight.

There was venom in the man, a controlled pitch of understanding of language and power that he had never encountered before. He was filled half by admiration and half by disgust.

Altogether, he believed he had conducted himself in a suitable manner. Either Sheppard was still in Newgate, or Wild had made no connection between his visit with Defoe and the subsequent escape. The wind blew so freshly that it found its way through his powdered wig and cooled his scalp. He straightened his back, tapped his cane upon the ground and, twisting the pomander, tucked it under his arm and walked between the dried crusts of mud raised by cartwheels.

'Joseph,' called Sixes behind his shoulder. 'You are walking home?'

'What do you want?' said Bendix drily.

'What kind of anger is this, my friend?'

'"Friend",' quoted Bendix.

'My father,' said Sixes, 'always told me that there was pleasure to be found in a visit. If not in the arrival, then in the departure.'

'I had no desire for that introduction,' said Bendix curtly and began to walk up Newgate Street towards the Fleet Bridge.

'You blame me for your presence today,' said Sixes, matching Bendix's quick pace with steady long strides. 'But know that without me you would merely have delayed your visit by a day. You spiked the man's interest, accompanying that hack, and he would have knowledge of you one way or other. Always best to hear one man's tale from one man's mouth.'

'Indeed.'

'He did not lie about his troubles either,' continued Sixes, walking comfortably at his side, disregarding the fact that Bendix stared straight ahead. 'He has much interest in your ointments.'

'It was information he might receive from a hundred doctors.'

'He is not fond of physicians.'

'I trust the feeling is mutual.'

'What has Defoe told you of him?' asked Sixes softly.

'Enough to know that he should have been hanged twenty years ago.'

'No matter who you choose to believe, Joseph, it is always wise to measure both tales. Defoe cares only for money. Wild, in his manner, is similar. They are two men devoted to their love of gold.'

'Yet Defoe is a writer who must pursue the truth of information.'

'Come now, any brother of the quill has as much love of the truth as a horse has for saddles. At best they are scribes. Jonathan is of much more import.'

'This comes from his centurion.'

Sixes flapped his hands at his side. 'You were not about thirty years ago. You do not know this city. If some records were kept of murders, you would know the peace that Jonathan has brought. You object to his methods. You think a planned theft is immoral. Further your thoughts, Joseph. Man will steal forever. The rich from the poor, the poor from the rich, all unto each other. Once you admit this to yourself, Jonathan can be seen in his true light. He is a moderator.'

'Moderator,' mocked Bendix quickening his pace. 'Theft? Theft might well be pardoned, for we are all fond of gold, but what of all the men he has hanged? This is moderation?'

'Only thieves and murderers have died.'

'Thieves whom he sent athieving. Murderers on his very missions.'

'Untrue,' protested Sixes. 'You trust the information of this man, Defoe, who admits to imagined works? Come now. If you're thirsty for authentics, you would do well to examine your new patient further. About Jonathan's stomach is tied a book of truth, yellow with the man's sweat. Truer than any of Defoe's words. The crimes of every thief are marked in that book, Joseph. The days they were sent thieving, the goods they received, the men who came in search of them, the monies they paid to recover them. Now that is a book of truth.'

'Do not follow me, Sixes, do not tell me another false word.'

'I trust you, Joseph, we have worked together. You and I – forget your righteousness, you have dug the body of a buried man . . .'

'. . . as did you,' said Bendix, turning to him for the first time.

'But you wave your hand at me in protests of innocence,' said Sixes, looking down upon the smaller man, his eyes moist with kindness. 'Come now, Joseph, you refuse to look at yourself. Defoe has seen Newgate, Wild spent three years in Bridewell. The only difference between you and them is that you have not paid for your sins.'

'I hardly think that is a just equation.'

Sixes laughed and placed his hands on Bendix's shoulder. The apprentice allowed the weight to bring him to a halt. Sixes forced his hand into Bendix's and they shook hands for several seconds. 'We have come to an understanding, have we not?'

'And what is our understanding?' asked Bendix.

'That we are not as far removed from each other as you presumed. We are aware of the history we share. Besides, today, you were well paid, were you not?'

'Overpaid,' corrected Bendix with some suspicion but no complaint.

Sixes bowed low, swivelled his body and tipped his tricorn at a passing servant girl. Bendix resumed his walk home. He listed his acquaintances of his two months in London. Calcraft, Defoe, Sixes, Sheppard, Wild. For every thought he had in support of one of these people, another contradicted it. Calcraft, a kind and generous visionary. An addled patriarch, thirsty to continue his experiments of anatomy. Defoe, an experienced and devout writer. An amoral hack devoted to the clink of coin. Perhaps everything was true of everyone. Was his own life not filled with contradictions? A poor rich man, a qualified physician and an apprentice, an unloved lover. They were all made of warring opposites, lambs and wolves, sand and raging seas. He remembered the doctor's words. That the eye was constant and it was only the interpretation of what is seen that is in flux. If this was so then he would observe sharply, for the man that you must trust may also be the man you must doubt.

He could sense the formation of a division of loyalties. Entities that had seemed foreign to one another were now converging. Bendix was not even sure if there were any connective strands apart from his own existence. He resolved to talk less, or at least consider his words wisely before he spoke. Men might open themselves for him, but he would remain closed for observation, lest he be used as the bridge to connect two bodies that should not meet.

The doctor, informed Mrs Hemmings, was in his study reading. Bendix could think of no appealing alternative, so returning to both his room and studies, he tried to reorder his life by focusing on his original intentions and, predictably, fell asleep in his chair.

CHAPTER ELEVEN

'Where is Lemon?' asked Bendix after his breakfast.

'On an errand,' smiled the doctor graciously. 'He shall return shortly. Joseph, look what our friend Defoe sent over this morning.'

It was a copy of the news-sheet, *Applebee's Original Weekly Journal*. The right-hand column was devoted to Jack Sheppard, describing his escape. It was a dramatic piece, depicting the visit of two of Sheppard's paramours, his removal of the spikes from the condemned hold, the scramble through the bars and his easy movement from the jail between his admirers. All in all, no matter how the escape had been achieved, Defoe had concocted a tale of humour and daring, and not a little pathos at the Thief Taker's expense.

'Defoe calls him the greatest of criminals,' said Calcraft slowly.

'And today he shall be heralded as such,' admitted Bendix.

Calcraft peeled the shell from an egg. He held the white fleshy oval between thumb and forefinger.

'I have been counting,' said Calcraft. 'This is the third time Sheppard has fled. Three times from gaol. Would that not suggest something strange to you, Joseph?'

'He is of flesh and blood,' said Bendix to appease his master. 'Sooner or later he shall hang.'

'It must be soon,' spoke Calcraft.

Lemon entered the room and announced under his drooping eyelids that the doctor's guest had arrived in person.

'Wonderful,' said Calcraft. 'Come Joseph, we are taking an active role in the apprehension of felons. Will take a minute of our time and match it with a parcel of our money.'

Jonathan Wild stood in the hallway, his scarred head covered by a short, grizzled wig. He was wearing the same black silk suit that Bendix had first spotted him in, carrying before him a silver staff, a pretension reserved for the city Marshals and a bold affront to the legal authorities. He was accompanied by a man a touch taller and considerably thicker than his master. His suit was of dirty grey, his nose pounded to flatness from years of pugilism. He wore no wig but had pulled the remnants of his hair into a louse bag at the base of his neck and grinned uncomfortably as if he were not sure what expression suited the grand house he found himself within.

'Sir Edmund,' said Wild, with a slight inclination that was supposed to pass for a bow. 'Mr Quilt Arnold, an invaluable source of strength and information.'

'Good, good,' said Calcraft. 'This is my apprentice . . .'

'Mr Bendix,' said Wild, 'it is a pleasure to make your acquaintance again so soon.'

Bendix bowed stiffly.

Calcraft looked from one to the other before deciding that any questioning would have to be postponed until his business was at an end. The gentlemen were conducted by Lemon into the library, where Wild luxuriated in a deep-cushioned chair and a cup of posset, while Quilt suffered on the edge of a cane-bottomed chair, hands soldered to knees. Almost all his fingers had been broken and poorly set, so that they faced Bendix like legs crossed upon a bench.

Though Wild had assumed a relaxed position, his words of criminals and their capture were filled with frenetic energy and the posture of anger. Soon Calcraft became quite coloured by a form of titillated osmosis and forced himself to interrupt the Thief Taker so that they might pinpoint their business.

'I believe it is in the public's interest,' said Calcraft, 'that a man such as this Sheppard should be recaptured at once.'

'You might ask your apprentice,' smiled Wild, 'as to the danger of the criminal, he being with the aforementioned only the day before his departure. Gentlemen as has been around as long as the two of us know the menace of such a man. Now a fool, a fool would tell you he is but a thief, a stealer of trinkets and barely worth transporting. But the sage will tell you what he is indeed.'

'And what is that?' asked Bendix in some surprise, sensing that his own aggrandisement of Sheppard's achievements were being shadowed by the Thief Taker.

'An example,' continued Wild, 'am I not right, Edmund?'

The doctor winced to be addressed in this manner, but managed a strong bob of agreement.

'Examples are for children,' said Bendix.

'Exactly,' said Wild, 'and what a poor model Mr Sheppard would be. He was an apprentice the same as you, Joseph, to a carpenter in Drury Lane. Six years of his seven he served and then begins his malice with his devil's hands. You will concur that Sheppard's betrayal of his master shakes the foundations?'

'Naturally,' consented Bendix, 'I do not encourage a nation of thieves.'

'A worthy position,' said Calcraft, 'but barely a gesture. I would prefer to *dis*courage the nation of thieves. Though it is against my nature to indulge in talks of economics, I would offer a considerable reward for the recapture of this felon.'

Wild opened his palms to encourage the doctor's exactness.

'A hundred pounds.'

'A honey stick,' said Wild, 'that will have the bees buzzing. May I ask a question?'

Calcraft nodded.

'Is your interest in the escape solely a question of civic duty?'

'Of course,' said Calcraft too quickly. It disappointed Bendix how easily one might spot a man's fabrications.

'If your interest was more than civic, say, if it bordered upon the anatomical, then I would add that it is a civic duty as well, to save a man a burial. I will not press you on the matter, Doctor, but should you be warm,' and here he flicked an eye at Calcraft's scarlet ears, 'then there is plenty of time to calculate another proposition to ensure safe delivery.'

'Let us keep our understanding tacit,' said the doctor softly.

Wild rose, nodded his head in a fashion that seemed more like the shake of a sneeze than a genuine bow and retreated, trailed by his shadow, Quilt Arnold.

'Why did you not tell me that you had been called for by Wild yesterday?' asked Calcraft as soon as he heard Lemon close the front door after their visitors.

'I did not think you would deem it proper to consort with such a man. He called upon me professionally.'

'A physician must heal all. All,' repeated Calcraft. 'Besides, he is the Thief Taker and not the thief. Were you to attend a man such as Sheppard, it would cause me disturbance. But the Thief Taker must be healed, he must be healed.'

'What did you make of the man?'

'I believe,' said Calcraft, 'that he will execute his job with expedition. Though we are all fond of gold, it is rare to see a man's eyes change colour at the mention of money.' The doctor's own eyes retained a healthy twinkle that relayed his satisfaction with the Thief Taker.

'One would almost think Mr Wild believes this a political affair with the amount of energy he spends in pursuit. And yet,' continued Bendix, 'he has chosen to meet a man who cares not for the game at which he plays.'

'It has often happened,' said Calcraft, 'that, for the sake of politics, men of no politics are disposed of.'

'And does it not strike you as unjust?'

'Merely inevitable,' replied the doctor.

Neither man had long to consider their differences, for by the end of the following day criers announced the recapture of Jack Sheppard. Bendix could not help but feel as if the man had disappointed him, allowing himself to be taken within the day. There had been a surety and composure about the thief that Bendix believed would translate into good sense and yet he had not lasted a single night. Surely it would be hard with more than two hundred and fifty pounds on his head to find a man to trust, but his looks were not so singular that he might be easily recognised. Bendix was staggered that the guile employed in his escape might evaporate so suddenly upon the streets of London and hoped desperately that Calcraft did not share his doubts of Sheppard. His only relief was that Wild had been following a false scent to Stourbridge at the time and could not collect the doctor's money.

Calcraft was elated. His humour in the following week was only piqued when Sheppard was not hanged on the originally appointed September the 7th. That day came and went, emptying the condemned hold of all but Sheppard. According to the laws that reigned even above Jonathan Wild, the prisoner might not be hanged until a new warrant was obtained at the next sessions. It was required that the original defendant might be recalled to confirm that the man retaken was the same felon originally committed to Newgate. Despite this a watch was kept on the Tyburn gallows by the more distrustful citizens, lest Jack Sheppard be hanged incognito.

Every morning the *Daily News*, the *Courant* and the *Journal* brought varying accounts of Sheppard. How he had been found by a Newgate turnkey, dressed in a blue butcher's apron hiding in a bed of hay off Finchley Common, a silver watch strapped under each armpit. The public were stirred to a fever on two more occasions, a week apart, first when the *News* reported that a file was discovered within his bible in Newgate, then again when a small hammer was found in the rushes of his chair. To satisfy the appetite for sensation, Defoe's *Journal* ran a column on how the Newgate turnkeys had been forced to move him from the condemned hold to the most secure part of the prison, a room called the Castle, three floors above the gate.

Calcraft read with disappointment how Sir James Thornhill, the Court Painter to His Majesty King George, had been commissioned to portray Sheppard. Indeed, Sheppard was perhaps the only man in London who shared Calcraft's despair. At seven every morning, Thornhill arrived to work quietly for three hours, assuring Sheppard every now and then that he would most surely receive the king's pardon. At ten the turnkeys would open the doors to the public, charging two shillings for a brief sight of Sheppard. There was the odd visitor who brought some happiness to Sheppard, but mostly he showed his back to the gawkers, the mohocks tapping their canes upon the floor to capture his attention and throwing coins upon the ground in front of him. Pitt, the keeper of Newgate, took no more chances. The first hours of the day with Thornhill were his only at liberty. The remainder of the time his feet were linked by sixty-pound chains, his arms bound in iron. About his neck he wore a brass collar attached by a three-foot link to a bolt in the floor. His waist was circled by a padlock used in the breaking of horses. Altogether Sheppard was weighed by almost three hundred pounds of metal and, though he managed smiles for the more charming of his female visitors, he thoroughly regretted his immediate return to the domain of Newgate.

Calcraft was not fond of the city nor its inhabitants, nor did he care for kings and kingdoms, desiring above all peace for his progress. He was even less enamoured of London's underbelly of perpetual filth, noise and anguish, but he could not risk his only charge on the word of his apprentice. His carriage sat outside Newgate. The doctor joined a small herd of pilgrims who paid their way to Sheppard's cell, saw the prisoner's bowed head, the chains and weights about him. Sheppard was in high spirits the day of Calcraft's visit, amusing the crowd with hoots and wild cries then confessing his sanity with a mocking smile.

The performance was watched with great interest by the doctor and had Sheppard known that he was being viewed as flesh without skin, meat without bones, he might have toned down his display and chosen a contemplative silence instead. Calcraft left most contented. It proved not only the impossibility of escape, but also confirmed the danger of the man. Only the most menacing of felons would merit such restraints.

It was in a more sombre state that Defoe and Bendix

found Sheppard in the last week of September. Defoe had once more resumed his weekly dinners at Lincoln's Inn and it had taken little encouragement from either Calcraft or Bendix to ensure that the apprentice might accompany the writer on his next visit. Bendix was growing accustomed to Newgate, mainly, he thought, because the presence of Sheppard had brought about a profound change. Neither he, nor any of the occupants, seemed to believe in the permanent incarceration that it had previously represented. Bendix believed that he owed Wild an apology he would never give. Sheppard's example *was* invigorating. Only days before their shipment for transportation, ninety felons had sawed through their fetters to the sound of drunken verse before they were discovered by a fortunate turnkey.

Even the pervasive darkness was reinterpreted by Bendix. Before it had weighed upon him, but now it was merely an assistant in the aid of freedom. If Bendix had questioned himself a little further, he would immediately have discovered how unattractive the prospect of Newgate spilling her contents on to the streets of London might have been, but, like the rest of the city, he thought only of Sheppard and could not disguise his wish for yet another escape.

There were no windows to cast their light about the room, only the single lantern that Defoe had borrowed from the turnkey for a shilling. Bendix raised it to illuminate two cane chairs that had been provided for the visitors. Otherwise it was a bare room of stone and brick, save for a large, disused fireplace heading the north end of the room. Sheppard lay stretched upon the floor, the heavy padlock resting against the side of his ribcage. Bendix was, for a moment, appalled at the counteraction, almost turning on Defoe as the cause of these exaggerated repercussions.

'I told you, Mr Bendix,' said Sheppard, turning his head

as best he could towards the lantern, 'that you'd find me in finer accommodations should you come again.'

'They are indeed sizeable,' smiled Bendix.

'If you wish for a quartern of gin, Daniel, you'll ring for the footmen yourself.'

'My Geneva days are gone, Jack. If I should have another stone, I would be forced to cut my own throat.'

'Jonathan would hang you for it,' smiled Sheppard.

Bendix let out a great snort of laughter that seemed to propel Sheppard's mood and tongue.

'Do you know why they hang me, Bendix? According to the laws? Because I am harmful to trade. That is what they tell me, how it's all down to finance. I don't understand much of finance. Defoe is an expert upon the subject.' Defoe nodded at the compliment. 'Figure on this. I harm but one man a time, a man not terribly indisposed by theft,' continued Sheppard. 'I'm thrown into prison, a fact never resented. Then I've broken out of prison, which I've not resented either. I have, on my three occasions of escape, caused damage in my breaches, work for many men. Never sir, have the goods stolen exceeded the cost of my damages. I conclude, Defoe, that I am, in fact, of worth. That thieving's a work of labour and talent. Indeed, it encourages the smithies and quills of London to better themselves.'

'Well said,' murmured Bendix, amused and partially convinced by the argument, even though Sheppard's wide grin confessed that the thief was only in jest.

'Tell me, Defoe,' said Sheppard, 'how many papers have you sold since my escape?'

'We print two thousand more a week.'

'And do they sing of me?'

'It is precious hard to find a porter. They sit with the

coachmen and coopers debating the chance of another escape.'

'And what do they determine?'

'They are for it. Except those who have paid their two shillings and passed before your own eyes. They wager against you, Jack, for they do not believe.'

Sheppard held his eyes closed for a moment as if he was pressing doubt from his mind.

'Mr Sheppard,' asked Bendix, interrupting Defoe, 'I must inquire, for it has rattled me since I first heard of your escape. Why were you taken so soon? Why did you not hie to France or northward?'

Sheppard gave an embarrassed shrug. 'I was caught between two minds. 'Tis a foolish position. I will confess, and Defoe knows this well, that I'm not adverse to being the sole subject of society. However, I'd have wider smiles and would take your cane if you would care to wear my chains.'

'A kind offer,' said Bendix with a bow, 'and one I shall have to decline.'

'May we do anything on your behalf?' asked Defoe.

'You've already done too much,' smiled Sheppard. 'Beg the warden for a dying man's peace. Let me not spend my last hours in a state of continual disturbance.'

'I shall back the request with gold,' said Defoe bowing.

'Goodbye, Mr Sheppard,' said Bendix, his voice brimming with saturine sympathy.

'I'd accompany you to the door,' said Sheppard, 'but physicks recommend rest.'

They had barely walked out of the Castle and along the Press Yard when Bendix tugged on Defoe's cuff and animatedly whispered, 'I saw it. When I asked of his capture. I saw it then.'

'His body is now searched twice daily,' said Defoe discreetly under his breath, steering Bendix towards the gate, 'I was searched myself not three days ago. For a crown a young friend of mine carried it in her child's swaddling. She bent and pushed it between the boards.'

The two men ignored an avenue of beggars released from the common side and strode through the slouched forms like titans neglecting their creations. Bendix heard the groans, saw the dark blisters on thin white limbs, but they spoke against his notion of Newgate as a slight obstacle and he walked through the gate at Defoe's side.

'It is such a small file,' continued Bendix, 'and his chains so heavy.'

'It was not a file,' said Defoe, 'but a nail. When his wardens come in, he manoeuvres himself to lie above it. They pull at his chains, his lock, talk and laugh at his continued good humour and leave.'

'A nail,' repeated Bendix, 'and the door is as thick as a horse's thigh.' He shook his head sadly. 'I fear that Mr Sheppard shall soon be hanged. If I were a gambling man I would end all wagers.'

'Sheppard,' said Defoe, 'is the centre of much interest. His fate has yet to be decided.'

'You talk as if you were the carpenter and he the marionette.'

'I would take some credit in his construction,' said Defoe. 'Both in departure and return. Was it not I who led Jonathan Wild to Stourbridge and away from Sheppard. A false scent, of course, but of my own emanations.'

'We were speaking of his escape,' said Bendix with the utmost concentration, 'and now you tell me you had knowledge of his capture?'

'Of course,' said Defoe, 'we were the only men who knew

he would flee. I had five culls follow him. Took him peace-
fully rather than leave him to Quilt Arnold and saved Sir
Edmund a hundred pounds.'

'You are at play with his life,' responded Bendix with genuine concern, 'and should he escape, shall you take him
again?'

'You do not give him enough credit, Joseph. He is sharper
than us both and more. Should he wish to outwit me, it
would be but a shake of his tail. He was retaken by his own
consent, you have heard it from his own mouth. He preens
in glory, Joseph. Has found that fame appeals much more
than fortune. A man does not gain notoriety stealing an
ounce of silver or a roll of calico.'

Though Bendix and Defoe walked slowly side by side,
Bendix had begun to slow.

'He thrives upon escape, Joseph,' continued Defoe, 'and
to escape again and again, as our friend has done, one must
necessitate one's own capture.'

'You might have left him twenty files in the Castle and he
will not escape it. You have killed the man, Defoe.'

'Four guineas,' said Defoe, proffering his hand, 'that he
shall be out of Newgate within the sennight.'

'Six guineas,' said Bendix, and shook the hand vigorously.

'And where does an apprentice get six guineas?'

'He does not need a penny if he cannot lose the wager.'

Defoe returned Bendix's grimace with a pleasant smile, as
if the apprentice's protestations and abhorrence at his
manipulations were nothing more than the naivety of youth.

CHAPTER TWELVE

Bendix circled the kitchen twice in search of Mrs Hemmings. A cursory glance at first, then a more detailed examination, in case the cook had slumped to the floor in a dead drunk. It was not until he had finished his second circumnavigation that Bendix remembered it was her day off. Neither Julia nor Lemon were in the servant's quarters at the bottom of the stairs and Bendix began to feel as if he were an expendable pawn in some household conspiracy. The only other conclusion he could reach was that all the servants and the doctor had retired to the western wing. Though this seemed entirely unlikely, Bendix knew that he had not learned all the mysteries of the house and its operation within two months, and prepared himself for his search.

The hours of summer already shortening, Bendix stopped to light a candle before turning the door to the doctor's wing. His heart was giddy as he proceeded to the siren sounds coming from the doctor's study. He felt his nostrils flare in strange anticipation. To his enormous disappointment, and their considerable surprise, Bendix found the figures of Julia and Lemon standing over the prostate body of the doctor, laid out upon his blue velvet sofa.

'My,' muttered Julia, her mouth dropping low enough to hide her neck.

Lemon's lips curled into silent protest at the apprentice's intrusion and he turned his attention downwards, towards the doctor.

'Doctor?' asked Bendix from the doorway.

Calcraft moaned in response.

'What has happened to him?' questioned Bendix, already suspecting.

'He is asleep,' said Lemon, waving away the first assault of Bendix's powdered scent.

'At rest,' confirmed Julia, finally closing her mouth.

'A man does not bring his servants to the foot of his bed to encourage his dreams. Is it the laudanum?'

Lemon hesitated a moment, 'He was found in the front hall. He was lying upon his back. I thought he might have died.'

Calcraft groaned as if to confirm his existence.

'I dragged him here,' added Lemon with a coldness that suggested if it had not been for the doctor's excessive weight the footman might have enjoyed the moment of ascension.

'You are to head to Streatham's apothecary,' said Bendix sharply. 'Or find a boy to send. Bring me the leaf of trianna.'

Lemon looked as if, for a moment, he might refuse to take an order from the apprentice, before moving towards the door.

'And I?' said Julia, still staring at Bendix's powdered visage. Though he did not need it, Bendix ordered her to fetch the coldest water she might find, hoping that it would keep her busy for some time. She moved through Bendix's perfumed cloud on the way to the door, inhaling it as if she wished it to flavour her blood.

'Child,' whispered Calcraft, as the door closed behind Julia. 'Child, stay close.'

'I am here,' said Bendix and knelt beside his master.

The doctor's eyes were a pair of lambent marbles that seemed to weep despite the wide smile at Bendix's approach. He could not focus on Bendix, nor his strange appearance, but depended upon his other senses, touching the cut of his fine silk cloth, breathing the perfumes of his apprentice.

Bendix watched as the doctor's eyes travelled over unseen scapes, mind awash in opiates.

'How much?' asked Bendix. 'How many drops did you take?'

'No mistakes,' said Calcraft. 'Precision. Perhaps the single chance.'

'At what?' questioned Bendix.

'Vital,' added Calcraft. 'Your thief. Most important.'

'Why?' insisted Bendix.

'A single chance,' said Calcraft, drifting helplessly before the arms of sleep.

Bendix reached forwards and slapped him gently on the cheek, but his eyes rolled up to hide the pupils. As Bendix grasped the fleshy part of the doctor's triceps and applied a very hard but ineffective pinch, Julia burst through the door carrying a brass basin filled with water. A small wave lapped over the side and fell between two stacks of books. It was the first time Bendix had noticed even the faintest sign of haste in the housemaid and he looked up to see her trembling above him. He got to his feet and relieved her of the basin before she drowned the doctor's papers. The freezing temperature of the water ran through the brass to Bendix's hands and he quickly placed it on the floor.

'I have brought cloth,' she said and thrust a collection of kitchen rags at Bendix from under her arm.

'Thank you, Julia,' said Bendix. 'You may leave.'

'Yes, sir,' she muttered and departed.

Lemon appeared soon afterwards with a small boy of twelve who had run from Streatham's so hard that he looked like a red hot kettle, steam pouring from his nose. He stood by while Bendix discovered the doctor's purse in his waistcoat, then let forth a second gush of steam through his three front teeth when he broke a smile at the sight of silver. Lemon looked down suspiciously upon the apprentice until he returned the purse to his master's pocket. He took the trianna leaves and chewed them into a green paste. The taste, repulsive as it was, was bearable to Bendix as he locked the back of his throat. Lemon watched with affected disinterest as Bendix smeared the substance over the cleft of Calcraft's top lip before rinsing his mouth in the basin of water. The doctor's nose twitched and, though he did not wake, he coughed, turned and slept with obvious discomfort.

Lemon stood because he would not sit before Bendix, until eventually his tiredness overcame him. Without a word of encouragement he left the two men together.

Bendix could not sleep. He thought of stepping along the corridor, up the staircase and opening the doors to the rooms one by one. Patience was the anodyne that calmed him, allowed him to rest in the darkness without counselling sleep. He had received no answers, merely an inflation of worry.

Bendix spent the following day travelling between the roof above his study and the western wing. The doctor was in an exhausted state of recovery, his unending energy finally sapped to the point where he could do little but lie against the barricade of cushions that Bendix had prepared for him. He answered his apprentice's questions in monosyllables. Only after his lunch of Mrs Hemmings's special soup, which Bendix had followed the wise course of diluting, did Calcraft elaborate. He offered an apology, the first that Bendix had ever heard from the doctor, despite his previous errors. Indeed it was more of a confession than an apology, Calcraft admitting, in two sentences, that his behaviour had become alarming and he regretted the poor example he displayed to all of his household.

When he did not sit reading in the doctor's presence, Bendix carried his books to the spice garden, where he remained with ceaseless patience, fully expecting that the apparition would now appear in her true form, rather than the wraith-like glimpses she had previously bestowed on him. He waited a good part of the day, then carried this alternating vigil into the night, until, defeated by a gathering cold rather than ill humour, he descended to his own bed and slept heavily.

He was awakened at six the next morning by Lemon, who informed him that a carriage containing Defoe awaited him in the Fields. Lemon also added that Defoe had expressly told him to let Mr Bendix know that he should bring his six guineas with him. If Bendix had not been struck by such true amazement he would have enjoyed the frustration carved in Lemon's face, as the footman ached to know the meaning of the money and uproar but could not deign to ask. He swallowed, beat himself twice on the chest, then coughed hard. Bendix had never dressed so quickly, so poorly, forgetting powders altogether, not even buckling his shoes. So fast was he that had he had six guineas, he would almost certainly have forgotten them.

Defoe had never looked healthier to Bendix. He shone without his usual paste of sweat and remained smiling even when he believed he had relaxed his face from its happy good morning. The apprentice was not upset at the loss of the wager. First, he was unable to pay it. Second, it had always been his desire that Sheppard should escape and escape for good, away from the doctor's intentions, away from Defoe's attentions. He would have fond memories of Sheppard should he never see him again.

Defoe informed his friend that he had been woken not even an hour ago by a boy he had paid a half crown to sit outside the condemned hold and eavesdrop on the talk of the keepers. After a good clap on the back, Defoe let his hands rest between his considerable thighs in an effort to keep them warm.

'Do you know how?' asked Bendix immediately.

'Of course not,' returned Defoe, grinning, 'we saw the room together. Not a chance. Six guineas bets a man without a guinea to his name, so sure are we.' Bendix nodded fast to encourage the dismissal of the wager. 'Come, coachman, come,' continued Defoe. 'Not a soul in London knows yet, but by tomorrow, Joseph, thousands shall read of the methods of his escape.'

'And what of his recapture?' asked Bendix suspiciously.

'My boy slept,' said Defoe, his palms open in innocence. 'He might be on a packet to Calais by now.'

The October morning merely brought a light-grey shadow to the walls of Newgate. Bendix nodded his head to the prison out of the window, as he might have done to an old curmudgeon he suspected of a secret softness. It cost Defoe three guineas of persuasion to tempt Austin, the under turnkey, into guiding them. He pocketed the coins, then rushed them onwards, anxious lest the keeper of Newgate or Jonathan Wild should appear. Leading the way up the stairs above the prison gate to the Castle, Austin maintained a constant whispered patter of awe. Bendix half expected to be greeted by galloping disciples eager to spread the news.

'The sessions had begun,' said Austin unlocking the door to the Castle, 'we were busy. Back and forth to the Bailey. But you would not have thought, never have thought, that a man could be capable of this.'

The manacles and fetters lay neatly about the ring bolt

where Sheppard had been tied. At the far end of the room, spilling from the hearth of the fireplace, was a cascade of brick and mortar. Above the chimney Sheppard had torn a large hole in the wall that reached almost from the mantle-piece to the ceiling. The three men approached the rubble in silence. Defoe knelt, with some difficulty, and extracted three broken links amid the bricks and mortar. The end of the links were blunt and whitened from where Sheppard had scraped between the bricks.

Austin kicked the bricks to the side and cleared a path to the chimney. He peered inside, removed his head and shook it, perhaps in continued amazement, perhaps from the dust that descended from above.

'There was an iron bar fixed six feet up to stop a man like him,' said the turnkey as Defoe and Bendix took their turns to examine the chimney, 'and now it's gone, isn't it?' Sheppard had broken the entire wall of the room to avoid dealing with the bar.

'A notable implement, I would wager,' said Defoe. 'But why did he not break the door to the Castle?'

'The Master Debtors are opposite,' said the turnkey. 'Too kind a man to raise them from sleep.'

'And what is above?' asked Bendix, keeping his voice as low as his fellows, touched by the sacred.

'Come,' said Austin and led them from the room, up to the fourth floor above the prison gate. 'This is the Red Room,' he said, stepping over a lock box on the floor, and opening the door of his lantern. 'Dust of eight years in here.' In the far corner of the windowless room was the small arch where Sheppard had broken through where the wall met the floor-board. A mouse hole, thought Bendix.

'Was there a moon last night?' asked Defoe.

'Not even a star,' said Austin.

'How did he work in such darkness?' marvelled the writer.

'There's no tinder box nor candle left even in the chapel.'

They followed Austin through the condemned cell in the chapel where Sheppard had punched a hole in the wooden door then cleaved a pair of spikes that separated the partitions. A second lock box lay at the entrance to the door between the Chapel and the Leads.

'His iron bar, I wager,' said Defoe.

The next door, assured Austin, was the strongest in Newgate, and yet Sheppard, whom Bendix had dismissed as squirrel-like, had levered his iron bar into a position against the colossal metal fillet to which both the lock and bolt had been attached. They followed the thief's path out on to the Lower Leads, surrounded on every side by high walls that were supposed to shut off any escape.

'He's climbed on this door,' said Austin, indicating the one they had just pushed open.

'How do you know?' asked Defoe.

'At your years and cow shape, you're not likely to discover,' said Austin, and with surprising agility placed both hands on the top of the door frame, a foot on the handle and balanced on top of the door before propelling himself on the roof above. Bendix's ascent was more awkward, aided at first by Defoe, shaking his head with exertion, so that his wig leaped up and down like a begging dog. Once he had gained the top of the door, Austin reached down and pulled Bendix from his perch before he was ready, having to haul him on to the Highest Leads through sheer strength, costing the apprentice the right sleeve of his lawn shirt.

Austin led him twenty yards to the west, from where Sheppard had left a blanket hanging from the side of the prison wall, slack and damp with dew to Bendix's touch.

Sheppard had used one of the spikes from the Chapel to drive it into the prison roof. Even with the aid of the blanket, it was a drop of some fifteen feet to the neighbouring house.

'Who lives there?' asked Bendix, creasing the cuff of the torn shirt and pushing it up inside the sleeve of his frock coat.

'Called Turner,' said Austin. 'He heard a thing before the midnight cries, but thought it dog or cat and that is that. Gone. Free as wind.'

Wondering what odds he might have commandeered from those who had seen the thief in his chains, Bendix looked again at the sharp drop. Twenty pounds against his one, he estimated. An immodest bet, such as he would have witnessed among the Comtesse's clique.

The apprentice was surprised to see that Austin was also grinning as he surveyed the city of endless rooftops before him. 'Why do we smile?' he asked.

CHAPTER THIRTEEN

Bendix found himself closely questioned by Defoe on their descent and then again by Calcraft on his return to Lincoln's Inn. Defoe had taken notes at Bendix's description of the Leads, of the blanket, of the final drop to the neighbouring house. They were both in a state of excitement, eyes bulging and tongues loose so that they constantly talked over one another and did not notice the content of their conversation. It mattered little, for the only sentiment displayed was amazement.

The doctor's reaction was antithetical to Bendix and Defoe's. He had remained in bed late that morning, informed by Lemon that the apprentice and writer had left together at dawn. Predicting the reason of their visit, he suffered many violent emotions in anticipation of Bendix's return. But he did not turn to laudanum, choosing to outlast dread premonitions and depending on a thread of hope that could not be cut until his apprentice entered his study. When Bendix opened the door, fresh-faced from October air, Calcraft attempted to contain his disappointment. At first, the apprentice presumed that the doctor was still exhausted from his heavy dose of laudanum, but on closer inspection Bendix believed that he saw Calcraft shaking with an intensity that he had rarely observed and never felt.

'By your own admittance,' comforted Bendix taking a seat beside his master on the blue sofa, 'Defoe is always correct in these matters. Why, it was not an hour ago when he told me he thought Sheppard would be taken within the day.'

The surgeon continued to tremble. Bendix thought to put his arm about the doctor but pulled it back. He gave him an odd pat instead.

'Little strength,' managed the doctor, pressing a finger against his own chest. Bendix saw the bowed head, the fingers of fat that lay across the back of Calcraft's neck. The doctor looked pregnant with the need to speak. A dreadful sense of power overtook Bendix, one he hated to possess, for he felt as if he might ask any question of the doctor and would receive the truth in return.

'I am weak, Joseph. I have not fulfilled my promises.'

'Tell me, Sir Edmund,' said Bendix and he was relieved by some stirring of affection, a filial kindness that haloed his head.

'I have a child,' whispered Calcraft and suddenly stared at

his apprentice with such vehemence and self-hatred that Bendix struggled to contain the flicker of his knowledge. The apprentice reached out to hold the doctor by his forearm.

'She is twenty years,' said Calcraft. Bendix could feel the tremors in the doctor's limbs.

'And her mother?'

'Died bearing her,' said the doctor softly. 'A superstitious woman. Dismissed me for the birth, thought my absence would reduce her pain. I walked by the river as she died.' The sentence was delivered in the coldest of voices, Calcraft staring at the ground. Bendix suspected that the merest glance of sympathy would crack the icy facade and that the doctor would melt under hot tears.

'When I returned,' continued Calcraft, 'there were sixteen towels of blood outside the room. Each one weighed more than the child. Blood does not move me, least ways moves me no more.' Finally, he looked up at Bendix with a thin smile as if to ask, '*Do you understand? Can you understand?*' And how could Bendix answer, he who had suffered no greater tragedy other than the loss of love and youthful heartbreak? Nodding with appropriate solemnity he closed his eyes for two long seconds of silence. He felt like weeping, not for the doctor's anguish, but because Calcraft had trusted in him. Bendix was filled with a sense of worthiness. The doctor saw the tears fill his eyes and reined in his own emotions, surprised by the depth of his apprentice's sympathy.

'I did not love my child,' said the doctor softly, 'not for many years, but now she is the limit of my happiness. I serve her, Joseph, I act only on her behalf.'

'If your love is so great,' asked Bendix, 'then why bring such suffering upon yourself?'

'She is here, Joseph, within this house,' the pitch of Calcraft's voice rose and Bendix flinched as if he had woken to find a stranger beside him, 'has always been here, was born here. Her mother died in the bed I sleep in.'

Calcraft was overcome by the need to breathe. He let the air come rushing in deep breaths. 'I have told no man. One man, before.' He let all the air subside, then pinched his nose between his thumb and forefinger. 'She was not born right, Joseph. She is not whole.'

For the first time in the conversation Bendix's reaction was not rehearsed. 'How so, not right?'

'She cannot see. She can see, but she cannot.'

'I do not understand,' murmured the apprentice.

'It seemed scrofulous, but it cannot be treated as such. It derived from wens upon her neck, that I am sure of, though they left her when she was but three. I have tried for twenty years. The light halts her from the outside. I live with her,' continued the doctor, 'I see little more than she does. I spend my time with her. She does not know the full extent of her difference, believes most young ladies of fashion adhere to the same rules she does. She thinks only the common folk go about.'

'We must correct this.'

For the first time since Bendix's entrance, the doctor smiled with relief. 'I knew, from when you knocked upon our door, that goodness would flow from you, Joseph. We must work hard, we must work together. I have been so long alone at this.'

'How so?' he asked.

'I am close. You shall see. I am close to letting light shine upon her with an absence of pain. There is little time enough. The sight she has is fading. Soon, Joseph, it shall be gone. No more remedies, the blindness would be absolute.'

'What course do you follow?' asked Bendix, even as his own mind began to stir potential remedies.

'The Old and New,' said Calcraft, his voice returning to its customary calmness. 'Does it not strike you strange, Joseph, that Harvey refers almost entirely to Galen and Aristotle? Galen dead some fifteen hundred years, Aristotle two thousand. Much has gone unrecorded.' He shrugged and elicited a nod from his apprentice. 'A man has beliefs,' continued Calcraft, 'and he must pursue them. Before Galen, Aristotle thought the veins held air. Before Harvey, Galen believed the liver drove blood. Ignorance is swallowed whole, again and again. Knowledge, Joseph, must be challenged and recreated.'

The apprentice managed an awkward nod. 'I had heard that scrofula might be cured from the touch of a king.'

'Or that of the hanged,' added Calcraft. 'I would not have believed it had I not seen it with mine own eyes, Joseph. I was younger than even you, of Amelia's age, was down visiting in Dorset. At the crossroads hanged the body of a highwayman, his hands tied, a day dead, perhaps more. A hundred women had brought their children for his touch. In death, the hanged are blessed. This felon had murdered a pair of women on the Dover road, cut one so badly her guts were strung in the bushes. The worse a man, they say, the greater his power. Perhaps,' smiled Calcraft, 'the same is true of kings.'

'One of these children, one with hair red as poppies, suffered terribly with scrofula, his neck swollen with tubercula. I attended his mother, to pull at her teeth only three days later, and I saw him playing whole. Under the sun, Joseph. He was cured from evil. His neck no thicker than a swan's.

'Dr Nicholas has witnessed the miracle of touching. Sergeant Surgeon Wiseman saw it on sixty occasions, noted them all. I have both their accounts, shall give them to you. There can be no doubt that one body may contain what is necessary to cure another.'

'So we are to do with Sheppard as we did with Pink?' asked Bendix.

'We must have him,' said Calcraft, 'they will come no worse than he. Only the Devil himself might have flown from Wild. If we might find Sheppard, the restoration would be immediate. Imagine, Joseph, a house transformed.'

'We would reduce him?'

'As we did Pink. Condense the sins of a man to a potency of sublimeness. It is not only Amelia who must be considered, but my own blood. I am the end of it, Joseph, the last, and my blood must be continued through her. She will be restored, she shall be married. She will be married well.'

Bendix managed a nod of conspiration.

'Of course,' said Calcraft, 'you are familiar with Harvey's theories of circulation.'

Bendix shrugged.

'I seek transfusion, Joseph, to add to her own blood the essence of our felon. Remember the animacules? They are contained in the skin, the bones, the flesh of man. It is not the touch of the king or the hanged that cures, but the trace that is left, something too small for the eye to see. It is transferred, it is what heals, jumping from one man to another. The only reason touch does not always heal is because they need condensing. Touch is simply too meagre.'

It was impossible for Bendix to judge the doctor. He knew his Lithotomical procedure to be unorthodox, moving against what was known and practised. Calcraft was obviously well read, had a library of almost two hundred creased and worn books. Most convincing to Bendix were his own beliefs and his unproved theory of the cure of the imagination. If he did not doubt his own theories, then how might he presume to doubt those of a more experienced man? Indeed, the doctor's hybrid notion of lore and medical advancement directly appealed to Bendix.

Besides, had he not seen the animacules with his own eye? They had lived, unknown to man, all about him since time began. Bendix simply did not know what they contained, though he presumed Descartes with his machinist beliefs would have agreed with Calcraft that the smallest parts were invisible, their purpose unknown. While it was not as revolutionary as his own concept of self-healing, the doctor had already moved his ideas into a practical arena. What greater success than the salvation of one's own child?

'Should we visit her?' asked Bendix.

'Visit her?' said a confused doctor. He contemplated the possibility. 'Soon, I suppose it must be done. She is a stickler, Joseph, a stickler for routine. It will not do to go bursting in on her. We shall make our request. There is so little of novelty in her life that I believe it shall not be a slice of time before we are admitted.'

'This evening?'

'I understand your eagerness to look upon the strangeness of the case, but do not forget, Joseph, we are counselling my daughter. My only child. Your approach is professional, but temper it with concern. On my behalf.'

'Yes, sir,' said Bendix, 'forgive my haste. I thought only of her worsening condition.'

'We have some time, a finite amount, but most likely enough to preserve decorum,' said Calcraft, cheeks inflated with promise, buoyed by the effects of catharsis.

Yet tomorrow brought different concerns. That day's *Evening Post* carried a large advertisement that Bendix read aloud to his master in an effort to maintain his good mood.

'"*John Sheppard did break out of Newgate in the night, with double irons on his legs and handcuffs on his hands, with a bright horse pad lock under his irons. He is about twenty-two years of age, about five feet and four inches high, very slender, of a pale complexion and did wear a butcher's frock with a great coat over it and is a carpenter or house joiner by trade. Whoever will discover or apprehend him, so that he be brought to justice, shall have twenty guineas reward, to be paid by the keeper of Newgate.*"'

'Good, good,' said Calcraft, 'every man in London shall seek him.'

'It adds,' continued Bendix, 'that, "*if any person should conceal him from justice (knowingly) since he has made his escape it is a felony and they will be prosecuted for the same.*"'

'A fine coda,' said Calcraft.

By the end of the day Calcraft was surrounded by accounts of Sheppard's escape: the *Daily Post*, the *Daily Journal*, the weeklies of Mist, Read and Applebee. Defoe's efforts, printed in the latter, were the most detailed and descriptive, containing more than a hint of sympathy for Sheppard that had Calcraft huffing with indignation. The two men sat together in front of the fire, constantly fuelled and revived by Bendix, their hands blackened with cheap ink. Calcraft could not subdue the venom he felt towards Defoe, believing his account the most damaging and mendacious.

'My own friend, the man whose pain I spared, moves against me in this manner. Listen, Joseph, he calls the escape miraculous, wonderful. As if it were the birth of the Lord. Listen to this, Joseph,' said Calcraft uncrossing his legs and leaning in towards the light of the fire. 'Defoe admits, and prints, that, "*One file is worth more than all the bibles of the World.*" Daniel will blacken his own soul to write such things.'

'It is but the report of what Sheppard says,' calmed Bendix.

Calcraft folded the paper into a thick square and pushed it between the logs on the fire. It caught and blazed brightly. 'Then it shows the darkness of the man directly,' said the doctor with sadness. 'Strange that Defoe should turn against me so.'

'He does not turn against you,' said Bendix. 'Never have I heard him utter your name but among words of highest respect. If he knew your desires he would not encourage the man's freedom.' Bendix paused, not entirely convinced by his own argument. 'To Daniel, it is but an opportunity to print a hundred extra papers, increase his fees from Applebee.'

'Perhaps it is darker still,' said Calcraft. 'He may not move against me deliberately, but in spirit we are opposed.'

'Tell me, Sir Edmund,' said Bendix, pushing himself against the rear of the chair, 'if there is change in Amelia's condition?'

'Change?' smiled Calcraft. 'We do not have Sheppard, how might there be change?' Bendix shrugged and leaned forwards, taking the bellows and sending a shiver of sparks up the chimney. 'She has asked much about you,' continued the doctor.

'Has she?'

'It is but natural. There have been few to stir her imagination. You are of much interest to her. She appreciates the smell of your pipe. Believes you must be an odd-looking man.'

Bendix smiled, but remained facing the fire to let the glow mask his amused indignation. 'How so?' he asked.

'Your youth, Joseph,' smiled Calcraft, 'she has grown accustomed to the aged. She judges all men to be of my age, whether it be Lemon or that man, Defoe.'

'She knows Defoe?' said Bendix, resuming his seat.

'She has doted upon him since she was a child. He indulges her, an uncle if you will. You may have observed how fond Daniel is of his own writing, his own voice. Amelia is equally fond of information. Inquisitiveness incarnate. A trait they share.'

'Yet she has never fled the house?'

'Once,' said Calcraft, 'but her world is within the house and shall remain so until we restore her.'

Bendix waited patiently through the second day. When he thought of meeting the doctor's daughter, his palms would begin to glisten in anticipation. He did not fear the idea of her, knew that he had held the hands of comtesses, walked around the château at Blois with Princess Anne Marie and charmed them all on the cusp of sobriety. It was simply that his time in Paris had followed a similar pattern, the first year hovering on the edge of the court, then falling gently away from the highest circles, until empty pockets had tarnished him and pushed love from his life. It had been so long since he was in a room with a lady deserving of respect that he was not sure how he would behave so close to temptation. If he might keep his mind bent towards the future he wished to earn, then he hoped the rest of him might follow.

Calcraft did not mention his daughter again, but instead gathered the newspapers and pored over the smallest column discussing the possible fate of Jack Sheppard. It was as if Sheppard had become the only lens through which he might define his daughter. Without one, the other could not exist. It was with great pleasure then, that he read Thursday's papers announcing the recapture of Sheppard. He had been found dead drunk in a brandy shop off Drury Lane. Bendix was no longer horrified by the matter. Defoe had obviously been correct – Sheppard repeatedly allowed himself to be caught. This consistency was only matched by his ability to escape.

Defoe was announced by Lemon, and after letting his friend wait in drizzling rain for a good five minutes Calcraft allowed him inside. However, his reception inside the house was almost as cold as it had been without. Only Bendix saw the humour in the situation. Both men could not have been happier to have Sheppard in Newgate but only the apprentice knew that Calcraft wished for the hanging, Defoe for the next escape.

They attempted to talk of other subjects, Defoe describing his travels about the countryside, offering Bendix some details of the North of England where his father had settled. Calcraft remained aloof, nodding as if he were entertaining the dullest man in the kingdom, smiling with thin lips. When Lemon announced dinner, Calcraft did not offer Defoe a seat at his table, nor did he make an attempt at an excuse, but marched quietly to the dining room, signalling for Bendix to follow.

Defoe waited until his host was out the door, then turned to Bendix by the fire and said, 'I do not like it when he turns his rich man's grin on me. He is quite ill behaved.'

'He dislikes your comments in *Applebee's Journal*.'

'Preposterous,' said Defoe. 'He is unusually fond of the news these days.' Defoe picked up a print of the *Daily Post* and aimlessly surveyed the competition.

'Perhaps he is still at the drops?'

'No,' said Bendix, 'he controls his desires very well.'

Defoe nodded. 'Perhaps the change in weather.'

'Perhaps his daughter,' said Bendix, awaiting Defoe's reaction.

Defoe turned rather calmly and smiled with great amusement. 'Have you been digging at the secrets of the house?'

'Sir Edmund related the facts to me.'

'Indeed, you are in favour at many tables, Joseph. It must cause you indigestion.'

'He is still unsettled,' said Bendix.

'Unsettled?' repeated Defoe. 'The man is damaged. Damaged and fascinating and cracked to the core.' Defoe shook his head at Bendix's understatement, then looked up to meet his eyes, 'Have you met Amelia?'

'No, sir.'

'I assure you she will have a profound effect on you.'

'How so?' asked Bendix.

'I presume only that you and I are alike. Seeing as I do not find myself held in appreciation this week with Sir Edmund, I shall have to rely on you to pass on my good wishes. Tell her I have a tale from the French court that shall be much to her liking.'

'If I am granted the opportunity, I shall do so.'

Lemon appeared at the door, 'Mr Bendix, dinner is served.'

'I beg only a moment,' said Bendix and dismissed Lemon with a wave.

'What news of Jack Sheppard?' he asked Defoe.

'Mr Sheppard is not only weighed by locks and chains, Joseph, he is now guarded day and night by two men.' He took Bendix by the arm, and they walked slowly to the door. 'It would, naturally, be easy enough to bribe the men who hold vigil, save for the constant visits of the wardens and Wild. Besides, bribery would be a dull escape and frowned upon by the people. If there has been one common thread in the career of Jack Sheppard, it is the escalation of daring. His chances for escape from Newgate are slight.' The stress on the word 'Newgate' caused Bendix to look up as they approached the front door. Lemon was busy serving the doctor his supper, so Bendix opened the door himself.

'He is to escape upon the Tyburn Road?' asked the apprentice softly.

'Perhaps at Tyburn itself.'

'How so?'

'It has happened before. I saw Half-Hanged Smith swing at Tyburn fifteen years ago. Two hours, Joseph, before he was bled, revived and then reprieved. There was a murderess called Greene, awakened by the surgeon's scalpel some hours after she was turned off. It can happen again, Joseph. The hangman will be bribed, he will tie an uncertain knot. So if the mob does not rescue him upon the road, they shall cut him down. I will have a carriage close by, we shall take him to a house off Tyburn where you will bleed him and he shall be revived. It shall be the first time we sell the confessions of the dead who are determined in their resurrection. You would, of course, have a share in the profits of the sales for your involvement.'

'You begin to sound like a zealot, Mr Defoe.'

'You have doubted me before, Joseph. What say we wager again?'

'Twelve guineas,' said Bendix.

'This time,' smiled Defoe, 'I shall be forced to collect.'

'You may take it from my wages on the hanging day.'

Defoe bowed and moved down the steps towards the hackney coach he had arrived in only half an hour before. Bendix waited until the horses were prodded to movement, then went inside to join the doctor at dinner.

Calcraft remained quiet throughout the meal, eating in precise movements. He divided the salmon in pastry, removing the bones with slight parries of his knife. Bisected his beetroot pancakes with one deft motion, speared his fried celery and sipped constantly at his wine. Bendix offered up suggestions of conversation, touching on some of the doctor's favourite subjects. He had even read Tooker and Clowes's trusted reports of royals curing scrofula through touch, but their mention drew little response. Calcraft answered in polite monosyllables, obviously deeming his apprentice's late arrival at dinner a nod in Defoe's direction. It was not until they were enjoying Mrs Hemmings's Everlasting Syllabub, when Bendix was digging through the warm cream to discover a scoop of orange whey, that Calcraft uttered his first sentence of the evening.

'We must leave our wine behind now, Mr Bendix, or else Amelia shall be most upset.'

Bendix put his spoon down with calm deliberation, but his heart beat like a hummingbird's.

CHAPTER FOURTEEN

The room on the top floor of the western wing lay in deepest shadow. It was unlike any other room Bendix had ever entered, entirely accustomed to darkness. In such dim light he could not be sure of the colour of any of the cloths or linens, but they maintained the softness of moonlight once the eyes adjusted. Amelia's world did indeed exist, consisting of only fragments and muted shades where the bright glory of colour was prohibited.

'Mr Bendix, it is the greatest pleasure.'

The figure moved towards him, rising from a chair as a gentleman might, but the motion was feminine. He bowed before Amelia, discomfited by the grace of her delivery. He had shaped his imagination with expectancy, creating a taciturn naïf of veiled beauty whose speech was as disjointed as her letter. The very timbre of her voice belied his conjecture. There was a firmness in the tone, a gravelled wisdom that was incongruous in one so young. When he rose from his bow, he studied her face in the weak light.

Her dark hair, perhaps black, perhaps brown, was made of ten thousand obedient strands. Her skin was of such fineness that the doyennes of Paris would have spurned her with a jealous twist of their fans. It seemed to draw the light of the room, unless, thought Bendix, the light emanates from within her. Her mouth was small, yet her lips full. They paused in a miniature O, then closed. It was only after the thin stripe of a frown crossed her face that Bendix realised how long he had been staring.

'Forgive me,' said Bendix, 'my eyes were not accustomed to the dark. It is my sincere delight to make your acquaintance.'

'Let us sit, let us sit,' said Calcraft. Knowing the unchanging positions of the furniture, the doctor took his apprentice by the hand and led him to a small cane chair. Bendix sat on the edge.

'Father?' asked Amelia.

'Yes, dear.'

'Did I not hear the sound of Mr Defoe's voice?'

'Aye, child,' said Calcraft.

'And he did not care to visit?'

'He was in the most terrible rush,' lied Calcraft, raising an eyebrow at his apprentice in a comical manner.

'A lie,' said Amelia. 'Has he ever disappointed me in a visit save when he was spurned from the house?'

'We differed,' admitted Calcraft weakly.

'You are not thinking of me, Father. Was it not for the introduction of Mr Bendix, I should have passed the dullest of days.'

Bendix bowed with some grace from his awkward position.

'Mr Bendix, you act as if you stand amid the most ancient ruins. Some gaiety if you please. My father tells me that you have studied in France? My knowledge, as in most things, comes only from my father and his friend, Mr Defoe.'

Bendix hardly knew what to say. He had imagined conversation and it did not move so fast. There was also a touch of inebriation in his confusion, for Amelia, the gift of sight apart, was more beautiful than he had imagined.

'France, Mr Bendix,' said a puzzled Amelia, who was beginning to think Bendix as poor with his tongue as she was with her eyes.

'A country of endless sophistication,' began Bendix. 'Perhaps not England's match in beauty should all her days be blessed with golden light, but once south of Paris an infinitely preferable climate.' He pointed to the shuttered windows, against which messages of rain had begun to beat.

'I am not fond of the sun,' said Amelia. 'We are not fond of each other.' She smiled to herself and Bendix felt himself a champagne bubble on a breeze.

'The nights,' he said, 'can be filled with stars and a moon larger and softer than you have ever seen.'

'Now you tease me, does he not, Father?' Calcraft managed a grunt of acquiescence. 'You do not understand my limitations, Mr Bendix. A single candle must be veiled in my presence. I am happiest when nature's light is tempered by man's design. My windows, even curtained, are thick in stained glass. You see that even a night of cloud and rain and a board of shutters afford enough light for us to see one another.'

'May I ask,' began Bendix, 'what happens when you are exposed to a greater light than that you wish?'

'Her head,' interrupted Calcraft, alarmed by the tone with which the couple addressed one another and anxious to move on to the more professional reason for the visit. 'She feels her head swell against her skull. Her skin blisters under the sun,' he said and saw Amelia look down in embarrassment and Bendix turn his head.

Calcraft was met with silence. 'My dear,' he continued, 'if you were to cover your eyes, might I light a candle? Mr Bendix has not called for tea and we must have illumination if I am to describe the focus to our friend.'

Amelia took a thick strip of satin from within her cuff and tightened it about her own head, giving a weary smile as if she were consigning herself to some children's game.

The match scratched against the rough wood and cast a small circle of light within the room. Adopting the flame, the candle lent a gentle glow, finally bringing colour to Amelia's muffled world. Calcraft placed the candle on the table by his daughter and summoned Bendix to rise. Amelia did her utmost to maintain her dignity while her father rolled up the sleeve of her gown to expose the length of her forearm.

Only now could Bendix see her true beauty. The sharpness of her cheekbones was warmed by the echoes of smiles that had etched themselves about her mouth. A thin neck and a hesitancy in the face, a marvellous uncertainty as to whether or not she was subject to his stare, the tempered slope that led from her nose to her lips. Her porcelain skin was lit by the candle to the glow of gold.

'Joseph,' said Calcraft to command the apprentice's attention. 'Observe. It is the clearest of blessings, a sign is it not? The skin so delicate that Mr Harvey might have proved his theory of circulation without ever cutting man or beast.'

Amelia's skin was an extraordinary colour. In fact, once the candle was held close, it seemed to have no colour at all. Calcraft turned the underside of her slender forearm to the light, letting Bendix see the blue lines of the veins that ran like marble streaks to her elbows.

'Is it not formidable?' asked the doctor. 'Now that transfusion has occurred to me I cannot believe I did not think of it sooner. It was the microscope of course that sparked me. Ingestion is not the answer. What is so passed in is passed out. But transfusion, Joseph, is a procedure originated for a body such as this.'

Bendix twitched to hear Amelia so addressed.

'It is as if skin were the map, the veins the roads that cross them. It shall not be a difficult task, do you think?'

'I defer to you in this matter,' said Bendix, 'though I seek to help in any manner that I may.'

'Good, good,' said Calcraft, now pushing her hair from the back of her neck. The skin beneath was scarred and smooth from the left ear down towards the shoulder, as if it had been dipped in a bath of creamy wax. 'She was outside, a year or so ago. Skin blistered immediately. Her eyes turned red. Since then, the condition of her eyes has deteriorated. A couple of years ago, the room was not so dark, the glass was not even stained.' The doctor blew the candle out with a salivated breath.

The smell of the extinguished wick caught in Bendix's nostrils. Amelia removed the stretch of lace from her head and slowly opened her eyes, pulling her hair back across the scarred shoulder.

'We are done, child,' said Calcraft. 'Joseph, you may retire.'

Grudgingly, Bendix bowed deeply before Amelia and, thanking the doctor for he knew not what, walked out of her room and back down the stairs of the western wing. He had not expected such beauty and was grateful to put some distance between himself and Amelia.

Chapter Fifteen

October ended, November moved past the defiance of her early bonfires and into the grey eve of winter. There were few men who did not struggle with their health. Sheppard, whose execution was postponed once more until the 16th, lived in permanent discomfort at the feet of his watchmen. Visits to his cell were no longer permitted, the Ordinary his only connection to the outside, and he only concerned with talk of the next world. Defoe had an awful week when he believed that his stones had returned, accompanied by sweated dreams of pain. After days of passing blood, his symptoms disappeared. Even Jonathan Wild was aggravated by his venereal diseases, but he was never so agonised to call Bendix to him.

Calcraft and Bendix worked together, the doctor edgy and concerned only with the capture of Sheppard's body and their subsequent procedure. Bendix's days no longer amused him. Often he was sent into the streets to procure dogs that, with the tips of quill pushed into their legs, would be made to endure transfusions. The liquids of the doctor's devising were of heavy opiates, so that he might judge the speed and success of the procedure by his patient's calmness or its occasional quiet death. Bendix was nervous on behalf of Amelia and yet the doctor remained buoyant where optimism was concerned. The apprentice believed that Calcraft's hope had been extinguished on so many occasions that the merest of chances now magnified his expectations.

Bendix was only allowed into Amelia's presence while the doctor was there. Calcraft had become, since their meeting, both jealous and suspicious. For the first time since she was a child, Amelia had complained to her father of the dullness of her life. She blamed her ennui on the absence of Defoe and, though Calcraft would not relent in this matter, neither would he substitute her longings for company with Bendix. He knew full well the difference between infatuation and courtship, and knew that Amelia was receptive to Bendix because of his youth. Once she was restored, she would see an array of young men who would astound her. His house would blaze with sunshine. He would have new windows cut in her honour and she would, with his advice, choose well from the glut of suitors.

Amelia's days remained neatly portioned, as they had always been. In all her years there had been no surprises and no disappointments until the arrival of Joseph Bendix. The first voice she heard every day was Julia's, and where Julia failed in speech, she excelled in listening. Her ears were absorbent and memories or thoughts that Amelia dropped one month would be collected and returned to her at the most suitable time.

Julia would end the day by relating whatever she had seen through the windows that afternoon in return for Amelia's stories of the previous night. They had names for the familiar shapes that passed before them. A fat gentleman with a club foot was named Mutton, the sedan men who attended their neighbours were known as Stump and Stoop. Julia talked with them often enough and passed their stories upwards.

November was Amelia's favourite month, harbinger of shortest days and endless nights and pleasing to her sight. Spring and its cool breezes depressed her with false promises, and it was only ever the visits of Defoe that had alleviated her moods. If Julia were idle chatter, Defoe was exercise, where she was questioned for opinions, tricked and teased by the sharpness of his tongue. He would leave her with a kiss upon the forehead, mind still alight but as tired as the cart horses that passed beneath her window, beaten and broken but moving forward. Occasionally the kisses would linger.

Her father was clumsy in his daily visits. Never accustomed to her world of increasingly dark shades, he would bump and bumble and encourage her to bind her eyes in cloth so he might light a pair of candles for his own benefit. It was strange, Amelia would think, but he was like a visitor within his own house. From there it was simple navigation for her to conclude that they lived in two separate houses, father's and daughter's.

She saw little humour in her father, though often she could hear him share his laughter with Defoe. It was apparent that he took no pleasure in her. While Calcraft could not see her eyes in darkness, she could see his, noting their exasperation and disquiet, their shine of hope and the closed lids of mounting dismay. Her sight, or lack thereof, was a needle in his gut and though the doctor thought he hid well beneath smiles and daily visits, his awkwardness did not escape his daughter. His time in her world never lasted more than a half bottle of malmsey and was pleasant enough in its own way, as a mark of time or the toll of a familiar bell, but as soon as he left Amelia inevitably relaxed.

As a child, Amelia had delighted most in flowers. Julia still brought her daisies, foxgloves, bluebells, while Defoe would conjure a dozen varieties of tulip, jessamine, hyacinth or rose. Before the flowers died, Amelia pressed them, turning the ratchets and squeezing the last moisture from stem and petal. Cut flower and pressed flower had separate scents. A single cut flower could open a city room, but crushed and captured the scent was reduced, mild but appealing. The presses still stood in her room alongside one another, like her father's books, emitting the soft smell of the sweet and the dead.

Pleasures were internalised over the years, from what might be touched or inhaled, to what could be recovered through memory. Amelia's disease had not struck until the end of her third year, and at the oddest moments slim scraps of the brightness of her first days would return to her. A summer of deep green grasses, as high as her waist. Apples sitting plump amid drooping branches. Amelia knew that her father believed that sensation reached one first through the eye, but her whole body was alive to the conditions around her. The faint shake of the floor might course up through her bones and let her know that her father was in the study. Every tread could be differentiated. She developed a love of noise, rare sounds like thunder, or even the familiar pattern of London rain.

True freedom only came with sleep. All her dreams were bright and unrestrained, when she soared bird-like over imagined woods that let her forget the strict order of her room. And yet even the forests that she flew over at night, which she knew were wild, knotted and unmapped, appeared as patterns, dark stitches sewn far beneath along the green cloth of England. These dreams saddened her, but served to remind her to greet her father with smiles and why he must sense nothing but a daughter's love. He was the only source for hope of release. Often she thought of her departure from Lincoln's Inn, but it was precluded by the desire for her recovery.

From her days as a child, Calcraft had always respected the rules of her room. There was only one chair he was allowed to sit on. Nothing could be touched unless it was presented directly by Amelia. A flower press, a cup, a bow for her hair, a ribbon for her eyes. The regulations were immaculate and persistent, organised against her father like a series of moats or trenches.

Bendix was treated differently. He was a guest and the regulations did not apply in his case. When he moved a pillow, Calcraft blanched on his behalf, but Amelia made no protest. When he left a flower press the wrong way up, Calcraft winced at the expected assault, but she remained silent. Calcraft could not know that to his daughter Bendix represented an entire history of another world, books of stories she thirsted for. She could see the displeasure in her father's eyes and was alarmed only for Bendix's sake, but knew that as long as they were in her house her father would say nothing.

Though Calcraft believed Bendix to be unworthy of his daughter, he did not deem him unworthy of his profession. Often, during their discussions on transfusions, the apprentice had raised many questions of worth, mostly of a practical nature. The speed of the transfusion, the amount of blood to let before the operation, the viscosity of the essence they wished to transfuse. Calcraft described his previous efforts, from powders and nostrums to bleeding and binding. He even allowed Bendix to see something of the mounting depression that had weighed him through these trying years. Yet now there was a date for their release. November the 16th, the day of Jack Sheppard's execution.

CHAPTER SIXTEEN

It no longer occurred to Calcraft that Sheppard had any opportunity for escape. The doctor had been elated to read the reports of November the 10th when Sheppard had been brought before the judges and had been dismissed as a hardened ruffian, despite the fact that his career was just over a year old. Calcraft sought only to secure the flesh of the hanged. To this purpose, the doctor revived his relationship with Sixes. For many days he came about the house. He unnerved Bendix, who rarely heard a door close or open and yet Sixes would be there, in conference with the doctor. His hours were strange, which was entirely in keeping with the doctor's own habits. Bendix knew full well the illegality of their plot and under the ever shortening skies it seemed appropriate that their discussions should take place in twilight and darkness.

Between the reappearance of Sixes and Calcraft's obvious disapproval of contact with his daughter, Bendix was hard pressed to remind himself of his promise to keep his distance from women. He contented himself with their occasional meeting, perhaps twice a week, when the doctor and apprentice came calling upon Amelia professionally.

He was always delighted in his visits, finding her most intriguing and inquisitive, revelling in the fusillades of questions she would level at him. Between them lay the faintest edge of flirtation that made these rare visits the focus of the apprentice's week.

'Do you drink, Mr Bendix?'

'I do,' he had replied.

Calcraft would look up and a minute's silence would follow.

'Do you shoot, Mr Bendix?' she had asked.

'Not anymore.'

'Why not?'

'Because I shot an owl.'

'Were you drinking?' she had persisted. He could hear the smile in her voice.

He had paused and smiled. 'I suppose I had been.'

'What is an owl?' she continued.

'Two eyes, sharp beak, wings, a sturdy bird of wisdom,' interrupted her father.

'And what noise does it make?'

Calcraft coughed, then had found himself hooting like a barn owl to satisfy his daughter's demands. Bendix had joined in and the two hooted themselves hoarse in competition until Amelia's laughter infected them both and they joined her in joy at their foolish sounds. There had followed the uncomfortable silence that trails many jokes, good or bad, and they had been forced to resume their customary postures.

Once Bendix had even been bold enough to hold her arm, affecting the manner of the most proficient physician. He believed he felt her tremble in silent communication. When the candle was extinguished and she had removed the satin strip from her head, she had looked across to him as his eyes grew accustomed to the darkness, and she had dipped them briefly, as if to acknowledge a new level of intimacy. Bendix was at least sure that the doctor's sight was not equal to his, nor, in the darkness, his daughter's.

Bendix's basement room was, by mid-November, an arctic place of little comfort. He charmed a second woollen blanket out of Julia and purchased a third in a haberdasher's off Lewkenor's Lane. Holding one candle to the base of another, he stopped the draughts in his room every night. Yet by morning, the cold air had often cracked the wax, leaving it shattered upon the sill. On the 14th of November, Bendix dreamed of drum and fife, the passage of infantry through Little Turnstile and into Lincoln's Inn Fields under a rain that rattled hard as hail. It took Sixes a dozen pebbles to finally bring Bendix to his window.

'Come Joseph,' whispered Sixes loudly, 'we have need of you.'

Bendix could make out the anxious stooped figure in the darkness. 'I do not understand why a regular doctor might not be called.'

'Ten pounds and then some in for you, Joseph, so into your breeches.'

'I must sleep,' said Bendix.

'Twelve pounds.'

Bendix left through his own basement window, creeping up the tradesmen steps on the outside of his stockinged feet, his body shrouded by his great coat. The apprentice sat on the steps to his master's house and rubbed his wet feet with the lining of his coat. Sixes hurried him into his shoes, then took him by the arm and began him on the short walk to Covent Garden.

'What time is it?' asked Bendix.

'Two hours from dawn,' said Sixes. 'We'll have you back with wide smiles before sun up.'

'I am cold,' moaned Bendix, wishing he had been alert enough to wear the thickest of his frock coats against the November wind.

'Walk faster.'

Covent Garden did not sleep like the rest of the city, but

suffered from an insomnia encouraged by alcohol and coffee houses, houses of game and honourable brothels. Despite the rain, city sounds were altered by darkness, the clip of shoe and boot upon stone was exaggerated, drunken laughter was buttressed by echoes. Already the first carts from the country had arrived with their produce for the morning markets, the worlds of urban night and rural day shaken but stable. Bendix could hear the horses breathe, could see the hot wisps of their exhalations rise between the lines of drizzle. They stopped before a thin three-storeyed house and Sixes wrapped on the door.

''Tis a gaming house?' asked Bendix.

'Bawdy house of Mother Cates,' said Sixes. 'Your charge lies upstairs.'

The door opened before them.

'Mother,' said Sixes and tipped his hat in her direction.

'It's a long hour,' she said.

The madam was not the most persuasive advertisement for the house, her large breasts barely contained by stays but so soft and loose that flaps of her skin spilled over the edges of her dress. Her powders were, however, expertly applied, a thin paper to hide an unwanted present. The dismissive glance thrown in Bendix's direction let the apprentice know that their esteem was mutual.

'He will do,' presumed Sixes. As they wound their way up the central staircase Bendix could discern cracks of light stealing from six or so rooms on the first floor. Evidently the whole house had been awaiting him, even if they did not wish to show it.

The room that they entered felt hot, thick with the smells of incense and the sharper scent of sex. Bendix found it curiously arousing, reminiscent of his less lonely nights, until he used his eyes and not his nose for inquiry. Lying on the bed, framed by thick red Turkish carpet, was a large man, naked and pale, like a fat grub turned from rotting food. He was lit by a dozen candles that lined the headboard. The sheets he lay on were of red satin, which for a moment prevented Bendix from seeing the swathe of blood that had pooled around the base of his neck. Mother Cates stayed by the door frame lest her presence affect any life left in her client.

'Is he dead?' asked Mother Cates.

Bendix approached the body. 'He does not look well,' said the apprentice, with a professional smile and fixed a finger in the corner of his eye to clear away the grit of sleep.

Sixes followed him to the side of the bed and stared down at the heavy white flesh. 'He looks as if he's drowned, doesn't he Joseph? All swollen and sprained?'

'I fear that is his familiar state,' said Bendix and threw a pair of superfluous pillows from the bed before removing his great coat and leaving it upon the carpet. 'You know him?'

'See to him,' said Sixes, returning to gruffness.

Bendix leaned over to the man's mouth and pressing his ear close could hear a steady breath. He ran his hands over the man's head and removed them covered in a thick and gelled blood.

'What was he struck with?' asked Bendix.

'Most likely this,' said Sixes dropping to his knee. He rose with a brass candlestick in his hand, the corner of the base black with blood and hair.

'Mother Cates,' called Bendix, 'if you would fetch a pair of scissors, both I and the gentleman would be uncommonly grateful.'

'He lives?' she asked, equal tones of disappointment and relief.

When they were alone, Bendix turned to Sixes. 'Why did the whore strike him so?'

'Just mend him,' said Sixes, 'or Parliament shall notice.'

Bendix smiled and taking a damp wash cloth from the floor, dipped it in the basin and dabbed at the back of the man's head, removing blood.

'Will he live?' asked Sixes.

'He shall wake soon enough, with a damned headache that he shall not forget. Unless she beat the memory from him.'

Mother Cates returned with the scissors, entering the room only for the necessary seconds, then retreating to the doorway.

Bendix cut away at the man's hair until he had a good view of the wound. It was not so deep, merely a scoop of hair and flesh that ran laterally across the back of the skull. The bleeding had almost stopped by itself. Bendix believed he could not have lost more than ten to twelve ounces, the equivalent of a heavy bleed.

'Should he wake,' said Bendix, 'you shall have to hold him steady.'

'I would relish it,' said Sixes and moved closer to the bed.

Bendix used the remaining pillow to turn his patient's head towards the mattress, propping him on his side so that he might continue to breathe. Sixes watched with interest as Bendix began to stitch the man.

'I believe,' said Bendix, as he ran his needle under the scalp, 'that he has drunk a barrel of malmsey. We could strike him with the second candlestick and he would not wake.'

'Fortunate, no doubt,' said Sixes.

'There is little else I may do,' said Bendix. 'We shall dress his head if Mother Cates will see to the body.' The madam nodded from the door.

'I told you it would be quick,' said Sixes.

'And how does a drunk man pay?' asked Bendix.

'At once,' said Sixes, walking over to a mess of clothes and pulling a large pair of silk breeches from the pile. He found a small purse and removed three gold pieces, throwing them towards Bendix. They landed on the bed. Bendix paused in his administration to seize the money. Sixes tossed the purse to Mother Cates at the door.

'Should we not present him with a bill when he wakes?' asked Bendix.

'He has credit with Mother,' said Sixes, 'and would pay ten times that to keep this from the Dissenters or his wife. A most useful thing to remember.'

'I may go?' asked Bendix.

'Come this way, Doctor,' said Mother Cates and inched a finger at him.

'We shall meet below in half the hour,' said Sixes, and he steered Bendix and his instruments towards the waiting madam.

'What should I do with that gentleman?' asked Mother Cates.

'Stop the windows, close the door,' ordered Bendix. 'Let him rest.'

The apprentice found himself led out, around the staircase and past a great shuttered window and then levered into a second room. Reclining on the bed was a young girl, no more than sixteen, wearing only petticoat and shift. She looked so weary with surprises as to be positively bored with ennui. 'Is he dead?' she droned at the apprentice.

'Put a dress on,' ordered Bendix.

'And who would help me at this hour?'

'I shall,' said Bendix, putting his silver case of instruments upon the bedside table.

'If you tell me if he's dead, then I shall put on which ever dress you wish.'

'Was it you who struck him?' asked Bendix. She did not answer. Bendix presumed he understood. 'He lives,' said the apprentice and took a seat on the edge of the bed. 'Stay as you are,' he ordered. 'Snuff the candles.'

She licked her fingers and hissed the four wicks until the room was blackened. A minute and Bendix's eyes were accustomed to the gloom. The whore was of good figure, tall, the same height as Amelia. He watched her hoist her shift over her shoulders and saw the gentle sway of her breasts in the darkness. There was little hesitancy in Bendix once he had justified the act to himself. His fading promise to keep away from the wiles of women could only be bolstered by such a carnal transaction.

Bendix raised himself and stepped out of his breeches, then walked back to the edge of the bed. Hearing her spit in her hand, he was prepared for her touch and pushed himself forward as she angled him inside her. Imagining Amelia beneath him, Amelia's hands gripping his thighs, Amelia's soft moans filling the room he drove himself in and out. Bendix held her hips and laughed in temporary wonder as he withdrew, leaving a thin white rope across her thighs. She joined him in his laughter until he pulled away from her grip, silencing them both.

Taking himself in hand, Bendix walked to the chamber pot where he relieved himself loudly. He heard the strike of the match and the room glowed in orange shadows. The ring of piss against china causing the young lady to turn to him. 'I'm clean,' she said.

'I have little doubt,' said Bendix, 'but little doubt is enough.' He shook himself then buttoned up, raised his instruments, made a poor attempt at a bow and left the room, wishing to dismiss the event as a necessary aside to his continuing celibacy.

Sixes was waiting outside. 'She's good, isn't she?' said Sixes, as Bendix closed the door behind him. 'A dirty little bitch.'

Bendix nodded uncomfortably. 'Let us get you home.'

They left under the grateful eye of Mother Cates, who leaned forward to bestow a kiss on Sixes at their departure. He recoiled with an apologetic smile and crossed one of his bone-thin arms in front of him, as if he would repel any further efforts of her behalf. He alleviated his rudeness with a courtly bow, 'At your disposal, madam.'

'Send my greetings to Jonathan and beg him for a visit,' said Mother Cates, recovering her poise.

'I shall,' said Sixes, his smile now crooked with awkwardness.

Bendix watched the maladroit scene unfold with amusement. He took Sixes by the arm and steered him out of the front door and back into north-west corner of Covent Garden, where a carriage waited.

'A wonderful establishment,' said Sixes, hauling himself inside, first one long leg, head, torso, then the second leg, 'but a wretched woman. Richer than the king.' He eased his legs out in front of him as Bendix took his seat on the cushion beside. 'They say that you've been close on Defoe,' said Sixes.

'Of course,' said Bendix. 'Sir Edmund sent me to attend his convalescence.'

'What do you make of the man?' asked Sixes as the carriage pulled away from the Garden, the sounds of the coachman urging forwards the horses sharp against the end of the night.

'He has been most kind to me,' replied Bendix.

'Because he shows you the sights of Newgate?' poked Sixes. 'You may have them for a penny.' He paused, then added sharply. 'Though few have spent the days inside he has.'

'He already informed me of this,' said Bendix defensively.

'Did he tell you why?'

'Debt.'

'Yes,' said Sixes, 'I am sure that's what he told you. Openly confessing in vagueness and washing the sin away. The man has lost his own money. No crime in that. Then his family's. Then his wife's family. Now, forgive that. He's stolen horses, written against God and state. You should know about the company you keep, Joseph. Make sure that he does not want something of you.'

'I am hardly in a position where I might be taken advantage of.'

''Tis just as well.'

'Tomorrow,' asked Bendix, 'shall you be at Tyburn?'

'Aye,' said Sixes, 'along with the rest of London and her counties. Come with me in the morning, Joseph, and you shall have a seat as no other.'

'I was to go with Defoe.'

Sixes paused a moment, then smiled. 'Perhaps I judge too quick. Perhaps so. You and Daniel Defoe shall both walk with me.'

Bendix remained unshaken by his night of whoring. It was quite the opposite of guile and other guises of love that he feared. Nor had his night distracted from his studies, or subtracted from his purse. Amelia did not arouse the same simple heat of lust that had engaged him. Pure desire he understood, even if only in hindsight. His dealings with Amelia were stranger, producing a perplexing respect, an overriding desire to create the space for love. If, of course, it hadn't already arrived. Then all that had remained was the space for him to admit his love to himself. And now he realised that this had happened at the precise moment he had entered the whore. The gap between sex and love had closed. His myth of the Comtesse melted. Amelia needed both his protection and his knowledge. He considered himself as vital to her as she was now to him.

CHAPTER SEVENTEEN

Sixes had insisted that the three of them climb to the third floor so that they might get a better understanding of the crowds. Already Bendix had felt himself pushed and squeezed so that his frock coat wore the smells and creases of strange bodies. Sixes was correct. From the window of the tavern they looked down the Oxford Road to see the swelling crowds gather in the morning. Along the way young girls dressed in white were already throwing petals in the air in play. Defoe was obviously enjoying the respite from the bustle and leaned heavily on the window sill until Sixes hurried them along, anxious to be at Newgate by ten o'clock to catch Sheppard being escorted from the Chapel.

The prisoner was in the midst of an argument when they arrived. On one side stood a journeyman smith, waiting hard by to remove Sheppard's fetters. Defoe knew the customs; removal of the cuffs, binding of the prisoner's arms to his side with stout ropes. Watson, the Under Sheriff, was adamant that the condemned remained in manacles, calling Sheppard an imp of mischief who would have the occasion to be delivered in irons. Never before had Bendix seen the prisoner angered and it was a sight of much sadness quickly aggravated by the arrival of the hangman, who attempted to tie his rope about Sheppard's chest in the customary manner, only for the prisoner to twist and squirm like a child escaping the nurse maid.

'It shall be the same for me as for all,' shouted Sheppard repeatedly. 'The King's Orders. The same as one as for all.' Watson looked disconcerted at first, and then, catching sight of Defoe, distinctly upset that the writer should be there to witness this tantrum. Yet, finally, it was Sixes who reacted, coming from behind Sheppard and knocking him to the ground with a punch to his kidneys. He lay there, face against the stone until Sixes lifted him with his boot, putting him on his back like a beetle. Sixes leaned down and ran his fingers along the lines of Sheppard's breeches, then his waistcoat, when he suddenly removed them cursing. Bendix could see the bright blood flow. A much more careful Watson removed the clasp knife, which caused such a burst of laughter from Sheppard that it made the smithy wince. Only Defoe and Bendix knew that it was merely the first of his intended escapes.

'I was to leap from your cart,' said Sheppard, 'about Little Turnstile or so.'

Defoe beamed a smile at Bendix. Little Turnstile was a tight alley that led into Lincoln's Inn Fields. Had Calcraft been looking from his window, as he surely would be, he might have swallowed a bottle of laudanum in protest.

The prisoner was marched from the Press Yard, through the Middle Ward and along the passage that skirted the condemned hold into the Lodge itself. Cries of support from the Master Debtor's hushed the sound of their procession as they left the gates of Newgate. The street was filled with a confusion of constables attempting to arrange themselves in rank behind the city marshal and the under-sheriff.

Sheppard was hoisted into the tumbril, as Arnet, the hangman, raised himself slowly on to the driver's seat. A loose collection of javelin men formed a phalanx behind. The Ordinary, Wagstaff, offered Sheppard a hand to bring him to his feet, but the prisoner ignored it, preferring to sit.

'Have you stopped your drinking, Jack?' asked Wagstaff.

'Had you set the example,' said Sheppard, 'I might have followed.'

Wagstaff climbed over to where Arnet sat.

'Better you stay there,' shouted Sheppard, 'else the good man might be mistaken and hang us both.'

Falling in just behind the city marshal came the figure of Jonathan Wild, astride a roan horse. Sheppard was silenced by his arrival. Indeed, thought Bendix, his face assumed a momentary mask of gravity that the apprentice interpreted as either fear or hatred. Wild geed his beast about the cart, and wished Sheppard a good morning.

'We are sorry,' said Wild, 'to see you pursue independence to this terrible degree.'

'That is a fine cloth you are wearing Jonathan,' said Sheppard, breaking into his more customary smile.

'Thank you,' nodded Wild.

'Considering that it is purchased from the breath of thieves.'

'I have always said,' answered Wild turning his back on the prisoner, 'that hypocrisy is a low hurdle for a great man to leap.'

Between the cart and the constables walked Sixes, Bendix and Defoe. Sixes quashed the objections of the city marshal with a deep smile and a wave of the hand towards the adjacent figure of Wild that immediately brought about a mutual disregard. The procession trailed Newgate Street, past Giltspur and the Old Bailey, the city marshal steering them to the porch of St Sepulchre's Church, where they paused beneath the tolling bells. Even to Bendix it was a fearful sound, a dreadful boom that came from above and seemed to roll down Newgate Street to wash over them. Bendix's anxiety was relieved by the appearance of the sexton, carrying a hand bell, its tiny high pitch weak and human over the great waves of sound emanating from the church. Bendix could see Sheppard clearly, his face moving downwards from a hushed horror at St Sepulchre's to a large smile to hear the sexton calling above both bells, 'All good people, pray heartily unto God for this poor sinner who is now going to his death and for whom the great bell does toll.'

'Come,' said Defoe and, grabbing Bendix by the hand, they moved towards the prisoner's cart.

'You who are condemned to die repent with lamentable tears,' cried the sexton.

Defoe was stopped by a constable not three yards from the tumbril. At a signal from Sixes, he raised his javelin and the writer and apprentice continued to the edge of the cart, where they both hoisted themselves aboard, leaving their feet trailing behind so that they faced the spears and the crowd that hemmed their procession.

At the end of the sexton's words, the air seemed to fill with nosegays, petals and flowers cast into the air from ladies who had taken the porch away from the clergy. Bendix swivelled and, bending his legs in two, brought his feet into the cart, now sitting so that he could see the profile of Defoe's face. He looked to his right to watch Sheppard's eyes following the fall of the flowers. The prisoner shouted out to the ladies, but his words were drowned by the bell. Still, the petals filled the air until the horse grudgingly pulled them forwards and the flowers fell among the javelins behind.

They moved slowly down the steep slopes of Snow Hill before crossing the Fleet River to meet the wide streets of Holborn, where the constables moved up from the rear and surrounded the cart completely. Sheppard turned and winked at Defoe.

'Tis a fine crowd, Mr Defoe, is it not?'

'The finest.'

'We must hope we sell aplenty.'

Wagstaff heard their conversation and moved back into his proper position in the cart, remembering his charge. 'Do you know the Commandments, Jack?' said the Ordinary.

'I believe they lived in the same parts,' said Sheppard, 'but we were never close.'

Bendix could hear the hangman snort with laughter and could not prevent himself from breaking into the same wide grin that ruled Sheppard's face.

St Andrew's Church was draped in spectators, the walls and steps pressed three deep. Their own pace had slowed as they were forced to cut a way through the crowds. Bendix noted how the young girls in white had turned their gowns to dirty browns, the flecks of mud had condensed, creeping ever upwards. The great smile of Sheppard caused a roar that began by those who could see it and spread naturally in all directions, smothering Wagstaff's prayers.

At the Oxford Road in Marylebone Fields they paused so that Sheppard might fulfil a promise to an admirer. Figg, the pugilist, was waiting for the procession with a warm pint of sack in his hands, and pushed his way through the javelins to the side of the tumbril. The heated concoction left a vapour of spice in the cold air that had Bendix realising he was both numb from November and thirsty. He watched as Sheppard drained the draught in one and felt a jealousy that he noted for its absurdity.

Ahead lay the triple tree of Tyburn, to the north, the open fields of Marylebone and the spires of Hampstead, clear and marked in grey. Their procession ended not far from the walls of Hyde Park. Defoe and Bendix were removed from the tumbril and it continued alone until it came to rest under the triple tree. The enormous crowd was silent. Sheppard, looking up, could see that tiers of seats had been built in his honour and that they were crammed with silk and velvet gentry. Above his breath he could smell oysters, but wished only for a second pint of sack. Arnet dismounted and removed the rope from his side, slinging it over the tree and then around the neck of the condemned.

Sheppard had meant to perform with humour, but rising at Wagstaff's behest, he found that he stammered his confessions to his robberies. Perhaps it was the cold, his thin suit of silk, or the first seeds of doubt to Defoe's plans, but he knew full well he had begun to shake. He could not keep from glancing at the rope around his neck. Every time the horse shook its head, he felt the cart quiver and his legs stiffened with anxiety. At the end, he did not forget his promise.

'For those who wish the truth,' said Sheppard, 'the narrative of all the robberies of John Sheppard is written by myself and will be printed by Applebee's of Blackfriars. This is my confession.' From where Bendix stood, he could see that the condemned had conjured a strange batch of papers into his hands. 'It is the truth,' repeated Sheppard and, leaning down, greeted a figure who had pushed his way through the crowds. It was Defoe. The old man in the full-bottomed wig held the confessions high above his head like holy writ and carried them away from the tree. The Ordinary could not allow such a strange appeal to the public to be the last words of the day, and called forth a loud prayer to the silent masses before climbing down from the tumbril. Arnet stood before his horse and, receiving a nod from the under-sheriff, brought the beast forwards two steps. Sheppard did not have time to lower his handkerchief across his eyes.

Bendix stood horrified for over ten minutes. The crowd had uttered one collective gasp and a fading groan, then joined Bendix in silence. Sheppard twisted and kicked against the rope.

'Come along,' said Defoe to himself.

With the crowd ten thousand statues, the jerks and spasms of the condemned were exaggerated. The only other movement came from a carriage, coming down from Edgware, slowly parting the people. When Bendix finally tore his eyes from the body, as finally it came to swing limply, neither Sixes nor Defoe were present.

A man dressed as a soldier burst through the line of javelin men. He paused, as if surprised by the ease of his manoeuvre, then drew his sword and cut Sheppard down, accompanied by the gasped urging of his audience. Bendix looked through the crowd for Defoe and saw him not ten yards from his own carriage, leading it through the mob. A score of men followed the soldier through the constables and, raising the body above their heads, turned towards the approaching carriage.

They had not walked ten yards before the murmurs of the crowd grew, building from an ocean of whispers to a like-minded grumble of doubt.

''Tis the surgeons,' cried a voice from on top of the Newgate tumbril, and Bendix, recognising the tone, turned to see Sixes frantically pointing at Defoe's carriage. 'They'll have him to the surgeons.'

Bendix had never seen a crowd so close, nor so driven, but he knew that it had a current, had direction, wave and anger the same as a winter sea and watched as Sheppard's body and the men that carried it were lost among the rising peak of the crowd. He caught a brief sight of Defoe, separated from his carriage, and then he too was submerged.

The disturbance did not last long, but it had an intensity of emotion that had Bendix moving backwards, away from the vortex. He saw Sheppard's body rise again, passed from hand to hand from the gallows then south. It would disappear and erupt, none knowing where to pass him, none knowing that their own actions were murdering him for the second time that day.

Defoe's coach was wrecked. Bendix could spy the heads of the two horses thrashing and turning and the cries of the men and women near them. The carriage itself was broken and sundered, somehow reduced to pieces by the strength of the mob. One of the doors was raised and passed in imitation of the body. Bendix turned again to find Sixes, but he, like Sheppard's body, had now disappeared. Whatever had happened in those minutes, Bendix suspected that he had long since won his wager with Defoe.

The crowd was slow to disperse, weighing the rumours of Sheppard's whereabouts, then splintering, gathering, moving again until it was agreed that they should convene at Long Acre, not far from Surgeon's Hall. If the mob were a barking dog, Bendix joined as one of the last hairs of the tail, moving slyly and with interest from one side of the street to another. Presuming Sheppard dead and Defoe's intentions upset, Bendix travelled with Amelia's interests at heart.

The crowd made their way down Bond Street with surprising speed that had Bendix trotting ten steps for every ten he walked. He saw some poor fellow ahead, unaccustomed to their pace, his outmoded peruke flailing behind him. Had it been a warm day, he believed the man would have fainted. Some of the crowd ahead had seized links along the way, so now the twilight was postponed and the masses concentrated about the fires like moths. Bendix broke into exaggerated strides to keep within the cast of light.

'Joseph, Joseph?'

Bendix stopped and looked around at the man who had been struggling before him to find himself apace with Defoe.

'Where the Devil do they go?' huffed Defoe, taking Bendix by the arm and letting the apprentice lead their way.

'Mr Defoe,' said Bendix with some amusement. 'I believed you had been crushed.'

'Only my hat, sir,' said Defoe.

'And your carriage.'

'Was not my carriage,' smiled the writer, 'but Mr Applebee's. The true sadness of the day, Joseph,' continued Defoe, running silent for a moment to regain his breath, 'was that I was close enough to see the signs of life upon Sheppard's face. He would have done it sir, escaped in front of England, had he not been killed by kindness.'

'I presume then, that you do not know where the body lies?'

'Would that I did,' said Defoe, 'and I should be saved from pursuing this pack.'

Defoe and Bendix spilled into Long Acre to find that any leadership the crowd followed had now dissolved. They did not know which building might house the body and so began to stone first one house then another. Volleys of brick and mortar exploded across Long Acre, accompanied by the sharp tinkling of broken windows and the protests of the besieged. Small groups of elderly watchmen were engaged every yard as they fought their way from house to house, their movements eventually absorbed by the blur of the crowd.

Bendix and Defoe kept to the shadows of an alley and

observed the chaos rise. Long Acre still seemed to be filling with those drawn from Tyburn. The combatants had arrived first but now the audience swelled so that there was something theatrical about the enterprise. It drove the more active participants to greater heights, detaching railings, beating on doors, calling bravely for men to gather, though there were none to oppose them.

The riot disintegrated at the arrival of the Prince's Foot Guards from the Savoy. There was more than enough light left in the evening to make the bayonets wink and such order in their presentation that boldness evaporated as quickly as the crowd.

'Look at Wild,' said Defoe, pointing to the Thief Taker's figure moving amid the soldiers. Quilt Arnold followed in his wake, the two dispensing blows with cudgels as the crowd thinned and warped before them. Bendix watched as one of the more intoxicated rioters dared to stand in Wild's path. He swung a stick at the Thief Taker that broke against his shoulder, before being felled by Quilt's cudgel. Wild paused to test and flex his arm while his colleague continued to beat a path across Long Acre. Weighing his staff in his good hand, Wild brought it down again and again on the man who had struck him, beating into his flesh, bruising him then cracking bones. It was too loud to hear the landing of the cudgel, but both apprentice and writer winced with every strike. While Defoe watched in fascination, it was entirely too visceral a spectacle for Bendix and he quickly turned away in disgust.

Taking Defoe by the arm, he dragged them both further into the shadows then turned up towards Holborn.

'He might have killed the man,' whispered Bendix quite shaken.

'Was a bailiff, long before a Thief Taker,' said Defoe, his breath short from excitement. 'Not the first soul he would have delivered directly to the Lord. Extraordinary, is it not, to watch a man reduced to an animal?'

'Were he drunk . . .' started Bendix but could only shake his head as if he might drive the illogic of Wild's behaviour from his mind. The writer patted him on the back, then ducked into the Barley Mow Tavern and secured the services of a link boy. He led them through thin alleys that Bendix had never trod before.

'I suspect,' said Defoe, 'that Sheppard's body shall rise. If he is not found and buried before the day is out, the crowds shall gather again. We can be sure of that.'

Defoe wished him goodnight at the head of Rope Maker's Alley and continued on his own. Bendix, following the light of the link boy, walked wearily back towards Lincoln's Inn Fields.

Lemon's gaunt visage greeted Bendix at the door as if it were four in the morning and not five in the afternoon.

'The doctor is below,' said the footman, 'and says that you are late for work.'

Bendix must have stood there, rooted by uncertainty or disbelief, because Lemon actually reached out and tapped the apprentice on the shoulder, urging him inside the house so that he might close the door against the cold.

Bendix moved down the stairs in a rush, so concentrated upon finding the truth of the matter that he did not remember his own progress. Calcraft stood over the body of Sheppard, slowly drawing a line across his chest with the finest of scalpels.

'I was there,' said Bendix in astonishment. 'The body was borne away by the crowd.'

'A hundred men,' said the doctor looking up, 'can move a body quickly. Was it rough, Joseph? 'Tis a wonder he is even in one piece.'

Bendix looked down upon the body and felt a great sadness rise from his stomach, a teary vapour he was embarrassed to release. The crowd had done much damage to their hero. Aside from the predictably cruel marks of hanging, Sheppard's graceful body was swollen from breaks and bruises, his right arm twisted, right ankle enlarged. The bright red eyes joined the downturned mouth in protest at his treatment.

'It would not surprise me,' said the doctor, 'if he died from these wounds and was not suffocated at all.'

''Tis what Defoe says.'

'See,' smiled Calcraft, 'we are in agreement once more.'

Sheppard's ribcage was sawn open in the same manner as Pink of the Waltham Blacks. As Bendix listened to the saw meet and part the muscle, bone and gristle, he removed his frock coat and, walking to the head of the table, covered Sheppard's eyes. Then, according to the doctor's wishes, he repeated the same tasks that he had completed with such enthusiasm only months before. The inside of the man was easier to look at than his broken skin and bones. Everything internal seemed untouched and Calcraft's notion of healing gained credence in Bendix's mind. If the hanged were sacred in any manner at all, it would be from what remained whole, not the blood-stained eyes, the marked neck, the limbs shattered by the crowd, but from the inside, from where a man's worth was stored.

'Mr Defoe once said that the father of Sheppard was a carpenter,' said Calcraft, as Bendix weighed the spleen. 'Being Christian folk we must believe that his execution represents the first step in salvation. God's deliverance from sin, Joseph, and victory over evil.' Bendix was torn between utter repulsion at considering Sheppard an evil man and the hope that perhaps Amelia would be cured and the doctor proved right. He recorded the weight in chalk and turned back towards the body with his eyes on his own bloody hands. 'At the heart of every miracle,' continued Calcraft, 'lies the transformation from what is deemed bad to what is deemed beneficial.'

'Yes, sir,' were the only words that Bendix could utter.

When all of Sheppard's internal organs were removed, the two men fuelled the fire, adding the series of small kettles to begin the necessary reduction. The basement held the acrid smell of bloodied sawdust that reminded Bendix of walking past the open doors of butcher's shops. Looking at the emptied carcass of the felon, Bendix could not help but think Calcraft the greater thief. Calcraft turned immediately to his calf-skin journal, and with hasty dips of pen and ink spent ten long minutes filling pages with the details of their work.

There remained, to the apprentice, something very base about the physical level of the doctor's work, a repellent aura that he equated with Wild's behaviour. Bendix continually struggled against his upbringing to adjust himself to the visceral side of physicking. Had his family not severed their ties with him he doubted whether he would have followed his education so far.

When Calcraft had finished his scribbling, he rose and walked across to his apprentice, still beady from his exertions. Together they sprinkled layers of sawdust over the deepest pool until the red stains no longer emerged.

'We are almost there, Joseph. Tomorrow we shall thin our decoction.'

'Aye, sir.'

'I am retiring now. Mr Sixes awaits us in the kitchen. I shall send him so you may go about the business of the body.'

'And what is the business of the body?' asked Bendix, spite muscling its way into his manner.

'Why, to bury him. I have been told we must give him a proper burial if the people are to be calmed.' The doctor collected his journal, tucked it under his arm and bowed a merry goodnight.

The two minutes that Bendix spent alone with the body were cruel to his mind. Now that the doctor was gone, another thought occurred to him. Perhaps what made Sheppard exceptional was not the inside, but the outside. The Dorset lore, where children were cured by the hand of a hanged thief, appealed more directly to the logic. He looked closely at Sheppard's hands, turning them up and down, wondering about the healing powers of the hanged. Two fingers of the thief's left hand had been broken during or after the execution. They were too large for his slim wrists, calloused from years in the joining trade.

'Mr Bendix,' said Sixes descending.

'A fine performance today,' replied Bendix, resting Sheppard's arm upon the table and taking a step towards his visitor, 'I believe that you instigated the chaos.'

'Money did,' said Sixes. 'What does a man not do for money?' He had a large object slung in a sack over his shoulder and rested it against the table where Sheppard lay. 'Money,' said Sixes, ''tis an old story . . . The beginning of human device, and alas, so sadly, the end of human device – money.'

'For you and I, perhaps,' said Bendix, 'but Sheppard did nothing for money.'

'And what does a thief desire,' asked Sixes, 'but to live off the rewards of another man's labours?'

'I trust you were well paid,' said Bendix.

'Considering my low desires,' replied Sixes, 'it were close

to a fortune.'

'Did Mr Applebee not bid for your services?'

Sixes began to untie the line that bound the sack. 'If,' he said, 'you are a man of independence and are blessed with a touch of sense you should work beside the law and not *out-side* it.'

'A thin justification,' said Bendix.

'Sheppard stood outside, he did. Tell me now, if this body could speak would he not wish the death of attention rather than a cold grave?'

'You have forgotten the attention Mr Wild receives from the news-sheets,' responded Bendix.

Sixes pointed at Sheppard's carcass. 'This was a toy for your news-sheets, played like a flute. Now if the news-sheets were pipes, Jonathan would be the accomplished musician.' Sixes leaned over and picked up the sack, emptying several pounds of viscera on the table by Sheppard's feet.

'You have attended other executions today?' asked Bendix.

'Aye,' answered Sixes, 'shall we fill him?'

'Fill him?'

'Give him new guts, stitch him, dress him. He must attend his own funeral, Mr Bendix and, though the service at St Sepulchre's shall be small, we must assure that none think the surgeons have been at him.'

'Of course,' said Bendix. Together, under the apprentice's instructions they replaced Sheppard's intestines with the large sack of sheep guts that Bendix noted for their warmth.

CHAPTER EIGHTEEN

The three days were both exhausting and chaotic for Bendix. He was not the doctor's equal in either energy or commitment, finding himself unable to conjure up a similar faith in another's abilities. And yet, when the two men visited Amelia together, he believed that he could almost see her restored. He pictured her at the gates of Hyde Park, walking through Defoe's orchards at Stoke Newington, by the Tuileries. The more fevered the doctor's intensity, the more Bendix was driven to judge himself by Calcraft's standards. The night of the disposal of Sheppard's body he had not slept, keeping watch over the kettles with the doctor, watching the minute observations with which Calcraft attended his procedure. He considered it most kind of the doctor not to make a single reference to his previous failure.

Calcraft's main concern in the transfusion lay in mimicking the pace of the heart. However, Bendix's dread lay in their attempt to imitate the density of blood. He read with horror of the consequences that the successes of the Experimental Philosophy Club had wrought eighty years ago. Imitators had transfused urine, beer, milk and wine. The best that could be said on behalf of the experiments was that not all the results were fatal. It was Lower who had made the obvious step, presuming that the most compatible liquid to transfuse with blood would be blood. Had the experiments not been banned in 1685, perhaps they would have had surer foundations. While the doctor's decoction contained the boiled essence of blood and tissue, its viscosity made it entirely unsuitable for direct transfusion.

Instead they would follow the course of Denis's original experiment, transfusing the blood of a calf into Amelia. However the blood would pass over the decoction, Calcraft predicting that its warmth would gather a concentration of the vital animacules as it passed into the veins of his daughter.

The night before the transfusion, they examined the details for the last time. Calcraft carried two steaming glasses of wine to the basement and the two men raised a glass to the restoration of Amelia. The doctor pulled a small box from his coat and gifted it to Bendix.

The apprentice open the black-lacquered lid and pulled a dried purple flower from within.

'Euphrasia,' said Calcraft as Bendix brought the flower to his nose. 'The Greek for gladness, a fine omen.'

Bendix smiled and nodded.

'Do you know what they call it along the southern coast?' asked the doctor. 'Eyebright. The Archangel Michael swathed Adam's eyes in it after the Fall. It too is within our restorative.'

Bendix put the flower back within its box and turned to the murky liquid in front of them. 'What of Sheppard? Elsholtz said that mutual transfusion between a man and his wife would make one's character more like the other's. The ease of discord and tension, once the blood was mingled.'

Calcraft shook with amusement.

'Why do you laugh?' asked Bendix, a touch offended.

'You believe that Amelia shall undo her stomacher and climb down the side of the house like Jack Sheppard?' The doctor tried to contain his joy, then erupted into laughter again. 'Preposterous,' said Calcraft. 'When Mercklinus received the blood of a lamb did he bleat and devour his garden?'

Bendix smiled and nodded. 'Still,' said the apprentice, 'there is no precedent.'

'And therefore no judgement,' replied the doctor, 'other than our own.' He raised his glass to his apprentice, drank a long draught and placed his drink upon the table. 'Before you came,' said Calcraft, with great sobriety, 'I believe that I did not talk so much. It was neither to my advantage or disadvantage. I read aloud, but they were not my own words. I enjoy silence. It is a hard belief to hold to in London, but I do enjoy it. It has made me wonder if there are those who enjoy darkness.'

'Perhaps,' smiled Bendix, 'yet there should be a choice between sound and silence, between sun and shadow.'

Calcraft tipped his glass in Bendix's direction. 'You have no choice at this moment, Joseph. Amelia has requested your company. She tires of me and is nervous of tomorrow. Calm her, calm her greatly.'

Amelia sat in her familiar chair. Bendix entered and could not stop himself from thinking of all the hours she had sat alone, of the extraordinary similarity between her todays and tomorrows. He was not an admirer of pity, but it was such an easy thing to forswear and infinitely harder to prevent. Without her father present to loom over her like a herald of etiquette, Amelia rose to her feet to greet her guest and begged him to sit. Bendix obliged, unaware that his mouth lay open, his lips parted as if frozen at some amusing point of conversation. She was a tall woman, and in the moment between his sitting and her standing she seemed like a pillar of light that cleaved the room. It was the first time that they were alone together and though their knowledge of each other's lives provided many points at which to begin a conversation, Bendix felt as awkward as when he first met her.

While Amelia seemed settled in the silence, Bendix's vacant stare belied an inner commotion that challenged his mouth into forming the correct shapes for speech. Finally he contained his nerves and said with utmost calmness, 'Are there flowers in the room?'

'There is little in bloom, Mr Bendix. Not even upon our garden.'

'Of course not,' said Bendix and was relieved to hear his voice emerge successfully from his mouth. Then, gaining confidence, 'You do not strike me as a lady in need of calming.'

'Is that what my father advised?'

'I know better than to equate calmness with felicity,' said Bendix. 'You may refuse to undergo his procedure. Your sight may be fading, but this is a question of life.'

'There is little point in choosing an eternity of hope over the moment of opportunity,' said Amelia softly, almost to herself. 'I trust my father.'

'Yet, you admit worries.'

'Perhaps I seek comfort.'

She knew that Bendix could not hope to understand, how almost imperceptibly the muted colours of her world had paled, drawn together in merging hues. To have never seen at all would have been a lesser burden to bear, but to know what could be seen, to rely on a memory that would fade as surely as her sight, brought Amelia great sadness. She would miss expressions most of all, the peculiar angles and reactions that differentiated one face from another. Bendix's awkward shadowed movements would be lost to her.

Bendix hesitated, thinking it ungentlemanly to encourage doubts.

'We do not know what shall happen,' said Bendix. 'I think only of when your father first followed his own procedures when cutting for the stones. I am sure his assistant was horrified by the digression and yet the doctor was most certainly correct.'

'Are you horrified?'

Bendix smiled uneasily. 'I have both faith and doubt, the same as you do.'

'What if the worst should happen, Mr Bendix, what more might happen to me? Only that I might wake again and the world will be darker. It shall happen soon enough. I would rather wager my youth now. Another year of hope would seem to me a very hollow meal.'

Bendix smiled in appreciation of her forthrightness. 'Your scar?' he asked. 'Why would you walk beneath the sun if you knew what would happen?'

'To be certain,' answered Amelia, leaving a ponderous silence behind her. She was ashamed of the scar, ran her left hand over it now in discomfort. The day she had walked out on to the roof she had known full well what might happen. It was not as if she was seeking attention, only an alternative to sameness. Weeks before she had made her decision, and the moment the door opened before her she was filled with wonder and regret. She had seen nothing at all, just a blaring brightness. She had turned her head away as the sharpest of pains had pierced her eyes. The skin on the nape of her neck had blistered immediately, forcing her back within the door.

As she found her own way back to her room, the pain moved on and concentrated about her shoulder and neck. Wiping tears from her eyes, she had dressed her own wound in the mirror, feeling with her fingers the swelling open blisters and sensing the redness of her flesh. Before she had finished, she had passed gratefully into unconsciousness. Calcraft's touch had awakened her. Reapplying the dressing, he had said nothing, though in the subsequent weeks he undoubtedly connected the deterioration of her condition with her token act of rebellion. Had he asked Amelia, she would simply have told him that it was not just her sight that was fading, but her hope.

'I do not know why,' said Bendix to disturb the silence, 'but I feel it shall work. I have seen you walking along the edge of fields. I have seen you within the gates of Hyde Park.' Bendix stopped suddenly and stared downwards, as if he had spilled irretrievable information.

When he looked up, Amelia's lips were pursed with amusement, the scar dismissed. Bendix's bumbling serenity was endearing to her. 'How old are you, Mr Bendix?'

'My name is Joseph,' smiled the apprentice.

'I know your name, sir, I wish to know your age.'

'I am thirty.'

'Where is your family?'

'My mother is dead,' said Bendix, diverted by the rapid turn of conversation and feeling himself once again the apprentice. 'My father lived here in his youth. He now lives in Northumberland.'

'Do you visit him?'

'It is a fearful long trip. I have not. I shall.'

'Would you travel by carriage or might you sail?'

'Do you plague Mr Defoe with so many questions?' asked Bendix, smiling broadly.

'Infinitely less,' said Amelia, relenting with a matching smile, 'for his answers are eternal.'

'How would you choose to travel?' returned Bendix.

'If my father lived in the North,' said Amelia and despite the darkness, Bendix could see her arch her back to attention and push her hands together, 'I would wrap myself in furs against the ice and travel by the ocean. I should not be taken ill. I should stand beside the captain and he should direct my view to ports of interest along the coast. There should be a gale, not a large one, but one that might cause a man to pray, and we should reach Northumberland under the brightest and bluest of skies.'

Bendix laughed along with his hostess, and for the first time since he had imagined her or since he had met her he was reminded of the discrepancy in their ages. Her tale seemed child-like to him.

'Tell me, Joseph, how much blood does the body contain?'

Bendix's smile was extinguished. 'We believe,' he said, then wiped his mouth and began again, 'we approximate about twenty-five pounds, twenty of which might safely be drained.'

'And should a lady faint?'

'Then she responds to the measure.'

'How much shall you bleed me?'

'The measure shall be small, twenty to thirty ounces, depending on your response. Your father has not bled you before?'

'He mocks the barbers.'

'I myself find it invigorating. Eight ounces brings about an ebullience.'

'There, Joseph,' chided Amelia, 'now you encourage me. You must do the same for my father before tomorrow.'

'He needs no encouragement,' said Joseph, 'he has been bobbing like a robin for days.'

'And what is it that you shall replace my blood with?'

Bendix made sure that their eyes locked across the darkness before lying, 'I do not know. It is your father's secret. I have seen traces of a small flower they call Euphrasia.'

'I presume what we do tomorrow is very different from Mr Lower,' said Amelia and Bendix looked up because it was not a question but a statement delivered with the full confidence of knowledge.

'Do you read much?' he asked.

'I read little,' said Amelia, 'but am often read to. You understand that the difference, Joseph, comes from the censure of content.' Bendix offered a small bow in appreciation of her understanding and to recognise her use of his Christian name.

'Why,' he asked, 'did you choose to address me with another's words?'

'I have none of my own,' said Amelia, smiling at the memory of their letters. 'It is a woman's lot, is it not? To be able to read, but not write?'

'According to your father?'

Amelia nodded.

'For the most part,' said Bendix, unwilling to counter Calcraft's opinion, 'but England is changing.'

'Even so,' asked Amelia, 'then who would I write to?'

Bendix shrugged, uncomfortable. He had wanted to suggest himself as the recipient of Amelia's letters, but to say so would have been so open, so pithy that he found himself embarrassed by the thought. A flickering image of Mother Cates's whore simmered in his mind and was immediately banished.

'Your father told me, a while ago, told me that you thought I was an odd-looking man.'

Amelia could not suppress a giggle. 'He should have not have told you.' She waved a hand across her face, still smiling. 'I did not mean to insult you. I think quite the . . . it is your youth. Compared to my father and his few friends, you are so young.'

Bendix could only see the conversation growing more uncomfortable for them both. 'Defoe is your constant visitor.'

'According to my father's humour.'

'And he is not adverse to the sound of his own voice?'

Amelia smiled. 'No, and I consider it my good fortune. Before Defoe there was only my father. I was foolish enough to believe whatever he read to me. Defoe taught me the fallibility of words, that one was not supposed to swallow every book whole.'

'There is little he has not written on,' said Bendix. 'I believe he can barely have had a thought that he did not commit in ink.'

'Have you read *Crusoe*?' asked Amelia.

Bendix nodded.

'And *The Fortunes and Misfortunes of the Famous Moll Flanders*?'

'I was abroad.'

'Of course,' said Amelia. 'Then it shall be new to us both.'

'He would not read it to you?'

Amelia leaned forward in her chair and looked at Bendix most earnestly. 'It was two years ago. The time of a similar feud between friends.' Bendix nodded in sympathy. 'You may buy it,' she continued, 'at the Cato's Head in Russell Street by Covent Garden. We shall start it for my convalescence.'

Bendix had the most perplexing sensation as he returned down the steps of the western wing that he had undergone a pleasant manipulation.

CHAPTER NINETEEN

The house, from the western wing to the basement, was bathed in a compromise of light. Neither was it illuminated by the bright candles that usually accompanied the doctor's work, nor dimmed for Amelia's muted world. Instead Lemon had placed lanterns lined with opaque glass about the steps to the basement, so that every ten yards yielded soft orange light as if suns were setting all about the house.

Amelia wore a thin strip of calico about her eyes and, taking her father's arm, descended with Bendix trailing them. There was some laughter during their descent, a cloud of good humour between father and daughter, while Bendix moved sober-faced behind them. Amelia had dressed simply for the occasion, a loose white gown with elbow-length sleeves. There was something so conspirational about the gaiety that even though Amelia knew the gist of the operation, he felt more accomplice than apprentice.

Only an hour before, Bendix had merely felt absurd, together with Lemon, beating a calf down the steps to the basement. So many households had fowl, sheep or pigs living among them, but Bendix wagered himself that they were the only such building in Lincoln's Inn. Worst of all, Lemon refused to share Bendix's humorous mood, letting the best of the apprentice's jests go unanswered save for the occasional bellow from the confused calf.

Calcraft let Amelia run her hand over the calf's nose, which seemed to have the effect of calming them both.

'Will it live?' she asked.

'Of course,' answered her father.

Amelia could obviously see from beneath her strip of cotton about the eyes, for when she took her seat by the table she looked about and said, 'What is this underfoot?'

'Sawdust,' replied Bendix.

'And why is it laid over stone?'

'It is warmer under the feet,' said Bendix, and then to support the lie, 'and provides a man with steadiness where stone might not.'

Amelia nodded. In truth she did not care what she said, or what she was told, it was merely the exercise of thought, the production of sound, that stopped her from an outright display of fear. While her father dampened a towel to place over Amelia's eyes, Bendix sprinkled a thick coat of sawdust about the floor around them. Calcraft draped the towel over his daughter's forehead, providing a screen so that she might not witness the cutting while telling her that it was to avoid any increase in light.

When, finally, they were prepared, Calcraft opened his daughter's arm near the wrist with a diagonal slice of his knife and began to bleed her. Bendix attended two large covered bowls on the table where their concoction lay and tested them for one last time between thumb and forefinger. He rubbed the insides of the silver tubes and catheters with their restorative so that the hot blood would rush over it.

The doctor filled three eight-ounce bowls with blood, and when Amelia described herself as feeling as if she were made of air he stemmed the flow and placed her arm gently upon the table. Moving quickly he made a second cut, drawing a tense flinch from his daughter. Bendix took hold of her arm and held it steady, despite her cry of protestation. It took Calcraft less than half a minute to locate the largest vein of the forearm, another minute to attach the silver catheter. A small burst of her blood arced to the floor. Bendix released Amelia's arm and quickly connected the second silver catheter into an artery in the calf's leg, sending the first pulse of restorative into her bloodstream.

Bendix could feel the sweat on his palms, knew that they hesitated between greasiness and resinous adherence. Should he drop the silver tube, they would fail. He looked down to Calcraft's exposed head, saw that he too was nervous with sweat, trickles rolling from down his jaw. Amelia arched her neck backwards. The tension between father and daughter shimmered, her patience and hope straining against their mutual desires. Anger caught in her throat and despite the pain she swallowed whatever words she wished to spill against her father.

Bendix could hear the stifling of tears. The calf stood dumbly by. Bendix had tied a leather strap about its mouth to prevent further bellows, but it seemed quite unconcerned with the draining of its blood. Calcraft looked up and nodded a smile of nothing but nerves and Bendix was struck with the indecision, the dubiousness of it all and felt a rush of hatred for the doctor to subject his daughter to such uncertainty.

'There is a great heat,' said Amelia weakly.

'Where?' asked her father.

'It moves upwards from my arm.' Bendix could see beads of pain rise on her neck. He motioned for Calcraft to look. 'I do not like it.'

Calcraft reached up and tapped the silver tube.

'Her pulse is at a gallop,' said Bendix.

Amelia merely breathed in and out, coaxed and calmed by Bendix until her pulse dipped once more. She pushed her right arm to the small of her back and choked in a cough of pain. She pushed her hand straight against her spine, then bent double in pain. 'Enough,' she said.

'She has twenty ounces in her,' said Bendix.

'She is quiet now,' said Calcraft.

Bendix leaned forwards and pressed his hand against her temple. 'It is because she barely breathes,' he said and without waiting for the doctor's permission pulled the catheter from her vein and knelt to close the wound on her arm.

While the apprentice was poised between patient and master, Amelia revived and vomited over herself. The sharp smell of acids pervaded the basement. Bendix continued his stitching, while the doctor wiped the vomit from his daughter's dress.

'We must take her to bed and bleed her,' said Bendix.

Calcraft looked to object, but the collapsed, blindfolded figure of his daughter seemed to reproach him, as if he were the sole instigator of her condition. Without even glancing at the doctor, Bendix knew the sight of Amelia was breaking him. He would make no more decisions on her behalf tonight. Bendix carried her up the stairs, past a close-mouthed Lemon and into the western wing.

Calcraft straggled behind, gripping his journal, lost in thought or perhaps merely lost, wandering like a banished lover. He remained alert enough to direct them to Amelia's bedroom. In his hurry to open the shutters, Calcraft tore a hinge, casting the yellows and greys of the evening into the room. Bendix had never seen so much lace. It was a room constructed from fashions that did not exist in London or Paris, a room of such finery and colour that, had it belonged to a queen, even the most sycophantic of courtiers could not have resisted a horrified rub of the eyes. Blue laces were draped over reds, swaths of coloured silk depicting busy gardens of the imagination hung about the walls. Even the ceiling was draped in a calico depiction of the heavens, sun and moon and stars all burning down upon them. There might have been a hundred cushions in the room, lying one upon another like low shrubs contesting the sun's rays. It was a room of such concentrated traffic that it upset the eye and jostled the mind.

Bendix laid his patient out upon the bright blue lace of her bed then left immediately, running down the hallways in search of his knife and cupping bowl. When he returned he was surprised to find that the doctor was sitting at the foot of Amelia's bed and had not attended nor even glanced at his daughter.

'Doctor,' said Bendix, 'surely we must bleed her now?'

He looked up and nodded, motioning for the apprentice to continue. Bendix hastily tied off Amelia's left arm with a tourniquet and, holding his lancet between thumb and forefinger, struck diagonally into the vein. He let the blood pour gently into the measuring bowl until he had drained her of eight more ounces before binding her arms and folding them across her chest.

'I believe,' said Bendix, 'that we should dose her with laudanum to encourage sleep.'

The doctor turned to Bendix, 'You shall find it in my study. Behind the row of inks in the desk. The dark-blue bottles.'

After they had raised Amelia to a level of consciousness needed to swallow the medicine, they departed from her room. Bendix had no doubt what the evening would bring and headed for his own bed in a black mood aimed directly at the doctor and his weaknesses. Should he find Calcraft at sea in dreams of opium in the morning, then Amelia's recovery, her life, would lie in his hands only. It was not a thought that encouraged sleep, and Bendix spent a great deal of the night humming songs of Paris to calm himself.

To his enormous relief, he found the doctor sitting at his breakfast table at six the next morning. He had not shaved, nor put on his wig. Indeed, had Bendix not been so tired himself, he might have recognised that the doctor had not slept either.

'Did you keep watch on her?' asked the apprentice.

'Aye,' said Calcraft.

'And did she sleep?'

'Deeply.'

'Good,' said Bendix and sat down.

'I unbolted the windows during the night,' continued the doctor, 'and removed the screen from her eyes as she slept. I fell asleep myself and when I woke, the sun had risen and Amelia had hidden behind her fabrics and closed the shutters that I had opened. There is no difference in her condition, Joseph. None at all.'

'We have to wait days to be certain,' said Bendix with little defiance.

'Her urine is black,' continued Calcraft, 'there is a great lassitude in her limbs. I do not know what we have done.'

'I shall see to her,' said Bendix.

'There has been no change,' said Calcraft, spitting each word with a charged regret as if he were both the judged and the jury.

'Amelia?' inquired Joseph at the door to her darkened room.

He could hear the rustle of a response, but no encouraging or reproachful words. Bendix lit a candle, covered it and entered the room. There was a beauty in the colours and layers of lace that he had thought so abhorrent in the light yesterday. They made an intense fabric of greys and blacks that offered small hints or deceits as to what their true colours were. Indeed, the army of cushions that he had thought so absurd in their abundance were now transformed into a landscape of gentle undulations. Even the bright calico that covered the ceiling deceived the eye into believing that one was outside.

He could not tell whether Amelia was asleep or awake, perhaps she did not know herself, but she did not resist his brief examination of her arm and eyes. Bendix was astounded at his own ability to perform as physician. In truth, Amelia, bled, transfused, sick, dosed and bled again seemed to have turned a shade of grey, her previous effervescence dissipated. Bendix was familiar with corpses and the warmth of her skin did not support her claims to life. And yet, they had no concept of the effect of their administrations, no knowledge if her reaction was positive or life-threatening. No matter how far they had attempted to push the limits of natural philosophy, Bendix resolved to follow more practised methods for her recovery. Tears threatened him. If he had even blinked, his wide eyes would have spilled them down his face.

He sat there and watched her breathe. Perhaps it was Amelia's delicate thread of life that moved Bendix. In all her beauty she lay before him. What frightened him most, on reflection, was not the possibility of her death or her continued sickness, but her recovery. If she were to heal, she would be open to the eyes of other men. The very thought angered him and he pinched away the wetness from his eyes.

It had taken weeks for Bendix to recognise that she was indeed a woman, a woman who might belong to anyone, whose beauty alone might attract a dozen men as surely as sweetened water tempts wasps. The simplest of thoughts occurred to Bendix – he must marry her. There could be no other way. He did not know if it was a good thought, if this was the bloom of love or its expectation, but possessing her became his only certainty. It was a love he did not want to declare, but wished to deserve.

Bendix found Calcraft at the breakfast table as he had left him an hour before. He looked up expectantly, but with an air of cynicism as if the apprentice could not help but concur with the master.

'I believe,' said Bendix, 'that she is suffering from an excitability of the blood vessels.'

Calcraft smiled and nodded his head. He might as well have bowed his head to the victory of old medicine.

'Three days of opiates,' continued Bendix seeking the doctor's approval. 'Then an emetic and cathartics. On the sixth day her chest must be blistered.'

'You will attend to her?' said Calcraft.

'If you will not.'

Calcraft nodded again. 'I have not slept. I must sleep.'

Bendix felt a rush of nervousness. Once more, he feared the doctor's return to laudanum and being laden with the responsibility of Amelia's health.

'You approve of the course?'

'We have failed, Joseph, it matters not what you do, but for every dose you wish to give her, reduce it by half. Her sight is lost. She will be blind, lost to us.'

'We may try again,' said Joseph.

'We have wasted the perfect specimen,' answered Calcraft wearily.

'With respect, sir,' said Bendix, 'we have not approached the perfect specimen. We have merely chosen an ill-suited subject. Sheppard was a rogue but not a murderer. It is Wild we want. Wild who runs London and hangs men. He suffers badly from the gleet. We might visit him together.'

'Look at you, Joseph, you have slept as well as I. We talk as fools, let us speak in the evening.'

It was no surprise to Bendix that the doctor did not appear at dinner, nor that he had instructed Lemon to inform his apprentice that he had taken ill and would remain in bed and did not wish to be disturbed. Mrs Hemmings cooked for Bendix alone. Faced by a large roasted hen and a pair of trout, Bendix was dismayed. To eat by oneself, he thought, was the most melancholic experience. It became a process, and one that Bendix hurried through. His thoughts were of responsibility, for if the suggestion of Sheppard had been his then perhaps he should also claim a share of the failure. However, had he not committed himself to the doctor's teachings, had he not buried his own beliefs and trusted in Calcraft?

The next morning the doctor did not appear. Bendix continued his visits to the western wing, walking along the corridors that had once caused him so much panic. Now he was among invalids, every man or woman in the household reduced by addiction or weakness and he alone to tend to them. He gave Amelia forty drops of laudanum twice a day, attempting to feed her broth. Julia attended her as well, though there was little to attend to, Amelia and her father both floating freely in a world of restless dreams that to Bendix's weary countenance became more attractive by the day.

CHAPTER TWENTY

At the end of the week, taking a brief walk wrapped in his great coat, hands clasped about one another, Bendix paused by a puddle of late November rain and, as the ripples eased at his feet, caught his reflection against the clouds above. He had forgotten both paint and powders yet he was as pale as virgin snow, a beggarly phantom. The only colour about his face were the dirty patches that shadowed his eyes. He turned immediately, curtailing his exercise and returned to Lincoln's Inn Fields, where he ordered Lemon to send for Defoe.

Defoe arrived within two hours and looked at Bendix with amusement. They sat by the fire in the doctor's library. The winds outside were swirling with mischief, forcing the occasional gust of smoke back down the chimney so that Defoe coughed and Bendix squinted and opened the door. It drained the room of heat so that they both pulled their chairs closer to the fire. It took Bendix only a minute or so to inform Defoe of the intent and failure of their procedure and the subsequent descent of both doctor and patient into dosed dreams.

'What is it you wish of me, Joseph?'

'I suppose I am the dog that looks for a scratched belly.'

'It is hardly success now, is it? Still, you have done well,' said Defoe, and leaned towards the fire. 'Do you feel better for hearing it?'

'Yes,' said Bendix and smiled for the first time all week. 'She has talked of you, she misses your company.'

'Do you read to her?'

'She has been in no condition for understanding.'

'And Sir Edmund remains abed?'

'Was he always this way?'

'I have known him years, but not all his life. Susceptible, I would say, always susceptible. Does Amelia sleep now?'

Bendix nodded and reached forwards to stab at the fire with the poker. 'How do you know the doctor?'

'Why?' Defoe paused, as if to consider the extent of his revelations. 'I do not know if you may understand, Mr Bendix, but the writer observes. A man needs a subject, many subjects, great subjects. I had heard much of our good doctor, rumours that the ways in which he worked were of his own invention and practised nowhere else in Europe. I was selfishly attracted, but soon absorbed.'

'You sought his friendship?'

'I wished knowledge of the man. We shared a certain amorphous politics. He had lost his wife, his vessel of idle chatter and chose me as replacement. Of course I wished to write about him, but friendship and examination do not mix. We became too close.'

'And this was all of your attraction?'

'This is all.'

'And his wealth?'

Defoe looked up and an easy smile broke over his face. 'At the time I was in debt. The doctor had made his fortune cutting the stones from beneath deep pockets. Welcomed in the courts of Europe. He broke my chain of debt. Yes, money is a concern, always a concern. It is a most attractive quality in a friend. Does it hold no interest for you?'

Bendix shrugged as if he had not thought of the doctor's wealth. Indeed, he had, but never had he thought of obtaining it. He believed himself ambitious and talented enough to procure his own fortune.

'Come now,' continued Defoe, 'there is little garnish gained from observation, from ink and paper. The doctor has been most kind. Do you deny the attraction of a heavy purse?'

Bendix shook his head. 'I was once accustomed to a carriage and six and prefer goose to bread, but if you sought to borrow from his pocket I believed I might thieve from the mind.'

'How very noble,' smiled Defoe. 'And what of Amelia? We are men, Joseph, the father sleeps, do you not think her a woman of great beauty?'

Bendix nodded slowly, as if he was not sure of what he was admitting. 'The girl is well enough.'

'The thought crosses all men's minds,' said Defoe. 'You think that I do not take a little of her youth and beauty with me each time I leave this house. You are alone in London,' continued Defoe, 'you have attended neither plays, drums nor masquerades. It is unnatural in a man unless his attention has already been absorbed. Tell me of her, tell me of all your intentions.'

Bendix opened his palms towards the older man in a display of confession. 'I wish success, what all men wish,' he spoke clearly, 'land, wife and a name that lives a thousand years. I wish it all.'

'Do you love Amelia?'

Bendix shifted, uncomfortable with such intimate information. 'I have loved before. It frightened me.'

'You were rejected?'

'Of course,' said Bendix in resignation.

'You wept?'

'Night and day,' smiled the apprentice, 'for weeks.'

'And now?'

'I am,' murmured Bendix, 'I am light. Little disturbs me.

With Amelia, even should I fall, I feel that no true harm would come to me.'

'Did you feel this before?'

'No.'

'Once,' concluded Defoe, 'you were in mourning. Now, you are in love.' He smiled kindly at the apprentice, with the greatest of warmth. 'Would you take Amelia?'

'If she would have me.'

'And if Sir Edmund would not?'

Bendix shrugged.

'She would come with five thousand pounds if she came with a penny,' said Defoe. 'It is a sum of consideration. Does it increase her beauty?' When Bendix did not reply, Defoe added, 'Does it increase her beauty to an apprentice?'

'Of course not,' said Bendix plainly.

'I am pleased to hear so,' smiled Defoe, clapping his hands in pleasure. 'And may your wishes be granted.' Defoe made as if to rise.

'What am I to do?' asked Bendix.

'About Amelia?'

'Physicking.'

'I would continue in your course,' said Defoe. 'You began with two patients, and a week later, you have them both. An enviable record. My only recommendation is for your own health. Find a reason to leave the house every day. Preferably in the minutes that it does not rain. Buy a ribbon for your love.'

'One moment more,' said Bendix. 'In the course that I have followed bleeding and emetics precede opiates. Soon I must apply a mustard press to the patient.'

'Where does the problem lie?'

'It is supposed to be applied as a blister to the naked chest.'

'Ah,' said Defoe, 'a most interesting situation. You wish to spare her blushes?'

'And my own.'

'I recommend two courses,' said Defoe. 'First, you may call in another doctor, though I wager that Sir Edmund would be against such steps. Second, if the thought is so horrifying, why would you not increase the dose of her drops and apply the press as she sleeps?'

The following day, the 1st of December, Bendix attended to both Sir Edmund and Amelia early in the morning and once again at noon. There was little he might do for the doctor, presuming that he would dose himself until he emptied the house of laudanum. Amelia, however, was weak but awake, though she had not attacked Bendix with her customary questions yet. She had only managed a murmured request for company or entertainment. Bendix had almost made it out of her bedroom when she raised her hand to hold him and brought him closer with the softness of her question.

'Where is my father?'

Bendix winced.

'I know,' she said. 'It does not need to be spoken.'

'He is disappointed,' said Bendix. 'We shall make no further attempt on your condition for the moment.'

'What if this is how I am meant to be?' asked Amelia. Bendix thought the question might be accompanied by tears, for her voice quaked with doubt. He could see little in the dark. 'What if I was intended by God to suffer this? It is so gentle, Joseph, simply a waning. I have seen Mr Defoe's pain from the stones. There are so many who have had moments that contain more suffering than I have experienced in all my days.'

'You must not resign yourself to what is curable,' said

Bendix, feeling very much the physician. 'If God gave man both the disease and the mind to cure it, is it not an insult to the Almighty to suffer? That is self-righteousness over right-eousness.'

'I believe in my father,' said Amelia. 'I believe in his methods. We shall try again.'

'Not until your recovery is complete,' smiled Bendix. 'If you have no objections, I wish to leave and see to your entertainment.'

Amelia bestowed him with a kindly smile that warmed him as he emerged from the front door into a flat drizzling sky. He headed to Russell Street, beads of water gathering on the rim of his tricorn, found the Cato's Head and bought a print of Defoe's own *Moll Flanders*.

Bendix had more need of the London air than he had thought. An anger against the doctor had taken hold of him that he had not recognised until his last visit with Amelia. Her survival seemed to have occurred in spite of their procedure. It was inconceivable to Bendix that he had almost abetted in her death. Like the doctor, he wished for her restoration, but he did not think he could repeat the process again. And yet, he knew that the doctor's theory remained untested. The choice of Sheppard had been of his own engineering and was to his shame. If the doctor were correct in his assumptions, it would take a darker soul than Sheppard to prove him right.

Chapter Twenty-One

Though Bendix was never a man who enjoyed showering his friends with praise, he could admit to anyone who wished to hear it that Robinson Crusoe's image of a single footprint in the sand had stayed with him since the day he had read it. It was, he thought, a wonderful examination of the philosophy of Locke and yet cloaked in palatable adventure. *Moll Flanders*, as he discovered when he turned to the first page and read aloud the full title to Amelia the next morning, was the extraordinarily inappropriate story of a prostitute, thief and bigamist. His patient, bolstered by a hedgerow of cushions, sat in shift and gown, her band of lace tied neatly over her brow. It was of much relief to Bendix that her eyes were covered, preventing her from seeing his embarrassment.

'Do you not wish to continue?' asked Amelia with a sloping smile, sensing his discomfort. The voice was weak, but strong enough to mock him.

'It is the tale of a whore, Amelia,' said Bendix.

'I know,' said Amelia, 'and knowing nothing of the life, am anxious to hear.'

'I do not wish to continue,' said Bendix flatly and slapped the book shut.

'Have you ever visited with such a woman?' asked Amelia.

'No,' lied Bendix sombrely, without raising his eyes.

'What manner of man does?'

'The ill advised,' said Bendix. 'Whores are traffickers of plagues that can eat a man's face. We shall find something else to read.'

'Did the disease begin with a whore, or the men who traffic in them?' asked Amelia.

'The whore,' said Bendix.

'And why is that?'

'Because subjecting the body to wilful assault by any man with two pennies will sooner or later weaken the mind. Once the mind is gone, the body submits to contagion.'

'This is common knowledge or your own belief?'

'How long do the questions last?' asked Bendix.

Amelia smiled. 'Until you resume the book.'

'I cannot.'

'It is written by a man as good as my uncle.' Amelia's was a very clear, almost practised whisper. 'I wish to read every word that he has written. I consider it a matter of politeness. He has been most kind to you since your arrival. I believe you should feel a similar obligation.'

Bendix reopened the book with an awkward smile.

'He would not read it to you, would he?' asked Bendix.

'Begin,' pleaded Amelia with a laugh, and he did.

To the apprentice's relief, the first pages contained none of the filth that the title suggested. Indeed, Moll's goodness convinced him for three days of reading that the words 'whore' and 'thief' had only been added to the title to attract a wider audience. He was, however, soon disappointed, yet the further Moll fell in her world of marriages and gold, the more engaged Bendix became, even reading Amelia to sleep and past. He would not call Defoe's writings erotic compared to the woodcuts he had seen in Paris, and yet he could not deny the stirring he experienced as he read the words aloud to Amelia.

'At last repeating his usual saying, that he could lie naked in the bed with me and not offer me the least injury, he starts out of his bed and now, my dear, says he, you shall see how just I will be to you, and

that I can keep my word, and away he comes to my bed . . . thus the Government of our virtue was broken.'

Moll was rewarded with gold, Bendix only with an ache for carnal pleasures. He would memorise the words a sentence ahead, then watch Amelia's reaction as he read them, seeking signs of shared excitement. There were none that he could interpret. No licking of lips or French sighs of love, only a smile or a straight face and no eyes to read.

Moll was obsessed with money. He could barely read a page without some mention of a settlement or a box of guineas. Defoe's questioning of his intentions and Moll's constant pecuniary fascinations soon swelled inside the apprentice's mind. He could not help but see his every move through stains of gold, just as the Comtesse had. Yet he had more to offer Amelia. Not a purse, but love, knowledge and time.

Moll loved guineas, Moll loved gold, Moll loved possessions. She understood it was a bad market for her sex and married money five times over. Moll loved silver, Moll loved wedding rings and watches and lockets. Defoe had swathed her in a conscience, but what was a conscience but a provider of alibis and excuses? Bendix wondered again if he was any better than this whore and thief. He walked the house as if it were his own. Rode in the doctor's carriage, ordered the doctor's servants as if they were his own. Had looked upon the doctor's daughter as wraith, then responsibility and finally as a woman.

To clear the matter from his mind, Bendix followed Defoe's advice once more and set about his London wanderings, walking west through Bloomsbury and by the frosted works at Soho Square. He passed south along St Giles and then through the crowds of Drury Lane. There had been no rain for two days and, despite the chill of the season, several storekeepers had left their doors ajar. Bendix, attracted by the colours he could see through the opening of one such door, entered to find himself in a mercer's shop.

'Cold day, sir?' said the squat proprietor, bristles like broom weaves poking from his nose.

'I wish . . .' said Bendix, who did not really know what it was he wished. 'I wish a gift for a lady.' It was a sudden idea, a manner in which he might allay worries about his own intentions.

'I have fine pieces of flowered silk,' said the merchant, turning towards a rainbow table of fabrics.

'Their worth?' asked Bendix.

'Forty-six pounds.' It was a hefty sum, more than his tuition in Paris for an entire year.

'I wish a mask.'

'You attend a masquerade?'

'I wish you to make me the most elegant mask. A pair of them.' Bendix tapped his physician's cane upon the uneven splinters of the shop floor. 'The first in the shape of the sun, the second as the moon. Can this be done?'

'It shall be of some expense.'

Bendix pulled his purse from his coat and let the gold obtained from his own doctoring clank and rattle for the merchant.

'Where you make the cuts for the eyes of the moon, you shall paint over them.'

'How will you walk?'

'It is no matter of yours,' said Bendix. 'I shall return in seven days.'

Though Bendix continued in his walks, visiting Streatham's apothecary for mustard plasters and laudanum, the majority of the last week of the year was spent in finishing Defoe's sordid tale. Finally Moll found herself within

Newgate, full of pity and remonstration for her upcoming
trial for theft at the Old Bailey.

*'My temper was touch'd before the harden'd wretch'd boldness of
Spirit, which I had acquir'd in the Prison, abated and conscious Guilt
began to flow in upon my Mind: In short,'* read Bendix, *'I began to
think, and to think is one real Advance from hell to Heaven; all that
Hellish harden'd state and temper of the Soul, which I have said so
much of before, is but a deprivation of Thought; he that is restor'd to
his Power of thinking, is restor'd to himself.'*

'Do you believe that, Joseph?' interrupted Amelia.

'I had not thought of it. It is well phrased,' conceded
Bendix.

'I think Defoe wrong,' said Amelia. 'If hell is but a lack of
thought, how may a man be driven there by excessive thinking?'

'Perhaps he talks of those who moan that they think too
much. Then I would agree. It would be ample evidence that
they do not think enough.'

Amelia was not listening to Bendix. 'Do you think that Mr
Defoe was referring to my father?'

'Defoe is of considerable intelligence,' admitted Bendix,
'but he is not a prophet. A man can not forecast another's
fate.'

'Unless he controls it,' returned Amelia.

Bendix nodded. 'Shall we press on?'

'Tomorrow,' said Amelia, but when Bendix made to rise
she began to speak again. 'Do you know, Joseph, that when
I was a child and my father read to me I thought that reading was accomplished through hands and not eyes. I couldn't
understand why books did not talk when I held them.' She
smiled at her own story.

'And what do you think now?' asked Bendix.

'I think I was close to the truth,' said Amelia. 'Books have little to do with the eyes. They are not subject to the barriers of the senses. When you read to me, we are equal.'

Bendix sought for the words, a phrase that would turn her simple thought into something brighter and more buoyant. He wanted to tell her that they were not only unequal but that she was far his superior. A moment of doubt flattened his words and his confidence and he withdrew awkwardly with the promise of a rapid return.

Bendix administered her usual dose of laudanum against the subsiding pain but intercepted Julia carrying Mrs Hemmings's broth up the stairs. Once he had dismissed her, he poured sixty more drops of the opiate into the already alcoholic concoction, then sat with Amelia as she took her soup. After returning the bowl to the kitchen and bidding the cook to boil a pot of water before retiring for the evening, Bendix collected Streatham's mustard plasters from his room.

He carried the seething water up the stairs, along with the plasters draped about his shoulder. He had left a single candle burning outside her room. Amelia was, predictably enough, in the soundest of sleeps. The doctor lay incapacitated below in his study, his daughter awash in laudanum before him. It was as if the world about him had been frozen, and yet he was free to walk, to interfere, to pursue. Placing the boiling water beside the bed, Bendix leaned over his patient and, with fingers as light as Brick Lane pickpockets, he lifted the sheet from her body and peeled it back to the foot of her bed. It was a reasonable act, professional. With thumbs and forefingers, Bendix pinched the sides of her gown and gently raised them, so that only her shift remained. He could hear the soft breath of sleep. Bolder now, he let his hand touch the outside of her thigh, catching the shift and rolling it northwards like gathered snow, until it joined the gown about her neck. She lay before him, naked. Breasts, nipples, the centre of her sex. It was his own breathing and not hers that he heard. Turning away, he tested the water beneath the licks of steam that spilled above the pot. It remained too hot.

He looked above the rise and fall of her breasts, to the black velvet strip about her eyes, then down again along the line from her chin to the meeting of her legs. His right hand ran down her breastbone and his fingers glided over the softness of one nipple and then the other. They stiffened to his touch. He knelt at the side of the bed, lying his head against her stomach and breathing in the centre of her warmth, his head rocked by the undulations of her breathing.

The water remained hot, though the cloud of steam had relented so that it hung low like fog. Bendix dipped his hands inside, winced and withdrew them from the heat. He scrubbed them together to reduce the pain. Taking the plasters from the side of the bed, he doused them in the scalding water, then let them cool in the air for a moment before applying them gently to Amelia's chest. The shock caused her back to arch in pain; her fingers snapped shut to fists and her knees raised, yet the laudanum prevented an understanding. A moment, and the spasm passed. When Bendix removed the plaster he was pleased to see the redness of the skin and the beginning of a perfect blister upon her ivory skin. Calcraft himself could not have performed it better. If he had any doubts of the extent of her recovery before, they were now removed.

Bendix gathered the water, plasters and candle and, hushing the flame with a soft breath, waited to adjust his eyes to the darkness, until the grey of the open door showed itself. It was not until Bendix had returned the pot to the kitchen and retired to his own bed, not until his bare skin was exposed and the nightgown dropped about him that he considered his behaviour. He had felt both desire and intimacy and he knew that his action was one of love.

In the morning he could not shake the rumours of her nakedness from his mind. His cock was rigid beneath the blankets. He stood on the cold stone of the floor, deflating his display of lust, but not extinguishing desire from his mind. He dressed quickly, pulling on his thickest breeches and headed out into the early morning. Walking past Mother Cates's establishment in Covent Garden, Bendix decided that he would not return and establish himself as a whorer but instead continue his search down Drury Lane.

Turning from the early sunlight, Bendix entered a cobbled alley and, when a gin-soaked callet linked her arm in his, he did not shudder or resist as he might have done on any other day. Instead they walked further from Drury Lane until they stood behind the broken barrels of a cooper's shop. Bendix paid her a pair of shillings, never looked upon her face, but turned her against the walls, pulled himself from his breeches and spat on his cock. Entered her roughly, rode her, his hands on the grease and dirt of her skirt bunched about her waist. He could see grey strands twisting from the back of her neck and closed his eyes to block sun and shadows and sight itself.

In the following pair of days, Bendix behaved with absolute professionalism, keeping his patient dosed with laudanum as the blister rose, then fell. By New Year's Eve the blister had retreated, the redness of the skin dissipated like a forgotten blush. He admitted to himself the pleasure he had received in peeling back her gown and shift and surveying the softness of her skin, the wintered landscape of her body, but he had not submitted to the weakness of desire again. He returned to Drury Lane, not to quell lust, but to collect the masks, then returned promptly to Amelia's side to read the last dozen pages of *Moll Flanders*.

She had not known the length of her rest, presumed that she had passed a heavy night, a suggestion that Bendix happily confirmed. Instead she pressed him to finish the story of the itinerant whore. It took less than an hour to end the tale, yet once again Moll regaled her readers with a lengthy account of her takings and belongings. Defoe camouflaged her mercenary instincts with a coda of love, stability and forgiveness. Indeed, if Defoe could forgive whoring, thieving, incest, adultery and bigamy in his creation, then surely Bendix might forgive himself the slightness of his sins.

Amelia sat up in her bed and begged for Bendix to blow out the candles that sat either side of them. He closed the book for the final time, then pinched the candles out with licked fingers.

'What now, Amelia?'

'It was a beautiful book, was it not?'

'But how to follow it?'

'There is another I wish to read.'

'Enough with books,' said Bendix. 'It is too dull.' He sat up and placed a hand on either knee. 'I have had a glorious idea. You shall accompany me to theatre, or a rout, some masquerade.'

'I shall do no such thing,' replied an amused Amelia.

'Amelia,' insisted Bendix, 'you ask me to read and read so that you might gain knowledge of what lies beneath your window. Surely then, one evening abroad might be worth a hundred books?'

'I cannot.'

Bendix removed the mask from Drury Lane. In the murk of greys, the profile of the crescent, the bright cusp of the moon's smile, the constellation of stars upon the cheek grasped all the light of the room.

'It is beautiful,' admitted Amelia, running her hands across it.

'It is yours.'

Taking it from her hands, Bendix moved behind and, with a strained gentleness, tied the ribbons about the back of her head. She raised her hands to the blocked eyeholes and a smile ignited when she understood that the mask was made specifically for her.

'If we were to go out, if it were dark enough,' asked Amelia, 'should we walk together?'

'I should not leave your side.'

'We must ask my father.'

'Your father still sleeps his days, Amelia. He would not notice our departure.'

Bendix did not mention his offer of outside entertainment again, instead relying on Amelia's desire to prompt him. It did not take long, the dream fermenting slowly in her head, becoming concrete through thought. Bendix increased his absences, wandering the frost-laden streets, returning again and again to Tom's Coffee House in Covent Garden. He would sit, purchase his pot from the girl by the fire, have a pipe of Virginia tobacco carried to him and find a seat on one of the smaller tables where he would not be disturbed. Most gathered on the chairs closest to the fire, but Bendix preferred to keep his clothes thick about him and look out of the window to Covent Garden, across to the shadowed arcades that led to St Paul's Church.

Railings of ice ran about the cornices; even the warm gutters of tripe and shit were slowed by the cold, their smells no longer pervasive but coming in sharp snatches of odour soon replaced by winter wind. There had been an absence of rain and only the odd dab of snow, the skies peculiarly blue, the clouds remaining distant. Bendix would return to Lincoln's Inn Fields by way of the river, taking much delight as the Thames slackened then sealed with ice. Children were the first to test the strength, tentatively sliding on cloth-bound feet close to the bank. By the second week of January Bendix could see couples striding boldly from Horse's Ferry across towards St Paul's Cathedral. The coffee shop was filled with talk of a frost fair upon the frozen water.

The cold had also brought the doctor struggling from his bedroom, a great bear disturbed in his hibernation. While Bendix and Julia had seen to Amelia's recovery, Lemon had jealously guarded his master's attention. Bendix's daily perusal of the doctor's bedroom was always watched with suspicion by the footman, as if the apprentice might suddenly start exploring the mattress for coins. Finding the doctor in the library, Bendix could see that his eyes had reddened and retreated into his head, their lids fleshy with disguise. Bendix looked at his thinning frame, the heavy movements of his limbs and listened to his conversation. It was so far from sense, from any form of logic, that Bendix immediately feared what effect it might have on his daughter. However Calcraft did retain enough judgement to ask after Amelia, and when hearing that she had returned to health, if indeed, no better than before, he looked as if his apprentice had informed him of her death.

'I remember,' said Calcraft, sitting before the fire, draped in two gowns, feet wrapped in velvet slippers.

'What?' said Bendix, standing before him, his cheeks still bright from the Thames wind.

'Remembering everything,' said Calcraft. 'Examining again and again and again. Remember the errors. All of them. Have figured them. Decided that the master was apprentice. Decided that it was the simplest of errors. Simple, plain.'

'And that would be?' encouraged Bendix.

'I allowed the truth into my house,' said Calcraft, 'but would not hear it sing. We shall try once more because we are both at fault, Bendix. Not what we believe in, what she believes in. Each unto themselves, no common ground, no laterals or verticals, no days and nights but all the in-betweens.'

Little made sense to Bendix, though it was obvious from Calcraft's open eyes and confident tone of voice that he presumed he was speaking gospel truths. If Bendix understood anything, it seemed as if the doctor, in his haze, was attempting to appropriate the ideas of his pupil; that it was the mind that held the key to health and not his complex decoctions and theories of touch.

'I suppose I shall visit her,' said Calcraft. 'Is Defoe upstairs?'

'No, sir.'

'A pity.'

'Sir Edmund. I do not think it wise to see your daughter until you are fully recovered. Your sickness has been long and most exhausting.'

'What sickness is that, Bendix?' said Calcraft sharply. 'The sickness of thought, of understanding, of unravelling. Or the crime of subordination, petty treason, to have one's apprentice dictate one's whereabouts.'

'She is delicate,' said Bendix firmly.

'Delicate, most surely,' said Calcraft. 'She looks upon you as no better than a porter, Bendix. You are nothing more.'

The turn had been sharp, but Bendix remained calm. It seemed that the doctor's humours were so imbalanced by his month in bed that he flipped and turned between concession and suspicion in a single moment.

'Do you touch her?' asked Calcraft, voice choked with malice. 'Do you touch her inside?'

'I do not,' said Bendix. 'I wish only her restoration.'

Calcraft seemed to draw some comfort from his apprentice's statement. 'Restoration,' he repeated, 'is of primary importance.'

'We shall work together?' asked Bendix.

'Yes,' said Calcraft. 'It is me she believes in.'

'She has told me so.'

Calcraft nodded and then allowed Bendix the most perfect smile, as if all that had gone before, the mutterings and accusations, were a prelude to this warmest compliment, lips touched by the colour of fire.

'Help me to bed,' said Calcraft and took Bendix's arm with a kind and fatherly grip.

CHAPTER TWENTY-TWO

The *Daily Courant* announced that the Frost Fair would begin that evening. Figg, the pugilist, would fight at sun down. Mr Guilding would appear with his extraordinary sheep that would count cards upon the ice. There would be races from bank to bank, the starting call given by a genuine Irish giant. Acrobats, jugglers, quacks and clowns would abound downriver from the arches of London Bridge. Bendix read no further. He clasped his pot of coffee and let the heat rise past the whites of his fingernails, easing the numbness from the joints. Men rose and walked about him, called greetings to his familiar face, but the apprentice was lost in thought and expectation.

It took Amelia the better part of two hours to prepare herself for the cold. For years she had stood by open winter windows, felt the swirl and grip of northern winds, but had always had fires to retreat to. Now, the sun dipping fast behind the house, Julia attended to her strapping and lacing, clasping and binding.

The thought of leaving the house had always existed. Amelia's was a world of windows. What was within them lived, the view no more than a stream of objects that wound past her, that could not affect her. The inside and outside were entirely separate. Within the house, breath and life; without, strangers and marionettes. It had occurred to her that perhaps the roles were reversed and all others lived while she was merely suspended in a false world. What was she, she questioned, but pieces and thoughts borrowed from books? Might she not break into fragments if she was asked a question by a stranger? For Amelia, Bendix bridged the worlds, being the only member of the household to come and go, to have lived elsewhere, across cities and seas and lands that she had only imagined.

If Bendix wished to show her the life that existed beyond the glass and casements of Lincoln's Inn, then she could not resist. What if she were only offered one chance to sense London? It would be madness to refrain. There was fear, plenty of fear in her preparation for the cold. She wished she might slip unseen into his pocket and learn of the town in safety and muffled warmth. The initial idea of wandering through London had been so attractive, to walk beside Mr Bendix, to wrap oneself in garments, to know the feeling of snow beneath one's feet. Now the idea solidified before her, every moment gaining weight from the gravity of the unknown. She suffered from fear. Her fingers trembled besides the closed window. Julia witnessed the nerves, the twitches and teary eyes and could see that her entire body resisted the idea of leaving the house.

Finally Amelia emerged upon the darkened landing. Bendix stood there in silence, watching her smile, convinced she was the most beautiful of ghosts. He viewed her descent with an awesome pride. She looked, in cornflower silk, as if she were moulded of ice and snow and light, ethereal and splendid in her grace. Her skin was covered, though she stepped only into darkness.

Ten steps from the house. The purity of the air, the buffeting of the breeze and the knowledge that there were no walls behind her, that she was exhibited and could not see. The switch in senses overcame her. She seemed to crumple under the approach of night as if clouds were made of clay and the sky a threatening ocean above. Putting her hands over her head, she bent over, then reached out to touch the ground. She turned, whispered 'home' and, when Bendix paused in bafflement, Julia seized Amelia by the hand and turned her about. Amelia was gasping by the time that the door opened. Inside, she shut the door and leaned against it, crying before Bendix.

He stood there, perplexed and uncomfortable under a sense of guilt. Surely he did not wish any harm to Amelia, had not thought that the merest stroll would bring about such devastation.

'I apologise,' said Bendix to both Julia and her mistress. 'I had not thought.'

Julia nodded but Amelia would not look up.

Bendix turned his head up the stairs, as if he expected

Calcraft to come bounding down with his surgeon's knife to remove his nose.

Without a word to Bendix, Amelia let Julia escort her to the western wing.

He received no word from the western wing until the following day when he was invited to share a drink with Amelia at sundown. She sat in perfect composure and greeted Bendix with such equanimity that he did not think that she would approach the subject of their aborted outing. Instead she did not pave the path with trifling conversation but ensured he held a drink and said, 'I do not wish to be thought weak'.

'I do not think you weak,' said Bendix, 'not weak at all. Had I never stood before and attempted fast paces I would not think it weak had I fallen.'

Amelia nodded to acknowledge his kind words. 'I did not sleep last night,' said Amelia, then smiled. 'I do not suspect this of your life, but must confess it of mine. Each day has the same tempo, the same pulse of brief enjoyment and loss. I find peace in words but only ever wonder in the difference. The only differences, Joseph, come through my window at dusk. A familiar carriage with a new livery, the growth of a child. That is my only wonder.'

'All lives are lived this way,' said Bendix, laughing softly, 'every day echoes the day before. We find the familiar necessary.'

'I cannot believe that,' answered Amelia.

'You see the change in seasons,' replied Bendix, 'and there is a change in tide. They are ordinary, the process is repeated again and again.'

'Then I should not fear that I faltered? I should attempt a second effort.'

'There is no need,' smiled Bendix. 'I might describe it for you.'

'You said a moment outside was worth a hundred books,' said Amelia, 'and have I not already proved you right?'

Bendix shrugged.

'I was disturbed,' continued Amelia, 'by suddenness and novelty. If we repeat the procedure, shall it not soon become ordinary?'

Julia quivered before the door, hands warmed by the single crown that Bendix had pressed into her palm. Mrs Hemmings was abroad, Lemon tending to Sir Edmund and his bedroom fire. The afternoon sky was the colour of curdled milk, lit by the dying sun, a mirage of heat. Amelia, the mask tightly bound to her face, held tightly to Bendix's arm, his mouth fixed between apprehension and glory. Julia had chosen Amelia the same dress of lightest blue Flanders silk, the colour of pure water frozen and touched by sun. Her gloves were a similar hue, brightened by the open flower of her cuffs.

'The sun has gone,' said Bendix.

'I feel only the wind,' she replied, and pulled her cloak about her. 'It cuts through one. Right through one.'

'Shall we return?'

'No,' said Amelia.

'Not even for a coat?'

'Let us descend.'

They walked together down the steps and into the gardens before them.

'You shall have to talk to me, Joseph,' said Amelia. 'Tell me of our progress. Do we take a coach?'

Amelia managed a smile at the sounds of their gravelled steps as miniature pieces of ice yielded and held, letting them walk across the square with little problem. Bendix had not seen so nervous a smile in his memory. Her hands gripped his arm as if he were prey. Beginning to relish their steps, Amelia refused the first and only coach to pass them and insisted that they walk. Bendix feared her weakness but let her be her own judge and concentrated only on lending his utmost support.

There seemed to be a stream of people who followed their course, flowing south to the Thames, along Chancery Lane and past her courts of law, across the Fleet to Temple. Bendix reported all that he saw, save for the pair of beggars he glimpsed locked in love beneath a footbridge. The couple followed the river eastwards, passing the polished dome of St Paul's and Cheapside until London Bridge appeared, her countless arches each a lantern to the last of the light. Atop, the shops that lined the bridge formed a jagged silhouette. Amelia seemed to adjust to London, trusting Bendix, letting him lead, even hold her about the shoulders as they crossed in front of a carriage. She seemed to unfurl, a parasol opened against rain or sun, becoming sure in her step, confident in her escort.

All about them the crowd were gathering, some choosing to walk along the river itself, the evening accompanied by a shared delight. Bendix and Amelia were surrounded by laughter, the whooping and merriment that accompanied every slip, false step and recovery. It was, he overheard, the surest frost in forty years. A carriage glided by on the ice, shrouded by the breath of horses. With much patience he described it all to Amelia. Sunday had brought an uncommonly well-dressed crowd to the fair, most men in suits of wools, worsted or silk, all topped by thick hats that hid the quality of perukes. In such cold and joy it was hard to differentiate the Lord from his footman.

When they first stepped upon the ice, Amelia gripped his hands with both of hers, frightened by the unsteadiness, the sweep of feet upon something so solid and untrustworthy. Bendix looked about him. They were barely noticed amid the glee, none pausing to wonder at Amelia's mask, none presuming it an affectation. It was merely absorbed by the night.

The sun inched over the horizon, but a thousands links were lit in defiance. Bendix could hear fiddlers rise above the sound of the crowd and the low thud of drums. A gentleman in a frock coat, face split in good humour, swept by upon a pair of skates. The crowd gathered from both the north and south of the river, converging just beneath the bridge, close to the front door of Southwark's Bear Tavern.

Tents had been pitched together across the stretch of ice, a canvas belt that strapped the waist of the river, not a hundred yards from the arches. Bendix paused to sweep the toe of his boot across the scratching of frost and snow, giving himself a view of the frozen Thames. There, beneath the surface, he saw a pale face pressed against the surface, caught in a parody of surprise. Only when Amelia pressed his hand and his head inched in her direction did Bendix grasp that he was staring at his reflection. She pulled him onward, wanting to know, demanding to know what he saw. As they walked along the line of canvas, they would pause according to Amelia's desire. Sometimes she felt herself halted by a scent, the sweetness of chestnuts, the faint salt of oysters, otherwise by the cries of jugglers, hawkers of nostrums and news-sheets. She sorted through the cacophony, discerning voices, following conversations a moment, then leaping from the sounds of the equine lady to the spluttering man. Never had so much intruded upon nor delighted her. Early fears seemed quite forgotten.

Bendix could not help but feel a thrill of pride to be the guide on her virgin journey. It was a pride mingled with relief, a joy that she had taken so quickly to being among the London crowds. Her could see her head turn in so many directions, unsure amid the excitement of where next to go. She had not even mentioned the cold since they had left Lincoln's Inn Fields. Bendix felt an absurd happiness, his smile so wide that it was pushing tears to his eyes. It wasn't pride he was feeling at all, but the giddiness of love. The air was so pure that Bendix could feel it burn his throat every time he laughed at her delight.

'Is this London?' asked Amelia, cupping her hand and leaning towards Bendix.

'It has gathered to greet you,' said Bendix.

At Amelia's insistence, they stopped at the tent of a man who advertised on behalf of the smallest man in the world. Though Bendix could not understand her desire, they paid their three pennies, one for the lady, and were ushered under a flap of canvas. They joined a dozen people on a church pew and Bendix watched as the agent emerged from the back of the tent holding the hand of a small, waddling figure, wearing leather breeches and a jerkin, a tricorn pulled down around his ears. His face was aged, pinched and deformed, his nose dark and pointed, eyes black and full of understanding. A lady to the right of Bendix gasped in pity.

'Does he speak?' asked one man.

'Not since his mother was eaten by rats,' answered the showman.

'How old is he?' asked another.

'In his sixtieth year,' said the man.

'What is his name?' called Amelia.

'His name is Benjamin.'

As they were shown from the tent, Amelia insisted that

she must touch the man. Bendix, alert to every desire, approached the retreating showman and offered him two shillings if the lady, hard in sight, might have a moment to run her hands about his charge.

'Three shillings,' said the man and the deal was done.

Amelia ran her hand over his head, giggled with delight. Benjamin did not speak but stood with great patience and endured the procession of gloved fingers glide about his brow, his tiny limbs. She stooped and touched his boots. Thanking the man, Bendix knelt to press a penny into Benjamin's hand. His agent halted Bendix's reach with the tip of his cudgel and waved him towards the flap of the tent. Bendix gave him a knowing wink.

'Was a bear cub,' said Bendix back in the iced air. 'I have seen the trick in Paris. Was freshly shaved.'

'I touched it,' said Amelia to herself in amazement.

'They can be tamed,' informed Bendix, continuing their walk down the row of tents.

'Mr Bendix.'

Bendix heard the call and ignored it.

'Mr Bendix!'

Amelia heard and froze. She squeezed on Bendix's hand. 'You are called,' she said.

'Mr Bendix.'

'So I am,' said Bendix and turned with much regret to meet the familiar voice. With two long strides, Sixes, holding a lantern, propelled himself across the ice that separated them. He reminded Bendix of the water boatmen in a summer pond, the black insects that skim effortlessly over surfaces. He seemed to be dressed most peculiarly, wearing the ducks and oilskins of a sailor, his black hair gathered at his neck in a louse bag.

'You look as if you attend a masquerade,' said Bendix.

Sixes bowed towards Amelia in her mask and replied, 'I am thankful I am not the only one.'

'Am I not to be introduced?' asked Amelia.

Bendix stood stupidly, neither refusing nor making the introduction.

'My name is Mr Sixes.'

'This is Miss Amelia Calcraft,' said Bendix.

'Ah,' said Sixes, 'a cousin of our good doctor.'

'His daughter,' corrected Amelia.

If Sixes suffered any surprise, he discreetly swallowed it. 'I am an admirer of your father and am honoured to have worked for him.'

Sixes, obviously unaware of Amelia's condition, was performing a pantomime on her behalf. It involved much hand-wringing, a toothy smile and the false benevolence of the merry peasant brought before his liege. 'Kind and generous, most generous your father.'

Amelia smiled. It was a charming smile. 'Mr Sixes, have you ever seen a day such as this?'

'Never,' said Sixes, 'have I been abroad on a night ruled by two goddesses of the moon.'

While Amelia fluttered with the attention, Bendix bowed in appreciation of the compliment.

'We have not met before,' said Sixes, 'though I have often been your father's guest.'

'I trust upon your next visit,' said Amelia, 'that you will call upon me.'

'You are too kind,' he bowed again. 'I must leave you. I could not let you pass without wishing a friend good day.'

'We thank you,' said Bendix and turned Amelia away.

The chill of the evening penetrated Bendix through layers of silk and wool. The ice seemed to work its way up through his boots, freezing his feet, his calves, chafing his thighs within his breeches. Amelia, on the other hand, was still alive with the sounds and scents of the Frost Fair and, despite the thinning crowds, displayed as much interest in her surroundings as when they had first stepped foot upon the Thames. A brief flurry of snow swept over the river and disappeared upwards like the raising of a lady's veil.

It was another half hour before Amelia emitted her first murmur of complaint, which Bendix seized upon as an opportunity to obtain the services of two sturdy link boys to light the way home. There was a comforting procession of people ambling down Cheapside despite the lateness of the hour. The grinding sounds of feet against crushed ice rose up against the presence of St Paul's and returned as hollow echoes.

Bendix's evening had been ruined by the appearance of Sixes. It was not that he was so unhappy to see him, indeed, their relationship had always been of mutual benefit, but if he were to have some business with the doctor, if Amelia's name was to slip his lips, then Bendix would never be allowed within her reach again. He relieved the numbness of his fingers by giving Amelia's fingers a slight squeeze. It was returned with a tightened grip.

He would have to seek out Sixes in the morning, trust in him, or at least find some way to ensure his silence. They walked up through Holborn, then dipped through Little Turnstile into Lincoln's Inn Fields, away from the trail of pedestrians. Having dismissed the link boys with a pair of pennies each, they walked the last yards in darkness, lest busy eyes search from windows. The thin carpet of snow that had fallen in their absence served to soften their footsteps. Bendix removed the key to the house from his coat pocket and they escaped the wind.

The silence just inside the house was astounding. Gone

was the scrape of ice, the chiding of the winter gusts, now just the wooden echoes of their breath returned to them from the panelling. Bendix rubbed his parched hands against one another, then paused.

Amelia's hand reached into his. He cupped his hands around hers. There was the sliding sound of her boot pushed against the floor, then warm breath upon his cheek. The kiss was so brief, so light a touch, that Bendix was not even convinced it had happened until Amelia repeated the action, pressing her lips against his once more in the darkness. She did not know what a kiss was, merely knew which body parts should meet, but still Bendix could not have been more surprised.

He bent down, harnessing every ounce of energy he possessed to make a peacock's display of his desire, to show that he could deliver a kiss of such perfection and honesty that she would understand every thought he had ever had. Reaching out to hold Amelia, he was greeted only by the sound of a door closing. She had already departed, familiar to the dark. When he listened closely he could hear the soft tread of her feet inside the western wing.

Smiling at his disappointment, he refused to feel foolish in the darkness. Instead, he thought of how swiftly she had moved from him, how accustomed she was to the dark. The choice was obvious. Either he would have to move like her, in a shared world of shadows, or he would have to work harder, pushing for the cure of her condition. Any discouragement he might have experienced in sharing the decline of her sight was converted to invigoration.

CHAPTER TWENTY-THREE

At six o'clock in the morning Bendix rose, finding himself in an erratic mood from the height of Amelia's kiss and the guilty worry of discovery. He believed he had two options. One, to win Sir Edmund's favour. The second to persuade Amelia to elope. Both required Sixes's silence for the moment. Defoe had questioned Bendix's intentions concerning Amelia and her finances. Yes, it was a love, he told himself, but to disappear into the country without a practice and with a wife who brought not a penny with her? They would not survive a month. As Amelia's husband, he would inherit her father's fortune. To win the doctor's favour, would be to win his daughter and emerge from apprenticeship to mastery. It was love he had been frightened of, love and money and damaging his career. With Amelia, all three were secured. She did not distract him from medicine as the Comtesse had done. Instead her condition simply encouraged his work.

Despite the promise of last night's sunset, the day was a grey disappointment. Bendix could see his breath before him, though he could not feel his toes. Pulling on stockings and breeches, shirt and waistcoat, he hurried across to the kitchen, where he was relieved to find Mrs Hemmings using a large pair of bellows to urge the kitchen fire to life. Bendix stood by the grate and during a brief and polite dialogue about the iciness of the day they were interrupted by a stout knock on the front door. Lemon appeared moments later to inform the apprentice that Sixes awaited him in the hallway.

'Twice within a day, Mr Bendix,' said Sixes at the apprentice's approach. 'We shall tire of conversation.'

'I must talk with you,' said Bendix sharply, wishing to silence Sixes and push him from the house before Calcraft might hear of the Frost Fair.

'You misjudge me,' presumed Sixes. 'This is urgent business, not some play at love. Come with me.'

Bendix hesitated.

'It is Wild,' said Sixes. 'Plenty of gold. We are to move quickly, most interesting times. You shall need dressing, needles, thread, the instruments of your trade.'

Bendix gathered his equipment in a haze of guilty pleasure, not a little grateful to be called to business when he had felt himself only moments away from betrayal.

Sixes waited outside for him, one hand holding the door to the carriage open, the other beckoning good speed to the approaching figure of Bendix.

'You do not seem shaken,' said Bendix, pulling himself upwards.

'Would you weep at your master's demise?' asked Sixes with intensity. Bendix sat down and managed an innocuous shrug. The coachman put his horses to the whip and the carriage lurched forwards, then settled at a canter.

'Wild called for you by name,' said Sixes. 'Will allow no others inside his room.'

'His pox has worsened?'

'Pox will not kill a man like Jonathan,' said Sixes shaking his head. 'A friend of our Sheppard's driven steel in his throat. Leaped on him with a clasp knife. A short dull blade, thick in rust. Through the throat.'

Unconsciously, Bendix ran a hand about his neck. 'The noble gesture of revenge,' said Bendix.

'He may be dead before we get there,' said Sixes.

Bendix could endure only a moment of silence before he blurted, 'We must talk of Amelia.'

'She must be a pretty thing,' said Sixes, too loudly for Bendix's comfort. The apprentice flinched and waved Sixes's voice lower with his hand. 'Who would have thought the old man's soil was rich enough for such a rose?'

'You must not tell him,' said Bendix. 'She is not to be seen.'

'Why not seen?' whispered Sixes. 'Why not seen when she is so blessed in beauty?'

'It is her father's choice,' said Bendix. 'She is most sensitive to the sun. To any light at all.'

'Ah,' said Sixes in understanding and ran his hands about his eyes to show that he grasped the purpose of last night's mask.

'You court her?' he asked.

'I do not,' lied Bendix, shaking his head.

Sixes nodded and smiled. 'How could you not?' he asked. 'The doctor would find no favour in this now, would he?'

'It is why I ask for your silence.'

'He shall hear nothing from me. I swear it to you.'

Bendix smiled in relief. 'I thank you for your goodness.'

'None at all. You have aided me before, now it is my turn and soon the wheel turns again.'

'Could Wild still speak?'

'Aye,' said Sixes. 'When the Ordinary approached him, he dismissed the fellow with a curse.'

'The cut will not be deep,' said Bendix. 'I'd lay a pound he still breathes.'

'Not a wagering man,' said Sixes. 'Am content with hope.'

'You wish him dead?'

Sixes shrugged. 'I am an agent, comfortable in the shadows. What have I to gain from his death?'

'Then why show so little concern?'

'Tis a world of favours, Joseph, and favours take figuring
and weighing. You'll find a book about his belly. Filled with
knowledge of a city and half its men.' He faced Bendix and
pinched his thumb against his forefinger. 'Five minutes. Five
minutes, I want this book.'

Bendix let the words hang between them, letting Sixes's
desperation echo so that they both might see the extremity of
his desire.

'If I were to give you this book, this wheel of favours
might turn my way?'

'All within the day,' said Sixes. 'I would be positioned a
dozen rungs beneath you. Humbled, you see. Obliged to the
fullest extent.'

It was an odd picture, Wild sitting upright in his chair beside
a hearth of chilly coals. He had wrapped a blue blanket
about himself, a bloodied pleat falling down beside him. His
peruke was missing, the silver seal of his head a lustrous
black. He cupped his wound in his left hand, waving Bendix
forwards with his right. The blood had slid down the inside
of his cuffs, leaving thick trails of life along his arm. His
face may have been drained of colour, but its skin remained
thick and leathery, a stuck pig that had been cornered.

Bendix could only think of the figure that had stood
before him on the night of Sheppard's death in Long Acre,
not only distributing punishment on behalf of the law, but
relishing it. The simian excitement of Wild had revolted him,
now encouraging the apprentice to act in favour of Sixes.
Besides, thought Bendix, Wild's essence was exactly what
Calcraft sought.

'Mend me,' Wild said.

'We might discuss a fee,' said Bendix coldly.

Wild managed a thin smile.

'You are still losing blood,' cautioned Bendix as he approached his patient.

'You'll be well paid,' whispered Wild.

'You should have had a surgeon attend to you immediately.'

'Plenty as would finish me off,' whispered Wild, 'and received payment for it. You come from Sixes. Trusting.'

'Remove your hand,' said Bendix, and prized Wild's fingers from his wound. They came away with difficulty, adhered to his neck by congealing fluid. Very slowly, Bendix unwound the muslin stock that Wild had been wearing. It was wrapped in several plaits about his neck, and while it caused the Thief Taker great pain to remove, Bendix guessed that it had saved his life.

'Water?' asked Bendix. Wild pointed to the side of the hearth. Bendix retrieved the basin and, dipping a handkerchief in the water, wiped at Wild's neck until the wound began to show and the basin turned a muddied pink.

'Was a rotten little knife, wasn't it?' asked Bendix.

Wild nodded.

'Wiped some rust on your chin,' continued the apprentice. 'Will be better for us both if you lie lengthways. May we use the wake table?'

Wild looked at his own table, previously reserved for the dead, now draped in a fine calico cloth. He smiled as if he saw the humour of lying on the table of the dead, but then the smile evaporated as if he had been seized by a doubt that he might not rise again.

'A taste if you will,' said Bendix and offered the Thief Taker a cannikin of diluted beer, strengthened by a heavy dose of laudanum poured by the apprentice.

With Bendix's aid, Wild swallowed a part of the concoction, then struggled to his feet and lay out upon the table, eyes now wide with fear. Bendix enjoyed the moment, taking unnecessary seconds to gather his instruments, waving needles and blades before the Thief Taker. He pulled the blanket from his patient and dropped it beside the table, then cut along Wild's shirt, moving upwards then along the arm until he had split the silk in two. Quite unnecessary, thought Bendix, but always enjoyable.

Wild's chest was matted with thick curls of hair, coiled in perfect circles, touching one another from the shoulder blades to where his breeches hid their downwards journey. Bendix had never seen such a hide upon a man. About his hairy belly lay the book, kept against his pulsing flesh by a belt of black leather that was threaded through the binding. Even in agony, Wild's hand lay over it.

The apprentice, steeped in the blood of the Thief Taker, stood above him with silver instruments and red hands, once more clearing the wound of blood. He talked incessantly as he worked, often looking up from the wound to note the progress of the laudanum upon Wild's drooping eyelids. The skin of the neck was shaved, prickled with bright bumps of irritation. With considerable care, Bendix pierced the skin with his needle and began to close the wound. He was possessed by many thoughts weaving the forty stitches. Mainly he thought of how easily he might kill this man who trusted him. Of all the bodies he and the doctor might work with, all who might be used for Amelia's restoration, he was now sure that there was none more preferable than Jonathan Wild's.

Never before had Bendix thought to kill a man, least ways not when his own blood was cold and his thoughts smooth. And yet, with scissors and blades beside him, his mind remained fine enough to think minutes ahead of himself. Even if he drew his blade across the throat and finished the worthy job that had been instigated, it would remain impossible to remove the body from Wild's own lodgings. Supposing the murder was justifiable, Bendix could not forgive himself the loss of the body.

Wild's eyes were closed. Bendix snipped and knotted the thread. He laid his hand upon his patient's brow. There was no reaction. Moving down Wild's arm, Bendix ran his fingers along the blood and hair until they arrived at the hand clasping the book. He could not be sure if Wild slept. The favour he planned to secure from Sixes was so large that it overcame his hesitancy. He reached beneath Wild's body, the hair on his back slick with sweat, until he found the buckle of the belt. As gently as he could, straining to keep Wild's torso off balance enough to slip the belt from beneath him, Bendix pulled the strip free. He ran the loop of the belt through the book, then placed it beside Wild's body on the wake table and washed his hands in the bloodied basin, wiping them dry on the Thief Taker's breeches.

Each page of the book contained a name. Beneath that name ran a second list of names and addresses and notes of property. The first name Bendix presumed to be that of the thief, the names, addresses and property those of the victim. The first and last pages of the book were yellow with sweat and the leather binding stank of the unwashed. All the thieves' names were crossed once, some, such as Pink's, were crossed twice. At the bottom of each page were two sets of figures, divided into guineas and shillings. If either one represented Wild's portion of receipt, then he was a very wealthy man. Other pages contained nothing but coded signs, cock-eyed confusion to the apprentice. He closed the book, ran the belt back through the binding, then put it inside his coat pocket and, going to the door, called for Sixes.

Sixes closed the door behind him, gave the body of Wild a brief glance. 'He lives?'

'Most certainly,' whispered Bendix. 'I do not know how heavily he rests. Be quick about it.'

Sixes sat behind the wake table, so that if Jonathan should rise he would not see his confederate plotting. He ignored the scent of the book, the yellow smudged pages and, licking the tip of a finger, busily turned the leaves, clucking with delight most every page.

Bendix attempted a vague imitation of patience by wiping his instruments against a white woollen cloth and replacing them in their case. He began to clean instruments he had not used.

'I do not know what you are about,' said Bendix, 'but we must replace the book now.'

'A moment more,' said Sixes without raising his eyes, carefully ploughing the pages, absorbing information with an absolute concentration.

Not even half a minute later, Bendix, hovering above Wild's body, interrupted Sixes again.

'If I may quote Jonathan's own words to you, Joseph,' said Sixes, closing the book, 'Tis more common to be sacrificed to your conscience than your roguery. Always best to commit to the worst endeavours with the greatest determination.' So saying, he handed Bendix the book and watched as the apprentice, with fingers slipping on the damp leather, threaded the belt back through the loops of the binding.

'I thought you said you wished him well,' said Bendix.

'Never did I say such a thing,' said Sixes, 'I would not kill a man myself, but do not quiver to watch them perish.'

When Wild awoke, Sixes had long since fled and Bendix was asleep in a chair by the fire that he had carefully revived. The coals were a summer print of orange and white.

Wild rose on the wake table, swung his feet to the floor and stood and swayed. His hands found the comfort of his belt, the reassuring bulge of the book. Next, they travelled to his neck, where his fingers ran about the knot of stitches, the perfect suture performed by the apprentice. A smile of satisfaction dawned upon the Thief Taker's face. The knowledge that patience and delegation might bring such immediate rewards caused him a dull joy.

Always a man who knew the measure and sense of money, Wild decided to settle his fee with Bendix immediately, so sure was he now of his own recovery. Hours ago, his shirt stained with his own blood, he had wondered at the painless approach of death, how judgement had passed him by and chance had ensured his martyrdom to crime. And yet this apprentice had opened a second life before him. Wild counted fifty golden guineas out before him and, drawing them up in a purse, weighed them in his hand before dropping them in Bendix's lap.

Bendix sat up with a start to see Wild standing above him, bare-chested, a mat of blood and fur, the absurd grin of survival.

'Should you stand much longer,' said Bendix, 'you shall collapse and tear the neck open.'

Wild sat down opposite the apprentice. 'I have no glass to see myself, but I feel well.'

'It is temporary,' replied Bendix, 'you shall be weak for days. This is a brief moment of elation.'

'A celebration of life,' mused Wild and looked about the room. 'Let's have ourselves a spill of malmsey.'

'I would advise against it,' said the apprentice, wagging his head. 'We must put you to bed.'

'Will put myself abed,' said Wild. He pointed to the purse in Bendix's hand. 'Is heavy is it not?'

'With obligation?' asked Bendix, gauging the weight in his palm.

Wild laughed, then gripped his neck in a brief twinge of pain. 'Either gold or obligation,' said the Thief Taker, 'but never both.'

Bendix rode home in a hackney paid for by Wild. He was lost in thought, ignorant of the way the wind sought to topple the coach, ignorant of the cries of the coachman and the oaths swapped on the way to Lincoln's Inn. He ruminated upon the responsibilities of a doctor. Calcraft had told him before that his role was simple – either to cure a man, or to ease his pain. Yet surely it was more complex than that. Some deserved pain, perhaps even death, and yet Bendix knew that it was not a man's responsibility to make this decision. Or rather, it was not a moral man's responsibility to decide, less he was a magistrate with the power of the Crown and God behind him. And yet who was Jonathan Wild to keep his book of sin about him? To use lives as fulcrums by which to manipulate men as machines, hanging those who fought against him, running crime as business. Did the moral have the right to punish the immoral? He wished for Defoe's company, for his clarity. Perhaps he had done enough to bring the book to Sixes.

He paused before Calcraft's house at Lincoln's Inn, considered the dark shutters and curtains that sealed the windows. Inside, treading lightly, he found Mrs Hemmings asleep in the kitchen, the doctor at rest in his bedroom. The sight of the restful breathing made him want to throw open the windows and strike a gong to proclaim his independence. Only Amelia was awake, sitting amid her darkened state. The rest of the household was ephemeral, thought Bendix. Compared to Amelia they were as thin as paper and if a wind were to sweep the house they would be scattered.

Amelia heard the steps, could recognise his tread, knew him lost in thought from the measure of his pace. She had spent the last few minutes first closing one eye, then the other, trying to determine if one eye was weaker than the other. It was near impossible to tell any more, but all thoughts of darkness were pushed from her mind by the sound of Bendix's steps. Some kisses, she had heard from Julia, did not merely last a moment, but moved against the laws of time and could drift between a man and a woman for days. She liked to think she could still feel the softness of his lips against hers, the faint taste of tobacco that she had licked at with the tip of her tongue, just minutes after their kiss.

'I will have to presume that you are thinking of me,' said Amelia, 'or else I should have to be moved by jealousy.'

Bendix smiled at her words. 'I think of you.'

She signalled for him to approach and sit beside her. When he was within reach, she ran a hand across his brow.

'At the Frost Fair,' said Amelia and she withdrew her hand from Bendix's brow, 'what manner of people were about?'

'Every kind,' replied Bendix, 'Lords to lackies, night soilers to the king's tailor.'

'What lies outside of the city?' asked Amelia. 'How much have you seen beyond?'

'You mean Paris?' Bendix noticed that her smile was strained, the good humour a false projection. He decided that it was his responsibility not only to cure her, but to provide constant distraction.

'No, not cities. The countryside. What animals have you seen? Have you ever seen a fox?' Always, when Amelia began her questions, Bendix was reminded of her youth. No matter the faintness of her touch, the stealing of a kiss, she remained a child in so many ways. It increased the delight he took in her, as if her innocence had been maintained by her condition. Perhaps she now ran undercurrents of resentment against her father for her internment, but had Calcraft not preserved purity?

Bendix did not hesitate to embellish his answers. 'I once saw a duchess in Devonshire, carried to church by a carriage and seven oxen. Under the shadows of the Alps, I saw a bear, white in colour, from nose to paw. I climbed into the treetop and watched as he fought with four wolves and feasted on their bodies. "Ahoy, Monsieur," I called to the bear, "if I climb down from my tree, will you treat me as if I were wolf or man?" "Why," he answered in German, for he had travelled far, "do you mistake me for an animal? I am a bear of rare civility," he said. "Indeed," I answered, "you have a tailor of uncommon talent, for I have never seen a suit of such quality."'

'Where was his suit made?' asked Amelia, smiling.

'Leipzig, of course,' said Bendix with a grin. He had not talked such nonsense in years. Not since he had had gold in his pocket, as much as Wild had weighed him with and more. It brought back his youth and his appetite for charm. Besides, Amelia's own smile was now refreshed.

'I inquired immediately for the name of his tailor, and told him that I wished a suit of similar quality. "There is," he said, "but one suit so fine, and if you wish to keep your head, I shall keep mine." I climbed down from my tree, the bear treated me most civilly, and yet, I could not help myself but draw my sword and attempt to separate him from his suit.'

'Did you succeed?' laughed Amelia.

'Do I wear the skin of a bear?' answered Bendix.

'Why no, sir.'

'Indeed,' said Bendix, 'for my hostility, he removed my

suit and left me naked as birth in the coldest place upon this earth.'

'How did you survive?' asked Amelia, now grinning with enjoyment.

'I pulled a wolf from within his skin and wore his suit a hundred miles, through children's laughs and farmers' smiles, until the fur wore out from a case of gout. I found fine silks to replace the pelt, feel twice as good as I had ever felt. Unfortunately, I have no witness, to the bear's fine suit or the wolf-skin business, and beg of you to believe my tale, which is no more odd than Jonah's whale.'

Amelia clapped her hands and bent forwards to kiss Bendix upon the cheek. He reached up to touch his own face, noticing the kiss only after it had touched and alighted.

'If I chose to travel, Joseph, would you accompany me?'

'Of course I would,' said Bendix.

'I am in earnest,' said Amelia and leaned her head so close that he could not only see into her eyes but feel the warmth of her breath.

'As am I,' he whispered.

'Good,' she said and backed away a foot. 'May we go about again, as we did at the Frost Fair? I shall wear your mask until I am restored, and we may go about the same as anyone else.'

'We may indeed.'

Bendix had been subjected to the coils of many coquettes and though he had always believed that the female arts of persuasion were learned and practised, he thought there was an impressive natural quality to Amelia's artifice. What could be better than learning one's own way to one's desires?

'What if I were to live in the steppe of a mountain?' said Amelia. 'Would you visit?'

'Even were you surrounded by white bears,' smiled Bendix.

'I am most grave,' said Amelia.

'About the bears or the mountain?' laughed Bendix.

'About leaving here,' said Amelia.

'You cannot leave,' replied Bendix calmly and, when she seemed to take offence at this notion and turned her cheek across the room, he sought her understanding. 'You are your father's daughter. The rights of property and capital cannot be passed, save to a son.'

'Unless,' said Amelia, 'the daughter were married. Then she might do as she wished.'

Bendix did not answer.

'Will you leave me now?' she asked, worried that she had spoken too directly.

'No,' said Bendix. 'How could I leave a woman I am in love with?'

The following night there began a series of walks. Still the days were ruled by darkness, night falling in the middle of the afternoon. Bendix maintained the services of two link boys, one who walked far enough ahead so that the light did not disturb Amelia, the second who walked a dozen yards behind them, his sword hanger gripped in calloused palm. Amelia and Bendix were ignorant of the dangers of their chosen passages, both intoxicated by Bendix's declaration of love. Still, her sight had not improved but neither had the decline increased, just the same steady fading that always separated them, never mentioned.

Amelia insisted on the regularity of their walks, even when the London weather became so foul that only dribbles of cows could be seen heading to Smithfield through the night and the Thames, turbulent and boiling, would not allow a single fishing smack upriver. Even upon nights as dark and unpopulated as these, when all with sense and wit relished roofs and fires, Amelia insisted on braving wind and rain. Bendix developed a feral cough and aching throat, soothed only by one of Mrs Hemmings's more potent hot concoctions. Sickness could not touch Amelia. She might be soaked through to the skin, her bones quivering with cold, yet her enjoyment, the constant novelty of London, of peeking from her mask down the darkest of streets, buoyed her above all contagion. In these moments the desperation of her dying sight was quite forgotten to both of them, though it seemed as if Amelia thirsted for experience, as if blindness threatened to strip her of all her senses. When they were apart from one another, both dwelled on her loss of sight. Amelia's moods swayed heavily, yawing between troughs and peaks that could only be steadied by the presence of the man who loved her.

Only on the tenth night, when Bendix's cough had become so thick and viscous that every breath was strained through water, did Amelia forgive him his duty and sit by him, eyes covered by velvet ribbon, feet warmed by fire.

'I have been thinking, Joseph,' said Amelia. 'Of what we talked the other day. Of my desire to leave this house.'

'You wish it to be sold?' wheezed Bendix.

'No,' she said calmly, 'it is my father's house and shall remain so.' She turned in her chair, rearranged the pleats of her dress. 'I wish only two things, my sight and the freedom it shall bring. My own house, Joseph, in the countryside, not far from my father, but far enough to discourage daily visits.'

'We did discuss this,' said Joseph, and swallowed a cough, 'and we also discussed the impossibility of such a move. Even if you were a ward of Chancery, rather than in the calmer hands of your father and Mr Defoe, it would still be an impossibility.'

'If you and I were to form a contract,' said Amelia, 'a matter of business if you will, which would grant me independence . . .' She could not bring herself to return Bendix's words of love. There was nothing wrong with doubt, she thought. Julia had often said that romantic declarations were dangerous for a lady to breathe. It did not occur to her how odd it must have sounded to Bendix for her to discuss marriage without mentioning love. Yet she knew how deeply she felt for him, thought it might be immodest to utter such words and left Bendix to presume on the depth of her emotions.

'Every contract,' said Bendix, 'leaves a line where the signature of the parent must be applied.'

'Julia has often talked of Lamb's Chapel,' said Amelia, 'you need no signature there. Just a guinea or two.'

'Do you know of what you speak?' stressed Bendix.

'Marriage,' said Amelia, 'I wish you to marry me.'

'Do you know what it implies?' laughed Bendix.

'Flight,' smiled Amelia.

'It is a vast change to consider,' said Bendix, rising. 'Perhaps you should think on it.' He paused before her. She suddenly felt very young, sensing him above her, her mental strength opposed to his physical presence. 'Will he kiss me?' she asked herself, but knew, as soon as the thought had formed, that Bendix would not bend. She could tell that she had disturbed him with her suggestion. It had to be done.

'I shall not change my mind,' she added, her chin pointed at the apprentice. He bowed before her and retired to the coldness of his bed.

She was not disturbed by Bendix's reaction, though he walked on tiptoes between her concerns. She felt it was improper to confess her love to Bendix and yet entirely within the bounds of propriety to express her desire for marriage. Since it was impossible for a young lady to govern herself, Amelia thought of marriage as an obvious answer, a vote against the divine right of the father, in favour of the popular election of Joseph Bendix.

Bendix used his sickness as an excuse for the next two days, avoiding Amelia and creating time for thought. He did not doubt his love, but the progress of his courtship had now been accelerated and quantified. It was no longer his decision. It was Amelia who had, so inappropriately, mentioned marriage. If she was not so uninformed of the ways of the world, Bendix would have been deeply offended. Yet if he might forget the etiquette and rituals expected of his class, then why had he not simply accepted? He wished her, all of her, from the body he had laid his head against, to the mind of endless questions – and yes, to the depth of her father's purse. Yet it seemed as if marriage were nothing more to her than a contract that ensured her escape despite her father's wishes. What if the kiss, her touch upon his brow, were nothing more than artifices to ensure his devotion?

It did not bear thinking on. If he might cure Amelia of her condition, then surely it would guarantee her father's acceptance of their marriage. And if he might document his case and publish an account of Amelia's restoration then it would bring fame that could carry a man to the king's court and fill his purse. Though Bendix feared his own mercenary inclinations, he still believed that marriage to Amelia might be earned, that it should be earned. In a way, he was grateful that she had not yet whispered words of love. When they came, he wanted to deserve them.

What was needed, thought Bendix, was a catalyst to propel the household forwards, to drive Calcraft from bed to work, Amelia from her world to his. With this in mind, he approached the doctor to discuss his intentions. Calcraft's eyes were closed and his face showed not the slightest acknowledgement to any of Bendix's greetings. In a most professional manner, Bendix sat on the edge of the bed and, with a gentle movement of his thumb, rolled back the doctor's right eyelid to see if he were submerged in dreamy opiates. The eye looked back at him, red, but cold, silent and understanding. Bendix removed his hand in shock and the eye snapped shut. There was no sweet smell of laudanum about Calcraft, and only the redness of the eye would have suggested the presence of medicine. It was as if Calcraft were merely hiding behind a facade of disintegration. The apprentice stood to repeat his questions, but did not even receive a wrinkle or arched brow in response, soon forced from the room by the wall of stony silence.

As he walked to the Blue Boar, he was certain that he knew the step that Calcraft would take had his mind not been so addled by laudanum. He strode with the paces of a man so intent on where he was going that he gave no heed to his progress. His shoes were soiled, mud creeping up his breeches, the oaths of journeymen and cattle drovers silent in his ears. Relief was only attained at the sight of Sixes by the fire, the shoe and stocking removed from one foot, his sole pointed towards the fire, busy picking at a callous. He had the good grace to lower the offending foot at the apprentice's approach, and offered a hand that Bendix forced himself to shake.

'You told me once,' interrupted Bendix, 'that favours work in circles.'

'Indeed they do,' said Sixes, 'and the wheel is turned in your direction.'

'You are much indebted to me,' replied Bendix. 'I do not know, do not wish to know how you deploy your information. I do, however, need a favour.'

'You wish her hand?

Bendix ignored the chivvying. 'The book about his belly. Shall it lead to his hanging?'

'What do you think?' asked Sixes.

'I would presume that the Thief Taker General has made fine friends in his years of business. One, perhaps, may intervene on his behalf. He might take a whipping or transportation, but shall he hang?'

'Some have suggested,' said Sixes, 'that he has few intimates about. They say there is proof he sent thieves to Windsor. Had a man take a watch from the Prince of Wales. Support as thick as fog clears quickly with a strong wind. I believe the mist shall rise and Jonathan will find himself alone.'

'And you?'

'They know where I can be found. Come, Joseph – would a man lay a felon on a Tyburn cart without knowing his own way clear?'

'I need Wild,' said Bendix.

Sixes looked up. 'In the same manner that the doctor desired Messrs Pink and Sheppard?'

'In an identical manner.'

The notion seemed to amuse Sixes, breaking a grin on his face that the shadows could not hide. His teeth shone as yellow as the sun tinged cloud. 'It shall not be easy,' said Sixes. 'Not convinced it can be done at all. Do you know what Sir Edmund paid out in gold for Sheppard? Where shall a man like you find such money?'

'You forget,' said Bendix, 'your previous inquiry. If I was to marry, then my pockets would run as deep as Calcraft's.'

'They would be Calcraft's,' smiled Sixes.

Bendix shrugged.

'Clandestine marriage,' mused Sixes, 'and though Defoe

keeps hold of his tongue for once, your story might excite some sensation elsewhere. Most obviously it is not the case, but might not some poor soul be led to believe you had betrayed the father and carried off his child to some low priest? Stolen her dowry altogether?'

'They may believe what they wish,' said Bendix coldly.

'Yet if Chancery were involved,' said Sixes, 'they might tie an estate in so many knots that it takes generations to unwind them.'

'You must speak more clearly,' replied Bendix. 'Your intentions confuse me.'

'Only the best of intentions,' said Sixes, 'just making you as aware as a man needs be. How bad's your need for Wild?'

'I would say,' answered Bendix, 'that it is central to my happiness and, more importantly, to the happiness of Amelia and her father.'

'Inquiries are necessary,' said Sixes. 'We'll meet at Tom's tomorrow.'

'Remember the law of favours,' chided Bendix.

Sixes bowed. 'It is why I shall even consider such an act,' he said. 'And I shall spend my evening weighing it.'

That it would cost him a sweet penny Bendix had never doubted. But without the body of Wild there was no future, or, at least, no acceptable future. If there was any truth to the doctor's theories, the reduction of a man to his essence may only result in a potent restorative if he were stained black by sin. Bendix thought he might travel throughout Europe and spend a hundred years looking for as fine an example as Wild. If he might engineer the gift of sight for Amelia, then he would have repute, reward, a deserved pride and, most importantly, the love of his wife. He remembered Sixes's words, that it was more common to be sacrificed to conscience than roguery. Bendix did not, of course, wish to be sacrificed at all, but there was no doubt his actions were criminal. What other course was open to him? His deeds were no more illicit than the doctor's, certainly more lawful than Wild's, but these men were old, accustomed to such work, where for Bendix it was a fresh fall. It carried with it the affliction of an uneasy temper.

Thoughts of Sixes held him from sleep that night and ensured that morning arrived with inconsiderate slowness, gifting him with saddlebags beneath the eyes. He could not escape the thought that he was too young and inexperienced to involve himself with men who had been playing at mortal games for half their lives.

The next morning Bendix waited an anxious hour, knowing that if Sixes would betray his confederate of twenty years, then he would have little difficulty disposing of a year-long acquaintance. After another twenty minutes or so – Bendix approximated the lapse of time with the turn of pages and coffee sips – he looked up and found Sixes coming towards him. At his side was a man dressed in the simple black cloth of business, who walked with his feet turned outwards, as if they wished to pull him in different directions. At first Bendix had tensed, presuming he might be a peon of some magistrate. His expression, however, was too forlorn and carried none of the confidence often adopted by the servants of the great. He wore a look of sad gratitude as if he was merely thankful to survive on other men's table scraps.

'Mr Joseph Bendix,' said Sixes, 'may I present Josiah Worth, Esquire.'

'Of Chancery?' asked the apprentice.

'Of the law,' said Worth.

'Surely,' directed Bendix to Sixes, 'our intended conversation is now prohibited.'

'Not at all,' said Sixes, 'not at all. Mr Worth is entirely familiar with our intentions.'

'And what are our intentions?' asked Bendix.

'Let us not be coy,' said Sixes, 'we all know of your desire.'

'Indeed,' said Bendix, 'but I do not know of yours.'

'Shall I?' asked Worth.

'Earn your keep,' smiled Sixes.

Worth dipped into a leather wallet and extracted a small roll of papers. Unfurling first one and then another, he seemed quite lost among the scroll of letters until with a satisfied flaring of the nostrils, he seized on a letter and pushed it under Bendix's nose.

'What is this?' asked Bendix.

'A contract,' said the lawyer.

Bendix read it very slowly.

'*Delivery of the case*?' questioned Bendix.

'We cannot refer to the deceased in particular in ink and paper,' said Sixes. 'Else the contract might hang all three of us.'

'Five hundred pounds a year?' whispered Bendix.

'To be exact, to add expedition to your understanding,' began Worth, 'the terms are simple. If you receive what you desire, then the aforementioned, Abram Mendes Ceixes, known to you as Sixes, will receive the sum of five hundred pounds a year. Should you cease to breathe, succumb to the next world, die, if you will, before the period of five years has elapsed, the aforementioned Mr Sixes will receive a single sum of five thousand pounds, thereby terminating the contract between you.'

Bendix laughed and pointed to the paper before him. 'And this is supposed to be Latin?'

'Would hold in Chancery,' said Worth.

'Good enough for me,' added Sixes.

'Mr Sixes,' said Bendix, 'while to pay you five hundred pounds a year would be a heavy but manageable burden, to forfeit five thousand at one time would jeopardise Amelia's estate. Besides which,' concluded Bendix, 'have you not forgotten your wheel of favours? Do you not remember that it was not many days ago when you admitted that the favour you owed me was inestimable.'

'I did speak such words,' said Sixes, 'and studying them closely found that they could *indeed* be estimated. Before you lies our estimation.' He smiled kindly at Bendix. 'I still consider it a favour,' said Sixes, 'despite the contract. You said yourself that your happiness depended upon it.'

'I did not mean to suggest that I thus begged for exploitation.'

'It is business,' said Sixes. 'The favour I shall do you may never be returned. Therefore it must be measured in gold. We shall stand before the fire,' said Sixes, 'and give you time to consider. We leave the writ before you.'

Bendix watched them walk to the fire and light their pipes as casually had they gone to purchase a cut of lamb or a cabbage. It was an outrage, thought Bendix, and yet he was not entirely outraged. After all, Wild was unique, altogether priceless in Bendix's estimation. He must not think of himself as an impecunious apprentice, but a landed husband, concerned for his wife's happiness. If he had been pouring the money into his own theories or follies it would weigh upon him, but would Calcraft not have paid half his fortune to secure the body?

He waved Sixes and Worth over.

'We are settled?' asked the lawyer.

Bendix nodded and Worth produced a small bottle of India ink and a quill. Joseph Bendix etched his name with a flourishing sweep of the hand.

'You will get him for me?' he asked Sixes.

'It is now,' said Sixes, 'my only concern.'

Bendix felt equal parts apprehension and relief. There could be no safer hands than Sixes. He had no doubt that the man could effect the lowest acts with the highest degree of skill, but Bendix had wagered a fortune that was not strictly his. The tense knot in his stomach revealed his discomfort, but this was no time for morals or ethics. From now on, it was simply a question of medicine and of love. After some thought, Bendix concluded that there were no better reasons to break the law.

To Bendix's surprise, on his return to Lincoln's Inn Fields, a black carriage waited before the house. The horses' flanks were haloed by steam. Only doctors and bailiffs possessed the urgency for morning visits, thought Bendix. Even tradesmen had the grace to await the afternoon. Defoe was alone in the kitchen, standing by the fire. He was hardly recognisable at first, his customary tangled peruke replaced by a grizzled, ponytailed cousin. A poor cousin, thought Bendix. Defoe turned and studied Bendix with no sign of affectionate greeting. The apprentice patted his own head and pointed to Defoe.

'I made the mistake of having it washed,' answered Defoe. 'That stupid man of mine left it away from the fire and this morning found it stiff as the dead.'

Bendix must have let slip a small smile.

'There is little to laugh at, Joseph,' said Defoe. 'I was raised an hour ago from my bed because you were not to be found.'

'I had an engagement.'

'Lemon fetched me. He does not know what to do.'

'What is it?' asked Bendix.

'He makes no sense,' said Defoe. 'I have just attended to him.'

'Sir,' said Bendix, 'he has made no sense for weeks now. He is drowned by his own dosing. If you wish change, then simply remove the bottles from his reach.'

'Lemon did this a week ago. I believe we must send for a physician.'

Bendix looked thoroughly offended.

'Where is Amelia?' asked Defoe.

'I presume she still rests,' said Bendix peevishly. 'May I visit him?'

'The only response of the day, of the week if we are to believe Lemon, was upon the mentioning of your name. To all my questions, I might have been addressing a sleeping dog. Yet when I asked if you might enter his chamber he gave his head the most vigorous shake. 'Tis best we submit.'

Bendix did not nod but stood in mute wonder, considering his misdemeanours but hardly convinced that they might lie at the root of his exile.

That first day brought not one physician but two, neither of whom thought to consult with Bendix. In fact, neither consulted the other, judging themselves as competitors. Bendix could hear the authoritative stomp of their canes above his head, then the drone of diagnoses as they relayed their thoughts and discoveries to Defoe. The writer dismissed them both. The following day heralded the arrival of Dr Monroe, the ruling physician of Bethlem, a figure of some respect and much notoriety.

Apparently he and Defoe were on friendly terms and greeted each other with a warm handshake. When Bendix approached, he was handed the doctor's great coat. The apprentice thought he saw a smile upon Lemon's lips. He passed his burden on to the footman. Monroe was a tall man, his cheeks glowing like a pair of polished apples. There was such a sturdiness, such an aura of ruggedness so foreign to London, that the apprentice was unsurprised to hear the thick brogue of a Scotsman. Monroe remained not half an hour and then he too departed.

Defoe did not relieve Bendix of his questions and anxieties until the evening, when finally he descended and emerged from the western wing to join the apprentice in front of the library fire.

'Where have you been?'

'Attending Amelia and her father.'

'What news?'

'None,' said Defoe, 'except that the gates of law have been opened. Monroe shall return tomorrow. As will Sir Edmund's lawyers.'

'What need of lawyers?' asked Bendix, thoroughly perturbed.

'Your days of apprenticeship are ending, Joseph, for, according to the law, you no longer have a master. Amelia wishes to speak to you on her father's behalf.'

'Will Sir Edmund see me?'

'He wishes to see no one. Not even his daughter. We are all exiled from communication. Dr Monroe shall pass his judgement tomorrow. I suspect that as long as Amelia shall pay the costs, he shall be removed from the house shortly.'

'Absurd,' said Bendix. 'His place is here. His work is here.'

'Tomorrow,' said Defoe, 'you shall understand.'

It was a gathering notable only for the absence of the only two members of the family subject to discussion. Monroe had arrived in a modest coach, a fur collar adding a touch of romance to his hale and hard features. Accompanying him was a second Scotsman by the name of Macready. If Monroe had withstood the insidious nature of London life,

Macready had voluntarily submitted to it. His eyes were a bright fiery blue, but the remainder of his face had faded, nose drooping to mouth, lips to chin, chin merging with neck. While the physician Monroe was a man concerned with the understated finery of his clothes, Macready might as well have arrived in a hessian sack for the figure he cut. They congregated in the library, Defoe seated, Bendix and Macready standing with their backs to the fire, the apprentice outfitted in his customary silks, the lawyer swathed in black wools, nodding in Defoe's direction. Monroe, sitting comfortably in Sir Edmund's favoured chair, seemed to have adopted the aura of a magistrate attending his sessions.

'It is, of course, a difficult decision for men to make,' said Monroe, his accent slightly obscured by respectability. 'Macready has attended to the doctor's estate for thirty years. Knows well his business. He is called before us because, in times of indecision, what better sacrament to defer to than the laws of a nation.'

He bowed in Macready's direction and the smaller Scotsman buried himself among papers for a moment, excusing his lack of preparation and mumbling something about numb fingers. Finally he regained his place before the fire and spoke softly, 'You are familiar with the 1714 Act *for the more effectual punishing such rogues, vagabonds, sturdy beggars and vagrants and sending them whither they ought to be sent*? You know of it?'

'I do not,' confessed Defoe.

'Of course you don't,' said Macready and bowed in apology. 'It is a matter for the law.'

'Perhaps it might be some help if I were to address you both in terms of physick,' interrupted Monroe. Turning to the apprentice, he raised his voice, as if the apprentice were both foreign and slow of understanding. 'Your master suffers from a distemper of the spirits. A strangely female hypocrisy of the spleen, a fever of the spirits if you will. He remains positively vapourish.'

'You believe so?' questioned Bendix.

'Joseph,' chided Defoe, 'Dr Monroe knows much of these matters, while you and I have no such precedents.'

'I do know that a man reduced to silence does not endanger his household,' said Bendix.

'Mr Bendix, you do not understand,' said Monroe closely. 'All that has been said and shall be said will not be mentioned outside these walls. It is in Amelia's interest that the doctor attends me in Bethlem.'

Bendix twitched at the sound of Amelia's name, as if Monroe had no rights to know of her, let alone refer to her in conversation.

'You live a hundred yards from the Courts of Chancery,' began Macready, 'but are ignorant of her ways. If Sir Edmund's condition were known by those less understanding than those within our walls, the Lord Chancellor would issue the writ *De Lunatico Inquirendo*. A test, if you will, of the mind's acuteness that Sir Edmund would most certainly fail. The heir is not allowed on the Chancellor's committee, only surrounding family, of which there is none. Sir Edmund's estate would, at best, pass to the Crown, at worse to Chancery. Amelia would become a ward of the court, a public figure, exposed to fortune-hunters and the like.'

'And if he is not mad?' asked Bendix.

'According to the law, he already is,' explained Macready. 'The footman Lemon has informed us of the doctor's fondness for laudanum. We term this a Voluntary Contracted Madness. To submit yourself freely to echoes of intoxication. Again and again is too much. A man may no longer manage his accounts, as we have proved this morning.'

'Madness,' said Defoe to Bendix, 'is not a matter of the mind or heart, but of the purse.'

'Similar to marriage, if you will,' said Macready.

'How long shall he remain in Bethlem?' asked Bendix.

'We do not admit the incurable,' said Monroe. 'He shall remain for one year, after which date he shall be judged again. If he is cured he shall be released, if he is not cured then he is incurable, and shall also be released.'

'Most sensible,' said Bendix sourly and shook his head as if he was trying to rearrange their arguments. 'If his madness involves lying abed and refusing to engage in conversation, then of what concern is it to us? What if this is simply a deliberate retreat from company?'

'Mr Bendix,' said Macready, 'we have explained. Sir Edmund cannot increase his personal estate. We have asked him the customary questions to weigh our verdict. There is no *mens rea*, but a defect of understanding. If he does not head the household, then who can?'

The subsequent silence closed the arguments.

'You have visited Bethlem, Mr Bendix?' asked Monroe.

'I have not,' said Bendix. 'Though I have heard much.'

'All have heard much,' continued Monroe, 'and not a word of it good. A visit would be most enlightening for you. The doctor shall have freedom of the gallery and may bring a considerable portion of his library. Every patient has his own cell, even those we suspect of being incurable. I have already made Amelia a promise, and I shall make the same to you, since you seem guided by the same affection. Every day, Mr Bendix, I shall attempt to restore Sir Edmund.'

The two Scotsmen walked to their carriage, their passage broken by the odd gesture or nod of agreement. Bendix watched them from the library window until they passed through Little Turnstile.

'Did you call upon them?' asked Bendix.

'After consulting Amelia,' said Defoe, 'it did not seem so much of a decision as an inevitability.'

Bendix nodded. 'He is no more unstable than the pair of us. Simply defeated.' Bendix shook his head in disgust. 'He has withdrawn, ceded victory.'

'Be careful of what you say,' advised Defoe. 'You have made a deep impression on her. I presume you are not ignorant of the fact. She is strong-minded, but it is a moment of delicacy. You heard Monroe when he pronounced Sir Edmund suffers from a female malady of the spleen. We do not wish to encourage a similar predicament.'

'Naturally.'

'She admits to being starved of your company. Shall we?' said Defoe, and the two men walked together through the door to the western wing.

If Amelia had indeed spoken of her high opinion of Joseph Bendix it was not at all apparent to the apprentice on entering her rooms.

'There is much to be considered,' said Defoe.

'Mr Bendix,' asked Amelia, 'are you comfortable in your lodgings at the moment. I am sure that my father would not wish his health to be the result of your sudden dismissal.'

'I am sure you are right,' said Defoe.

'Your father was obsessed by a single subject,' said Bendix, 'yourself.'

'Not myself, but my health,' said Amelia, a trifle sharply. 'There is more to women than weakness and thin blood. My father is most devoted to my cure. In that, I trust him completely. Indeed,' said Amelia more softly, 'I wish to encourage you to continue in his work.'

'Between us,' said Bendix, 'we came close to ending your life.'

'What if I lose all my sight?' asked Amelia. 'I will wager it again – when you are prepared.'

Bendix looked to Defoe for support. The writer shrugged and patted himself in the belly. ''Tis a reasonable enough request, Joseph. Secures your lodging for a time. A vast laboratory. What more might an apprentice desire?'

The answer was clear. 'Nothing,' said Bendix.

The household had been exhausted by the doctor, even Lemon. It was Lemon who had endured his self-imposed silence since the failure of their restoration, leaving Bendix with some fragment of hope that a personal visit might stir Calcraft's tongue. Against Defoe's wishes, without anyone's knowledge, Bendix waited until the heart of the night, then opened the door to Calcraft's bedroom. He found him reading, not the familiar bound tomes of medicine but a novel. He closed it, examined his visitor, then placed the book on his lap and stared ahead.

'You know they shall take you,' said Bendix perching on the edge of a straight-backed chair. 'They will take you to Bethlem.'

Calcraft rubbed his palms together, stretching the fingers away from each other. The apprentice could hear the stifled sounds of breath escaping from the doctor's nose.

'Forgive me, sir,' continued Bendix, 'but you are a fool. I have secured the body of Wild. He is to be hanged. We might carry out your theories. Attempt your daughter's health again.'

Calcraft kept staring at him. It was a look of full understanding, a confirmation of deceit. Bendix could not be sure what the doctor thought he knew. That his apprentice was betrothed to his daughter, that it was impossible to save her, that she could not be saved? Even if Calcraft had concluded that he had wasted half a life galloping down the wrong paths of natural philosophy and condemned his daughter to blindness, why not confront failure rather than stare at it in silence? If he opened his mouth, thought Bendix, then everything might be changed with a word, and yet he lay silent.

Monroe arrived the following morning in a carriage with black-curtained windows. Standing up to their fetlocks in mud, the horses shook their heads with impatience. It was the first time Bendix had seen Calcraft in daylight for weeks. The suits he had stretched with his solid belly now fell loose about him, the globe of his stomach reduced to a shrinking paunch. Most noticeably his face had aged, with lines plowed deeper, cheeks hollowed impressions, eyes devoid of their customary shimmer. There were no signs of instability, merely the sort of figure Bendix remembered from Paris, the stooped shoulders of those who had lost their hearts to love, or squandered fortunes at hazard. Calcraft did not look at Bendix but passed by him without a word, trudging down the steps and into the carriage. Bendix could hear the mud suck at the horses' hooves as they pulled their charge towards Great Queen Street.

CHAPTER TWENTY-FOUR

The first week without the doctor brought down a foggy mood on the household. Lemon spent many hours away from Lincoln's Inn, always dressed in Sunday perfection,

obviously in search of a new position. Julia and Mrs
Hemmings were not so animated, sharing opinions of the
length of their tenure and warming mugs of gin by the
kitchen fire. Amelia was the only person to react positively
to her father's departure as she expanded her domain by
darkening the entire of the western wing, having Lemon
pull all the shutters to, then shielding the few candles with
stained glass so that the private side had the cosy glow of a
tiny country church.

The weight of Calcraft's absence bore most heavily upon
Bendix. There had been little direction to his studies since
the attempt to transfuse Amelia, but now there was no
teacher to instruct or guide him. His mind seemed fallow.
When ideas did not flow, during those panicked moments
when Bendix was positive that he was incapable of fresh
thought, doomed to echo failures, he found it sensible to
read. He raided the doctor's library of concepts and theories
a month or a thousand years old. What was a new thought,
he asked himself, but a reaction to an animated and imperfect idea?

At four, when the sun had already given way, he would
stop his work and visit Amelia in her rooms. It was an odd
thing, to feel no sense of threat or dread when stealing
moments with the doctor's daughter. And yet, rather than a
sense of release, Bendix was plagued by a new notion that
without the doctor he lay stagnant.

'A poor day?' asked Amelia.

'My eyes are swollen,' moaned Bendix. 'Exhausted.'

'Come sit,' said Amelia and through the darkness, Bendix
moved close until they shared their sofa. She reached up
and ran a hand over his brow, pausing above his nose and
applying pressure with the ball of her thumb. The pain of his
eyes thawed.

'The house is so large,' said Bendix.

If Amelia agreed, she added no words of support.

Though the word 'marriage' was not mentioned the following day, Amelia did express a desire for further
entertainment, rather than their customary nocturnal walks.
Obediently, Bendix sorted through the news-sheets, trying
to figure the major mountebanks from the minor. When he
had narrowed the list of possibilities down to a matter of
horses or a three-legged duck, he presented the options to
Amelia. Though horses were the more familiar sight from
her window and ducks (let alone three-legged ducks) somewhat rarer, she could not resist the advertisement: *'Shamyl
Lubanov, the godless Circassian, will stride not one, nor two, but
three horses at once on the south side of Moorfields off Chapel Lane,
at noon, four and again at six. Threepence for your pleasure.'*

Amelia insisted on walking, and where before Bendix had
found himself stout of heart with courage for two and more,
he found this particular excursion worrisome. The night was
thick in cloud and they had but one link boy, a pocked man
with a blackened eye whose tongue was loose with gin.
What perfect culls they were, thought Bendix, for any
butchering footpad who might watch their progress. Amelia
squinted from beneath her mask, unaware of the dangers the
city might have to offer, believing them locked tight within
the pages of books.

They reached Chapel Lane, found no crowd but merely a
pair of shadows sitting atop a low brick wall.

'You there,' shouted their link boy, hand on hanger,
'where's the horseman?'

They did not reply.

Bendix thought his more cultured tones might elicit an
answer. 'We look for Lubanov, the Circassian horse-walker.'

'Do you now?' replied one shadow, the unthreatening

shape of an orange. 'I think he's gone, don't you sir?' he said, addressing his colleague. 'You've come to throw coins at his horses?'

'No man is fool enough to walk with more than he can part with,' said Bendix, attempting to retain his composure. The link boy stood rooted under his torch, unsure of the direction of the meeting.

'Are you a man of velvet pockets?' asked the thinner of the two. 'You look a touch French under this light.'

'My name is Joseph Bendix,' said the apprentice, and when the pronouncement did nothing to alleviate tension, he added, 'physician to Jonathan Wild.'

'Your horses are gone,' said the circular shadow getting to his feet. 'Had an engagement. Where was it, Smithers?'

'Oxford, I believe,' said his colleague.

'Gone to Oxford, then.' Bendix could feel Amelia's disappointment.

'We have a woman with the legs of a rabbit staying a door down,' offered the fat little man. 'Or a gentleman from the East as walks on burning coals, should that be to your interest.'

'The gentleman from the East,' said Amelia, and though Bendix could sense that she was still disheartened from the absence of the twenty-hand horses and the wild Circassian, the fire-walker intrigued her.

'You should follow us,' said the rotund figure, stepping towards the light of the link boy. 'Shan't bite, not with ladies about.' He gestured for them to follow. The link boy looked distinctly sober and waited for Bendix's orders. He nodded and the company of five progressed down the black alley of Chapel Lane, past the sounds of a gin shop and halted before the door to a cellar.

'Down here he is,' said the fat man, swinging open the

door to the cellar. He pointed at the link boy and, at Bendix's directions, the fellow disappeared slowly downwards. Bendix aided Amelia in her descent, step by rotting step.

Smithers cleared the straw, forming a slim walkway of bricks down the centre of the cellar, while the fat man went in search of their entertainment. It took only a moment for Mr Rhyme, fire-walker of the East, to be located within the house. Bendix held his tongue, though it was obvious from half a glance under the flicker of the link that Mr Rhyme had arrived at his foreign look by staining his hair with coal dust and his skin with tea. Wisely, he did not speak, but nodded frequently as he went about his work, spreading a thin line of coals within the bricks while Smithers lit them. The fat man proceeded to fan the audience with grins and dramatic sweeps of his cloaks. Soon the coals were glowing with warmth. Bendix, no longer fearful of a dirk between the ribs, brought Amelia's palm down close to the orange coals until she flinched and withdrew it, her face broken by a wide smile at the strangeness of the sensation.

'What is he doing?' asked Amelia.

'He is standing atop the brick, before the coals.'

Mr Rhyme pointed at the man called Smithers.

'Lady and gentleman,' announced Smithers, 'for your pleasure, from the mountains of ice on the edge of all that is civilised, comes a deed of horrific consequence. Sage of a Land so far East it is beyond the sun itself shall practise what his fathers taught him and tread, at a most deliberate trot, from one end of the burning coals to another. His name is Shadrach, his name is Meshach and we are within the fiery furnace.'

Mr Rhyme stretched one foot out like a cautious wading bird and then stepped out on to the bright orange coals. At Smithers's dramatic gasp, Amelia joined in, then the link

boy and the fat man, and finally Bendix as Mr Rhyme gri-
maced most fearfully and continued his crossing.

'Is he afire?' asked Amelia.

'No,' said Bendix, half in disbelief, bending down to touch
the tip of his finger against the coals. He yelped and pressed
the finger in his mouth. Amelia quaked with excitement. Mr
Rhyme may not have been from further than Clerkenwell,
but his talent was most foreign to Bendix's knowledge.

'Again,' said Bendix, once Mr Rhyme stepped safely off
the coals.

'Another guinea,' smiled Smithers.

'Again,' repeated Bendix, and once more the feat unfolded
before his eyes.

It was, to Amelia, a dazzling entertainment. Her senses
were engulfed by the sounds of foreign cries, the pungent
smell of burning coals and the rise of heat that seemed to
scorch her. The darkness behind her mask was turned to an
image of rising flames, with the large black figure from the
East standing in the centre of the fire.

After the second crossing the fat man emptied a bucket of
water across the coals and the cellar was filled with a cloud
of steam that curled Mr Rhyme's moustache into a heart-
shaped bow. He nodded at the applause of his audience and
watched carefully as Bendix wisely emptied almost the
entire of his purse into the grasping hand of Smithers. The
link boy watched just as closely to ensure it was worth his
wait to return the couple to Lincoln's Inn.

Bendix and Amelia returned home in silence under a cold
rain, both their minds busy with the evening's excitement.
The fire behind Amelia's mask was waning, as was her ela-
tion, but Bendix's mind was frothing with possibilities. Mr
Rhyme, thought Bendix, had suggested an answer to
Defoe's challenge so many months ago. The writer had said

that Bendix's theory of imagination could neither be proved nor disproved, but the fire-walking fakir of Clerkenwell had proposed an examination of his views that might convince all, even an old cynic such as Defoe. Bendix would, of course, require subjects.

After little sleep and a cockcrow rise, Bendix wrapped himself in his great coat, swathed himself in his thickest neck cloth and walked out into the mud of London in search of Sixes. The sky was an unwavering grey above him, not even a hint of the sun's existence for two weeks and more. Constant showers, swept sideways by winds, ensured that the roads had not been given a moment to drain or dry. The wider streets, with their canals of mud, resembled a Venetian parody. Hackneys seemed to have evaporated into cokey mists or been lifted and taken by the wind, so that Bendix had no choice but to dip his head into gales and lean for every yard. The usual walk of fifteen minutes took almost an hour, his legs, coat, arms splattered with mud and dirt.

The Blue Boar was almost empty, Wild's business obviously affected by the weather. Even if he still sent his thieves athieving, the victims had not been prompted to take to the streets in search of their property. Sixes was asleep in his customary chair by the fire, his legs resting on a three-legged stool, his louse bag looped over the back of the chair, mouth agape noisily drawing breath.

He opened one eye when Bendix removed his stool and sat on it. His voice was smooth and relaxed, as if he had slept for a month and woken to find all troubles gone.

'Joseph Bendix,' he said, 'on the dirtiest day of the year. Have you come in search of me or Jonathan?'

'I want nothing of him,' said Bendix, peeling his coat from his shoulders.

'Yet,' smiled Sixes.

Bendix pulled off his wet gloves, then lay them close to the fire. 'It is you I seek.'

'A pleasure, I am sure. Have said nothing to the doctor about his daughter. Have had no requests for my company from Lincoln's Inn. Feeling ashamed to call you both my friends when so little news comes through. Most glad that you seek me out.' Finally, he pulled himself out of his slouch, straightened his back and enjoyed a long yawn, providing Bendix with a view of blackened tonsils and scrawny neck. 'What may I do for you?'

'I need a subject or two,' said Bendix under his breath. Though there were no others in sight, Bendix would not have trusted a plank of wood in the Blue Boar.

'You are most impatient,' said Sixes. 'It is a poor place to talk.'

'You misunderstand,' said Bendix.

'You wish them of similar condition?'

'No,' said Bendix, 'I wish them walking and breathing.'

Sixes looked faintly surprised, even horrified.

'Not only shall they walk into the house,' said Bendix reading his mind, 'but they shall walk out. No harm, little harm shall come to them.'

'What am I to tell them?'

'That they are to earn the easiest two shillings of their life.'

'How so?'

'You may tell them that they are to be branded.'

'You cannot brand a man,' said Sixes, shaking his head at the apprentice, ''tis the benefit of the clergy in Newgate. What a court will do to a thief it does not wish to hang. 'Tis a mark of crime, no man will submit to it.'

'They are branded on the hand, are they not?' asked Bendix.

'Aye.'

'Well you may tell your fellows that they may choose where they shall have their brand placed. Or bring me those already burned.'

'I do not think that I might convince . . .'

'Of course you can,' said Bendix, 'merely offer them one shilling, then tempt them with the second, snare them with a third if you must. I do not care what you bring me, just as long as they speak enough English to understand and are not so rotted by gin that they feel nothing.'

Sixes laughed. 'You are much changed,' he said.

'Will you do it?' asked Bendix.

'Aye,' said Sixes, 'and I shall not charge you a penny.'

Bendix thrust himself forwards and shook Sixes firmly by the hand. If the contract for Wild's body had been a deliberate action of illegality, Bendix's pursuit of his own experiment was dogged and blinkered. He knew now that to achieve a wondrous end a facade of cruelty was required. In truth, it did not bother him at all. Amelia's sight was at stake and with it, he presumed, his own chances for happiness.

Bendix conducted his first two experiments alone. The men were paid a shilling before they submitted and another after they left the house ten minutes later. Sixes had argued them down and had not had to yield Bendix's third shilling. It was just as well, for Bendix did not have many guineas left. Bendix was as equally stunned by his first encounter as he was disappointed with his second. Though Sixes had promised him sober men, he had told the apprentice that it was a hard thing to convince a sober man to endure such an ordeal. Instead he sent drunkards; a gael, unable to speak a word of English, and a labourer so poor that his feet were wrapped in pieces of canvas.

Both men left in tears, one from laughter, the other pain. Bendix was convinced that the state of drunkenness had much to do with the effect of his experiment. Believing that he could succeed on the third attempt, he decided on obtaining a reliable witness. He chose Daniel Defoe. On hearing that Bendix had thought of a manner to prove the power of suggestion, Defoe could do little to contain himself, coming the same day on a visit to Amelia, though Bendix received the brunt of his attention.

The apprentice did not wish to ruin the surprise and kept Defoe at bay with a mixture of quixotic gestures and vague references that had the writer hooting with impatience.

'At least,' said Defoe, 'have the grace to tease me gently.' Both men were smiling. 'Shall your great discovery be enough to cure Amelia?'

'I shall not be able to convince you with words,' said Bendix, 'but can only ask for your patience, so that your own eyes might convert you this Saturday.'

'I look at you,' replied Defoe, 'and I see that you do not doubt yourself.'

Bendix's smile widened at the accuracy of Defoe's presumption. 'Half of me believes Amelia's disease to be an illusion. Perhaps it is not so much a condition as a fear contracted from the doctor. Does the child not listen and trust the parent?'

'It does not matter,' said Defoe, 'how she came to be affected by the light. It is so now. Your beliefs are inconsequential, as are Sir Edmund's. Only hers matter.' Defoe scratched behind his ear. 'She was burned terribly. The scar proves it.'

'Even if her condition is incurable,' answered Bendix, 'then why did he not show her more? Why did he not bring her about in darkness?'

'You forget,' said Defoe, 'that when you show London to a young lady, you also show the young lady to London.'

'Then, you admit,' replied Bendix, 'that hers is merely a condition compounded by a father's selfishness.'

Defoe laughed at the apprentice. 'I say no such thing. A father is to the family as a king to his nation.'

'You have written against kings before,' said Bendix.

'But never signed the papers in my own name,' bowed Defoe.

Though Defoe had not been invited until the Saturday afternoon, so that Bendix might have the morning to negotiate with and calm his subject, he could not restrain his impatience and arrived well before lunch. He paid his respects to Mrs Hemmings in her kitchen and then visited Amelia, carrying a calf-skin book of papers that he wished to read to her. Bendix thought that Defoe had not looked so well in all their months of friendship. Perhaps it was simply the chafing of the March wind upon his face.

Sixes arrived at noon by the servants' entrance. Behind him was a woman dressed in a simple calico dress. Once it might have been worn by a lady of grace, but now it carried the black dirt of winter. Bendix looked at the woman, thought her between forty and sixty. Her wrinkles were crusted with soot. The faint smell of gin seemed to rise from her dress.

'Her name is Lizbeth,' said Sixes. 'She wants to see her shilling.'

'She shall have two,' said Bendix looking into her eyes. The left was brown, the right grey. He did not know what he saw. She communicated nothing to him. The bridge of her nose was syphilitic, gnawed on and devoured. Bendix had passed such women in Newgate, in the shadows of his walks. The poorest of whores, a hedge whore, to be taken while standing, unable to afford tuppence for floor or hay.

'Hello, Lizbeth,' he said and managed a smile.

'You'll burn me?' she asked.

'A small mark,' said Bendix and he brought a shilling from his pocket and turned it from palm to palm. 'No bigger than a penny.'

She looked at Sixes.

'Aye,' said Sixes, ''tis a good man. Listen to him and you shall have your shilling. He'll not cheat you.'

Satisfied by Sixes's reassurance, Lizbeth stepped forward.

Upon entering the basement Defoe was horrified to see a poor shade sitting upon the block table, facing Bendix as he fuelled the fire. The apprentice attended a quiver of pokers that stood among the coals. As the writer stood by the bottom step, Bendix removed an iron from the fire and fed it to a large oaken bucket. The resulting hiss seemed to course down the woman's spine. Is it not enough to torture the woman's body, thought Defoe, without taunting her so?

The woman ignored Defoe as he approached, staring only at Bendix and the fire, trapped in between thoughts of need and dread. One moment wishing to run up those stairs and burst from the front door, the next resigned to a minute of pain that might excuse her days of duller submission. She tried to look away, first to the shelf of bones, then to the books, finally at the brackets of candles against the wall. They too were filled with fire, so her gaze fell upon the shilling in her hand.

Bendix greeted Defoe with a nod. He had removed his peruke, the short grizzled stubble of his head swirled with sweat. There was an air of theatre about Bendix's performance, thought Defoe, a broadness in character previously unknown. Either Defoe had learned nothing of the man in their months of friendship, or Bendix was assuming a role simply to petrify this old woman. Should Amelia see him in such a state, all her feelings might evaporate.

'Lizbeth?' said Bendix.

She turned over on to her stomach, lying flat against the table. Defoe could see her close tearful eyes against expectation. The apprentice leaned over and tied one of Amelia's ribbons over her eyes. Then, with a delicacy incongruous to his wildness, he pulled the dress off Lizbeth's shoulders, until it bunched in dirty waves at the small of her back. Defoe could see a long scar across her back, a clean single stroke of ivory that ran from hip bone to shoulder.

Bendix raised one iron from the fire, extinguished it purely for the effect of the ruptured hiss of steam. He walked quickly to the row of pots, through a well-trod sawdust path and removed a small block of ice. Returning to the fire, Bendix grasped another iron from the fire and carried it to the table where his subject awaited. He held the iron to within inches of Lizbeth's face, watched her mouth curl away in reaction to the heat, then laid the iron gently upon the floor.

Lizbeth screamed as Bendix pressed the ice to her back. It was a sound that startled Defoe in its intensity, made his eyes strain, his shoulders hunch in remembrance of the agony of his own operation. Bendix held the ice against her for not more than five seconds, then pulled it away to leave a remarkably angry welt. Before the writer's eyes the skin swelled and blistered, an intense burn caused by a splinter of ice. Bendix was waiting for him to match gazes, a look of calmness and vindication that held only a slight sympathy for the pain he had caused his subject.

'It is over,' whispered Bendix to Lizbeth. 'Do not move. I shall apply an oil and dressing. You shall have an extra shilling for your bravery.'

Without a word to Defoe, Bendix crossed the room and gathered a blue bottle of oil and a ball of white dressing. Bare-handed, he applied the oil to the square inch of the burn. Defoe could not understand which of his senses were operating. His nose, for instance, could not decide if it smelled the pungent odour of roasted flesh. One moment it was there, the next it was replaced by the coal fire and scented oil. His mind already doubted what his eyes had seen. He wished to reach out and touch the wound, but did not wish to share any more in the woman's pain.

Bendix wound the dressing about Lizbeth, passing the material under her breasts, then wrapped it about her back, covering the small burn thoroughly. He pulled her dress up over her shoulders, then offered her his hand, bringing her to a sitting position. The skin of her cheeks was damp with tears, yet she looked at Bendix and stretched out her hand. When two more shillings were pressed in her palm, her hand closed in a fist.

'Whose mark is it?' she asked, gesturing towards her own back.

'No one's,' said Bendix.

She continued to look at him.

'Enough now,' said Bendix, 'our deal is done. Away with you.'

He pointed towards the steps of the basement and obediently, though with a trudging reluctance, Lizbeth climbed the stairs, escorted by the apprentice to the servant's entrance and out into the afternoon.

'Well?' asked Bendix on his return. 'What do you think now?'

Defoe stood rooted, arms crossed. He blew a blast of air from his lungs. 'I do not know what to make of it,' he said. 'Do you?'

'Not entirely,' said Bendix. 'Or rather there is so much to be learned from such action that the knowledge is too vast to apply to a specific.'

'Amelia?'

'Exactly,' said Bendix. 'In this case, we can be sure that expectation resulted in the expected, rather than the logical. It is not always so.'

'Before?'

'One burned, the other laughed so hard at the ease of his shillings to humble me entirely.'

'What shall you do?'

'Continue to experiment,' said Bendix.

'Do you continue the doctor's work?' asked Defoe, in an avuncular tone.

'I do,' said Bendix, 'as well as my own.'

'And which holds credence?'

'I doubt his path, I doubt mine.'

'Certainty is for fools,' smiled Defoe. 'Besides, it is not yourself that you must convince, but Amelia.'

'You see no harm then,' asked Bendix, 'in pursuing both paths?'

'You know me, Joseph,' said Defoe, opening his palms to the apprentice. 'In a race with long odds, one often backs a pair of horses.'

Bendix did not bow to sleep that night, but sat in his study, guarded by the light of a dozen candles. His mind was unable to slow, ticking like a timepiece. By sun-up his head hurt so that it seemed as if his spine now tapered into a cloud of pain. He concluded that Defoe was right. Amelia maintained her belief in transfusion though it had almost killed her. It was, he presumed, tantamount to belief in her father.

He could not, therefore, neglect the doctor's methods,

though his own hypothesis had already proved more successful. Throughout the night, the more he thought on the two theories, the more he believed they might share common ground. If Bendix's theory rested on what the patient was expecting, then Calcraft's relied upon a doctor's expectation of his subject. It was with considerable pride that Bendix determined that his method was more logical than Calcraft's.

The weakness of the doctor's position came on its reliance upon the soundness of the judge's mind. In Calcraft's case, their choice of Sheppard could not have been worse. Had he spoken to the thief, he might have recognised that Sheppard was a man of some wit and kindness and not the devil he sought. Wild, on the other hand, was a man of intricate artifice, who with his black book tied about his belly carried the weight and evidence of his own sins with levity. Had the doctor considered the Thief Taker over the thief, then perhaps Bendix would not have been abandoned to lonely and unspoken thought.

The temptation, thought Bendix, was to conclude that an untested theory was an intellectual exercise. Yet experience without interpretation was worthless. He believed that the question might only be resolved through repeated experiment. However, patience was not a quality that Bendix either possessed or esteemed.

Bendix repeated his theories of suggestion, of fire and ice, every day for the next week. By the following Monday, he was forced to confess to Sixes that he could not afford another subject, prompting his acquaintance into low murmurs of sympathy, followed by the offer of a loan. Few men are thrilled by obligations and none by debt. Bendix considered the offer for a moment before dismissing it. He thought it more prudent to pause in his experiments and consider the details of his findings. To try and examine, why, out of his ten subjects, the blisters had risen on six, while the other four had remained untouched.

It seemed to have little to do with sex, two men and two women free from burns. The problem lay, thought Bendix, in the fact that he was meddling with the mind, not Calcraft's animacules, decoctions or empirical minutiae. And what man could guess a reaction, unless he knew the mind on which he operated? Who had the faintest concept of what these drudges had seen and suffered before appearing in Lincoln's Inn? Or perhaps it was more simple. Perhaps gin dulled the imagination, perhaps stout rotted the brain, or pox, gleet or fever affected the power of suggestion. Bendix felt as if he lived in a world of 'ifs' and 'maybes', a world of such loose possibilities that it made a man's head throb to follow the thread of a single thought through his trail of subjects.

Upon his daily visits Amelia noted Bendix's distraction, plagued him with questions, always content to know that he suffered so on her account. The apprentice, in return, was grateful for her smiles and favours. Since her father had left the house, Julia had taken to sharing Amelia's bed. Although Bendix knew this was a custom long held by young women to ensure that no indiscretions occurred in a household, he could not help but wonder why the custom was revived *now*. Perhaps because she did not trust him. At first it angered him, not because he presumed to make any midnight excursions to her bedroom, but because *she* had presumed he might. And when anger had spread through him and indignation had dabbed his forehead red and sped his heart to a gallop, he forced himself to remember the night he had laid his head upon her naked stomach, and knew that she took the most sensible precautions.

Money concerned him. Bendix spent the next days paying closer attention to Amelia than to the studies that might cure her. He had written a desperate, begging letter to his oldest brother in Northumberland. In return he received an encouraging sermon, fortifying his attempts at change with sombre words and evocations of God on high, but the letter arrived without the necessary scrapes of silver. Bendix had expected as much and burned the paper slowly amid coal.

In Paris, when his father had first sent him words instead of gold, he had avenged himself by drinking enough to blur his memory, delaying full understanding for a pair of dizzy days. The only pain this latest letter caused was in its seizure of moral ground. It strongly suggested that, if like a dog he continued in obeisance, then he would one day deserve the bones.

Before his outlay on suitable subjects, when he still had coins to click in his pocket, money had not disturbed him. Indeed, he had begun to adopt Calcraft's own stance that talk of money was unnecessary for gentlemen involved in the higher pursuits of natural philosophy. Of course, he had not objected to earning his own guineas when employed with Sixes's help, but shillings and coinage did not obsess him to their current extent. At the resumption of their walks, he found himself looking at Amelia's mask, wondering at the number of subjects he might have had for its commission.

He looked upon Amelia as the cause and cure of his complaint. They were strangely reliant on one another. Only when they were alone for some time could Bendix put all his fears and pursuits aside and return to his customary calmness. It always carried with it a smile of love for Amelia. He could not be sure if his experiments were conducted only for her or for both of them, yet there was nothing insincere in the manner in which they held hands, or sat in silence, exchanging rare kisses. Neither could read the other's mind. Bendix always attempted restraint, wishing to treat his future wife with the utmost respect, in awe of her innocence. Amelia was more curious, a little frightened of the sheer physicality that might be expected of her. She was still not used to touch and was caught between desire and composure. Instead she would merely fill her head with the tiniest erotic memories that were exaggerated by time. The different scents brought to her on Bendix's lips: teas, chocolate, tobacco. Hints of soap, brandy and woodsmoke were noted and stored and when remembered caused as much pleasure as when they had first happened. Still, despite their closeness Bendix could not ask Amelia for money, knowing that it would be such an open display of his impecuniousness that he would show himself as not just an ill-advised match, but a disastrous one.

Amelia had risen at ten, seen to her dress, taken a small breakfast and emerged from her chamber at noon for her daily appointment with Bendix. He could tell from her poor imitation of aloofness that Amelia had measured an agenda for their conversation. Modesty, he thought, was about to be levelled by directness.

'What is this being read to you? Etherege?' said the apprentice picking up the tome. 'Slight entertainment.'

'I would agree, Joseph,' said Amelia, 'if there were alternatives to occupy my mind.'

'I have been working,' said Bendix and put the book back upon the table.

'On my behalf?'

'Always,' said Bendix.

'Then I suppose it would be in vain to complain how little I see of you. We do not walk so often as I would like.'

'All the pleasure that I receive,' said Bendix with the start of the smile, 'I receive in your company. All else is work for me.'

'Tell me,' said Amelia, breaking a smile in conspiracy, 'what does love mean?'

Bendix seemed taken aback, as if she had once more accelerated his line of courting and etiquette. 'A question answered a thousand times a day, and never to one's satisfaction.'

'Well,' said Amelia, undeterred, 'what does love mean *to you*?'

'To some there is no such thing,' said Bendix, gesturing in distraction.

'To you, Mr Bendix,' chided Amelia.

'I used to think it was a sickness,' confessed Bendix. 'It makes a man go to sleep and awake with the face of his beloved before him. Worst of all, a man in love believes he has never thought so clearly, that he has never before appreciated the world as he does at that moment.'

'And does he?'

'Undoubtedly,' said Bendix, 'at worst it is a blindness, at best it proves to be a high fever caught by the young.'

'And what age are you?' asked Amelia.

'Neither young nor old,' said Bendix.

'And what age do you consider me?'

'Surely you are young.'

'And thus subject to this fever as well as a blindness?'

'I cannot answer that question for you,' said Bendix.

'I can,' said Amelia, 'but wish you would spare me and declare yourself.'

Bendix knew that he had parried until he had been forced into a corner. 'You know my intent,' he said. 'I am your father's apprentice. The only thing I wish more than you is your recovery. And though between us we have no contract, the apprentice is not free to marry until his time is served.'

'You have no contract with the father,' said Amelia, 'but would you not make one with the daughter?'

'Not without the father's permission. If he were to recover, she might be disinherited for so rash an act.'

'Then he must not know. We have little time,' stressed Amelia. She knew the true extent of her diminishing sight better than Bendix. The games of reporting that she and Julia used to play on their neighbours were distant memories. Colour itself was long forgotten. Yet she could not panic. She enjoyed his reactions, the straight back and strong character that would not be hurried from the proper path. If she were honest, she would have admitted to Bendix that time concerned her less than she let on. Blindness now seemed a certainty to her, a heavy door closing that she was too weak even to keep ajar.

'Still,' said Bendix, 'I insist that we attempt his permission.'

Amelia took a small gold coin, a doubloon, and pushed it in her teeth, bent it to half a harvest moon. She offered it to Bendix. He paused, astounded at the offer and its significance.

'You are sure of what you do?' he asked.

'Yes.'

'And we shall visit your father and declare our intentions?'

'If, as my future husband, you insist.'

'Nor shall we go before God until we have attempted your health.'

'Of course not, though I hope that you shall show some friend the evidence of my devotion.'

Bendix fished in his purse, finding one of the last of Wild's guineas. He put the coin into his mouth, and like Amelia had done a minute before, twisted the soft metal in his teeth. He offered her the coin. In silence, and a semblance of tears from Amelia, their contract was established.

'Is this love?' she asked, understanding that she now valued it more than her sight, more than her freedom from Lincoln's Inn.

'I promise you it is,' replied Bendix.

It was a sudden proposal, one that had been engineered by Amelia and accepted by Bendix. He knew a little of the laws of marriage, as did any bachelor who had ever thought of seeking advancement through vows. Amelia, unmarried, might have no say in the disposal of her father's property. The estate would be held together until she was married, then passed into the hands of her husband. If she were not to marry, she would be free to spend the income Calcraft's estate provided, but the estate would be kept in trust until her death, then divided among relations, or ruled upon in Chancery. Bendix, then, knew what he was; not only loved, but an instrument of freedom for Amelia.

It was a pleasant manipulation and one that any man might be grateful to submit to. In return for providing her with a degree of freedom, he would become the executor of the entire estate, married to the woman he desired. It was a circumstance so unusual that Bendix laughed aloud. Wrongly, he felt his love was not returned as purely as it was delivered. It was not a great worry, for he knew that Amelia was weighed on not only by the desire of freedom that he himself had planted at the Frost Fair but by the wish that her eyes be cured. If he might provide both her wishes, then her love would follow as surely as rain to thunder.

At Amelia's urging, Bendix scribbled a note to Defoe begging his company on both of their behalf. Defoe treated the news of their contract with the greatest good will and though Bendix knew him well enough to know that his face was unlikely to betray his true emotion, by the time he drank to their happiness for the third time he had convinced the apprentice of the purity of his joy. Amelia seemed infected by the presence of her friend. She made a great show of presenting their coins to Defoe for viewing until Bendix found himself attacked by a similar contagion and smiled with appropriate inanity. To hear their contract confessed seemed to alter the air they breathed. Indeed, Bendix felt as if the spoken words had forged a clearer path to love, almost forgetting his anxiety for their visit to Bethlem.

They travelled at dusk in Calcraft's own equipage, Lemon wearing a simple livery, a hired coachman driving their horses through a light rain. If Amelia had to suffer the pain of light, thought Bendix, it was just as well she was born in England. He did not know if his fears had been exaggerated by the prospect of seeing the doctor again, but the single cloud of coke and grey that had been suspended over London for a month seemed to have been lowered to the rooftops. It looked so thick that a spire couldn't puncture it.

Defoe made several attempts at conversation on the way, but Amelia was entirely caught up in the novelty of travelling inside the carriage and Bendix was concentrating on his hollow stomach and stuck throat.

'I must warn you,' said Defoe, 'that, like most public institutions, it is run for profit of the staff and not its patients.'

Bendix nodded from habit. In the dark, he caught Amelia squinting through the windows as they passed down Thames Street. They wound around Monument and up through the Royal Exchange and the stalls of ivory teeth for broken mouths and spectacles for weak eyes. Cutting through the crowds of porters and pippin mongers, they ran past the stables of the Flying Horse Inn before their carriage slowed then stopped. To the north lay Moorfields. How different a carriage ride, thought Bendix, than his first meeting with Sixes, when wooden shovels had moved the earth and given up the body of the hanged.

So large did Bethlem loom in the consciousness of London that when Bendix finally descended from the coach he was staggered by its slight size. As one of only two public institutions for the mad in all of England, he had expected a sprawling mass of bricks, a confusion of style and construction to echo its purpose. However Bethlem seemed fit for the Lord Mayor himself. A foreigner, thought Bendix, might think the English deemed madness a quality of Society.

A small parcel of hedge whores hung outside the gates. To either side of the entrance sat two colossal statues. The figure to the right was chained, cheeks drawn in anger. His cousin across the gate sat in pitiful melancholy, which Bendix supposed was to convey a syphilitic dissolution. To either side of the entrance hall two long galleries stretched east and west. Their little group, headed by Lemon, stood patiently by, awaiting Monroe's arrival. It was not the place of cacophony that Bendix had heard rumours of as far away as Paris and yet the sounds unsettled him. He thought he could hear fifty men breathe as one. Above them wailed the strings of a fiddle, not badly played. Only one voice was discernable and that was raised in prayer. All in all, thought Bendix, it seemed as much a monastery as a madhouse.

'So cold,' said Amelia.

Defoe smiled and attempted to amuse. 'Might expect the mortification of one's extremities.'

All thoughts turned to Sir Edmund and polite smiles fractured. Lemon looked over his shoulder to present Defoe with a withering look.

Defoe tugged the apprentice on his cuff and together they walked some yards eastwards. The first door had a windowed grid of bars that the two men peered into. All was darkness, nothing to be seen and only low breaths of rest were emitted. They continued to the next door. Defoe noted that it was not locked and pushed open. From the light of the gallery, they first smelled, then saw, a man lying naked, dribbles of his own excrement stuck to the backs of his legs. He rested, unaware or uncaring of his condition, lying in the straw, two blankets on either side of him, immune to the cold. Bendix noted the iron cuff about his right ankle and the chain that climbed the wall to the rusted bracket.

Defoe nudged the man with his foot. The madman stretched like a cat from sleep, then pushed himself on his haunches and began to talk to his visitors in a language of clucks and low whistles. Defoe clapped his hands to silence the man, then raised his hand as if to strike him. Instead of retreating the man sprang across the stone floor, halted by the chain from reaching Defoe. Still he managed to deliver a slop of messy spittle in the writer's face. Sensibly, Bendix took Defoe by the arm and drew the door close behind them.

'Provocation,' explained Defoe, 'will teach you much about a man. What good would staring at the sleeping body have done us? Now we know how he sits, speaks . . .'

'Spits,' added Bendix, offering Defoe his handkerchief.

The echo of footsteps caused all the visitors to turn and watch Monroe's steady progress down the gallery. He must have had metal tips attached to his heels, for he clicked and clacked his way past all the doors off the gallery, providing a sharp and unmistakable echo. He seemed to glow from vigour at twenty yards. Bowing low in front of Amelia and shaking hands with both Defoe and Bendix, Monroe ushered them up the central staircase, the edge of the steps worn smooth from use. Upstairs, the geography was identical. They followed Monroe west along the wing.

'Progress,' said Monroe softly to his charges, 'has been slow. It is devilish hard to deal with a man committed to silence.'

'Does he have the freedom of the gallery?' asked Amelia.

'Aye,' said Monroe, 'he comes and goes as he pleases. Never outside the gates of course, but he has not caused occasion to be restrained. Merely dedicated to being uncommunicative.'

Bendix noted that it was only the second door that they had passed that had no lock on it. They passed inside and immediately Lemon set about darkening the room for his mistress's convenience. No light came between the high iron bars. Lemon simply turned the bull's-eye lantern that lit Calcraft's domain towards the wall, then draped a thin piece of orange silk over it. Had it not been so cold, Bendix thought he might have been inside a fire.

The doctor sat on a low bed of straw, dressed in the same suit that he had worn on leaving Lincoln's Inn. He wore no wig, but had his head wrapped in bandages, like a turban from the East. Looking neither sickly nor content, he did not rise at the intrusion. He did glance up, but the sight of three members of his household and his best friend seemed no more startling to him than the April rain. Bendix was pleased to note that the doctor was portly, believing the appetite a gauge for the desire to life.

' 'Tis best to be direct with him,' said Monroe, 'for he is no longer apt in conversation concerning the climate.'

'What is with his head?' asked Bendix.

'He signalled that he wished it shaved,' said Monroe, 'then bought the dressing from an attendant. Seemed most grateful for it.'

'What does it mean?' asked Amelia.

Monroe shrugged. 'There is little discernible meaning within these walls, child.'

'Yet his disease is curable?' inquired Amelia.

Monroe gave his nose a tug, then blew on his hands against the cold. 'Aye,' he said, 'they are all curable, else they would not be granted admission.'

'And how do you seek to cure my father?' asked Amelia.

Monroe turned and addressed Amelia directly, his chest puffed like an angry rooster, yet his tone silky with professionalism. 'He is not exposed to the daily visitors, eats well twice a day, takes walks for his health, sleep for his rest. I cannot think of a single other patient within my walls who exhibits such sure signs of recovery.'

'Yet,' said Amelia, 'he will not talk?'

'No,' said Monroe, 'not to me.'

'Father,' said Amelia, turning from Monroe and kneeling before Calcraft.

He looked at her, which, thought Bendix, was some improvement since last they had seen him.

'I have come for a reason.'

Still, there was no response.

'I wish to marry Joseph Bendix,' said Amelia. 'I know that you have thought highly of him.' Bendix nodded to the use of the past tense. 'And hoped that you might speak to give us your blessing, if not your signature upon the contract of marriage.'

Calcraft sucked his lips in, so that they were pursed in thought. Finally, he breathed out, but still he did not speak. If the news was of any surprise to him, he had swallowed it.

'Sir Edmund,' said Bendix stepping forwards. 'I endeavour to treat your daughter. I continue your work daily and believe I am close upon a cure.'

To this, the doctor revealed his understanding through a full and amused smile.

'I shall not marry her until there is improvement in her condition,' continued Bendix, 'Of this you have my word.'

Calcraft relaxed his smile and resumed his former stare.

'May you grant us your permission?' Bendix felt awkward, could sense Lemon staring at him with disgust. 'It would mean much to your daughter's happiness.'

Amelia leaned forwards and tried to grasp her father's hand. He did not resist, but Bendix could see how he withheld life from the limb, as if he had stopped the very blood from flowing to it. Amelia pressed her lips to the back of his hand. Calcraft looked upwards, over the body of his daughter, and very slowly shook his head at Defoe. The writer did not move an inch, staring at the scene before him.

The rains had risen during their visit inside and after Monroe had walked them to the gates of Bethlem and Lemon had shuttered them up within Sir Edmund's carriage, the horses dragged them through the gathering mud, back along the London wall.

'Was not entirely as disturbing as I had expected,' said Bendix, if only to relieve the silence.

He looked up at his company for some support in conversation, and saw only a pair of tears leak from beneath Amelia's band of silk.

Defoe noticed her distress and politely began to talk so that he might blanket her sobs, should they begin.

'He seemed well fed,' said Defoe. 'Altogether peaceful tonight. Often,' continued the writer, 'the patients are so stirred by the provocations of their visitors that they magnify their insanity towards the expected entertainment. I have seen guineas thrown at them.'

'The conditions seem to alter from cell to cell.'

'As in Newgate,' said Defoe, 'one's state is tempered by gold. I have seen a man of some importance who thought himself the king. Allowed to wear his crown about the gallery and drape his cell in silks and velvet.'

'And the others?' asked Bendix.

'A sailor for ten years,' said Defoe. 'A man of grunts and flaring nostrils. Most entertaining to the young ladies. Strapped in a leather harness. A horse that was never broken.'

'Is silence,' asked Amelia, 'a rejection or an acceptance of the proposal?'

'The disavowal of the mad man is similar to the acceptance of the sane,' said Defoe.

'But he did not deny the marriage,' said Amelia. 'Nothing at all.'

'He did not seem unhappy,' suggested Bendix.

'By law,' said Defoe, 'he is removed from decisions concerning his estate. This includes you, child, and no matter how well the intention to seek your father's approval, it was as unnecessary as bowing before a king who has no throne. Appreciated at some level, by Sir Edmund, but not requisite.'

'We are free to marry now?' asked Amelia.

Defoe shrugged. 'You are both of an age. To marry is no more difficult than walking or breathing. A guinea and a visit to Lamb's Chapel and you shall be one before God's eyes.' Defoe's words seemed to restore an equanimity to the carriage that let them prosecute their journey in comfortable silence. Amelia's gloved hand snaked across to hold Bendix, linking them by their little fingers. Defoe nodded approvingly.

At Lincoln's Inn, Lemon escorted Amelia to the western

wing, where Julia had prepared her fire and heated water should mud or dirt have touched her skin. Mrs Hemmings had stirred a batch of warm milk punch. Both men took one drink with Mrs Hemmings, then retreated to the library, where the fire seemed to have been burning without end for close on six months. Defoe and Bendix managed to swap smiles and good-natured talk despite their early evening visit to Bethlem. It did not seem to occur to either of the men that the nutmeg that flavoured the punch, the fire that warmed their faces, the roof that saved them from the rain, all belonged to the man they had visited and forgotten.

'You have your wish,' said Defoe. 'She seems most eager.'

'To wed, indeed,' shrugged Bendix. 'I have fallen in love, while she perhaps has only fallen in love with the prospect of change.'

'I think you do yourself a great injustice,' said Defoe. 'Obvious to a man my age that though her affection is hard to descry, her attraction to you is considerable.'

'You have seen this?'

Defoe nodded.

'Still,' said Bendix, 'others have worked for their glory, mine falls to my lap.' He took a sip of the milk punch. 'Undeserved fortune is often cursed.'

Defoe laughed out loud. 'Too wary of the very things you wish for. You shall have property, marriage, station.'

'And a lack of reputation,' said Bendix. 'I would wager it all upon curing her condition. If it is just blindness that we shall face, I am capable of persevering, but Amelia's bodily condition grows weaker and weaker.'

'From what you have shown me,' spoke Defoe, 'I would not think that reputation will be slow in calling your name. If you might show the court, or a ducal patron, the very experiment that you showed to me, you would soon be elevated to kingly circles. It is nothing less than a new branch of medicine, Joseph. Whatever doubt you feel about your marriage will dissipate in the heat of future glories.'

Bendix considered the writer's words. 'Why does the doctor deny me?'

'He is merely waiting for your failure,' explained Defoe. 'For you to return to his level. Preferably beneath.'

'Perhaps you are right,' said the apprentice. 'It eats at me, when I should rise above.'

'Well done,' said Defoe.

'Still,' replied Bendix, 'I shall cure her.'

Defoe opened his palms as if he were not the sort of man who would stand in the way of the desires of upcoming generations.

CHAPTER TWENTY-FIVE

Once again, Bendix knew that he was being driven by Amelia. It seemed as if Defoe had barely left them alone for a night and a day when Amelia decided that the two must set a date for their marriage. She was drunk with the desire to leave Lincoln's Inn and believed the oath Bendix had made to her father, that they would attempt her health again, could be leaped as easily as a rill of summer rain. Love must be confirmed. Her own vision seemed less important to her than her freedom, no matter that she confessed to Bendix her eyes seemed weaker still.

The wedding was not to be a grand affair. It was not to be

any kind of affair whatsoever. A pair of witnesses might include all their friends in London. The excitement of marriage, and it was an excitement that Amelia managed to convey to Bendix, lay not in the day of celebration but in the search for a new house. It was a house that would be theirs, and only theirs. Lincoln's Inn, for all Amelia cared, might be knee-deep in dust before she would return again. She wanted fresh air, grass, the sight of woods and river; all the things that had eluded her in childhood she wished to live and breathe as a woman.

She would take Julia with her, of course, and Lemon if he so wished, though he was a London man and would most likely choose to find alternate service. As for Mrs Hemmings, Amelia confided to her future husband that she cared not whether she followed or remained. Bendix presumed that the sentiment was mutual, or perhaps Mrs Hemmings would not notice whether she stayed or went, so clouded with alcohol was her vision.

Their evening walks were transformed into evening rides, the clemency of early May lending the country a warmth, if not actual sun. They would leave as Mrs Hemmings began to prepare the evening meal. Bendix would put his nose into the kitchen and make sure that the lobster was boiling, or the eels ready for skinning. It was, of course, not possible to stray too far in the hours between meals, but Amelia's appetite was not as voracious as Bendix's. Her hunger was for sensation and not consumption.

They viewed land near Chelmsford, several acres in Fulham and Vauxhall and took more than one turn about Richmond. Always, Bendix would time their visits to the disappearance of the sun, describing the contours of the land. Amelia would spend the next half hour walking by Bendix's side, extolling the beauty of the country buried in the darkness, inventing acre after acre of uninterrupted woodland. Waiting until the carriage ride home, Bendix would correct her dreamy imaginings and together they would decide if they were intrigued by the vicinity.

Spending the majority of his time with Amelia, Bendix still managed to dedicate a portion of his time to himself. Always jealous of his hours of reflection, Bendix maintained the habit of his walks. It was a daily practice, but prolonged twice a week by a visit to his original haunt at Tom's Coffee House. Perhaps, he thought, Amelia was not the only one so eager to depart the familiarity of Lincoln's Inn Fields.

Most of his energy on his walks to Covent Garden was drained not in thoughts of medicine but in the disposal of money. The purchase of a house was the realisation of a dream that he had not earned, but, he thought, how many had earned their fortunes in England? It was a country of landed favour and grasping inheritance. Perhaps Calcraft and Hooke, Wren and Boyle had deserved their fame or fortunes but countless others were passed land, incomes, tenants and farms. Often, in Paris, one heard the amounts discussed; the daughter of the duke was worth four thousand pounds a year. The count's second child had two thousand pounds a year and an estate in the Loire.

As the youngest son, he had expected nothing but endless patience and gold. He had abused position, trust and money and fallen to the physical labour of medicine. Without family, a man could not be expected to rise unless he was blessed with the smile of fortune. Finally, it made sense to the apprentice. A doctor, fresh with innovations, gave his daughter to a promising disciple, a half-moon waxing towards greatness. It was as if Sir Edmund had established a separate society, estates garnered by thought and progress and not the unearned parcelling from father to son. It was an entirely preferable manner of succession.

Bendix passed under the shadow of St Paul's Church and the humped arcades of Covent Garden. He walked through the doors of Tom's Coffee House, bought his pipe full of Virginia tobacco and a cup of steaming chocolate and took a seat by the sooted glass window, looking out into the early damp days of May. He flapped open the *British Journal*, giving it a loud rustle as a defence of his territory.

The words hooked Bendix's eyes and stuck them to the page. It was a small paragraph on the front page, four days old. '*The Famous Jonathan Wild was on Monday committed to Newgate.*' Bendix sped to the front table and, spilling a gentleman's glass of port, gave a curt apology and then robbed him of the collection of news-sheets he had gathered before him, replacing them with the slim *British Journal*. The affronted man tucked his feet under his chair and prepared to stand in protest, but his companion, as slight of build as his friend, laid his hand upon him and together they kept to their chairs, all the time casting angry glances at the absorbed Mr Bendix.

On the 22nd it had been reported in *Parker's London News* that Wild was charged with '*buying jewels, knowing them to be stolen at the late Installment at Windsor*'. It added that '*he was pretty secure, and very much afflicted with the gout, which may in time, by a receipt from the hangman, be effectively cured*'. Then again, on the 26th, *Parker's* continued, '*Various are the opinions about the famed Thief-Catcher, as to his trial. Some say it will be at Chelmsford, others at Burntwood, others here and some elsewhere*'. Bendix read backwards and forwards across the days and only learned that the crime for which Wild was arrested could not be agreed on by any two papers, nor, in some cases, by the same paper on consecutive days.

Bendix had no knowledge of what Sixes had seen and interpreted during his five minutes with Wild's book nor what he had done with his information, but the quick demise of the Thief Taker seemed to point in only one direction. The confusion concerning the crime for which Wild had been brought before the magistrate also pointed to Sixes. Who but Sixes might match crime with criminal, property with owner, instigator with employees? It was most likely, thought Bendix, that they had so much evidence to hang Wild with that they did not know which felony to force on him. The more Bendix thought of the demise of the Thief Taker, the more his world came back into focus once more. The blur of the marriage contract and the visits to Bethlem and the countryside now melted away. He was left alone with the desire to possess the hanged body of Jonathan Wild, to continue his experiments, to restore the health of his wife and secure both peace of mind and a sun-bright entrance into the court of King George. Perfectly aware that these were cold thoughts, he also knew of the warmth that such cruel devotion to progress might bring.

There was enough time between capture and trial for the pamphleteers to circle with varying accounts of the life of Jonathan Wild. Narratives passed from stall to coffee house, barber shop to tavern and round again. *Parker's London News* and the *British Journal* contented themselves with noting the apprehensions of many of Wild's associates. Every day, Bendix checked the lists for Sixes's name. Finally, on May the 10th, he read that Sixes had been committed to Clerkenwell Bridewell, where he was living in the most splendid manner. The trial was set for the 15th of the month. Justice, it seemed, had been woken and whipped for the Thief Taker's sake.

Bendix attended only one hour of Wild's trial, buying a seat from a well-placed straw booter with one of the Thief Taker's own guineas. A neck cloth hid the scar across his throat, a sensible wig covered the silver fissures of his skull and his portliness was well disguised by a fine suit of black silk. The crowd was thick in the Old Bailey, the light May rain disturbing none who had settled in to watch the settlement of Wild's fate. Rain had bled the powders from the Thief Taker's peruke, the mixed hues of grey, black and ochre lending the man a semblance of illness. The face beneath maintained a jowly assurance. So familiar was the Old Bailey to Wild that he seemed unconcerned with the proceedings.

Bendix was certain that the court and King's Counsel performed in harmony against the prisoner. Wild's line of questions were halted or turned aside, so many witnesses called and dismissed that the prisoner must have been dizzy in his memory. The Thief Taker's lawyers, Baynes and Kettleby, seemed more distracted than Wild. Much of the language, told in speeding tongues of law, escaped Bendix. It seemed as if the King's Counsel concentrated on a single crime, the theft of fifty yards of lace from the parish of St Andrew's, allegedly organised by Wild. When the witnesses and the counsel could not seem to convince the court that Wild had been present, they changed their tack, insisting instead that he had most certainly received the goods, itself a hanging offence. He was acquitted of the first indictment, found guilty of the second.

The rains had lifted, the evening sun appearing to mock the Thief Taker as he was addressed by the court. 'What have you to say why judgement of death should not be passed upon you?' Wild's brow was creased in confusion, the surprise of a good man whose faith in justice had been betrayed. My God, thought Bendix, the man believes himself innocent. The Thief Taker moved to his feet. He swayed under the sun, studying the face of the court, of the counsel and witnesses, of the crowd that lay before him. Bendix felt their eyes pause in recognition and thought that of all the spite and disdain that exuded from Wild, he had been granted a particular charge of venom.

'Do not forget the service I have done this country,' said Wild. 'I've delivered it from malefactors. My body is crossed with scars I received in these undertakings. My Lord, I have done good. You know this, you do. This is a strange rig they've run upon me. Was esteemed a man of merit by the government. Therefore, my Lord, I expect compassion. Will submit myself to His Majesty's mercy and humbly beg a favourable report of my case.'

'You may depend on justice,' said the court, 'and nothing more.'

The hangman stepped forwards and tied Wild's thumbs together with whipcord. The knot was tested, then the guarded prisoner pushed forwards and marched towards the walls of Newgate.

Bendix had not walked many yards eastwards when he spotted a familiar shadow lurking beyond the reach of the sun, standing still as a post between an oyster seller and a black carriage. The apprentice peered at the shape for a moment, then followed his nose forwards.

'Sixes?' said Bendix in genuine surprise. 'The *Post* said you were making home in Clerkenwell.'

'The papers will print what money pays them to,' said Sixes. He waved Bendix forwards into the shadow of the carriage.

'I thought I might have to pay you a visit,' said Bendix. 'After the trial of course.'

'The falling of the mighty,' sighed Sixes. 'A sad sight when a man's sins overwhelm him. I shall, of course, be seeing you again soon enough. After your nuptials, I trust.' He bowed his head, looked about and walked against the crowd of sightseers, back towards Newgate.

Bendix walked home. He was in no hurry, the sun high and bright and far away. It had been dark for so long that Bendix had quite forgotten how many colours the city held; the red bricks, the reflecting glass of windows contorting and refracting, the quiet, blue flow of the Thames. Even the sky above seemed to consist of a hundred shades that had no name. The only disappointment Bendix could find was in his own dress, which seemed betrayed by the light, the thinness of the silk, the frayed patches openly accused by the sun. Perhaps, he thought, he did not cut quite so fine a figure as he had presumed.

The glory of the day had lifted the mood of Lincoln's Inn. Windows had been thrown open as if the house swallowed sweet breaths of freshness and pushed the dampness of spring from her walls. Bendix could spy Julia on the spice garden, hunched in careful administration to the plants. Lemon was in the kitchen with Mrs Hemmings, sharing a glass of wine. They greeted Bendix as if he were almost welcome. Finally, Bendix headed up to the western wing. Though it remained shrouded in familiar darkness, Amelia's windows were open, the whole wing relieved of the miseries that those winter months had brought. Julia had chosen Amelia a pale pink dress, a happy rosebud hue that played gently with her ivory skin.

'Daniel has good news,' said Amelia. 'A house in Chiswick, built not seven years ago by a milliner as lost his fortune in the South Seas.'

'This is good news?' asked Bendix.

'For us. Would you like to visit? Daniel should accompany us.'

'I can think of nothing finer,' said Bendix, with perfect sincerity, for he had not enjoyed a day as pure in a year of enduring the British clime.

Chiswick, so Bendix discovered on an evening of high orange clouds, was a small village sitting off a looping bend of the Thames. It was not far from the forests of Richmond he had admired so the week before, and had a busy neighbour in Turnham Green, a string of inns and stables and modest houses. Across the river was a dock carved out of a bank of osiers and willows, from where small malting houses spilled the scent of barley. Defoe was the ideal guide, filled with tales, some utterly unbelievable, of the local gentry. It seemed that they could not turn down a lane that he had not trod before, could not come across a church that did not hold the body of a beloved friend.

The traffic on the Thames was thick that night, boatmen and ferries pulling about the shallow river, disappearing behind the eyot, small masts remaining in sight. Children ran among the rich mud and barges that had been beached with the tide. All was prettiness and calm. Amelia, with her back to the setting sun, heard the splash of water, believed she could feel the river running deep under her feet and knew that she had found her home.

The waterside was cramped with fishermen's cottages and yet the neighbourhood boasted more than enough manor houses to settle Bendix's concern with station. Defoe walked the couple past Prebendal Manor at the bottom of Chiswick Lane. He told the apprentice that Sutton Court lay close by. Defoe emphasised the potential of the district. It was not fashionable yet, but Bendix relished the fact that they might be present at Chiswick's transformation from exclusivity to a broader selectivity.

The house they viewed was not grand. Bendix would not admit to his intended the weight of disappointment that sat in his stomach. For a moment he was flushed with anger at Defoe, believing the writer slighted them with his low presumption of their wealth. He could not, however, deny the house's charm. They approached it from St Nicholas's Church, walking past mossy gravestones and country yews until they met with the high wall of the property. The gateposts were flanked by a pair of mulberry trees and within the walls a long triangular garden led to the door. It was a three-tiered building, neither cottage nor mansion, choosing comfort over grandeur.

All the windows looked away from the city to gardens, orchards and meadows. There was a kitchen, dining room and scullery on the bottom floor; above, gabled windows that bathed the bedrooms in morning light. Every empty room conjured a wealth of possibilities. Wherever Defoe waved his arms, there appeared before them tables and tapestries, settings of silver and liveried footmen. There was not a splinter of furniture about, but it was well swept, free of signs of vermin. Best of all, thought Bendix, it was contained within tall walls; privacy coupled with modesty that might hide the true humbleness of the seat.

''Tis pretty,' said Bendix.

'We shall have it,' answered Amelia and her smile held no room for further conversation.

'I shall ride out tomorrow,' said Bendix, merely proclaiming what Amelia knew must happen, 'tell the lady of the manor our intentions and reserve the house for our marriage.'

'We shall ride together,' said Defoe.

Amelia took Bendix's arm in her hand, and pressed her lips against his cheek. It would be a happy house, thought the apprentice. Defoe moved himself between the couple and, linking arms together, walked them back through the gates of their property, beyond the church to where Calcraft's carriage awaited them.

CHAPTER TWENTY-SIX

Their proposed journey was delayed until the afternoon, for on their return to Lincoln's Inn Fields a footman lay waiting for Joseph Bendix. He carried with him a note from Newgate and had been informed that he might not leave Sir Edmund's house until he had extracted a promise from his apprentice. The impoliteness of the intrusion offended Bendix, but quite intrigued Defoe.

'If it is Mr Wild who calls, then surely you must go,' advised Defoe.

'He is hardly in a position to insist,' answered Bendix.

'Curiosity, Joseph,' said Defoe. 'I am feverish to know his desires.'

'You are writing an account for his hanging day?'

''Tis already written,' smiled Defoe. 'But you might add symptoms of peculiarity that might set it apart from the rest. He must have wishes, you might fulfil them in return for confessions. I would see you paid.'

'I shall go,' said Bendix, 'if only to see how the mighty fall.'

'Shall I accompany you?'

'To Chiswick, yes,' said Bendix. 'To Newgate, only as far as the gatehouse.'

Bendix travelled alone. There were none of the crowds at Newgate that had flocked to see Sheppard attend chapel or merely sit in his cell. Wild was too familiar a figure, his misdeeds so broad and intricate that perhaps too many felt accomplice to his guilt. Bendix knew what awaited the Thief Taker on his hanging day: hosts imbued with righteous anger, a passage to Tyburn of such ringing hatred that not even the stoutest heart could be saved from doubt.

Surprised to find that Wild was kept in the condemned hold with the other prisoners, Bendix paid his threepence and moved unsteadily down the stairs into the gloom. The bars that Sheppard had escaped through had since been bricked over on Wild's orders. Now no air could freshen the pestilence below. Bendix raised his borrowed lantern, illuminating the dirty faces of the five inhabitants. He passed the light over them again, believing he could not see the Thief Taker.

'Joseph?'

Bendix turned back to the voice, then moved towards it. Wild looked as happy to see him as if he were his only son. He reached up in his chains and pulled Bendix close to him, wrapped his dirty arms about the apprentice and pressed his bulldog face close. The light of the lantern jogged wildly about the hold. Wild whispered thanks in rotting breath of old onion. His discomposure unsettled Bendix. It was as if he viewed a different man than before, who suddenly deserved the compassion of understanding. Bendix saw the hopelessness of his case. Knowing Newgate well enough, he had presumed frightened turnkeys would not treat their Thief Taker so. Only if they knew that all his appeals had failed, that every friend had turned away, would they dare to treat him as if he were already dead.

Wild looked at him in admiration, then sat back down in his bed of dirty straw and signalled for Bendix to follow suit. With great reluctance, the apprentice gingerly lowered himself to the floor. The Thief Taker moved as close as a lover and spoke to him in whispers so that the condemned could not hear him.

'Was you, was it not?' asked Wild.

'I?' posed Bendix.

'You that gave me up. Put me to rest with your opiums and took my book. Who'd you show it to? Who?' Wild spoke in the oddest tone of acceptance Bendix had ever heard. It was as if all he sought were an explanation of his fate and he were no longer concerned with avoiding the rope.

''Tis true,' whispered Bendix, 'that I put you to rest and is true that when I had sewn you up I left you resting. I even know the book you talk of, strapped about your waist. I did not take it. I did not show it to a soul.'

'You put it back wrong side up. Is how I am prepared for this.'

Bendix looked away, dimming the lantern's light. A loud coughing began across the hold.

'If I wished you dead,' said the apprentice, 'would it not have been simpler for me to further open your wound, rather than close it?'

Wild dipped his head into his own hands, then ran his hands about his gouty leg.

'You owe me,' he said. 'Was your medicine as put me asleep and made me delicate to my undoing.'

Bendix bowed in acknowledgement.

'Get me more of it,' ordered Wild. 'Today.'

Bendix did not answer.

'You think it ungodly?' smiled Wild. 'There are noble Greeks, learnèd Romans, who slew themselves and are remembered by history. A man still enters the kingdom of God does he not? Matters not if he enters by rope or in sleep. They cannot keep him out.'

'What makes you think that the Devil himself will not be standing at Tyburn?' asked Bendix. '*Cursed is every one that hangeth on a tree*,' quoted the apprentice.

'You'll get me more sleep, won't you man?' pleaded Wild. 'As much as will never let me hear the bells.'

'You have appealed?'

'To the king himself,' whispered Wild. 'The Dead Warrants have come. Cured this city of crime, had it tamed like horses and now they wish me gone. London will burn without me. There is none left but you, Joseph. Bring me the liquid. Let me pass in peace.'

Bendix wondered whether, if Tyburn had not been necessary to his own course, he might have searched out laudanum for Wild. As a man of compassion, he decided, it was most probable. ''Tis against God,' said Bendix.

'Do it for me,' whispered Wild, gripping his hand so hard that the Thief Taker's chains began to cut into the apprentice.

'I shall think on it,' said Bendix, 'with great reluctance.'

'Good,' murmured Wild. 'Good man. Angel. Soon as can be.'

Bendix hoisted himself from the straw, swiped the tails of his coat free of straw and muck and, holding the lantern before him, navigated the stairs towards the light of day. Any man of violence, removed from his crimes, was capable of stirring pity, but pity, once detected, is easily dismissed.

❉

Outside, Bendix attempted to put the plight of Wild from his mind. It was an excellent effort, replaced by thoughts of Amelia and the details of ensuring the purchase of their house in Chiswick. The Thief Taker disappeared even from the periphery of his mind once Bendix was struck with the splendid notion that on so fine a day there could be no better way to travel to Chiswick than by water.

The two men secured a boatman at Horses' Ferry, choosing a squat, bearded fellow whose English was so rough that they described their destination with a flurry of gestures and shouting. Defoe carried with him a copy of the *Daily Journal*, which had printed Wild's petition to the king on its front page. He irritated Bendix by spending the first five minutes of their journey reading it aloud. The apprentice would far rather have forgotten about his afternoon visit to Newgate, but Defoe was most eager for information with only two days left before the execution. Reluctantly, Bendix gave a partial description of his visit, concentrating on the depravity of the man, his wish for laudanum and his desire to take his own life.

Within minutes, Defoe was satiated and the two men stretched back and watched the boatman break a sweat against the current. Defoe's shirt flapped from beneath his waistcoat, his peruke askew atop his head. Age, thought Bendix idly, is an able replacement for vanity. He wondered if Defoe owned a looking glass, and if he did, would he be seen about so often?

They paid their boatman an extra shilling to keep him by the barges until their return and strolled down Chiswick Lane, spending a lazy half-hour walking among the buzz of flies and knee-high grass. Occasionally, they called to a passer-by for directions. They found the current copy hold owners of the house, Mr Rupert Quinn and his mother, already at the court of manor by Chiswick's bowling green.

In suitably direct tones of business, Mr Quinn declared in front of the court that he had sold the whole estate to Mr Joseph Bendix of Lincoln's Inn Fields, his heirs and assigns forever. Bendix had not expected the moment to overwhelm him, but when both he and Defoe signed their names against the contract and shook hands with the departing owner, tenderness washed over the apprentice and he shook Quinn's hand until he had reduced the man to concerned smiles. Defoe kindly guided him back across the bowling green and down to the banks of the Thames.

'I have never seen you so happy,' said Defoe. 'Cannot remember myself so happy.'

Bendix gave a guilty shrug of pleasure. 'I do not know what it is,' he said. 'Perhaps pride. I should like to write to my family. Let them know of my joy. Perhaps invite them to stay after the marriage is complete.'

'I would wait a year,' said Defoe, as the barges and their faithful boatmen came back into view. ''Tis best to let your wife become accustomed to yourself before plaguing her with family. Children, however, should be encouraged immediately.'

'There shall be many,' said Bendix immodestly. 'First, we shall have Amelia walking under the sun, then I will fill her belly with greater concerns.'

Defoe gave him a paternal slap upon the back, then clambered over a barge to save his shoes from the mud, taking the boatman's outstretched arm and collapsing into the vessel with an exhausted sigh.

CHAPTER TWENTY-SEVEN

As hard as Bendix tried to squeeze Wild from his mind, the Thief Taker would not disappear. He remained, not as the suffering figure deserving of opiates, as he had hoped, but as a commodity, an ingredient of restoration. Bendix, relying on his memory for the decoction of Messrs Pink and Sheppard, was soon convinced that his knowledge of the process was incomplete. He had paid attention, but had not always been present. Absorbed in his own work, Calcraft had often sent Bendix from the basement to collect spices or run inconsequential chores. The doctor had, of course, kept his meticulous notes in the calf-skin journals. Bendix searched his study, his bedroom, the basement. Towers of knowledge were reduced and rebuilt in his search, but not one word that Calcraft had written in the past two years survived in the house. Bendix did not know if the papers had been burned or sat beside the doctor in his Bethlem cell.

He rode on horseback to the gates of Bethlem, through a strange humid evening where all the smells of the city were kept close to the ground undisturbed by the movement of wind. The cotton of his shirt grew damp with sweat, releasing a musty scent of dirt. He gave a stablehand fivepence to wipe his horse down, then was forced to grease the watchman with twice as much to allow him through the gates.

It was past eight in the evening and the inclement weather and lateness of the hour had kept all visitors at bay. The patients seemed to have been stirred by the pressure of the weather and great whooping calls came up and down the gallery, a pair of madmen at opposite ends of the building striving for constant communication. Bendix walked up the stairs and noticed the stone steps were sweating, the heat of the earth pushing its fluids upwards. The door to Calcraft's cell was open, the doctor reading quietly by a pair of candles, his head no longer wrapped in the turban but ragged with rough stubble.

'Doctor,' said Bendix, and stood in the shadow of the open door. He knew there was little chance of an invitation to enter, so he waited a polite moment and then proceeded. To the right of the doctor, upon his narrow desk, stood a stack of journals, perhaps twenty in all. It occurred to Bendix that he might have to seize them. The doctor followed his eyes.

'I am in need of help,' began Bendix with a smile. 'I am close upon the attempt of your daughter's health. Please, sir, I am unfamiliar with the detail of decoction, if you might allow me some words, or perhaps use of your journal, then . . .'

He opened the palms of his hand in supplication and sought to match his pleading eyes with the doctor's. When they met, he was surprised to find Calcraft's filled with an ugly amusement.

'I do not think I can cure her without your help,' added the apprentice.

Once again, Bendix was greeted with a stare of intentions, but not a word. Bendix pushed back against the wall of the cell and prepared himself to besiege the doctor with his presence until he met with a response. Without asking Calcraft's permission, he lit a pipe and attempted to look as if he were lost in a world of dreams. They were disturbed after a few minutes by the nightwatchman, requesting another shilling and a wad of tobacco so he might deflect any possible complaints. After the echoes of his receding footsteps melted amid the howling on the gallery below, the doctor let his tongue snake out of his mouth and wet his lips.

'Have you married her?' he asked.

Bendix managed a cool exhalation of smoke that he hoped might hide the mild shake of surprise. Calcraft's voice was deeper than he remembered, but his words had been shortened and sharpened by his silence. 'Amelia?' the apprentice asked quietly.

Calcraft nodded and Bendix shook his head.

'No, I have not,' continued the apprentice. 'I made an oath to you I have not broken. I would first attempt her health.'

'Has her condition worsened?'

'Undoubtedly,' replied Bendix. 'If she worsens, it will not be merely her eyesight that fades. She is not so strong as her father.'

Calcraft nodded, almost in pleasure of Bendix's similar inability to affect the course of Amelia's illness.

'Why do you speak?' asked the apprentice.

'Do you wish silence?'

'No,' said Bendix softly.

'How much have you spent for Wild?'

'Five hundred pounds,' said Bendix, omitting the pertinent detail that he was contracted to Sixes for five hundred pounds *each* year.

Calcraft laughed. 'And where would you acquire such a sum? Not from Defoe, surely he can not have such money available.'

'No, not from Defoe.'

'Ahhh,' said Calcraft, 'the family understanding is re-established. The runt is welcomed back into the fold and your father provides the fund.'

It caused a hot flush of denial to rise up the apprentice's

neck. Every word the doctor had spat had made him want to stand in anger. He had learned the lessons of temper before, and to deny Calcraft's accusation would only be to admit something worse, such as the truth.

'Yes,' Bendix said, knowing it was only half a lie, 'the money comes from my father.'

'It is wasted,' said Calcraft. 'You will not cure her.'

'I wish your books, your journals. Let me attempt her health.'

'Before you attempt her flesh?'

'I have not laid my hand upon her, I promised you that.'

'You wish my help so badly,' said Calcraft, 'when we have already proved me useless. I presume then, that your own foolish notions of the mind are also dismissed.'

Bendix shrugged.

'I've thought hard on it,' said Calcraft, 'and it finally occurred to me, this attraction of yours for the medicine of the mind. Nothing but idleness. Your past, incorporated into your present. None of your beliefs can be proved or disproved. It is an argument that has nothing to do with the body, only the mind. That is purely philosophy, not a hint of the labour of medicine – the use of words to chase tails. You are, of course, no more foolish than me, but you do remain an ass.'

Bendix held his tongue. He longed to boast of his own discoveries, of the fire and ice and blisters that proved the power of the mind. He would not give it away, information guaranteed to provide him power and money. And yet, despite his discoveries, he had not formulated a manner in which they might be used to restore Amelia.

'You have not answered my question,' said Bendix.

'And what is that?'

'May I have your journals?'

'Please,' said Calcraft pointing to them.

Bendix moved towards them, and with Calcraft's help tied them in two separate calf-skin bundles.

'There was a king,' said Calcraft, testing the knot of his bundle, 'the first King of Thebes, called Cadmus. He brought the alphabet to Greece. He also planted dragons' teeth, which ripened into a crop of armed men. When you are done with these books, burn them all.'

Bendix nodded in consent.

'Lastly,' said Calcraft, 'should you tell Monroe that I have spoken, it shall only be greeted with silence. You will not be believed, his vanity would not allow it.'

Bendix nodded in concession. 'You want nothing of your daughter?' he asked.

'Why would I,' answered Calcraft snidely, 'when she has found such an able companion?'

CHAPTER TWENTY-EIGHT

Bendix did not falter in his determination to ignore the plea of Jonathan Wild, for the next time that he saw the Thief Taker he was in the company of several hundred others, crushed outside the walls of St Sepulchre's. Nor had he been mistaken in his prediction of the crowd's reaction. It seemed as if the air above Wild's head was forever occupied by gravel and pebbles and sharp stones. Bendix was thankful that Wild did not catch his eye, but noted with regret the cuts upon the Thief Taker's forehead and his pale demeanour, as if he had not slept since last they had met.

The sheriff's sergeant kept his horse well ahead of the

cart, as did the city marshal. The javelin men lagged well behind, leaving only the hangman and two fellow thieves to suffer in a share of Wild's vilification. The Thief Taker sat in his callimanco nightgown, his eyes open but not in sight, unconcerned with the cuts about his brow. He wept openly. Bendix followed the cart, back in the gathering wave of the mob. They moved at the same pace as the cart, stopping at a tavern near Gray's Inn and watching as Wild struggled not to spill his glass of wine. His hands were not tied as Sheppard's had been, but nor were they composed in hope. The trembling, evidence of the crowd's effect, caused the mob to increase their howling.

The tumbril stopped twice more. Once at the White Lion, again at the Oxford Arms, which increased the crowd's anger. Bendix was deafened by those gathered about him and pushed his way to the west of the tavern, where he had agreed to meet Defoe. The writer, pressed against a porter's rest, had much to relate, none of which Bendix could hear for the constant shouts aimed at Wild. They let the girth of the crowd pass ahead, then continued with the stragglers towards Tyburn.

'We shall not sell well,' said Defoe. 'Most disappointing.'

'Madness,' replied Bendix, waving away a dirty child, 'there are thousands about. Thousands.'

'Might have been more,' said Defoe. 'I passed some laudanum to Wild last night.' Defoe waved his hand at Bendix's huff of disapproval. 'Applebee would not reprint to include the story. He swallowed it all, Joseph. Fell asleep in the Chapel, dragged back to life by the Ordinary and a pair of thieves. He spent his last evening sick and fevered. Shakes this morning like a virgin bride.'

'You interfere,' said Bendix sharply, 'where you are not welcome.'

'No harm,' said Defoe, linking arms, 'the creation of an episode, no more. The public demands an end and they shall have one.'

The friends hurried their pace, until the thickness of the crowd slowed them. They fought their way to Mrs Candrey's wooden tiers and spent a crown a piece for the final seats on a sagging plank that overlooked the triple tree.

The three men were hanged together. As Wild fell he reached outwards and grabbed the thief beside him. His rope slackened and life was retained for precious seconds, until the hangman beat him off with a staff. He twisted away alone to the crowd's delight. Wild took almost a quarter hour to cease his struggle, every flicker of pained life cheered. There was no surge of support to save him from the surgeon's carriage. Presuming that all had been arranged safely by Sixes, Bendix turned to Defoe and, excusing himself on Amelia's behalf, he hurried to Lincoln's Inn Fields to await the delivery of the body.

There was more black than blue above by the time that Sixes called at Calcraft's. Bendix had spent the afternoon in his own study, looking down on the street most every minute in expectation of the gangling shadow. He saw no horse or carriage, but was not aware of the subtleties of transporting the dead and ran quickly down the stairs, two steps at a time.

'You know how to age a man,' said Bendix with a smile, greeting Sixes at the door. He waved him through to the library. 'Impossible to work on such a day. I believe I counted the cobbles three times over.'

Once inside the library, Bendix slowed for a moment and for the first time noticed the manner in which Sixes avoided his eyes.

'Shall we go to the servant's entrance?' asked Bendix. Sixes shook his head. 'You do not have him, do you?'

'My device was foreseen,' muttered Sixes. 'A matter of accounting I assure you.'

'Who has the body?' asked Bendix.

'His wife.'

'I was not aware he was married.'

'She's a bitch of superstition,' said Sixes, taking a seat on the fire dog. He pinched first his nose and then his lip. 'Won't let him go. Bury him herself if she could. Will hold on to his body. Sit with it a day or two. We shall have patience, Joseph, patience and we both shall profit.'

'It shall rot.'

'The nights are cool,' calmed Sixes, 'and she'll care for it. She'll hold it as long as she can stand, then move it again. We shall be watching day and night. Always.'

'The rot shall drive her out,' said Bendix. 'Who watches the house?'

'Faithful to me only,' said Sixes. 'You are not the only man who wishes the corpse. Others watching too. False scents shall be laid. Patience is all I ask.'

'You'll get nothing else,' said Bendix coldly.

Matters were confused two days later at the attempt by Wild's widow to take her own life. She was cut down within moments, gaining only the briefest of glimpses at her husband's fate.

Every day Sixes reported to Bendix, the two men growing so weary that by the end of the week they seemed to have developed their own language of exhaustion. A dip of a tired eye, the drop of a sagging head and the continued futility was understood. On the evening of the seventh day, Wild was buried at Pancras Church Yard, but still the widow and her family kept watch on the grave throughout day and night. A full four days after his interring the grave of Jonathan Wild was broken and emptied.

The arrival of the body did not bring the rapture that it might have done the week before. Instead Sixes was consumed only by relief, matched exactly in intensity by Bendix. Working alone, in constant reference to the calf-skin journals, the process of decoction proved lengthy, taking the exhausted Bendix a day and a half of sweated toil. Most surprising to him was Sixes's constant attendance, as if he were afraid that Wild would rise, push his intestines back within his adipose carcass and cheat him of his contract. Every hour, Sixes dripped vinegar about the floor to keep the stench of the dead from rising. While Bendix worked, Sixes opened all the vessels in the room, pushing his nose into spices and powders, none beneficent but all preferable to the rotting Wild.

The body was a waxy shade of cream. It was only ever the details of the dead that kept the anatomist alive to their humanity; the hair that covered his body, the well-lined palms of his hand, the silver plates that sealed the fissures in his skull. Bendix could see signs of gout in the Thief Taker's feet and about the sides of his nose, the distinct erosion of syphilis. It was as if death had brought about an acceleration of the disease. Even on a living host, syphilis was determined to rot a man. Bendix had seen many men who had lost their noses to the disease. It was odd how important the nose was. Without it, the image of the skull was overpowering.

The belt and book, worn so faithfully throughout the years, had thinned the hair about his waist, leaving a clear outline of their existence. It was, thought Bendix, a remarkable body in the intricacies of its oddities. With regret, he cut from the shoulders to the breastbone and down to the infected pubis.

When Bendix had cleared the corpse of all the intestines, weighed and measured them, lit the fires and warmed the kettles, Sixes set about the disposal of the body. He was curious in his treatment of his former employer. At first Bendix presumed it was a gesture of respect, but only after dismissing this notion did he understand that while he had been the customer for the contents of the cavity, there were others who would wish to study the skull, skin, brain and bones. Sixes was merely applying the greatest of care to a package of value.

CHAPTER TWENTY-NINE

After two days of decoction, Bendix made a familiar error. Leaving the liver to boil, he retired to catch the briefest of naps that might ensure a sound mind. Exhaustion harnessed him, clamped down on his eyelids, secured his body to the bed and did not let him rise for twelve hours, during which time Amelia sent Julia down twice to check on his condition. She reported to her mistress that he slept in peace and, though Amelia was anxious for words, she thought it prudent to let him sleep.

Rushing from his bedroom, Bendix slid his way to the basement in stockinged feet with blurry eyes of tiredness. The fire was cold, the liver a shrivelled black prune. He did not see how any of the doctor's animacules could have survived. Bendix's body was choked with such pulsing disgust that he could not keep still, nor believe that he could have echoed his year-old mistake. Arms to his side, hands on his waist, arms crossed, hand on temple. Fingers always twitching. And yet no position provided him with even the faintest encouragement. Very simply, he did not know if he had destroyed his experiment.

He rebuilt the fire, pushed the coals about the hearth in varying heights of cairn, then reassured himself that his sleep had not ruined the work already done. The remaining organs seemed to have survived their decoction. As if in penitence, Bendix bled himself immediately. It brought him a heady clarity and with six ounces of his brimming blood in his cupping bowl Bendix set about the creation of the various mixtures in his hopes of seeking the perfect restorative. He raided their garden for euphrasia, plucking and slipping the flowers between a press, then rummaged his way through the doctor's pots, searching out sassafras and calomel.

Eighteen of Calcraft's twenty journals were stacked in two columns on the shelf of disordered bones. The remaining two were spread across the table. They dealt with the thickness and texture of the restorative, encouraging the employment of all senses in the pursuit of the ideal proximity to blood. The ink that described the taste and touch, the sight and smell of the fluids, was fresher, a different shade of blue from every journal that had been written before it. Neither, thought Bendix, was the hand that had written it as steady as before, but shook as if shivering from cold.

The apprentice left the house only once in the week, when his eyes felt so weak and his brain so muddled that he had quite forgotten the season. In the basement, the stone had retained the chill of winter damp and Bendix dressed accordingly in a woollen suit and great coat. When London greeted him with peculiar sunshine and the blooms of June, he looked about himself on the street and saw men of quality stare at him with detached interest, as if he were the shaved bear at the Frost Fair. He stopped a porter in Covent Garden and tipped him a shilling to return his coat to Lincoln's Inn. He did not care if the man absconded with coat and coin, but calculated the risk on the trustful nature of the man's face.

Tom's Coffee House had opened its windows, customers perched outside and in, a content rumble of conversation reminding Bendix of the loneliness of his occupation. He warmed himself with the thought of Amelia, then chastised himself at once with her neglect. What good, thought he, to cure the woman one wished as one's wife, when her cure might jeopardise her love for him? He resolved to visit her immediately on his return, but wished for some news of the city to alter the scope of his knowledge. A man cannot mix and test all day.

There was only one story that amused him. He found it in the *British Journal* and thought it was the perfect epitaph. It made his blood rise. He looked about him at the chattering men. Writers and idlers, merchants and gamblers, all who read, none who knew. He studied them with contempt for their ignorance and raised his head so high you might have been forgiven for believing his nose suffered great disdain for his mouth. Company meant little if it favoured gossip and mutual admiration. Reflection, thought Bendix, could only be obtained alone and no man was more used to his own company than Joseph Bendix.

He read the paragraph again: '*Last Sunday Morning there was found upon Whitehall Shore, in St Margaret's Parish, the Skin, Flesh and Entrails (without any bones) of a Human Body: the Coroner and Jury that sat upon it, ordered it to be bury'd, which was done on Tuesday last, in the Burying Ground for the Poor, and the Surgeon who attended, gave it as his Opinion, that it could be no*

other than the Remains of a dissected Body. It was observed, that the
Skin of the Breast was hairy, from whence People conjecture it to be
part of the renowned Jonathan Wild.'

Bendix suffered from the thrill of law-breaking. The ethics
of the majority had been ignored. Bendix knew that he pursued higher ground that stood above sheriffs and magistrates
and their silver staffs of authority. Despite his burst of supe-
riority brought on by the *British Journal*, Bendix humbled
himself through the memory of Amelia. He had cured
nobody, discovered only an imperfect idea. He folded the
news-sheet and pushed it inside his pocket while the lady of
the house was waiting on those outside.

At home, Bendix changed from his suit of wools, wiping
the birth of summer sweat from his torso, and dug for a
white silk shirt in his chest. He was too harried to bother
with powders, but chose a blue suit of silver brocade then
buckled his shoes and headed for the western wing. Amelia
was delighted to see him, or at least said so. While spring
had brought freshness to her abode, summer had shut her in
again with its rise of heat and light.

Bendix took his customary position on the sofa. Amelia
dismissed Julia with a wave of her hand. The maid seemed to
melt slowly from the room as if she might catch some snippet
of love-making should she drag her heels. It was, however,
not an afternoon reserved for coyness and approaches.
Allowing the merest of addresses as to her health, Amelia
reproached her intended husband with a flurry of accusations, echoed by a scowl and underlined by silence.

Bendix provided her with all she had wished to hear. How
he had done nothing for a fortnight but work towards their
happiness, how he neared his goal, how soon they would be
free of house, of darkness, of work.

Relenting, Amelia let a smile break across her face. 'I wish tomorrow were today,' said Amelia. 'I wish it everyday. That time might be wound forwards.'

'It is,' emphasised Bendix, 'only a matter of days.'

'Can you imagine the river tonight?' asked Amelia. 'We might walk past St Nicholas's and watch the ferry and her horses.'

'Soon,' promised Bendix, 'you shall spend your days walking, until you will agree with society that the ground is for the poor and the four-legged. You will have sedan chairs and a pair of footmen to carry you from seat to seat.'

'Never,' smiled Amelia. 'I shall walk. You shall teach me how to take the water.'

Bendix nodded and laughed. 'It is all so soon.'

Of course, Bendix did not leave his meeting before the question of their marriage was raised, and though it was not an issue he sought to delay until he had finished his work, he knew how disappointed Amelia would become if he havered. Once agreed upon, Amelia became childish in her enthusiasm. Bendix was, predictably, charmed and felt his love rise again.

'We shall do it today,' said Amelia. 'We might send a note to Daniel. Have Lemon witness. Julia knows how to find Lamb's Chapel. Tonight, then.'

'Not tonight,' smiled Bendix. 'We made a promise to your father. To attempt your health.'

'And,' replied Amelia, 'it will not be a promise broken, but a promise altered. By a matter of days. Come now, what difference can it make?'

Bendix shrugged. He knew that to Calcraft marriage was merely a question of his daughter's innocence. If he were to ensure her virginity, then he would also keep his promise to the doctor. 'We must send ahead and ensure the presence of the curate,' he smiled. 'Some food upon the table. If it is not to be a wedding, it must at least be a decent sort of marriage.'

'How long might that take?' asked Amelia.

'It is merely a question of alerting the correct people, then just a brush of money.'

'Might we do it tomorrow?'

'It is possible.'

'If it is possible, then it is certain,' said Amelia, which brought another laugh from Bendix, who held both his hands up in surrender to her determination.

There was no doubt that once again Bendix had been pushed by Amelia, but thinking on it the same evening he concluded that if a man were to crawl, walk or run towards you with good news, he would be welcomed whatever speed he travelled. There was no need to hold Amelia's innocent insistence against her. Since she had no knowledge of etiquette, it was impossible to judge her by such standards. She was, Bendix believed, a woman of an open nature. Her freshness should be relished, her buoyancy encouraged, her whims granted, for, if his belief in the imagination proved correct, the happiness of her mind would have the most direct effect upon her body.

Bendix was not a man accustomed to relying on anyone else. In Paris, he had trusted others, trusted them with his education, his insolvency, his secrets of love. Never had the trust been returned. Yet Amelia relied upon him entirely. Her father lay in self-imposed silence, suspicious of his intentions and wallowing in a cold pity. Defoe, however avuncular, had only ever been a temporary anodyne. And yet he, Joseph Bendix, with his penniless second-hand heart, had won the love of the purest young lady. To Bendix, it was merely proof that progress brought reward. It was a simple enough theory and easily supported the evidence of mutual adoration.

Chapter Thirty

The Reverend Doctor Henry Holloway was an acquaintance but by no means a friend of Daniel Defoe. They had met when they were thirty years lighter, both weighed by wife and children and then sunk by debt. The Fleet Prison provided the colour for their shared misery and while Defoe had spent his life bouncing from prosperity to adversity and had discovered the benefits of stability in his dotage, Holloway's path had been much less jagged. He earned a precarious living, Defoe informed Bendix, teaching the tongues of Latin and French and sometimes playing chaplain to the ships.

Debt was part of Holloway's character, owner of his clothes, his purse and keeper of his freedom. He lived within the Rules of the Fleet, unable to leave their bounds without immediate arrest by his creditors. It was then, hardly surprising, that he bowed to the request of either friend or stranger. For a pair of crowns, he promised to perform the marriage and provide the certificate. No, he said, he did not mind if they married at noon or night, did not mind if they had faith in God, did not mind at all. Two crowns would guarantee God's blessing.

Amelia had read of marriage and of clandestine marriage, and preferred the latter for its ease, excitement and suitability to her current predicament. When Calcraft's carriage pulled up after dark before the Turk's Head Coffee Shop, Amelia looked much less worried than her groom, maid and liveryman altogether. Only Defoe shared her state of happiness. He liked to think that in his sixties there were few sides of London he had not already experienced.

Their party was greeted by the landlord, a Lancaster man with a nose flattened by an early and short career in the prize fights. He showed them up the back stairs, to a room on the second floor, filled with worn cushions and the light of a generous fire. The only table in the room was draped in imitation of a feast. Half a scrawny chicken, the body of a lobster, fatty slices of mutton that leaked their lipids on to the dirty table cloth. A pyramid of oysters rose behind the meats.

The rotund Reverend Doctor Holloway stood before the fire preventing a good portion of the light from finding its way to the corners of the room. To say his clothes were shabby would do a shabby man a disservice, for his coat was barely an improvement on rags. Bendix did not know when he had last been paid, but imagined that he had seen the waxing and waning of at least one moon since his pockets had been filled. He watched as the Reverend Doctor dropped a half-eaten chicken leg into the fire in preparation for their handshake. Holloway wiped his hands on his breeches, which did not increase Bendix's desire to greet him. Decency required the exhibition of etiquette, so Bendix shook the soiled hand, bowing slightly before the gentleman.

'Welcome, young man,' said Holloway and gave him a familiar clap on the shoulder. He did not offer Defoe his hand, nor did the writer extend his own. They seem to have settled on a silence between them, as if the knowledge they retained of each other precluded any affectation of gentility. The landlord itched his flattened nose, wished them to take their time and partake in the foods, then excused himself. Lemon shut the door behind him.

Holloway did not seem to know how to approach Amelia in her mask of ribbon, but had certainly seen stranger sights and married odder couples, so he complimented on her dress then nibbled upon a corner of mutton.

'You have the ring?' said Defoe to Bendix, who nodded in confirmation. 'Keep it in your hand or it might find its way to the Reverend Doctor's pocket.'

'I suppose,' said Bendix, 'that speed is, in this case, the most essential part of the contract.'

'Did you see those spilling from the tavern?' asked Defoe, smiling. 'A convention of ken crackers, the odd greased watchman and the dirtiest whores not dead in a ditch.'

'I believe the Turk's Head was your recommendation?' inquired Bendix.

'For her happiness,' said Defoe and nodded towards Amelia.

In fairness to Defoe, it is true that Amelia did not seem the least perturbed by their situation, nor by the man who was to marry her. She fussed with Julia over the arrangement of her hair, while Lemon stood stoically by the door, as if he were not so far from the more familiar tureens of silver.

'Shall we?' asked Holloway. He wiped his fingers on the tablecloth then took a sip of some draught that he must have ordered long before the wedding party arrived.

Bendix produced the ring and turned away from Holloway to face his bride and Defoe, who held her by the arm. The odd thing, thought the apprentice, was that Holloway had a marvellous timbre to his voice, which almost made his fall from grace forgivable. He read from the Prayer Book with as much sincerity and enthusiasm as Bendix had ever heard. Before he knew the words his mouth was forming, Bendix had consented to marriage. He looked at Amelia and she seemed only to be a perfect smile. The rest of the room, the fusty corners, the coughing fire, the stares of one and all dissolved and in a moment of joyful silence so sharp he forgot to breathe. Bendix could see nothing but the face of his bride.

Only a fire crackle released Bendix from his state of exaltation, then as he smiled at his sentiment Amelia reached forwards and squeezed his hand and their uncertain union was complete. The apprentice swallowed hard to banish any insidious tears. When Bendix broke the moment by surveying the room, he saw the most remarkable sight: sobbing from Julia and a smile beaming from Lemon. The apprentice noticed for the first time that the footman had few teeth. Holloway interrupted the household bliss with a request for signatures in his register and for the certificate of marriage. Bendix blew the ink dry with his own breath and pushed the certificate deep within his breast pocket. It was the paper that linked him not only to his own wife, but to her fortune and to their property. It was not surprising, then, that it should command a place so close to Bendix's heart.

Though Bendix offered the Reverend Doctor an invitation to Lincoln's Inn for supper, he knew full well that Holloway could not leave the boundaries of the Fleet.

'Engagement,' said Holloway. 'A terrible hurry.' However he displayed no intention of leaving before the wedding party, one eye on the red shell of the lobster, the other on the oysters.

Amelia seemed so happy that she cared not where she was. With the sound of a hoarse whooping emanating between the boards from below, both Defoe and Bendix remembered the clientele lurking in the tavern and their thoughts turned to immediate departure.

Holloway walked them to the top of the stairs, where they waited for the return of the landlord before venturing downwards. To the mellifluous accompaniment of Holloway's wishes for luck, happiness and fortune, the broken-nosed Lancastrian escorted them to their carriage. Bendix felt eyes upon him, or rather on Amelia. He heard the crowd emit low snickers of presumption at their clandestine union.

Bendix had no intentions of claiming his conjugal rights before he had restored Amelia's sight, or at least improved it. Her disappointment would be great, but he hoped her innocence in these matters might help to soften the necessary displeasure. They mounted one by one into the carriage, Lemon riding beside the coachman, the others swapping smiles and congratulations. A small following emptied from the tavern and walked after the coach, shouting for a wedding gift from the groom. Bendix could hear Lemon turn them off with a shout then encourage the coachman to see to his business before they pulled away from the Turk's Head and broke a canter towards home.

To Lemon's horror, the door at Lincoln's Inn Fields lay ajar. Only Mrs Hemmings had remained at home, but had she tippled and slept, or had she lapsed to incoherence, then a gang might have stripped them of all worth. The rest of the party followed, sharing Lemon's cautious stance and worried look. He pushed the sleeves of his coat up his arms as he crossed the hearth. There, in front of him, lay a complete service of silver, polished to a mirrored sheen. Lemon could tell from the briefest of glances that this was not a service he had ever seen before. On top of a handsome cream jug lay a folded letter, addressed to Mr and Mrs Joseph Bendix. Lemon plucked the note from its place, then waited until all had expressed their astonishment with various cries or silences and promptly handed Bendix the letter.

Had Lemon not quickly lit a pair of candles, Amelia would have torn the note from her husband's hands, so great was her desire to discover the name of their benefactor.

'*Wishes for happiness and long life*,' read Bendix, 'signed *Abram Mendes Ceixes*.'

'Who is it from?' asked Amelia, standing beside the regiment of forks and spoons, trencher salts and serving dishes. 'Is it beautiful?' The light of the candles sparked like fire from one silver surface to another so that the hallway sparkled like a treasure chest. 'Who is it from?' repeated Amelia.

'Mr Sixes,' said Bendix.

'The gentleman from the Frost Fair?' asked Amelia. 'How extraordinarily kind.'

Defoe's humour crumpled. 'How could he know?' asked Defoe. 'Your marriage was clandestine and is not an hour old.'

Amelia seemed delighted by the coincidence and stood there, spewing strings of superlatives.

Bendix merely shrugged. 'Holloway was your own choice,' he said, 'but I would guess he is not the most stable of tongues between gin and coin. Indeed, I think he would swap his own child for a suckling pig.'

Defoe was studying a fork from the service. 'Wonder where he stole it,' muttered the writer.

'Do you recognise the mark?' asked Bendix.

'Older than me,' said Defoe angrily. 'I can do no better than that. I suppose it will add a certain shine to Chiswick.' He resolved at once to wait before presenting his wedding present. He had, he knew, been thoroughly trumped in grandeur.

'So generous,' said Amelia.

Had she known how generous her husband had already

been with her estate she might not have thought so well of Sixes's presents, though Bendix knew she did not place a price upon her sight.

Defoe sidled up to Bendix's right shoulder. 'I am not certain,' whispered the writer, 'what has been done, or what is to be done, to deserve such treatment. Suspicions come naturally to me. Let me say only that to employ Mr Mendes is to prescribe a poison as the antidote. It is a dangerous equation for the uninitiated.'

'You wish me to return his gift?' asked Bendix.

'Heavens, no,' said Defoe, flooded with his old humour. 'One might finance a war with such finery.'

Long after Defoe had finished his fourth glass of malmsey and complained that he would soon be victim to the gout, long after they woke Mrs Hemmings and heard of the horse and cart that carried Sixes and his silver to their door, long after Lemon had snuffed the candles of the ground floor, Bendix made his way to his wife's bedroom. It would be, he knew, a difficult subject to bring to conversation, but as husband and master it must be done.

'We must speak,' said Amelia and blew the light of the sole candle out. Slowly Bendix's eyes adjusted to the darkness and he watched the shades of blues and blacks as Amelia peeled the ribbon from over her eyes.

'Indeed,' said Bendix. 'There is much to say now that we are man and wife.'

'It is an awkward matter,' said Amelia, 'but if you love me in a manner that reflects my love of you, then it is a bagatelle.'

'What is it?' asked Bendix.

'The matter of husband and wife,' whispered Amelia. 'I know what is expected of me, only I cannot. Not in this house.'

Bendix smiled. However his smile was no more than a flicker, for as pleased as he was not to have to engineer the conversation around the awkward topic of intercourse, he did feel that it was a husband's right to prosecute or excuse the act. He was as unfamiliar with marriage as his wife. Neither knew if their behaviour was acceptable, only that it was acceptable to one another. Besides, he had not broken his promise to her father, nor did he intend to. She would remain untouched, until he had at least attempted her cure.

They slept by one another's side. Bendix grasped her hand during the night and she made no objection to his manoeuvres. In the morning she kissed him as he slept, thinking him handsome. She ran her hand along the skin of his arm, touched her lips to his shoulder and could not believe the pleasure she already took in her state of matrimony. The excuse for the postponement of their consummation was only half a lie. It is true that her greatest desire lay in escape from the house, but she also feared intimacy more than she desired it. Yet, she could not deny the excitement of waking with her husband beside her. To touch his face, trace her fingers through his hair and about the curve of his ear, to know any man so well thrilled her. Amelia, who had spent her life in unconscious loneliness, studied her husband with the same fascination that she brought to her walks in the country or her strolls through London streets. His unfamiliarity fascinated her; the manner in which he breathed quietly between his lips, the way his arms crossed in sleep, the waning moons of his fingernails.

The only person who was disappointed in the wake of the wedding was Julia. After Bendix had shared breakfast with his bride and disappeared to the basement and Amelia sat with her back to the fire, mind busy with memorising the details of her husband's skin, Julia carried their sheets to the kitchen. With Mrs Hemmings's help she examined the evidence and was most disappointed to find no evidence of Amelia's blood upon the sheets. Julia was comforted by Mrs Hemmings, long familiar to the effects of drink, who sensibly suggested that perhaps Mr Bendix had taken too much port and been ineffective.

Bendix had not drunk too much. In fact, he had been reasonably abstemious in keeping Defoe company on their return from the Turk's Head. He was glad, for his happy state of marriage and clear mind resulted in progress, during which he became convinced that he would be ready for an attempt on Amelia's health within a matter of days. It was at four o'clock, shortly after he had taken a cup of chocolate with his wife, that the idea was conceived. Amelia had been pressing him, in the most convincing and flirtatious manner, as to how much better it would be for their marriage if they were to move to Chiswick that very day. Both knew, of course, that it was impossible, but the display of eagerness on Amelia's behalf charmed Bendix to the extent that he promised their departure as soon as possible.

On returning to the basement, he passed a case of wine that Lemon was preparing to decant. The smell of spices assailed him just before the dirty odour of Wild's decoction. In a frivolous thought, Bendix pondered how much better it would be to recover with a draught of Calcraft's wine than with their base and ill-gained restorative. He had been unsettled since his last meeting with Sixes, presumed it was the impending sentence of marriage, but now it had come and gone and brought smiles and relief he knew that this discomfort lay elsewhere.

He uncorked a bottle and brought it to his lips, then retreated to his study for peace. It was not the marriage, but the consequence of marriage that gnawed at him. He had fulfilled the letter of his contract with Sixes; received the body, achieved Amelia's hand. Yet he had obtained Wild almost more for Calcraft than for Amelia. If he might cure her without Calcraft's restorative, then all he had done was to make an outrageous gift of his wife's money.

The patient, continued Bendix sipping at his drink, did not know the smell and taste of wine from that of the decoction. What if he were to wave a sack of wine beneath her nose, pretend it was the decoction, then make the cuts about her arm and dose her with laudanum? He would never insert the catheter. She would undergo only the illusion of a transfusion. If it failed, there would be no month of recovery, but he might immediately resort to Calcraft's theories. There could be no harm whatsoever in prescribing his own remedy first. Besides, was this not the perfect combination of his own and Calcraft's ideas?

When Amelia was informed that evening by her husband that he would be ready to make the attempt on her health as early as the next day, it brought memories of the last operation down upon her. On top of these fell concerns for her father and soon Amelia could not hide her tears.

Bendix took pride in comforting her. Holding her close to his chest, he absorbed the sobs and stifled them with words of confidence and premonitions of their life in Chiswick. By the time that he had soothed her to sleep, he had also obtained her permission to transfuse her on the following day.

The equipment was laid out upon the table, the sawdust freshened with vinegar and the table filled with nosegays, carried by Bendix himself from Covent Garden in the early morning. He took her by the hands and carried her to the same chair in which her father had placed her so many months before. Gently he bled her of ten ounces. Once more, she felt faint and began to tremble with memories.

It had taken Bendix less than an hour to concoct his fake solution. He would not have been able to replicate the recipe, taking no notes on the mixture. It contained wine, lemon, heavy milk, doses of sassafras and euphrasia, calomel, stout and laudanum, but in what order, what quantity, he could not remember. It did, however, taste sublime and he had no doubt that Mrs Hemmings would agree. He had based its creation on Wild's decoction, attempting a similar fluidity and a taste that while much more agreeable, might have the vaguest similarity in scent. Like all his revered natural philosophers, Bendix used his mind and sense and tested both decoctions again and again. He rubbed them both in the palms of his hands, passed them under his nose, sipped them. With Calcraft's final journal before him, he obeyed the inky rules to the letter. Always he tasted Wild's decoction first, for the flavour and the thought was so unappetising that it had always to be followed by his own potent solution.

He filled the pig's bladder with the milky wine, then came close to Amelia.

'Much has changed,' he said, 'from what your father offered you and what I offer you now. The solution is a pleasant one. You might taste it upon your tongue if you wish.'

Though Amelia did not wish it, Bendix pursued her interest until she capitulated. He squeezed a drop into her palm, then watched as she tentatively lapped at the pinkish fluid. As he had presumed, she was favourable in her judgement. He did not submit to her inquiries as to where the multitude of tastes sprang.

If Amelia had been reluctant to taste the concoction, she was very content to swallow the fifty drops of laudanum that Bendix offered her.

'Not enough to cause sleep,' said the apprentice, 'but it will bring quietude to your mind. It shall let the transfusion occur most rapidly.'

At first Amelia was buoyed by the medicinal quality of the opiate, but as Bendix took her arm and, shielding the cut from her eyes, traced his knife across her skin, she began to lull into a dreamy reverie. She did not wonder where the calf might be. The bones on the shelves seemed to shift. Sawdust gathered in miniature hills before her eyes, then scattered with the soft blow of her breath. She could hear the footsteps of Lemon walking above and they resounded like a giant's hobnailed tread throughout her head.

When Bendix saw that her eyes no longer focused and drifted across his face without the slightest sign of recognition, he made a second incision along her arm and quickly sewed it up. She would have a matching scar from the cuts her father made along her other arm and yet no transfusion would occur at all. She would remember the pleasantness of the liquid, see the scars upon her arm and feel in much better health than during her last operation. There would be no blackened urine, no fevers or blisters. She should, hoped Bendix, believe the transfusion to be a resounding success.

For two days Bendix kept his wife dosed with laudanum. He informed all of the household that they were to be kept on at their new home in Chiswick. Lincoln's Inn Fields, he said, would not be reopened until the doctor returned from Bethlem. He gave a strong hint in his voice that this should not be something that should be relied upon. While Amelia slept, Bendix chose some of her favourite furniture from the western wing.

CHAPTER THIRTY-ONE

Lemon looked ill at the invasion. Hordes of porters seemed to pass up and down the stairs, Mr Bendix forever following one or other. Defoe had arrived to assist and was instructing the men as to where each piece should be placed within the wagons. Slowly, the two wagons sagged from the weight of armoires and stiff-backed chairs. By the early afternoon, they creaked their way from Lincoln's Inn Fields, the kindly Defoe travelling ahead by boat to supervise the unloading.

Ceasing to dose his wife by nightfall, she slept without the benefits of laudanum until early the next morning. She did not hesitate to wake Bendix, who lay fully clothed beside her, supposedly on watch for her waking. At first she was groggy, staring at the dressing Bendix had applied to her arm with strange wonder, then turning to press her head to her husband's chest. There was no ribbon about her eyes, nor light to disturb her as he bent, hardly woken from his own sleep, and kissed her.

'How are you?' he whispered.

'I feel, I do not know,' she said. 'I feel as if I have slept a dozen years. There were people in my dreams and colours and rivers that ran so fast. How long have I slept?'

'Two days,' said Bendix, 'and one night more.'

'Where is the sun?' she asked.

'Oh,' said Bendix teasing, pointing to the open window, 'I believe he's an hour or two late. To think they call him a gentleman.'

They waited together to watch the rise of the sun and it

came through a thick baste of cloud that turned gold with the dawn. Amelia did not hide her eyes from it but kept them narrowed against the soft light. She watched the first hour of the day in silence, her husband beside her, and when finally she spoke and asked for the shutters to be closed, she wept at the beauty of what she had seen.

Bendix was filled with a different kind of amazement. There was no doubt that when she had asked for the shutters to close it was because of the rise of pain and yet she had suffered, if it was even suffering, through an hour of daylight. Should that be all that she might be convinced of, Bendix considered his experiment a success. Damn the doctor, damn a thousand years of thought, said Bendix to himself. The mind contained a heavy dose of medicine, unwritten tomes of wisdom and the knowledge to cure or harm. He had but stirred a thought within Amelia and already it had taken hold.

They spent the day together in the dim light of the western wing. When finally they rose from bed and Amelia saw the emptied state of her drawing room she laughed out loud and thought that truly she had been blessed with a man above her expectations.

It was as if they had traded energies with one another. Amelia's high spirits, Bendix's exhaustion. He excused himself for the remainder of the day and retired to the basement. Before entering his bedroom, he set about cleaning the kettles and bottles. Though the morning had brought much encouragement, Bendix was not yet convinced. He kept both his adulterated wine and the decoction side by side on the shelf beneath the bones and books.

He passed the bottles beneath his nose, barely believing he could have tasted so vile a mixture. Perhaps it was his burning of the liver that caused the offensive odour, or perhaps the doctor was correct; whatever was within the man could be concentrated and this was the smell, the taste of a multitude of sins. The scent of a man who had committed over fifty men and women to the gallows, transported many to the New World, driven money from thieves and thieved alike. Yet, thought Bendix, there was an organisation to his deeds. How would London live without him? If crime was not regulated, would it rise above them?

The idea of a London thick with thieves sent Bendix into sleepy thoughts of peaceful Chiswick. He retired to his bedroom and packed his instruments in their chest. The day crept in his basement window. He watched a pair of mud-crusted boots pass by. Then a doctor with his cane and the base of a sedan chair. When he lay down on his bed, sleep washed over him. He felt the dreams begin, the mind spinning odd images together.

At five o'clock he awoke and was relieved to find that the sun had banished the clouds and remained in the sky. He pulled himself from bed, feeling the rise of a sharp headache in his right temple. Sleeping during daylight hours had always been his forte as a student and this pain was, to Bendix, no more than a sign of his utter conversion from idleness to utility. Those that achieved also suffered. He massaged his temples, wiped his body down with a wet cloth from the basin, then pulled on his black silk suit.

Amelia was not in her bedroom. He found his wife in her father's study, the windows shuttered against the light. She had separated the room into two halves, what should stay and what must go to Chiswick. They worked together for no more than five minutes when Bendix took her by the hand and motioned her towards the bedroom. Though Amelia did not wish to resist, she felt it was her duty to uphold her own honour above her husband's impatience. Once more she had misread Bendix's intentions. He opened the shutters. The sun filled the room with a glow of orange, casting both their faces in gold. For a moment Amelia reached up to shield her eyes, but gently her husband pulled her hand from her face and together they stared from the window at the death of the melting light. Casting a shadow across Amelia, Bendix leaned over and let his lips glide over her cheek. They looked at each other in the sunlight. Neither broke their gaze, but their mouths broke into smiles, then soft laughter, which Bendix silenced by joining their lips together.

CHAPTER THIRTY-TWO

Once again, they slept in the same bed, Bendix curving his body about hers, the thickness of their cotton gowns seeming as light as gossamer to the apprentice. It was as if his skin already imagined itself in the act of love. His face was buried against the back of her neck, against her scar. At first, she had tried to move, but he had held her until she relaxed and pushed back, accepted.

Amelia had never been so awake. She did not dare to sleep. Tomorrow would bring her to Chiswick, to life and love that she had been prevented from imagining. She felt her husband's breath on her neck and pushed back against him like a fireside cat. She could feel his cock, warm and stiff, pressing against her. Julia had warned her, and amid giggles had attempted to describe exactly what it might look like, as if it were an animal separate from man. But Amelia was not as alarmed as she thought she would be. Instead she was flattered, smiled quietly to herself, knew that she was a woman equal to every other and married to a man better than any she had met or read about.

Amelia watched the sunrise by herself, then woke her husband with kisses along his arm. She told him of her orders to the household that she had issued the previous day while he slept. Bendix felt a mild irritation on the soles of his feet. Fearing that Amelia's bed might be suffering from a minor infestation but too polite to mention it, Bendix waited until she left the room then had a satisfying scratch, raking his feet with his fingernails.

It was a magnificent day for their journey to Chiswick. Bendix spent the morning with five porters, instructing them on packaging and carrying until they grew quite bothered by his fussing. Their irritation was tempered by a handful of shillings. Julia and Mrs Hemmings travelled with the coachman on the well-laden cart, Bendix, Amelia and Lemon rode in the carriage. It was a hot day, not unlike the one that had first escorted Bendix to the outskirts of London, but he could not say that he would genuinely miss the centre of the metropolis. As they passed down to the river and along Thames Street, the throngs of people surrounding the banks, the small sails crowding the water, the snorts and shuffles of animals all filled Bendix with a great longing for the peace of their walled home.

So much had changed in his days since Paris. He had known happiness before, but it had always been dwarfed by the subsequent misery. To have earned, to have achieved, gave Bendix a surer foundation. It was as if he had only ever lived in the basement of Lincoln's Inn and was suddenly brought up to the roof garden. No longer was it a world of boots and horses' hooves, but an open vista of possibilities.

They stopped at the height of the heat, in the early afternoon, at Mrs Hemmings's insistence. Passing a market that she knew to provide the poulterers in Leaden Hall, she could not resist the purchase of two fat geese and a stout capon, all for the remarkable bargain of nine shillings. The men took advantage of their pause and, while the horses were tended by the grooms of the local tavern, they sipped at small beer and cold meat, carrying a portion outside so that the ladies might share in their fortune.

Bendix felt exhausted again, the toil of his last weeks still weighing on him despite the buoyant signs of their success. His headache had returned, accompanied by a sore throat and a possible swelling in his neck that he tried to ignore. He finished his glass then asked the groom to replace it with cold water. Though they had not travelled far enough from the city to avoid the sight of it, the green-acred horizon before them was alone an encouragement to continue.

Too concerned with his own ailment, Bendix failed to appreciate his wife's extraordinary expression of concentration. Her features were frozen as if she were trying to follow the sound of a particular violin through a chorus of strings. Like her husband, she was contemplating the difference between the city and their future surroundings. It seemed to her as if London, though miles behind, chased them with its echoes, while a smooth world of peace stretched ahead where sounds might travel forever without meeting walls of any kind.

They purchased the services of porters and grooms at Turnham Green who trailed their carriage on foot for the last mile of its journey and entered the gates like tired hounds at the end of the hunt. While Mrs Hemmings saw to it that they would be provided with some of the beer she had wisely purchased at the tavern, Lemon began to instruct them in the unpacking of the cart. None worked especially hard, for they were in no rush to leave. They knew the land well and were not restricted by the setting sun. Instead they delayed their actions in Lemon's presence, but every time that Amelia passed a great rush of energy gathered between them and the heaviest bookcase was raised like a feather. Had they not looked where they placed their hands, they might have raised the cart by mistake.

Bendix was not blind to the effect of his wife and took great pleasure in the willingness of the men to turn themselves to beasts of burden before her. There was no sunset to speak of, just a gradual darkening, where the night lowered herself across the land. Still, Amelia's cream dress seemed to harness the final light of the clouds and, in order that the men should disappear in time for him to have his dinner, he took Amelia by the hand and walked her about their garden. It did not lead directly to the river banks, but rose gently, cresting in a view of the Thames. The previous owners had cut the water view from a bank of willows, so that the river was framed by wilting boughs.

They sat together on a stone bench under a surviving willow, looking south. In the gathering darkness Amelia rubbed Bendix's back at his request, fussing over him at his mild complaints of fever. She could not express her gratitude to her husband for the freedom of her day, or even the joy she took in his moment of sickness compared to her health. To nurse another brought her a sense of competence and use. There was no sensuousness in her touch, no trace of desire in her fingers, merely an innocent benevolence and a hint of pride.

Bendix did not sleep in the first hours of the night. The room echoed with every cough. He felt the steady and undisturbed breathing of his wife, but the unfamiliar shadows, the odd creaks and the faint sound of the river kept him from sleep. He rubbed the soles of his feet against one another, felt their heat and sweat and knew that it could not be a question of the bed's infestation but his own.

Defoe arrived the following morning and announced himself by screaming at his coachmen, bringing Lemon rolling out the door of the house in mixed livery, which drew wry smiles and peace from the onlookers. The two coachmen and Defoe were attempting to remove the writer's wedding present to the young couple. The looking glass was an awkward shape, almost as tall as a man, lined in oak and inlaid with mahogany and ivory. With Lemon's help they succeeded in angling it through the front door and into the largest of the downstairs rooms, where it stood like a skinny sarcophagus.

Amelia had risen long before Bendix, the apprentice finally falling to sleep when the sun was waking. His wife rose with the dawn, watched it from the bedroom window with unchanged amazement, then roused the rest of the house and began the elaborate process of unpacking. She forced Lemon into moving or dragging some of the heavier pieces of furniture so that, should guests call, she would not be embarrassed to greet them. It was testimony to Bendix's exhaustion that he was able to sleep through the groans of Lemon and the floorboards, the cries of alarm from Julia and the barked orders of Mrs Hemmings.

When Amelia appeared before Defoe, in the dim but by no means dark drawing room, he was finally lost for words. Amelia may have seen little of the light, but the light had also seen little of her. It revealed her beauty to the writer so that his tongue thickened and his thoughts were hardly avuncular. She enjoyed his shock, presumed it was aimed only at her state of sight, ran a shy hand across her face and then kissed him so hard on his cheek that she elicited a blush from beneath the full-bottomed wig.

'This is news,' he said. He wanted to pour forth words, but was reduced to, 'How?'

'My husband,' said Amelia proudly.

'We shall have to visit your father,' replied Defoe and watched Amelia's face fall. Such a natural thought had not occurred to her. 'And where is your saviour?'

'He rests.'

'As did God,' smiled Defoe and, rearranging his emotions to their ancient positions, stole a second, more innocent kiss from Amelia.

They took a plate of smoked fish and then a cup of chocolate in the drawing room. Many pleasantries were exchanged between them over Defoe's gift of the glass and twice he made Amelia stand before it to consider her own dark-eyed beauty. Bendix did not appear until the afternoon. He had made himself up as if he were going to pay his introductory visits to the local gentry, face hidden beneath powders, peruke well combed and dusted, shoes capped by a pair of polished buckles.

Defoe greeted him with an affectionate clasp of congratulation and informed him that he was every ounce the equal of his father-in-law. Refusing the offer of chocolate, Bendix nodded at all of the writer's kind words and happily agreed to discuss the decorating of the drawing room.

'No chinaware?' asked Defoe.

'Father had little,' replied Amelia.

'A fine man,' said Defoe. 'You could not find a piece of china in all of London till Queen Mary found humour in it. Now I find it on cabinets and scrutores and chimney pieces piled to the very ceiling. Fatal excesses.'

'They can be ornamental,' said Amelia.

'As a flourish, but no more,' continued Defoe. Bendix knew that no matter what the writer talked of, he was being studied closely if only because of his own silence. 'They have shelves for china. Imagine, only for china. Now King William had more particular judgement and favoured gardening. Decided that evergreens preserved the beauty of a garden in winter. A simple thought and a fine one. Can any country boast of finer gardens?'

'Our own,' started Amelia.

'Shall, in time, be beautiful,' finished Defoe, and the three joined in a unanimous smile of politeness.

After Amelia had insisted that Defoe stay for dinner and the evening, Defoe asked Bendix for a more thorough tour of their property.

'Surely,' teased Bendix, 'you have trod these paths before?'

Defoe laughed as the two men emerged into bright afternoon sunlight. They walked slowly to the crest of the hill, then out through the gates of the property and down to the river where they sat to watch the barges on the western banks grow heavy under the produce of the malting houses.

'Are you a good physician to yourself?' asked Defoe.

'As fine as any man,' said Bendix.

'If you were to take an old man's advice,' said the writer reaching over to pat his hand, 'I would suggest you submit to another's eye. May I interfere and send a friend from London tomorrow?'

'It is not necessary.'

'I disagree,' intoned Defoe, 'I think it is essential. Moreover, I do not know the particulars of your marriage, nor do I wish to know, but if I were you I would excuse myself from my wife's bed for a day or two.'

Bendix nodded solemnly.

Despite the weight of their thoughts, both men presented Amelia with pleasant company at the dinner table and, with Mrs Hemmings adjusting to her new spit and kitchen, they chewed their way through a burned lamb and an eight-pound capon. Bendix insisted that his wife sit at the head of the table and, though it was an odd request, he angled his head continuously to the right as if he were ashamed of one side of his face.

Defoe was gone before Bendix rose and the promised doctor did not arrive until the following morning. Understanding her husband's fatigue and noticing that his sore throat seemed much better for his day out of London, Amelia did not question his lack of desire but tended to him in their darkened bedroom. She did not expose herself directly to the sun at the height of noon, only at the first and last of the day. Her eyes, she thought, were not wholly cured, but improved a hundred times. If she felt the stirring of a headache, she would merely walk in from the garden and sit in a shaded corner of the drawing room. Or better, she would walk up the stairs and see to her sleeping husband, only a little worried by his poor health, but determined to swathe him in duty and love.

Waking in the middle of the night, his schedule of sleep upset by such constant attendance, Bendix lit a candle with great difficulty in the dark and wandered down the stairs. His walk was hesitant. The candle shook in his hand, even though he tried to steady himself in the warm air by taking deep breaths of night. He entered the drawing room and, placing the candle on the table, stood before the looking glass.

Any doctor, any student, might have told him what attacked him. Defoe's gift of a looking glass only confirmed matters. Syphilis had begun to eat its way through the side of his nose. Worst of all were the open chancres at the back of his throat. He was only thankful that they were not upon his lips and that he might keep his secret from his wife. Snuffing the candle with pinched fingers and not even registering the flicker of pain, Bendix took a seat in the drawing room and could not bring himself to return to bed.

Dr Beecham arrived earlier than most gentleman rose and found Bendix in his garden, studiously avoiding his wife and household. He introduced himself to the apprentice as a specialist in the diseases of Venus. If his wife was too innocent to observe, Defoe had been too experienced to misjudge his condition. Bendix's health had already declined between Defoe's departure and the doctor's arrival and it took the visitor only a brief survey to confirm suspicions.

'Most curious,' said Beecham, studying his patient coldly as Bendix had often studied others. 'You have visited prostitutes, you say?'

Bendix nodded.

'Within the last two months?' asked Beecham.

'No,' lied Bendix. 'Since I have met my wife, I have not been close to a whore.'

'The sores,' said Beecham, 'spring most often on a man's cock, or whatever part of the body first meets with the disease. Those who kneel before their whores are subject to chancres upon the lips. Most odd that it should be confined to your throat.'

'I suppose,' said Bendix, harnessing a smile, 'that if I am to be plagued by a disease it is comforting to know that it should be so singular.'

'Hardly singular,' answered Beecham. 'Couldn't be more common. Only the location is exclusive. Perhaps in severity your case might be called singular. It is a slow plague, but with you it is not so much creeping as leaping.'

Beecham opened the flap of his coat and removed a small pillbox.

'My own invention,' he said, 'a crown for each box. Thirty doses. I do not guarantee a cure, but have seen beneficial effects in cases of equal extremity.'

Bendix took the pillbox and ordered four more. The doctor promised to return at the end of the week to check on his patient and to make his delivery.

The riddle confounded Bendix for the afternoon. He walked alone by the river, ignoring his wife's cries for him from the open windows of the house. The Thames seemed unbothered by his fate, as did the men who ploughed their oars through her waters. Bending down, he cupped his hands and swallowed half a mouthful of water. With the remains, he opened the pillbox and took one of the small black pills. It had no taste.

When he understood, he sat down by the footpath. He moved only once in the hour, when he hurled the pillbox and its contents into the water. Calcraft had been wrong and Denis, fifty years before, was right. Transfusion did not bring a cure, but a transferral of character. He had read of Baptiste's worries, how the peaceful man might be turned mad by being given the blood of the lunatic. Qualities were passed within the blood. Bendix knew that the sips of his own decoction, lingering in the back of his throat, had indeed contained the essence of Wild. All that was bad in him, all that was black had been ingested. He had tasted sin, sickness and death.

It was odd that Bendix should, in his trouble, think of Calcraft's theories rather than his own. He had only just succeeded where the doctor had fallen before him and yet he did not have the courage to turn his lens upon himself. No matter where his syphilis had come from, be it Drury Lane whore, Mother Cates's girl or even the decoction of Jonathan Wild, it was the speed of the disease that was shocking. The velocity of his demise was not occasioned by any other factor but his own belief, the secret suspicion that what was happening to him was not only deserved, but fully earned.

He knew what he had done to Amelia. It was far more painful than the rush of syphilis. He loved her, he had reduced everything to love, every action he had taken was justified by his marriage to Amelia. Now he realised that it was a marriage that would never be consummated. His breath tickled his throat, made him want to weep. Had he made love to his wife, she would now have shared his condition. His abstention was small consolation. Instead his pact with Sixes would ruin her in a different manner. He had pledged his wife's happiness, wagered it on his own life and now ruined them both. Even his experiments were unrefined; he could not explain why some achieved success and some did not. Yet he had returned the gift of sight to his wife. Belief had been so strong in Amelia. Perhaps, thought Bendix, it ran even more vigorously in himself. Had he accelerated his own decline, knowing the power of the mind?

Amelia's voice came tripping down the banks. It brought him to his feet again and though he thought that it might make more sense to walk into the water than away from it he responded to the call of his wife. She stood within the bay windows, obscured by the shade. A second figure, deeper in the shadow, stood behind.

'Hurry,' she said, as Bendix headed down from the crest of the hill, 'you have a visitor.'

Already Bendix had thought of seeking a man of God.

Not the Reverend Doctor Holloway, but a man of grace and knowledge. He remembered his father's letters to Paris. How the local curate had come calling the day he moved to his Northumberland estate and introduced himself. Curates relied on the gentry to supplement their incomes, thought Bendix. Let us meet the master of St Nicholas's.

As Bendix lifted his weary feet over the threshold he saw the second figure was entirely familiar. Sixes bowed with pleasure at seeing him, his lean angles opening and closing like a pair of scissors.

'I have thanked him for his kind gift,' said Amelia.

Sixes raised his hands in protest. 'Enough,' he smiled. 'Was only silver for a lady more beautiful than gold.'

Bendix smiled weakly for his wife.

'Amelia,' he said, 'will you excuse us while we discuss a small matter of business?' He signalled Sixes to join him through the bay windows. Not having the energy to walk any further, Bendix paused on top of his crest and sat on the seat of his silk breeches in an ungentlemanly manner that he would not have considered the week before. Sixes sat beside him, his sharp knees pointing skyward, his feet towards the river.

'News,' said Sixes and tapped on the side of his ear. 'It travels faster than horses. Heard of your purchase of the house – beautiful garden. Knew of the doctor's visit. Hoped sorely that it was one of your domestics and not your good self that had taken sick. Ever so sad to see it. And your wife?'

'As happy as I have ever seen her,' said Bendix, forcing himself to spit the words from his mouth without a trace of the emotions that boiled within.

'You do not look well,' said Sixes. 'I can send many who know about these things. Mother Cates is most familiar with them.'

'No,' decided Bendix, 'I need only peace and my own mind.'

'You do not forget,' smiled Sixes.

'Forget?' said Bendix, then smiled to acknowledge the true root of the visit. It made his physical condition unbearable. He breathed sharply, then managed in little more than a whisper, 'You still think in gold?'

'Merchant in my darkest heart,' answered Sixes, returning the smile. 'Am happy with my annual income and your company. Hate to see you underground.'

'I am sure,' said Bendix, 'that you would weep for days, as you did for Jonathan.'

'You're different sorts,' said Sixes. 'Sinners and Saints. Contract is a contract, 'specially when it's signed and seen by Chancery.'

'Yes,' said Bendix nodding to himself.

Sixes clapped him on the back. 'Was not the reason I came. Just acquainting myself with house and wife, both most lovely. Much to live for. I shall send doctors. No reason to distress a household.'

'And who would you send for,' asked Bendix, 'when your doctor is already here?'

Sixes shrugged. 'I see you're in no mood. Mercury, my friend. We shall send it up from London. I'll be back to see how you fare.'

Sixes's was the last visit of the week. At his departure, Amelia went into the garden to retrieve her husband and found him in tears. He complained of tiredness, was ashamed of having his wife see him so poorly. Bendix was not strong enough to tear himself from her, but let her walk him upstairs to their bedroom and put him to bed. She saw the marks upon his nose, saw a rash upon his chest as she undressed him, smelled a foulness about him that had not even been there the night before. Thankfully, for her husband, diseases of Venus had not been included by either Defoe or Sir Edmund in her education.

It brought out wonderful sentiments in her. Every request by Bendix was met with immediately, though she would not hear of his desire to meet with the curate from St Nicholas's. Bendix grew angry on his first two days abed, but Amelia kept the shutters closed, the summer away and would not think to have any visitors. Defoe was the exception to the rule. Though Amelia may not have had any familiarity with the disease, it was apparent that Bendix's condition worsened quickly. Indeed, thought Amelia, it often seemed as if she left the room to freshen a strip of cotton with water and on her return her husband would be whiter, weaker than before.

When Amelia slept, Defoe kept guard of his patient. The signs upon the apprentice were unmistakable. Yet the peculiarity was the speed at which the siege of disease had broken him down. Defoe had seen the chancres of stricken men come and go within days. Had seen rashes fade, fevers pass, tremors quit the body all in a matter of months. Bendix was attacked by all simultaneously. The writer watched sadly as the apprentice's hair fell out in clumps on the pillowcase. He hid it so that Amelia would not see the deterioration. It was syphilis, no doubt, but of a voraciousness Defoe had never heard of. It was as if Bendix had contracted a concentrated case from a dark and poisoned whore. Whatever the cause, his decline was accelerating, almost as if the apprentice was now speeding his own demise.

By evening of the fourth day, Bendix ceased to make sense. Logic still came at him, but only in bursts and then collapsed into inanity. His eyes turned red before Defoe.

On the morning of the fifth day, after Amelia's departure and Defoe's arrival, Bendix bade him listen closely. He told him of the bodies of Sheppard and Wild, of Calcraft's transfusion. Bendix could tell, even through his fever, that nothing surprised Defoe. Finally he told the writer of his contract with Sixes.

'The paper,' said Defoe, 'is worthless.'

'No,' insisted Bendix, 'it bears my signature. Five thousand pounds. A Chancery man was there.'

'Joseph,' said Defoe, 'you have greater concerns than gold. I shall take care of Amelia.'

'With what?' said Bendix bitterly. 'With words?'

Defoe smiled kindly down at the patient.

On the morning of the last Saturday of June, when the sun was high and neither Defoe nor Amelia were present in the bedroom, Bendix woke from his fever. His brain seemed swollen against the side of his head. He ran his hand over his face and felt the erosion of his nose. He thought only of Amelia until the pain pulsed over him and its sharpness drew the last of his breath.

Defoe found the body. Pulled a sheet above his head. He had never cried over the dead, nor was he inclined to differ over Joseph Bendix. Always he thought of what the dead left behind. He himself stood a chance in memory, with only words. Bendix, who had the thread of greatness sewn in his seams, would be forgotten by all. It was almost enough to make a man cry, but there could be no exceptions. Going downstairs, he informed the household of Bendix's death, then left for the drawing room to inform Amelia. Lemon did not look up from polishing the gift of wedding silver.

Amelia did not cry in front of Defoe. He did not know if she cried at all. She excluded all from the drawing room and sat alone throughout the night. Bendix was buried on the evening after his death. Dr Beecham, passing by with his black pills to check upon his patient, could only bother the widow for a single payment. At Defoe's insistence he remained for the service and managed several glances at his watch as Bendix was buried at the top of the crest with the view to the Thames. When Defoe and the household walked the doctor to his carriage, Amelia remained standing above the fresh earth and wept at her loss.

There were few as good with grief as Defoe. He sent letters across the county. To inform his own family he would be several days late. To tell Bendix's father of his son's death. To let Dr Monroe know that he might, should he see fit, impart the news to Sir Edmund. Then he scoured the neighbourhood and discovered two widows of young gentlemen and begged them to take tea with Amelia. Though it was an affair as thick with tears as it was with sugar, Defoe thought it was sensible for Amelia to share her mourning with women.

The two visiting widows seemed to be involved in a competition of grief that Amelia watched with some understanding. She knew none could rival her memory of her husband, nor his gift to her, but she found female company diverting. Bendix had appeared in Lincoln's Inn a year ago. She thought of their fleeting acquaintance and flutter of a marriage as a graceful reverie before the day began. Having seen little of grief, Amelia barely knew how to interpret the swells of emotion that seemed to overwhelm her at odd moments of the day. Yet when her mind cleared, she felt nothing so much as gratitude to her husband and a continued wonder at the immediacy of her new world.

Not knowing how exhausted Amelia was by the effort of entertaining, the widows lingered over their departure, bestowing compliments on the fineness of her silver. When they finally left, she retired to her room. Defoe brought out pen and ink and wandered down to the stone bench to enjoy the late evening light.

He heard the carriage arrive and guessed at its contents long before the shadow darkened his papers.

'Good evening to you, Mr Defoe,' said Sixes. 'I was wondering if I might have words with the lady of the house?'

'Terrible that your visit should be so mistimed,' answered Defoe, 'but she has retired already for the evening. Surely, you would wish to visit with the master of the house?'

'I would, I would,' said Sixes, 'but have heard already. Wished to pay my respects. News flows faster than the Thames, they say.'

'Who says?' asks Defoe snidely.

'Them on Grub Street,' smiled Sixes most politely. 'I would have thought you might know that. Won't disturb, shall return. Goodnight, sir.'

'I am her guardian,' said Defoe, 'According to the laws of Chancery, if you have business, if perhaps, Mr Bendix was in debt a shilling or two, then it is to me you must apply.'

'Rather more than a shilling,' smiled Sixes, pulling the contract from his waist pocket. 'Most rash a decision. Young men, though.'

Defoe peered carefully at it. 'And the "case",' asked Defoe, 'that would not be an anatomy outside of the Royal College, a crime that would carry you to the Tyburn tree?'

'Not as it says there,' smiled Sixes. 'Not as it was witnessed by a notable man of Chancery.'

'Fair enough,' replied Defoe. 'A package it is.'

'I would not expect payment at once,' said Sixes. 'I believe it is a quarter of the doctor's fortune. Perhaps the house in

Lincoln's Inn might be sold. I have patience, can wait til the court returns.'

'Unfortunately the paper means little,' said Defoe. 'They were not married.'

Sixes smiled again and reached into his pocket once more, 'Mr Bendix's marriage contract,' he said. 'I do believe that would be your own mark to the east there.'

'A marriage is not complete until its consummation,' said Defoe. 'The sickness fell too fast upon Mr Bendix for him to indulge in the pleasures of the bed.'

'Since when,' smiled Sixes, 'has the report of consummation relied on anyone but a maid and a bed sheet. You shall contend they did not lie together, I shall contend they did. I can provide whores he tasted to confirm his manhood. Chancery will decide the fate of the widow.'

'Amelia's virginity might be confirmed by a midwife.'

'Or denied by another.'

'I am glad you are so familiar with our law,' said Defoe calmly, 'for then perhaps you will not have been as ignorant nor trusting as the late Mr Bendix. Those who seek fortunes should be well advised not to woo the illegitimate.'

Sixes shifted, a mild shake of the head.

'The child, Amelia, is Calcraft's bastard,' said Defoe coldly but with distant amusement. 'The marriage came a week before the birth of the girl. I believe your Chancery friends call it a case of "Special Bastardy". According to your blessed laws, when conceived out of wedlock, Mr Sixes, a child has no rights to their father's property. You may apply yourself to the parish records, but they shall only confirm that Joseph Bendix married a penniless girl, subject to the whims of her father's trustee.'

'The house?' said Sixes, jabbing his thumb behind him.

'Contract signed by Mr Bendix and myself.'

Sixes smiled.

'Which means,' said Defoe, 'that your contract with Mr Bendix is not worth its pen and ink.'

'Does she know her state, her bastard birth?' asked Sixes.

'No, sir, she does not. I wish to keep it so.'

'In time it might prevent a marriage,' smiled Sixes.

'It is not essential that she is held from the truth,' said Defoe, 'only preferable. The preferred is less dear than the necessary. Would a hundred guineas hold you silent?'

'A hundred a year until her marriage,' said Sixes, 'would ensure a golden silence.'

'Should I draw a contract?' asked Defoe, tapping his quill on the sheet of paper.

'I should prefer your word and prompt payment.'

'I do believe,' said Defoe, rising with some difficulty, 'that we have attained a state of mutual satisfaction.'

As Defoe walked away, Amelia watched Sixes from the window seat. Watched him move about their Thameside acre, watched him stand beside Joseph's grave. She could see his lips move, as if he was talking to the dead, and was comforted by the thought that her husband had been well loved.

EPILOGUE

To spend the summer months in black did not upset Amelia. She grew flowers upon her husband's grave, increased the circle of her acquaintance with the help of the young widows and was courted by a variety of gentlemen. She resisted all advances, finding comfort only in the continued visits of Defoe. The autumn forced Amelia to remember the beauty of shadows, of the different shades of grey. It began with the shortened days, when all of those about the nation huddled about their fires, thankful for roofs and thick walls. Defoe noticed the regression, the voluntary submittal to the darkening light, and sought to remedy it by increasing the regularity of his visits. Always he encouraged Amelia to take the air. To see her shadow in the twilight was his way of making Bendix live again for both of them. His name was not mentioned. It did not need to be, for it was ever present between them.

Twice they visited her father and after the year at Bethlem had passed and Monroe had failed to coax a word from his colleague, Calcraft was deemed incurable. Defoe did not even have to propose the idea for Amelia suggested it before Monroe himself.

The following week Sir Edmund was collected by his friend and daughter and borne to the house at Chiswick. He expressed no shock, spoke no words to find himself carried elsewhere than Lincoln's Inn. The household stood in the cold to welcome him and Lemon, at least, was certain that he saw a fraction of a smile. Throughout the first month Defoe would attend their house for days at a time, anxious lest melancholy repel the prospects of happiness that had first accompanied the purchase of the house.

Yet Amelia retained her good humour. She met the limited independence of her life with a cosseted grace. Indeed, thought Defoe, she seemed to thrive on caring for her father. There was a familial understanding that he simply could not grasp. On his way back to his orchards in Stoke Newington, he would often stop at the tavern in Turnham Green. His ears remained sharp, could pluck the thread of rumour from a raucous room, but Defoe did nothing to dispel the myths that rose of the house and its proprietors. He did not talk the local porters down from their suspicions that Chiswick was now thick with ghosts.

ACKNOWLEDGEMENTS

Many thanks to Mr Eric Elstob for his patience in showing me an eighteenth-century London I had walked past and never noticed. Thanks also to Doctors Carlberg and Willis for their help in the world of medicine. And to Joanna Weinberg, many thanks for the title.